Jayne and the Average North Dakotan

Jayne and the
Average North
Dakotan

To Steve ♡

Chandler My

Chandler Myer

atmosphere press

This book is dedicated to my husband, Peter.

I couldn't have written a word without your unending encouragement, support, and love.

CHAPTERS

ONE

The Pink Eye

A mile-high waterspout agitates the Minot High School indoor swimming pool. I heroically battle the dyspeptic current, spending more energy calling for Mother than implementing any swim training. In my defense, none of the swimming instructors ever mentioned waterspouts, indoor or outdoor, so I looked to my usual comfort source. The razor-sharp concrete deck tears my hand as I pull myself to safety. Intense seasickness reverberates through my body. If I could just sleep, this would all pass.

A thunderclap startles me to semi-consciousness.

"WELL, LOOK WHAT THE CAT DRAGGED IN!"

Principal Oglethorpe delivers her morning announcements louder than usual, something about a cat. I'm on a rickety wooden ladder with my ear pressed against the freshman homeroom loudspeaker. The class is laughing and talking to obscure the principal's voice. I push hard against the brown wooden speaker straining to hear her instructions. The incredible noise creates a rhythmic pounding in my temples that threatens nausea.

"RANDY LARSON! TIME TO FACE WHAT'S LEFT OF THIS WRETCHED DAY!"

I turn from the speaker to find the ladder has become a levitating mattress suspended above my classmates. I'm wearing Aladdin's sexy outfit from the Disney movie, my belly looking like a 40-year-old drunk rather than a (slightly) chubby freshman. The students laugh and point at a yellow liquid stream pouring from the floating bed onto an oblivious Principal Oglethorpe. I'm mortified, even if she doesn't seem to notice. I squeeze my eyes shut, and the laughing stops.

"RANDY!"

A jolt of consciousness brings another wave of nausea. Open eyes see nothing but a fuzzy, black bar running through my limited field of vision. The mattress has landed in an Army field hospital where Hawkeye and Hot Lips are performing surgery to cure my raging case of the pink eye. Clinger notes we are wearing the same green taffeta dress. It's just like me to create a fashion faux pas on my deathbed.

"I'd tell you to rise and shine, but neither of those seems viable," another nurse with a loudspeaker voice astutely observes. She must be next to my bed. "Jesus! You look like Bette Davis at the *Baby Jane* afterparty!"

Baby who? Party? Have I been to a party? My mind is racing, and I can't see or move. The bed is damp with an overwhelming aroma of freshly watered urinal cake – another rush of nausea. Am I dreaming, or is there a real woman beside my bed? I think I'm in bed. But I don't think I'm in an episode of *M*A*S*H* anymore. Nothing feels right. Speak, Randy. Speak.

"Pthpt." Yes, that's the sound I made. It could have come from any orifice.

"Heavens to Liz Taylor! Someone can't handle a drink or two, hmmm? The good news is you probably feel as bad as you look."

I don't think this is Principal Oglethorpe. I see red sparkles on either side of the black line as a body plops heavily beside me and slaps my face with a warm washcloth. The fuzzy vision lines disappear, and I begin to see red. The pink eye has gotten worse! It has become the red eye!

"There you go, little gargoyle."

My vision clears enough to see a towering woman in red sequins perched next to me. She's holding a washcloth with two squished spiders. Did she remove spiders from my eyes? Maybe I'm not awake.

"Next time, spring for the deluxe eyelashes, yes?" She squints at the arachnidian smudges and grimaces. "These are so cheap they're probably made of armpit hair." She throws the soiled cloth into a corner of the room and shudders. "Disgusting. Now sit up and take a swig of water."

An upright position is achieved, though the sizeable nurse-like person may have done all the work. This feels like consciousness. The nurse unfolds herself to a standing position, a creature so immense the room goes into a solar eclipse. My wide-eyed gaze signals awe from her knees to the top of her blond bouffant, nearly pressed against the ceiling. Or fear.

"Yes, I'm a big-boned gal," she smirks. "Six feet, nine inches unless I go crazy with the teasing comb. In this cave, I nearly scrape the dreadful dropped ceiling." Her red sequin evening gown – with matching heels and lipstick – shudders to accentuate her horror at my living conditions.

The red nurse pushes a cup of water to my mouth, and I attempt to drink like a person who has had multiple Novocaine injections. Hydration returns some of my speaking skills, releasing every thought in verbal diarrhea.

"Oh, god! I feel terrible. Is this a dream? I think I have the pink eye. Or the red eye! I probably need an ambulance. Can Hawkeye cure this? And I feel damp. Was my bed floating when you came in? And my mouth is full of cat fur. You are so tall! Are you Principal Oglethorpe? Did you bring a cat? I can't believe I licked a cat!"

A perfectly manicured finger covers my mouth. "I can

assure you no one here has licked a pussy. Ever." She grabs my face and looks deep into my eyes. "And no pink eye. Is this your first hangover?"

The room moves vertically, so I must be nodding. I have a hangover? Don't you have to drink to have a hangover?

"Well, you're in luck. Hangovers are my specialty. I've spent years partying with Marilyn Monroe and picked up a few inebriation tips. Step one is to get you out of bed."

"Wait!" My hand goes up in a fleeting moment of clarity. "Who are you? Why are you in my bedroom? This *is* my bedroom, isn't it? Are you the angel of death? Am I already dead?"

Her condescending look should involve peering over the top of glasses – if she wore glasses. "The Grim Reaper could never be this fabulous." A toothy smile flashes and instantly disappears. "And, no, you're not dead yet. You are experiencing the fruits of your labors, so to speak. Don't you remember anything from last night?"

I can't figure out where I am now, let alone last night.

"No."

"The Drag Race? The DIK Bar? The Brothel? Nothing rings a bell?"

"Brothel?" A dim bulb shines on my clearing memory. "I remember getting dressed up to run the High Heel Race. And I remember a bar and lots of drag queens."

"That's called a gaggle of drag queens, just so you know."

My brow furrows as I conjure events of the past evening. "There was no brothel, was there?" I see I'm wrapped in a soiled green taffeta dress – the same one Clinger was wearing. The bulb gets brighter. "You're Jayne Mansfield, aren't you?"

She raises her hands like she's about to sing 'YMCA.' "In the flesh! Well, you'll have to trust me. There *is* flesh under all this Lycra."

"You brought me home?"

"Oh, puppy, you wouldn't be here if the girls and I hadn't

6

dragged your sloppy ass back from Dupont Circle. I've never been the maternal type, but you looked so helpless. What was I to do? Besides, you kept calling me your fairy godmother. Now, I certainly don't mind being called 'fairy,' but 'god-mother?' This queen is no mother – god or otherwise."

It's true. The drag diva dominating my bedroom looks anything but maternal. And she could pass for Maleficent before any fairy godmother. "So, uhm, you spent the night?"

One carefully plucked-and-redrawn eyebrow rises. "Don't get your hopes up, horn dog. This is, was, and always shall be a platonic relationship."

"That's not what I meant...."

"I made do on what passes for a sofa in this tenement. Now, let's get you out of that hideous outfit, burn it, and scatter the ashes at Dollywood." She reaches to pull off the dress.

"Wait!" My mind may be cloudy, but I can feel what is – or isn't – under this demonic prom frock. "Could you give me a little privacy?"

Jayne cocks her head and cracks a crooked smile. "I'll bet my left tit – the new one – you didn't bother to wear proper knickers under this pathetic ensemble."

"Uh."

"Suit yourself. You don't want me all up in your business. Fine. When properly covered, come to the kitchen for brunch martinis."

How did I end up hungover in a green taffeta gown with a gargantuan Jayne Mansfield drag queen mothering me? That's a complicated story. You see, I was destined to live the life of an average North Dakotan.

Then, everything changed.

TWO

Under a Rock

My average life started on December 29, 1986, when I decided to come into the world before the new year started. I don't remember this choice, but everyone told me I made it so I wouldn't have the distinction of being 1987's firstborn. I'm the baby of the Larson family, arriving 20 years after the first and 15 years after the one who was *supposed* to be last. Yes, I was a great big, aren't-you-too-old-to-have-a-kid kind of surprise. My parents never admitted I was unplanned, but I once heard my aunt call me The Mistake.

Junior and Michael had already left home for St. Olaf College when I came along. My 15-year-old sister and de facto parent, Jennifer, raised me while Mother worked at the church and Dad at the Air Force Base. She started at St. Olaf when I was five, returning the responsibility of child-rearing to a couple of tired, aging Lutherans who wanted nothing more than peace and quiet. I did my best not to bother them.

The four Larson siblings would be together only three times. The first was an eerily quiet Thanksgiving when I was in eighth grade. The second and third were back-to-back gatherings for my parent's funerals. Each time felt like a gathering of strangers who knew little of one another and had no interest in learning more. The older three live out west, just far enough that coming home is inconvenient. No one ever told me how or why, but my parents lost touch with their first three children. Subsequently, I never got to know them.

My old parents – 40 and 50 when I was born – raised me as a middle-aged man. I listened to public radio, played solitaire, and read the *Minot Daily News*. Dinner was at 5:30 nightly – the usual casseroles and something encased in Jello that every Lutheran eats – followed by a heaping bowl of ice cream enjoyed in our trio of recliner rocking chairs. Old shows like *The Golden Girls, Murder She Wrote, The Andy Griffith Show*, and a regular supply of black-and-white movies from the 1940s and 50s were the usual evening entertainment. We were in bed by 10:00 pm and up at 4:30 am. Midwesterners know morning is an excellent time to get things done.

Mother, Dad, and I took only one family vacation. It was the summer after fifth grade, and we borrowed two tents for a week at Northgate Dam Campground near the Canadian border. My parents probably thought I should learn camping skills since I didn't excel in either 4-H or the Boy Scouts. All meals were cooked on an open fire – most burnt – and I was encouraged to play in nature rather than read in my tent.

A few dozen people around my parents' age stayed there, camping in RVs and other tents. And one boy my age: Erik.

Erik was just ahead of me on the evolutionary scale, standing three inches taller and possessing all his adult teeth. Hours in the summer sun had bleached his shaggy blond hair like a surfer. We rode our bikes, and he tried to teach me boating, fishing, and swimming with moderate success. He was the best! We made smores on the second night of vacation and sat together on a log, legs touching. There was something special about that moment. Erik was my first crush, though I didn't understand it then.

Erik stayed in my tent on Wednesday – my first sleepover.

We played cards, made shadow animals with the flashlight, and I giggled a little too hard every time he said something funny. Erik got a kick out of making me laugh. We finally drifted off with our sleeping bags close, sharing one pillow. That was our arrangement for the rest of the week.

We talked about the future on the last night of vacation. It was serious stuff – for fifth grade.

"I want to get married and have two kids when I get older," Erik offered. "It's better when kids have brothers to hang out with."

"I guess. I don't really know my brothers."

"They should be close to the same age so they can do stuff together. Like us. Best friends."

This made me smile. "Yeah. Best friends."

"Too bad you don't live closer. We could hang out all the time."

"Maybe we can get our parents to come back here every summer." I schemed. "That would be great."

"Yeah." We both stared at the tent walls, imagining a world where we could pal around all the time. "I'm getting cold," Erik finally said. "Roll onto your side, and we can keep each other warm."

I rolled over, and he pulled in close behind me, wrapping his arm over my side with his hand on my chest. I had never felt so warm in my whole life. Soon his breathing slowed, and I could tell he was asleep. I fell asleep sometime later. When I woke, we were in the same position. And I was still smiling.

After that week, Erik went back to Williston, and I returned to Minot. We never talked, wrote, or saw one another again. I hope he still remembers me. I'll never forget him.

Middle school proved I wasn't like other kids. For starters, I dressed like my father: buttoned-down white shirt, navy blue trousers short enough to expose my white socks, and black Oxford shoes. Sports and school dances weren't my interests. Instead, I sang in the choir, played clarinet in the band, and hung out with a small handful of friends from church. We made pizzas on Friday nights and played Scrabble tournaments on the weekends. Then there were Bible studies, church retreats, church choir, and Sunday School. I was the living definition of a "nerd."

That's also when I became interested in boys – you know, in the Biblical sense. I was obsessed with everything from haircuts to butts. Sometimes, when a guy talked with me, I found myself staring into his eyes, completely lost in the intimate world created by our conversation. I could tell it made them uncomfortable because some would suddenly stop talking or walk away.

"What are you staring at?" Dave Weaver once asked, stopping mid-sentence while telling a group of guys some outlandish story.

"Staring? I wasn't staring." My skin burned with embarrassment, and I wanted to hide.

"You're looking at me like I got a naked boob on my forehead." Everyone laughed except me.

"You said 'boob!'" someone repeated as they walked away, leaving me to my shame.

Unfortunately, that happened more often than I wanted to admit. Most people thought I was weird. To be honest, *I* thought I was a bit weird.

Soon I realized my weird had another name: gay. I'd heard about men who liked other men, and I knew it wasn't positive or acceptable. People said nasty things about anyone who was thought to be gay. I remember a local bachelor named Robert Klukendahl (never call him Bob), whom people called "fancy" and "light in the loafers." It didn't take a genius to figure out what they were saying. I started walking "like a herd of buffalo," as Mother said, to make sure my loafers were heavy.

It became harder to hide my same-sex attractions as I moved through high school. The nerd bit was largely effective against teenage homophobes, but did nothing for my popularity. The only person I ever told was my friend Millie. Her response was, "I always wanted a Gay Best Friend!" After that, we spent so much time together people thought we were dating. It was a great cover.

Everyone in the Larson family attended St. Olaf College for four generations. I broke the tradition because Mother felt I lacked maturity. "If we let that innocent little boy go off to school alone, he'll be the devil's plaything." Given St. Olaf is an Evangelical Lutheran college, this seemed unlikely. Everyone knew the real reason she couldn't let me go, and there was no fighting it. She had lost her other three children when they went to college and couldn't take the same chance with me.

Mother declared I would live at home while pursuing an accounting degree at Minot State University. She insisted this was the best path to my adulthood. As usual, I didn't put up a fuss. That's not to say I was thrilled to change family history. But home was comfortable, and her way was simpler than deciding on a major, moving to Minnesota, and all that.

After college, Dad secured me a finance job with Minot Public Schools. I continued living with them, sitting in the same recliner, eating the same food, and sleeping in the same bedroom. I slipped into letting other people make decisions for me, at work and home, so it was easy. I expected to become an old bachelor in my parents' recliner.

I was 22 years old, and all I knew was 15 square miles, 40,000 Lutherans, and my parents' way of life.

Everything changed last year in April when Mother died; Dad dutifully followed her two weeks later. My lifelong companions were suddenly gone, leaving me alone for the first time. There was no one to cook, clean, or tell me when to pay my bills. I felt like a 30-something orphan.

Mother called me to the living room for a chat the week before she died. The cancer had taken over, though no one knew she was sick. Mother thought it unbecoming to complain or gossip, and sharing a cancer diagnosis could be a little of both. Her voice sounded quiet and dry. She must have known death was coming and wanted to ensure I knew what to do next.

"Randy," she said, her long, gray hair neatly tied in a bun and reading glasses low on her nose, "if I had my druthers, all my kids woulda turned out just like you. A mother couldn't wish for a truer son."

I stared at my feet. Gushing sentiments like these made me uncomfortable.

"You know there's a world beyond Minot," she continued, rocking in her chair and knitting one final pink and orange sweater for the church rummage sale. "Your father and I won't be around forever to keep you company. It's high time you struck out on your own to discover what's there. Maybe live in a big city, like Chicago or Minneapolis. It isn't good for a man to be alone his entire life."

"Minot is fine for me," I protested. "Besides, you and Dad will need me when you get old."

"We're already old, son. And we live a handsome life without any assistance." The sentiment was genuine. Neither her advancing years nor exhaustion could round her unyielding shoulders. Even her ubiquitous calf-length house dress was perfectly ironed to hide its 30-year age.

"I'm talking about you. I don't know there's many like you in this neck of the woods." Her gray eyes, stern and incisive, betrayed no emotion as she looked up from the knitting and softly cleared her throat. "God never meant any of his creatures to hide under a rock."

"What do you mean?" I said nervously, looking out the window. Something deep inside knew we were having The Talk.

"Never you mind. I've made my peace, and you best do the same." She paused, squinted down at her knitting, and cleared her throat again. "The big city is a good place for you, far as I can tell. Besides, you've always said you wanted to ride the subway like the people in the movies."

"I *have* dreamed of riding the subway." I looked at the long lines in her brow and wondered when they showed up. This would have been a good time to touch her shoulder or give her a hug, if we North Dakotans were prone to such things. Instead, we sat perfectly still with these newly revealed thoughts. "It might be nice to have some new friends. Maybe try a fancy restaurant or sip cocktails at a piano bar like *Casablanca*. Not that I would drink much."

"Pshaw. And when can you do such a thing in this town? Never, that's when." Coming from a woman born in Minot, who spent nearly 50 years as the organist at the same Lutheran church, it must have been hard to say. Were her eyes moist?

Dad entered the room and sensed a deep conversation, the type he had spent a lifetime avoiding. So, he picked up his paper and started toward the bedroom.

"Pa," she said without looking up. "I was just telling Randy he best move to the city. Time to make some changes, get out on his own."

"You betcha. Listen to your mother, son." Dad was a career military guy who stuck with the look and routine he found in the 1950s. His soldierly flattop, infused with just enough Brylcreem to give it shine, morphed from black to gray to white without changing style. This was not a man who embraced change. Yet, he always supported Mother's wishes.

"Thank you, dear," Mother said softly.

Dad paused for a moment, looking out the picture window. "I hear tell Saturday's gonna be colder'n a brass john in the Yukon." He chuckled softly, shook his head, and determined enough time was spent in this conversation. "Well, then...." With that, he walked into the bedroom and noiselessly closed the door.

"So, it's settled," Mother continued. "There's no time like the present. Run along now and make plans for the next chapter in your precious life. I wanna know the Lord has surrounded my son with people who will take good care of him."

That's the closest we ever came to discussing my sexual orientation. Mother knew. Dad knew. I knew they knew; no need to put into words what everyone knew in the first place. Still, Mother gave me permission, a literal mandate, to find other gay people and start living my adult life. She lifted the rock I had been living under – just a little – and sunlight poured in.

My view of the world changed that day. Thoughts and emotions, long held deep inside me, began seeping to the surface. I finally met the Randy inside me.

Today is February first, a momentous day. I've spent the 10 months since my parents died in self-examination. Thirty-two years of suppressed feelings and a lazy attitude toward life have roared through my head in a way I didn't know possible. Mother and Dad left a gaping hole in my life, and everything I failed to examine rushed to fill the void.

I am a homosexual. Or a gay. Or whatever the people in big cities call men like me. I don't even know what those terms mean. I've never had a date with a guy, and I've never done you-know-what with anyone. These past few months have made me realize I *want* to know all of these things.

I think Mother was right. My life needs to change. This doughy, small-town boy has been in a closet in the middle of nowhere for his entire life, and it's finally time to step out. It's time I made some fundamental decisions about how and where I want to live. Is this what I want to keep doing? Is this my home from the cradle to the grave?

So, today I am making my first big decision: I'm leaving the Flickertail State.

THREE

Not Even Fort Wayne?

Is it possible I always wanted something but never knew? I mean, what if there was a voice inside me trying to encourage my independence, and I never gave it a chance to speak? Have I wandered through life with my parents because it was easy or because I've been afraid to go solo? Am I strong enough to live alone? What will the world be outside of Minot?

These are the thoughts banging around in my head recently. It's hard to believe I spent 30 years taking the easy road while others made my decisions. Mother chose my clothes, activities, college, and degree program. Dad decided on every job I ever had. Friends came from the people I knew at church – most of whom chose to include me because it was easier than ignoring the nerdy kid.

Millie understands better than anyone. Yes, she was one of the church friends. But I think we would have been buddies regardless.

"You're really leaving Minot?" she sighs and stares at me across the sticky Chuck E. Cheese table as we slurp the last drops of Mountain Dew. Millie is unconcerned that her three kids run unsupervised through the restaurant like feral cats on crack. One pulls the costumed mascot's plastic tail trying to make it cry, while the other two romp in the ball pit. "I'd quicker thought Ryan Gosling would marry me before you'd leave Minot! Lordy!"

"Right? No one ever leaves Minot." We both shake our heads at the sad truth.

"Oh, darlin', don't you remember Colleen Fishburn? She left about five years back for a 'spa vacation.' My left cheek! The only 'spa' in Rancho Mirage, California, is the one Mrs. Betty Ford created herself. Colleen was plastered seven days a week from eyes open to eyes shut, so we all knew the story. Honest to Pete! She met some rich fella out there who was the worse for wear and dryin' out. Strange bedfellows, I tell ya. They ran off to live the fancy high life in Hernando, Florida, and thought nobody was the wiser. Shoot!"

Millie speaks fast and rarely breathes. But, long ago, I learned she makes a tiny sniffing sound and says something like "shoot" or "lordy" when she's finished a thought. That's my cue to start talking. Just not too much.

"I always wondered where she went." My straw hits the bottom of the cup, creating a vaguely obscene noise. As usual, I blush like I was caught with my pants down. "Oh, speaking of leaving Minot, I could use your help with my move. I don't know where to begin."

"Where are you movin' to?" Millie stares at me as if this is a logical question.

"Well, uhm, you see, I don't know. I haven't figured it out yet."

"Randy Larson! You tell me you're movin' and don't even know where to? Sakes alive, I'd say you need some help!"

Everything about this moment reminds me of Mother. I can take a good-natured tongue-lashing from Millie, but this feels like a visit from the grave. My eye twitches ever so slightly. I take a deep breath and remind myself I'm an adult.

"You're right, Millie. I'm not even sure where to start. I

need a job, a place to live, a city, and...."

"Slow down. You came to the right place. You don't think the annual church bazaar organizes itself, do you? No one is better at making plans than me." Millie straightens her back until she appears to tower over me. "Now, get out your notebook and write this down. We'll start with what I like to call The Big Plan."

"Yes, ma'am."

Millie scans the room for her kids as I search my backpack for the red Minot State University Beavers notebook and pen. "Annabel! For cryin' out loud! Get Zach out of that ball pit. He ain't even bouncin'; he's just licking the balls. And where in tarnation is Jolene? Help Mama and watch over your brother and sister." She looks at me and winks. "Too bad my husband didn't spend more time developing *his* tongue skills in the ball pit!" We both laugh.

There was a day when I had hours to talk with Millie. Now I get minutes between child emergencies. Why does anyone want to be a parent?

"Take this down. First, ya gotta decide on a place to move to. Lordy!" She throws her hands in the air. "I won't be any help in that department 'cause I don't know Wichita from Waikiki. But, selfishly, I'd like you to live in a vacation destination so's Dave and I could visit. Somewhere close to Disney World would be nice."

"Keep Florida in mind. Check."

"Then you need a visit to hunt for a job and place to live. Give yourself a good three months to accomplish this. It might take more if you want to buy a place. Do you want to buy a house?"

"I haven't thought about it." I pause from frantic note-taking. "Maybe I'll just rent until I decide if I like living there."

"That's solid. You can't be stuck owning a place between a whorehouse and an opium den just because you don't know where the good neighborhoods are." This oddly specific prediction should be shocking. But, to be fair, I have no track record for wise decisions. "And that brings us to selling your place. What a sad day that'll be! We have so many memories of your house! All the pizzas, Scrabble games, and Christmas cookie decorations. Your mother was a saint; God rest her soul. Not a day goes by I don't regret leaving the freezer door open so's your ice cream cake melted and ruined your eighth birthday. Your mother shoulda whooped me good! Sakes!"

We take a few minutes to reminisce on the thousands of adventures Millie and I have had over the years. I wish she'd forget about when we were four, and I put earthworms in my mouth to see if they would come out of my butt. (They don't. Well, at least not in the same condition they went in.) So many of the stories just serve to embarrass me. I'll miss her.

"We need to focus," I say after a particularly mortifying story of a poorly timed eighth-grade erection. "This list isn't going to finish itself, Millie. How long do you suppose it'll take to sell the house and move?"

"Oh, give yourself three months. A cute little place like that should sell in a heartbeat. It's the packing that'll take time. And you can count on me to organize your garage sale. I'll chase those cheap biddies away and get you top dollar for every one of your treasures! I will, I tell ya."

I smile. "Let's see. That's three months to find a job and place to live, then three months to sell my home and move. It's that easy?"

"Sounds about right. Six months should do it. When do you plan to be settled in the new place?"

"Well, summers in North Dakota are the best, and I'd like to enjoy one more." That gets an agreement nod. "So, I should move by September. Does that work?"

"September, huh? It's already February. That only gives you one month to come up with a destination." She wrinkles her nose and shrugs. "You're an ambitious one; I'll give you that."

"Yeah, I guess...."

"And maybe a little naive." Millie suddenly whips her head around and stands. She has a sort of spider sense when it comes to her kids. "Annabel! I told you to watch Zach! He's gone and puked all over the ball pit. I knew that would happen if he kept licking every set of balls he could get his hands on! Lordy! Go collect your sister, and I'll take care of the little demon."

She dashes off, grabs her kids, and runs out the door. Not even a goodbye. Or money for her part of the bill. To be fair, vomit does require an immediate response.

The Big Plan now drives my daily schedule. I think about it every waking moment.

A broader travel experience would be helpful about now. Yes, I've been to the big cities everyone visits, like Fargo and Bismarck. I even spent two nights at the Minneapolis Super 8, where the fancy deluxe room had a coffeemaker and extra towels. But that's about all I know.

Come to think of it, there was also the post-college graduation trip with Millie before she had kids. We thought an exotic beach vacation to Bay City, Michigan, would be a dream. It was closer to a nightmare. The Creekside Inn, a reportedly charming hotel near a rustic creek, sat high-and-dry in the middle of the I-75 cloverleaf – next to the dusty creek bed. We could reach out the window and touch the guardrail without stretching. The beautiful Lake Huron beach was a sandless area beside the Dow Chemical storage facility. After an hour or so of sunbathing on concrete, we barely noticed the dead fish smell.

Beyond that, I've only experienced cities through movies

and TV. Something tells me that doesn't count.

Back to The Big List. I need guidelines to help me suss out potential cities from endless possibilities. My Capricorn brain concocts four clear bullets that should set me in the right direction:

1. Big City. I want a place to come out of my shell. It will have a fast-paced life, exciting people, and tons of trendy restaurants and clubs.

2. Gay Community. I can be around other gay people, meet Prince Charming, and get married.

3. Subway. I've never been on a subway, but I know it's a glamorous way famous and sophisticated people get around.

4. Interesting. This is essential, if somewhat vague. Minot is fine but not interesting. I can't define it, but I'll know Interesting when I see it.

Oh, and the city can't be in North Dakota. That seems clear because of the subway requirement, but it's worth noting.

No, I've never hung out in fancy restaurants or discos. But isn't the reason for this move to break my current life's rigid mold and make myself a fabulous gay man with tons of friends and a full social calendar? I'll be like Cinderella – or is it Cinderfella? – after her fairy godmother makes her the belle of the ball!

Enough daydreaming. I have to make a list of cities. I'll go backward through Dad's trusty 1991 atlas, starting on the west coast.

San Francisco is first on the list, of course. Don't all gay people end up there at some time? And Los Angeles is included just because I will go to huge parties with movie stars like Neil Patrick Harris, whom I've loved since watching *Doogie Howser,*

MD reruns. He invites me to hang out every day, we fall in love, and he leaves David Burtka for me. The entire cast of *Will and Grace* is at our wedding, and we live happily ever after in a mansion overlooking the Pacific Ocean.

LA is definitely on the list.

Cities are added to the contender's list for the next two weeks, including Denver, Dallas, Minneapolis, Chicago, Atlanta, Columbus, Orlando, Washington, DC, New York, and Boston. I can imagine living in any of them.

Narrowing the list requires testing against my guidelines. Each place meets the first two requirements: big city and gay community. More than half get removed because they either don't have a subway or have a fake subway — you know: the trains all or mostly run above ground. If it's not underground, it's not an actual subway. I also remove Los Angeles. Do I really want to be on a subway when an earthquake hits? Neil Patrick Harris will be disappointed, but it must be done.

The list is narrowed to Atlanta, Boston, Chicago, New York, and Washington, DC, but that's as far as I can go on my own. This is where MJ comes in.

Mary Jo Klerken is the choir director at Minot High School. She and I sang in the church youth choir, graduated from Minot High School, and went to Minot State, where she majored in music. MJ, as I call her, should be my best friend due to the time we've spent together. But Millie won't allow that. Anyway, she's done lots of travel and can be helpful, if not somewhat bossy.

"It sure has been a minute since we spent an evening together, Randy. I'm so excited you rang me up!"

MJ arrives on my porch at precisely 6:30 with her shoulder-length, dishwater blonde hair sporting vertical bangs like she slept face-down for a week. Her tote bag — emblazoned with "Jesus Nailed It!" in large block letters — carries Sprite and regular Doritos (she says the fancy flavors are pretentious).

"I hope you don't think I'm tacky for wearing my Easter sweater early this year. It might be too warm next month, with the holiday coming so late and all." Her oversize, homemade wool sweater displays a large, crocheted Jesus nailed to an actual wooden cross. It's her favorite sweater, making an appearance every spring. I have no idea how she washes it with all those thorns and things.

"Oh." I just nod my head in agreement. Unfortunately, the time of year is not what makes this sweater tacky. "I'm glad you could come. I've got to decide on a new city, and you're my only friend with real travel experience. I want you to help me pick a great place to live."

She throws her lime green Jaclyn Smith Collection puffer coat — purchased with a coupon from Sears — onto Mother's chair. Then, with a skill developed over years of serving church spaghetti dinners, she pours two red Solo cups of Sprite and settles on the floor next to the coffee table.

"Perfect. I created the complete list of cities I've been blessed to visit since middle school, so we can start there. I left off the Lake Erie cruise with the Lutheran Ladies since we only stopped in Vermilion and Ashtabula. Here goes. My world travels include, in alphabetical order:

- Branson, Missouri (three times!)
- Clewiston, Florida
- Duluth, Minnesota
- Fargo (of course, many times)
- Fort Wayne, Indiana
- Kenosha, Wisconsin
- Modesto, California
- Tulsa, Oklahoma

How many of these are on your list?"

This is awkward. MJ vowed to visit all the major cities in the US, but I don't think we share the same definition of "major." Is Modesto even a real place?

"It doesn't seem like our lists have any crossover," I say as politely as possible.

"Stop joshing! Not even Fort Wayne? What's on your list?"

I show her my final five. Her face scrunches in the usual way, like trying to get unconstipated while eating a lemon wedge. I don't know if it means she's thinking or is backed up.

"Not that it's my business, Randy, but why would a person in their right mind want to live in *any* of those places? Hundreds of people die every day in cities like those. Shootings. Falling off tall buildings. Rabid rat bites." She gasps. "It's just not safe. Maybe you should reconsider Clewiston."

I go point-by-point through the list of criteria while she continues to make the same face. I wonder if this is why she's 33 and never had a date.

"Well, in my opinion, you're putting too much emphasis on the subway thing. Those are death traps full of thieves and rapists. Now, on the other hand, you can't go wrong when you think of what Jesus would do. He traveled on land, water, and in the air." She piously touches the crucifix around her neck, dangling near the sweater crucifix, which gets snagged by the crucifix charm bracelet. I help her disentangle the clustered symbols of torture. "Jesus never traveled underground. So I can only deduce that subway travel is for heathens."

It's hard to counter her logic, such that it is. My mind conjures the superhero, Hedgehog Jesus, who evades Pontius Pilate by burrowing under Judaea. I giggle aloud, adding another layer of constipation to her face – nothing friendly in this look.

"MJ, millions of people are in the cities on my list. Most of them aren't even dead. Besides, you have to go to places like these to find a real gay community. Don't you think it's time I got out there to see what I've been missing?"

Mary Jo reaches her left hand to her chest in a pearl-clutching motion, careful not to do any more damage to her bevy of crucifixes. I'm afraid of what she will say next.

"You know I've come to accept your homo-ness, Randy.

And I still love you, even if I hate your sin. But if you move to Sodom or Gomorrah, the temptations will be great. I've heard they have parades every year where thousands of people run the streets naked as jaybirds! And what if you start having sex with farm animals? Or get suffocated in an orgy!"

Has she always been a walking cliché? I've lived near farm animals and never once considered having sex with one. She must be thinking of Will Jorgensen. People say he needs to send roses to the family's dairy cow every Valentine's Day.

"I don't think there are many farms in Chicago or New York." That should clear the air.

"Maybe this wasn't such a good idea." MJ takes a hefty swig of her Sprite. "I can't be a party to your eternal destruction. You've got a great house and life right here in Minot. No good can possibly come from moving away. Why don't you pray on it some, and we can chat again after church on Sunday."

MJ stands and puts on her coat. I look at this person with cherry lip gloss, saddle shoes, and ornamental symbols of capital punishment... and I know I have to get out of this place. We walk to the door and hug. My shirt gets caught in the thorny Jesus crown attached to her sweater, and we perform an awkward dance of disentanglement. MJ is convinced this is a sign I'm making a mistake.

"You can keep the Doritos but give me the Sprite. I shouldn't drink alone, but this has me too upset. Promise me you'll pray on this." I nod. "Good. See you Sunday, Randy. God bless."

The door closes, and I let out a frustrated sigh. I will make this decision, with or without help from anyone.

Armed with my yellow legal pad, laptop, Doritos, and a lite beer, I sit at the kitchen table to look over the five finalists. I can't live in all of them. Maybe I need to consider the 'interest-ing' requirement since the first three points are met.

Interesting.

How do I quantify this? (A good accountant always asks this question.) All five cities are interesting, aren't they? What are the ups and downs of life in each of them? I'll list four pros and cons for each place and see what emerges.

Atlanta. Pros: Coca-Cola, sunny, warm, and I think it's close to Disney World (so Millie can visit).

Cons: Southern accents, humidity, hurricanes, and Baptists (not the good kind we have in North Dakota).

Boston. Pros: Atlantic Ocean, American history, tea parties, and lobster.

Cons: Cold, weird accent, mobsters, and Catholics.

Chicago. Pros: Skyscrapers, pizza, Lake Michigan, and Marshall Field's.

Cons: Cold, Midwesterners, cold, and cold.

New York. Pros: It's freakin' New York City!

Cons: It's freakin' New York City!

Washington, DC. Pros: Dupont Circle, museums, cherry blossoms, and government jobs.

Cons: Humidity, politicians, murders, and politicians.

This exercise made the decision a bit easier. It's becoming clear I have favorites.

Atlanta comes off the list first. Baptists of the northern va-riety are just fine, especially in small numbers, but Southern Baptists? I'm afraid there are gangs of them on the streets just looking for people like me. And I don't want to develop a southern accent.

Boston and Chicago need to go as well. I have this one chance to get out of North Dakota, and I shouldn't waste it on another frozen tundra. Besides, it's hard to be fabulous when you have to wear a winter coat most of the year.

So that leaves me with just two choices: Washington and New York. Both are on the East Coast, the most sophisticated part of the country, and likely full of gay people. Using the Ten-Percent-of-People-Are-Gay Rule, Washington has nearly twice as many *gay* people as Minot's entire population! New York has over 20 times more gay people than Minot has Lutherans! These are very sobering statistics.

New York is supposed to be the center of the universe. It has everything. But, if I'm honest with myself, I don't think I'm ready to move to a place as crowded as the Big Apple. It sounds exciting but also scary. Can I really handle that place on my own?

Still, Washington has about 650,000 more people than Minot. By comparison, it's a big city – probably more manageable than New York. It has lots of cultural activities and the Smithsonian. Celebrities are always there speaking at rallies. And I can find a government job that will give me insurance and a pension. Mother and Dad would approve.

It's all here in pencil on a legal pad. The numbers don't lie. I know what I have to do. My new home will be in Washington, DC.

FOUR

Lipstick on a Pig

The Big Plan continues to develop despite me. If only Mother could have lived long enough to get me through this one last thing. Absent my parents, I may have inadvertently given Millie the reigns for this life-changing project. She calls daily for a status update – except when mothering her children takes precedence over mothering me – and usually adds a few things to my action list. What does that say about my independence?

March through May are reserved for finding a job, securing an apartment, and selling the family home. This is on top of my full-time job and other life activities, which are admittedly few. A yellow legal pad with a running To-Do list prominently resides on the kitchen table, keeping me focused between Millie's calls.

The first item is employment.

I never learned real job search skills – nepotism requires little effort. My parents secured every job I've had, from mowing lawns to the current Minot Schools position. My one-page college resume hasn't been revisited in over 10 years. It would be wise to get some help with this project.

Martin Mroczkowski graduated with me from Minot State and had a handful of jobs before we lost touch. He should put 'job seeker' as one of his professions. It's been a few years since we talked, but I'll bet he would help me out.

"Hey, Randy! You're a voice for sore eyes! How ya doin'?"

"Not too bad, Marty. You still living in Minot?"

"Nope. I'm living down in Fargo now. This guy quit working for the Man and opened his own business." I can almost hear his ego inflate as he speaks. "It's called Mroczkowski & Sons Taxes And Kapital Equities. I spell 'capital' with a K because it's ironic. M-S-T-A-K-E dot biz." He laughs pompously, like a movie caricature of a fat, wealthy man. Is it 'ironic' that people will get his website every time someone types 'mistake?'

"I'll check it out." I won't check it out. "Mroczkowski and sons, huh? You have kids?"

"Nah. I'm just planning ahead."

No, I definitely won't check it out. "I see. That's impressive. It's a step up from junior accountant at H&R Block. When did you make the switch?"

"Oh, I had a little disagreement with the management about a year ago. I thought we were dating, but she called it something else. My lawyer said I should find another place of employment. It was a good opportunity to become my own boss."

I don't ask for details. "I'll bet."

"Sorry to hear about your folks. My parents told me they passed recently. You got any plans now that they're gone?"

"Thanks. Actually, that's why I called you. I've decided to move to Washington, DC. Set out on my own in the big city, just like in the movies!"

"Good for you! Randy in the nation's capital. Who'd-a thunk? What's your job?"

"I'm working on that part. I don't even know how to start since the last time I searched for a job, Obama had just been elected."

"The good old days, as they say," he says with another pompous laugh.

"Yes, well, I pulled out my college resume, added my current position, and it still looks thin. I think it needs some tweaks. Maybe you could give me a little advice?"

"With your resume? Boy, that stuff changes all the time. People have video resumes now. Can you believe it? They put together a whole song-and-dance routine to describe their shit job at McDonald's. It's un-fucking-believable!"

I picture myself dressed as Ethel Merman singing my resume to the tune of "I Got Rhythm." My descent down a long, grand staircase is met by 80 gorgeous men in top hats and tails. They sing and dance each time I list one of my skills.

"I doubt I'll do something like that," I say while quietly rehearsing the choreography. "Best for me to stick to a traditional format. I only have one job and a college diploma if I remove lawn mowing, newspaper carrier, and Dairy Queen fry cook. It fits on half a page. You got any suggestions?"

"I guess it depends on what kind of job you want. Are you shooting for CFO, or are you more of a ground-floor type of guy?"

"I currently share a cubicle with the rotating intern."

"So, we'll say ground floor." I don't have the energy to be insulted. "Not much you can do about a thin resume, man. You'll just have to charm them."

I know less about charm than I do about resumes. Or choreography. "You think I can get away with something so flimsy?"

"Unless you want to lie about it. But stretching the truth only works if you take adequate precautions. I learned that the hard way."

I suddenly remember Marty had trouble getting a job after graduation, so he changed his alma mater from Minot State University to Harvard. The next application got an offer. He lasted one week before a real Harvard graduate reminisced about life in Cambridge. Marty thought Harvard was in New Jersey. Thus began his descent to H&R Block.

"I can't think of anything to pad it with. Can you make a school accountant job look especially good?"

"Can Queen Elizabeth look sexy? Low lighting, heavy gauze, and a good bit of distance, but it's still lipstick on a pig. Just use lots of adjectives."

I didn't understand anything he said. "Could I send it to you for a little editing?"

"Sure, pal. Use my new work email: Big@MSTAKE.biz. I go by Mr. Big in the office." Mr. Big in a one-person office? No wonder the email address came out so wrong.

"Great. I'll send it tomorrow."

"So, you got any special lady, Randy?" This question always makes me blush. "You can't be a bachelor your whole life."

Marty isn't in on my sexual orientation. I was in the closet through college, and it's been a selective coming-out process since.

"No, no one special. I've had a lot to do with Mom and Dad dying and all. Maybe once I get to Washington, I can get into the dating pool."

"Dive in, man. You were always going to have to settle, and age doesn't help expand your field of prospects."

This is one of my friends? "Great. Thanks, Marty. I gotta get going. Look for my email later."

"Ciao! Catch you on the flip side!"

Well, it's a start. I fritter away a half-hour creating adjectives that make my numerical accuracy appear significant. 'Precise.' 'Skillful.' 'Detailed.' 'Meticulous.' Is there any difference? I've got two-thirds of a page before giving up. It goes to Marty, and I move on to the job search.

FIVE

I Doubt You'll Do Any Damage

Marty's resume edits arrived early this morning. He stretched it to three-quarters of a page with creative font sizes and an impressive number of synonyms for 'accurate.' I'll take it. His email also included a DC escort service link – Tits-R-Us – should I want some 'extracurricular activities' while I'm there.

I want to look down on his stupidity, but this reflects more on my poor communication skills than his sense of propriety.

He *is* right that I should give myself a gift for significant progress on the Big Plan – it just won't be sex with a woman. A celebratory supper at the Dakota Square Mall Olive Garden, one of Minot's fanciest restaurants, is in order. I go alone – as usual – only to find MJ leaving as I arrive.

"Randy!" She hugs my neck so hard that I cough like a cat choking on a fur ball. "What do you think of my new hairdo?"

This is new? "It looks great."

"I feel like a movie star!" she says, unable to contain herself. I'll let her have this one, given she resembles the girl who gets bullied in an after-school special. Maybe she used a different freeze gel on her bangs?

"I'm off to Women's Pie Night at the Aldersen's. I swear we have the country's best pie makers right here in Minot!

Lordy! You should come over for a taste, and I guarantee you will re-think this notion of moving."

I haven't had homemade pie since Mother died, so the invitation sounds even better than endless breadsticks. "Really? I'm allowed at women's night?"

"Of course not, silly! I was just sayin'. Can you imagine a man at the women's meeting? Talk about a scandal!" We both laugh at the absurdity of this conversation. Only I don't think we have the same idea of what's absurd.

"Yeah, I suppose. We'll have to get together another time before I leave town."

"I have faith you'll re-think this move, Randy. We can talk about it when we get together. In the meantime, I'm praying night and day you'll see the glorious riches already raining down upon you." MJ strikes a piously condescending pose. "Jesus is giving you a golden shower right here in Minot, and you need to turn your face to receive it." I shrug and faintly smile. "Now, don't fill up on breadsticks!"

I'm relieved watching her skip – not kidding, just like elementary school – to her car. The more I interact with longtime friends here, the more I'm ready to move.

Life continues in its usual, mundane way for the next three weeks. Indecisiveness has returned, making it hard to commit to the search or even the move. I made a few job applications to Federal Government agencies Dad would approve of, but nothing excites me. I began to wonder if this was all a bad idea.

I'm about to bite into a typical hot dog dinner on a random late-March Wednesday when my phone rings.

"Mr. Larson?" says the nondescript voice.

"Yes."

"This is Laura Booth from the United States Treasury

personnel office in Washington, DC. We have your application for the position of accountant. Are you still interested in this job?"

"Interested?" I stammer. There's an awkward pause where I should say more, but I don't know how this is supposed to work.

"I'll take that as a 'yes.'" I can almost feel her sigh through the phone. "We would like to interview you. Would Thursday, the fourth of April, at 11:00 am work for you?"

An average person would check the calendar and maybe comment on moving some things around. Me? I just say, "Yeah."

"Okay, then, we will send you a letter with all the necessary information next week, including a list of area hotels. In the meantime, you will be responsible for your transportation, accommodations, and meals during the interview period. I recommend you arrive the day before and depart the following afternoon, should we wish to bring you back for a second interview."

"Okay."

"Thank you, Mr. Larson. We will see you on April fourth."

I said only four words comprising eight syllables and zero complete sentences. Still, the two-minute conversation brought excitement back to this change. The corners of my mouth curl into a self-satisfied smile.

The majestic arches and spectacular floor mosaics of Regan National Airport sparkle in the April sun – oops! Sorry! The people I keep banging into – or who slam into me – seem more interested in running to their destination than gawking at everything. The airport looks like a yellow Emerald City, and I need to take it all in.

My first *ever* subway ride runs from inside the airport to Metro Center. Years of dreaming have led me to the moment I go underground and board the sleek, silver trains of the Metro. Unfortunately, this station is high above the airport, with trains whizzing in bright sunlight. It's a different ride than I imagined, but I push aside disappointment. I'm still riding the Metro, right?

The train doors close faster than expected, slamming the brand new American Tourister suitcase I bought with a Walmart gift card. The doors re-open, but one of the wheels is stuck between the car and the platform. Another slam on the bag. They re-open as I yank the wheels free and stumble inside. It's sad to see deep scratches on the hard black sides. The Metro is not giving me a warm welcome.

"Get your ass on the train, Okie!" a guy yells to me. He looks like a bum who rides the subway all day to stay warm. I'll sit at the opposite end. The train jolts forward before I'm seated, throwing me full force into a woman holding the pole. My face lands directly between her boobs.

"Do you mind?" she says, shoving me away.

"I'm sorry. I didn't mean to...."

"Save it, pervert."

The fumbling continues until I reach a seat in the back. I'm facing opposite the direction of train movement, and it starts to make me slightly motion sick. No, a lot motion sick. It must show because the older woman beside me touches my arm. "Are you okay?"

Dizziness overwhelms me as I look into her sweet eyes. "Yes. I'm...."

Projectile vomiting. Right at her face. First is the tuna sandwich from lunch. Then airplane snacks. Finally, breakfast eggs and toast. Something in there looks like spinach. It's on her hair, face, jacket, slacks, and shoes. It's grosser when you put the smell with the visual.

She screams like she's being assaulted. Well, I guess she is, in a way.

"I'm so sorry!" I manage to say before I begin another round of regurgitation. This time it's on my shoes and the floor.

The train pulls into Crystal City, and the woman runs out the door in a waft of sour bile. Everyone is staring.

"I'm backward," I say to anyone listening. No response. I'll just exit and try to become anonymous somewhere else. This is not what I imagined a subway ride would be.

With only one shoe gripping the sidewalk, I make a step-and-slide motion into an adjacent hotel's lobby restroom. I smell like vomit cologne. The chunks wash off my shoes quickly, clogging the sink for the next person. Sorry. Ten minutes later, I'm back to looking and smelling as close to normal as possible.

The poor woman next to me is unlikely to have the same luck.

Once the JW Marriott stands majestically before me, flags gently rippling in the humid air, the subway challenges disappear. The future is all I see. Broad, bustling streets offer an automotive soundtrack for a city whose energy exceeds my imagination.

The superior room is considerably better than the Creekside Inn and Minneapolis Super 8 – the entire list of hotels I've seen. This one is elegantly decorated in gold and white, with a fantastic view of the Washington Monument. I think I can even see the US Treasury. This must be the way all Washingtonians live.

My first DC meal is a McDonald's Big Mac combo; I'm on a budget. Sightseeing is confined to the hotel lobby so I can get to bed early. As I lie wrapped in the cool, white sheets, the poofy comforter nestled under my chin, my brain tries to grasp the enormity of what I am doing. I'm leaving everything

I've ever known to start a new life in the nation's – no, the world's capital.

I fall asleep with a stupid grin only a small-town boy in the big city can manage.

The Treasury's stark marble reception area coldly greets me 10 minutes before my interview. It's an intimidating space but grand in a way appropriate for the United States Government. Nothing like this could exist in Minot.

A short woman with gray hair that says she ran out of conditioner approaches me. Colorless eyes find me over half-rim glasses. She's moving quickly, blowing frizzy pieces of hair sticking out from an otherwise neat bun. I'm reminded of Mother.

"Mr. Larson?"

"Yes," I say, standing to greet her.

"I'm Laura Booth. We spoke on the phone. Please follow me to one of our interview rooms." The firm handshake, absent eye contact, is more perfunctory than welcoming.

We walk rapidly up one flight of steps to a small conference room ablaze in neon light. Ms. Booth sits at the head of the table, and I take the seat to her left. She looks exhausted and disinterested.

"Normally, I would have the department head with me, but he had a family emergency and won't be in today," she says, looking down. "The assistant head is also out sick. That leaves me to do 14 interviews on my own. I guess that's better than the 16 I did yesterday. Also, alone." She lets out a quick laugh like a cartoon character going insane. "We've had so many jobs open I can't keep up with all the hiring. And I didn't get any sleep last night because my cat got sick." This finally merits eye contact. "You ever see a cat stand in front of the TV and spray diarrhea all over the screen? And I was watching *Game of Thrones*! It's the kind of crap that makes me regret joining AA."

"Oh." Empathy has never been my strong suit.

"Anyway, let's get started, shall we?" She is breathing quickly, eyes darting across the pages before her.

Laura asks simple questions about my background, schooling, and what I do at Minot Public Schools. Is she yawning because my answers are boring? And she never smiles. Her pen even breaks while writing notes. This isn't Laura Booth's day.

After about 15 minutes, she gathers my resume and other papers into a neat pile. She sits back in her chair, looking over smudged glasses in my general direction. "I just have one more question. You've spent your entire life in the same city far from here. Cincinnati?"

"Minot."

"Yes. Idaho."

"North Dakota."

"Whatever. This is a big move for you. What brings you to Washington, DC?"

I planned for questions about my credentials and past work, but not this. Funny. It's an obvious one now that I'm presented with it. Why hadn't I thought more of it before this moment?

"I guess the best answer is it's time for me to move on with my life now that my parents are gone. Yes, I have been in the same town for 32 years. It's a nice place with nice people. But when I look in the mirror, I can't help but wonder how I would look if I lived in Washington. Everything here is so interesting." I pause to consider telling her I also want to marry a rich, famous man but decide against it. I'll come out to people later. "I know my life will be wonderful and filled with good things if I move forward with a positive attitude and excitement."

That is as honest as I can get.

Laura Booth makes eye contact briefly, and I see her soften. "I'll drink to that. Don't tell my sponsor." She glances at her watch, rubs her hands together, and takes a deep breath. "So, Mr. Larson, you'll do just fine in this job. I can always count on Midwesterners to be hard-working and honest, even if they can't say 'soda.'" I shift uncomfortably in my chair. "Normally, we would take some time to talk with you longer. Still, I've got a dozen more interviews to conduct for similar positions across the agency, and I doubt you'll do any damage. We can offer you the job with a GS-08 salary. There's no negotiation at this level, so just take it, and I can move on with my work."

I'm stunned. First, I didn't expect to get an offer so fast. Second, I imagined there would be more celebration involved. Even a smile would be friendly. On the other hand, she said I wouldn't do any damage. "You mean I got the job?"

"Yes, Mr. Larson, you got the job." She lets out an exasperated sigh and makes a note in my file with the broken pen. "You'll start June first."

"June? Uhm, no, I don't think I can start that fast. I need to sell my house, find a place to live, and move across the country."

She sighs again. "How soon can you be here, then?"

I think about the Big Plan Millie and I put together. "Would August first work for you?"

"August? That's a bit longer than we want to wait." She thinks for a moment, likely weighing her tolerance for sitting through another interview against having a position sit empty for two months. Her hands make a circular motion like she's stirring a drink.

"Do you need to interview some more people and then decide? I can wait a little longer for an answer." This wasn't intended to push her over the edge, but it did.

"Interview more people? This place is so understaffed I'll never stop interviewing people for years to come." She shakes her head. "Screw it. I'll accommodate an August start. You have a big move, and I ran out of cigarettes, so I just don't care right now. Wait here, and I'll have my assistant come by with the paperwork. We will need to run a background check and call your references before the offer is finalized. It's all just a formality, really. Welcome to the United States Treasury." She extends her hand to congratulate me, though I can see in her eyes she has already moved on to the following interview. Or maybe she's fantasizing about cigarettes and bourbon.

"Thank you!" I say, shaking her hand.

About 20 minutes later, I walk out as the Federal Government's newest employee. The pay is lower than I hoped – and the cost of living higher. I'll need to keep a tight budget.

I grab a bite to eat on 16th Street and start walking toward Dupont Circle. Sarah Horowitz, the real estate agent Millie found online, is meeting me soon for a whirlwind tour of apartments. I'd like to see a little of the neighborhood before we meet. It's incredible to think I'll be living here in just a few short weeks!

SIX

At Your Age?

Sarah Horowitz should have no trouble finding me, a pie-faced North Dakotan sitting alone in a Dupont Circle Starbucks. Everyone else is paired with someone; most are men who look like they belong in the city. By that, I mean they look gay to me. I try not to stare. It'll take some time to get used to this new reality.

A diminutive lady, not five feet tall, shuffles through the door with a rolling motion like riding a unicycle. She pushes back long gray hair that hasn't seen a brush in weeks. Her face is nearly concealed by oversize, black-rimmed glasses sporting a prescription that triples the size of her eyes. She gives me a clandestine nod as she approaches.

"You must be my two o'clock," she says in a voice loud enough to be heard down the street. "I'm Sarah Horowitz, real estate agent to the stars." She barks an unsmiling chuckle while extending her hand. Did I miss a joke?

"Nice to meet you," I say, shaking her hand. "I'm no movie star, just a lowly accountant. I hope you're not disappointed."

She makes a strange guttural sound, like trying to clear phlegm. "Disappointment is my constant companion. Besides, movie stars would be looking at *nice* apartments. I'm not here

42

to judge." Sarah continues to stand, surveying the room nervously, like a fugitive. "You want a coffee or something?"

"No, thank you. I don't drink much coffee." Her stare tells me I've said too much.

Sarah is wrapped in a fur stole, oddly inappropriate for the late spring warm weather. She fluffs the expensive garment dramatically to ensure everyone in the vicinity has taken notice before haphazardly tossing it on the sticky bench seat. "I got this pain in my right foot like I should die before day's end," she winces as she slides into the booth. "Bunions. And probably varicose veins, or gout, or something like that."

"Oh."

"So," Sarah leans toward me, "you're moving to the nation's capital from one of the nondescript states, huh? And this is the first time you've rented?"

"Well, North Dakota. It's actually a nice place." She rolls her eyes, so I let it go. "And, yes, it's my first apartment."

She sits bolt upright, mouth open in a gasp. "At your age? Have you been in prison or something?"

"What? No!" My face contorts comically. "Why would you assume that? I've been living with my parents. They passed away, and I decided to move to the city."

"Living with your parents?" Another gasp. "At your age? I presume there's no girlfriend in this picture."

My eye twitches a little. I expected more questions about my income. "No. I'm single."

"Single? No girlfriend? At your age?" She pulls her mouth tight and hard to the left as she looks around the room. "You shoulda told me you're gay."

"What? I'm not... Why did you say that?" My face burns as a drop of sweat rolls from my armpit.

"Single guy lives with his parents and sits alone in a Dupont coffee joint. It's the definition of homosexual!" She folds her arms and nods at her clever sleuthing.

I feel cornered. "*You* suggested we meet here! I don't know anything about this city."

"Your kind is always so dramatic. Of course, you don't. I'm not trying to be a nudge." She rolls her eyes and pushes back her frizzy hair. "Now I gotta re-think where you should live. I hadn't planned on sticking with just the gay spots. You shoulda told me so I could prepare."

Another drop of sweat. "I only want a nice neighborhood. I made a list." I dig into my pocket when she puts her hand up.

"Slow down, there, fancy boy. I got a process." She puts her purse on the table and roots through it. "Here." She pushes some papers at me. "Fill these out quick while I get situated."

The forms cover basic information about me, my income, and where I want to live. "Do you have a pen?" I ask.

"So, this is how it's going to be? I should be your mother for all I have to do, what with picking your apartment in a neighborhood where you can meet a nice man and all." She pulls out a cheap Bic, nearly chewed to the point of leaking, and hands it to me.

"Thank you." I can't make eye contact anymore.

"It's my lot in life to serve other people." Another eye roll. A 1984 Washington atlas, lamination pulling from the corners, emerges from her purse. I suspect she could also have a hat rack hidden somewhere deep in the bag. "Never leave the house without this thing."

"Don't most people use the map on their phone?"

Sarah leans in and whispers, "*They* follow you with phone maps. Besides, paper doesn't emit signals that give you the cancer." Her eyebrows arch as she looks around to see who's listening.

Dad would have said the same thing — except the part about being followed. Maybe that's a sign to trust this person. I hand her my completed paper as she roots through her purse for a mint. "It's good to have fresh breath." She pulls lint off a mint-like object and pops it in her mouth. "So, where is it you think you want to live?"

"Probably one of these nine neighborhoods," I say excitedly, showing her my list. "Maybe we could see several places before narrowing it down."

Sarah's head drops as she looks over the top of her glasses. "What am I? Your personal tour guide? We'll look at two, maybe three places. Tops. Gay joints, so you're comfortable."

"Oh. It's just that I thought you would show me each of these areas so I can get a feel for the neighborhoods. I don't care if it's gay or whatever."

"You'll only get confused." She waves her hand dismissively. "Besides, some of them don't allow dogs."

"What? I don't have a dog."

"Good. Then we can take those places off your list. As your agent, I am highly skilled in finding the perfect place for you. I'm a bit of an apartment yenta if I say so myself. Now, stand up."

"Stand up? Are we leaving?"

"So many questions! Up!" I stand. She smirks as her eyes scan me from top to bottom. "Sit. I know all I need."

"From looking at me? How is this going to help find an apartment?" My voice sounds shrill.

"I have an eye. This shmatte," she brushes my shirt, "says you're gay, but the cheap fabric says you can't afford to be too G-A-Y. So, Dupont is out." She looks at the income line on the questionnaire. "This is your income or your shoe size? You can't afford to walk past most of the gay joints."

"How much does an apartment cost?" I try to focus despite the growing pit stains on my shirt.

"Already, you sound cheap! Look, Stephen."

"Randy."

"Randy." Another eye roll. "You'll be happy living in a place where you can at least smell the food from the gay neighborhood, yes? Maybe crane your neck a smidge and catch a glimpse of two or three colors in the rainbow flag?"

"What does that mean?"

"Good. It's settled. You'll live in Adams Morgan." She smugly pulls out a folder to show me a dingy apartment. "I got two listings there. You can have this one."

I shake my head like a confused dog. "I'm sorry. I can't follow what's going on."

"I found you an apartment. It's perfect. When the wind blows from the right direction, you can practically smell the Axe Body Spray wafting up from Dupont." A broad smile – her first today – makes her look like a poorly prepared corpse.

"Uhm, okay. Can I at least see it?"

"Of course. What schmuck rents an apartment without seeing it?" Eye roll.

"How much does it cost?"

"Too much. But you'll be frugal. Let's go."

We take a taxi to a small building in Adams Morgan – she insists I pay the fare. The apartment is a one-bedroom on the second floor with windows out to 18th Street. There's nothing wrong with it. I just don't know how it compares to other places on the market.

"You like it?" she asks.

"It's fine. Can we look at the other place?"

"It's already rented," she says, looking away.

"But I thought you had two places open."

"It rented while we were in the cab to this place. I got an email." She hasn't looked at a phone or computer the entire time we've been together. "So, you'll take this?"

We're moving a little too fast. "Can't we look at a few more places?"

"I'm a busy woman. Besides, if I don't get out of these shoes in the next 30 minutes, I may have to be buried in them." She groans. "Nothing in Washington is better than this dump. Trust me."

"I guess. But I still don't know how much the rent is."

"Twenty-five hundred."

"Per year?"

"Did I show you a storage locker? Of course, it's not per year. That's per month." She gives me a condescending look and slowly shakes her head.

I never imagined paying so much for a place to live. Let alone something as small as this one-bedroom. "I was thinking closer to the $900 range. That would be better for my budget."

"So, you'll live in Kentucky and commute. I hear there's a train on odd-numbered days."

Now I'm panicked. "There's nothing in Washington around my price point?"

"Maybe you should rent the back seat of somebody's car. But that means giving up closet space." She begins to fidget. I can tell she has no patience for someone like me.

I do quick math in my head. "This place will eat up more than 55% of my annual income. Shouldn't I look for something in the 30% range? Isn't that the standard?"

"Fifty-five percent? Eh, you're in the neighborhood. Spitting distance, shall we say? When you consider heat, electricity, and pest control services, the 30 is practically 55. You're good. Are you going to take it?" Another smile accented by puppy-dog eyes.

"Pest control? And don't I have to add heat and electricity to the cost of *this* unit as well? I'm already at 55% *before* adding them in!"

"Hot air rises, and you'll put down some throw rugs. I just cut your heat bill in half. And the draft under the door cools the place in summer. Besides, you can't open the windows with the deafening street noise. You want to sleep, don't you? And you'll save money when you get rid of the dog. Do the math, but I'm certain I found you a bargain." I'm frozen in disbelief.

Such a huge decision! There is some money from Mother and Dad's estate I could tap into if the rent becomes a challenge. And I'll be prudent with budgeting. Besides, Sarah is a professional. She wouldn't put me in something I couldn't afford. Right?

"Still thinking about it?" she says impatiently.

"This is a major expense. I don't want to rush into anything."

"You're an educated adult. We've been at this for over an hour. How much more time do you need? I say, shit, or get off the pot, David."

"It's Randy."

"See how you notice every detail?" Her third smile. "I have a gut feeling says you'll make it work."

"I am good with details. And budgets." I think for a moment. "I guess you're the professional who knows what she's doing."

"Maybe I put that on my business card," she quips with a deadpan expression. "Can we get on with this before my support hose give out?"

After much handwringing and insult-enduring, I finally sign the lease. It may not be the best decision I've ever made, but it means I now have a home in Washington, DC.

On the flight back to Minot, I stare out the window, daydreaming of a new life in the nation's capital. It's so exhilarating. And so very scary. The big adventure is about to begin.

SEVEN

Jesus Is My Co-Pilot

Weeks have passed in a blur of activity until moving day is suddenly here. I'm staring at this empty house, a concrete reminder my time in Minot is over – even if I'm not completely prepared for what's ahead. On one hand, I managed to sell the house and most of its contents while finding a new job and apartment in Washington. And I did it without Mother's help! On the other hand, I should have worked on goals for the new life ahead of me. I chose a city that's interesting and has a gay community, but I don't know what to do with all that.

Unfortunately, today is *not* the day to start work on this project. It will wait until I'm settled.

"Goodbye, old life," I whisper to the ghosts of the house. "There are so many things I never told you. Maybe some things you already knew." A sigh escapes. "And now it's time to move on. I'll miss you, and I won't forget you." I pause as the first moment of sadness hits me. "Don't forget me."

I slide behind the wheel of a 15-foot U-Haul truck – one that looks like it recently careened over a cliff, exploded in flames and kept going – to drive 1,600 miles. It's my first time driving a moving truck. Any type of truck, for that matter. Large vehicles scare me more than roller coasters, spiders, and sushi combined.

For that reason, and solely for that reason, I asked Mary Jo to make the trip with me. The conversation could be weird, and she probably won't help with the driving. I just want to have someone with me when the truck careens off the next cliff. The holier-than-thou conversation is a small price for avoiding a *Thelma and Louise* ending.

"Well, I s'pose it's about that time," MJ says with her seatbelt firmly fastened. She's wearing a neon pink t-shirt announcing "Jesus Is My Co-Pilot" like an insurance policy. "Snacks are behind the seat. Water is here on the floor. The back door is closed and locked. And I put a Saint Christopher medal on the mirror. He protects all travelers, not just those crazy Catholics, right?" This would be a joke if someone else said it.

"Maybe we should convert before leaving just to make certain," I say, trying to be funny. MJ has never found humor in religion.

"Don't be flip, Randy Larson. I would sooner join a Buddhist cult than get mixed up with the Pope-lovers. Catholics are condemned to eternal suffering because they worship symbols and idols," she says as she secures a Jesus-holding-a-chalice coffee thermos and adjusts the 24-carat gold cross around her neck.

The driver's seat vibrates as I take one last look at my home since birth. "Well, that's that," I say with a slight nod. "Look at us leaving right on time."

"No, we're already 15 minutes behind schedule. I've got my work cut out for me keeping you on a schedule, Mr. Larson." And so it starts. Maybe the truck vibrations will put her to sleep.

"You're the best." It's better to ignore her bossiness and take what I can get. "Thanks for coming with me. We've got a long road ahead of us." I squeeze her hand quickly before putting the truck in gear. "Goodbye, Minot. Hello, Washington, DC!"

Ten minutes into the drive my knuckles are a ghostly white. I brought MJ to ease my driving anxiety, but she sits three feet away, making constant noise and oblivious to my terror. She delivers a monologue on every thought in her head, most relating to Bible study topics, with little interest in engaging me. And she already needs a restroom to expel the 16 ounces of water she drank since we left.

There is a 60-second pause in MJ's talking somewhere near the Minnesota border. The sound void is filled with an ominous quiet that can't be good. A cold water drop slides down my right side.

"Randy," MJ says, staring straight ahead.

"Yeah." Another drop of sweat.

"Jesus just spoke to me, and I have to tell you about it."

I've never heard Jesus speak. I assume his voice is a cross between Mr. Rogers and James Earl Jones – with a dash of Bea Arthur – something hard to miss in a space this size. Yet, I heard nothing. Two drops of sweat begin a race down my left side.

"Jesus said you should turn this truck around and go back to Minot where he has true followers who can help keep you on the straight-and-narrow."

"Turn around? Now?"

MJ turns an indignant eye in my direction. "I'm only repeating what Jesus said. Don't get snippy with me!"

I swallow hard. "Sorry. I didn't mean to be snippy. But we're about five hours into this trip. Couldn't he have told us sooner?"

MJ purses her lips and nods. "He said you would question him."

The sweat has worked its way to my forehead, and sweaty

palms are ineffective at wiping it away.

"This is a sign," she continues. "If you won't listen to Jesus now, it will only get worse when I'm not here to protect you." She turns to face me. "It was right you didn't tell people about your homo-ness all these years. Private thoughts, while still sinful, are better than public actions." She's on a roll, raising the volume and pitch of her voice. "The people in Washington will lead you to drink and fornicate and reduce your church tithing! Soon you'll think you can *morally* marry another man! Who will save you from yourself?" By now, she's breathing hard through gritted teeth.

"MJ!" I say louder than expected. My instinct is to fight with her, something new for me. But I know the argument could last for as many hours as we share the same space, so I bite my tongue. "Did Jesus really say we need to turn around now?"

MJ scowls a variation of her constipation face. "Not exactly. It seemed implied, though."

"Well," I tread lightly, "if he wasn't explicit with the instructions, why don't we save the conversation to after our long drive?" I look at her hopefully. She continues to stare at the road. "I'm already tense with this big truck. It seems Jesus would want me to operate the vehicle safely."

That seems to work. MJ is silent for another moment before resuming her discussion of some Bible study topic. Catastrophe avoided.

By the time we reach Madison, I'm exhausted. My back and shoulders are knotted from maintaining a death grip on the wheel, and I have a headache from MJ's nonstop voice. My only thoughts are of sleep.

The Motel 6 is shabbier than expected; the room smells of every previous traveler's body odor. Room 12 is the last available (Did someone die in here?), even though MJ called five times from the road to confirm there would be two deluxe rooms awaiting our late arrival.

"First, we have to share a room." Dramatic pause. "And I see only one bed," MJ remarks with disgust.

"That bothers you more than the smell?"

"I don't smell anything." To be fair, she houses an indeterminate number of cats. "There is a bigger problem, Randy. We are two unmarried people with only one bed."

"I guess that's all they have. It's fine for us to share. Unless you snore."

MJ has never found humor in bodily functions. "Ladies don't snore! That's not the issue. I've never slept with a man, and I don't intend to start with you. No offense."

I could say, "None taken," but that seems obvious.

"By 'slept with,' you mean intercourse, right?" I ask for clarification.

MJ brings her hands to her hips in a stage-worthy performance. "I mean in any sense of the word if you must know. But especially in that sense."

"I assure you nothing will happen. We can even build a pillow wall between us," I say with a cheeky smile.

MJ has never found humor in pseudo-sexual situations. "It's a sin to sleep with you and later tell my future husband I'm completely pure. How would I ever live with myself?" This is from a 33-year-old woman who has never had a date. The 'future husband' is likely a mythical creature.

"It's just sleep, MJ. The bed is big enough we don't even have to touch."

"Nope. I can't do it. Jesus said unmarried people should not have relations. This would feel like we're having relations. And what if I were to become in the family way after this?"

"How would you get pregnant?" I take a step back.

"Randy Larson! You know there are tons of examples of girls and boys hopping into the same bed only to find they have a little one on the way. The Lord works in mysterious ways." There's no arguing with a Lutheran who invokes the mystery of her god.

"Fine. What do you propose?"

"The gentlemanly thing is to give me the bed, and you sleep on the floor."

"The floor?" The thought of lying on green shag carpeting that was probably installed – and last cleaned – in the 1970s makes me queasy. A hard shudder rocks my shoulders.

"I suppose you *could* sleep in the bathtub."

My shoulders sag as I see no way to win this argument. "I'd rather try the floor. What do I use for bedding?"

"There's an extra blanket." She unfolds the tattered throw to find a Rorschach test-like stain pattern and a used condom. Somehow ignoring the rubber, MJ lays out the blanket and pillows in an open space next to the bed. If I weren't so tired, I'd fight back.

"That looks comfy!" she says with Martha Stewart warmth. "Now, give me a few minutes in the powder room to complete my beauty routine." The lock clicks almost before the door is closed. As if I would barge in on her Noxzema ritual.

The best I can do is hold my nose and lie on the blanket, fully clothed. Exhaustion puts me to sleep in seconds.

"Rise and shine, sleepyhead!" MJ chirps six hours later. She is already showered and dressed.

"Did you even go to bed?" I roll over open-mouthed into whatever created the carpet's smell. Now I'm awake!

"Uff da! I always get up at five." She rolls her eyes. "The powder room is all yours. We should get back on the road in exactly 28 minutes, or we'll be behind schedule." She sits down to read her Bible — the 1 Corinthians section about staying away from sexual immorality.

Today's drive is a repeat of yesterday, minus the morality lecture. We arrive at the Super 8 outside Pittsburgh to find a room nearly identical to the previous night's dump. This time I don't argue about the sleeping arrangements.

"I think I'll be more comfortable sleeping in the truck. You can have the bed. Just let me have the bathroom for a moment, and I'll get out of your hair."

"You're going to leave me alone in this room? With that massive spider on the ceiling? And all manner of deviants running around outside? Randy Larson!" To be fair, this dramatic performance might have won her an Oscar in the 1930s. "Maybe we should both sleep in the truck."

I envisioned some small comfort in spreading out across the bench seats. With two of us, sleep will be upright. "Isn't both of us sleeping in the truck the same as sharing a bed?"

"Don't get cheeky with me, mister! They are completely different situations. We can use the powder room here and sleep in the truck. It will be just fine."

"As long as the spider doesn't lock us out."

MJ has never found humor in arachnid jokes.

By morning I can no longer turn my head to the right, and my spine is shaped like a lightning bolt. I limp like an old man toward the coffee machine – every joint in my body aches.

"Looks like you got a hitch in your giddy," MJ says in her annoyingly cheerful morning voice.

"Aren't you stiff from sleeping in the truck?"

"No. I think my clean living and personal blessings keep me limber."

The five-hour drive to Bethesda, Maryland, gets us to the Days Inn just before 1:00 pm. MJ insists this hotel is another upgrade, even without a number in the name. To her credit, the room smells of bleach, and the carpet appears new. There are even two usable beds!

"Randy, I hope we can spend some time seeing

Washington today. But right now, I just need to nap for a short bit. Would that be okay with you?"

"A nap would be perfect. I'm already exhausted."

Sleep overtakes us before our heads hit the pillows. I dream of all the monuments and government buildings I want to see. If we move fast, I think we can get to all of them, even with a nap.

The next thing I see is the digital clock showing 8:02. MJ is still asleep on the next bed.

"MJ. Wake up. It's 8:00. We slept the entire afternoon!"

She yawns, stretches, and wipes her eyes. "Well, there's still time to get a late supper. You can see all those tourist places anytime now that you live here."

As we walk into the lobby, the desk clerk asks if we enjoyed our stay. He then tells us the breakfast buffet will close in 15 minutes, so we should hurry.

"Breakfast?" I ask.

"Randy!" MJ is standing at the revolving exit door. "The sun is out!"

"Is it morning?" I ask the clerk.

"Yes, sir."

The 18-hour nap meant we missed a day of sightseeing, but at least we can make it to my new apartment on time. The adventure begins!

EIGHT

The Rockefellers Should Be So Proud

"I'm an old woman to wait so long on a stoop!" Sarah Horowitz, real estate agent to the stars, sits on the steps to my new apartment. She's visibly uncomfortable in the August heat, due partly to her fur stole and heavy shoes. Maybe people in Washington like to wear winter clothes all year? And she's irritated about waiting *two minutes*!

"I'm sorry," I say, running to meet her. "I wrote nine in my calendar, and it's only two minutes past. We got here as fast as we could."

"I distinctly remember saying 8:55, but what do I know?" she says with an eye roll. "I'm just the woman with the keys to Barbie's dream home." She turns to MJ and gives her a quick toe-to-head look. "Who's the shiksa?"

"What?"

"Will you be introducing this tragic figure, or should I just ignore her?" She looks at me while pointing her thumb toward MJ, sporting a green "Minot Lutheran Bible Camp 2001" t-shirt.

"Oh. This is my friend, Mary Jo. She's helping me with the move."

"Nice to meet you," MJ says with a big smile, extending her hand.

"Bible camp, huh?" Sarah shrugs, ignores MJ's hand, and continues looking at me. "I see a highway of heartache ahead. But that's not my business. Let's get inside before I'm too old for a walk-up."

She complains of a Texas-sized bunion as we ascend one short flight of steps. Sarah dramatically throws the door open to slam the wall, and I see an unrecognizable space. My first apartment, which I remember looking more like Mary Tyler Moore's Minneapolis home, closer resembles a closet.

"Shouldn't this be bigger?" I ask.

"Exactly what I said on my wedding night. But we take what we're given," Sarah sighs.

There are four small rooms – emphasis on small – with little light. Uneven wood floors lead through skewed doorways like a funhouse. It's the same place, I guess. Maybe I didn't spend enough time looking when I signed the lease.

"Make a list of anything that's not in order. But don't go overboard with the white glove test," Sarah suggests with a wince. Either her bunions hurt, or she caught the smell coming from the bathroom. "Here are your two sets of keys." She looks at MJ and rolls her eyes. "Everything you need to know is in your lease."

"That's it? It's mine now?"

"The Rockefellers should be so proud. Remember to call me when you're ready to downsize." She waddles to the door. "Mazel tov." Sarah waits for a response, but we just look at her with confusion. She throws her hands in the air and shuffles out the door.

I look at MJ. "Well? What do you think?"

She walks slowly and silently through the meager kitchen, modest living room, cramped bedroom, and minuscule bath. "It's small," she finally says.

"This is plenty of space for just me."

"I guess. How many square feet is it?"

"The lease says 610."

Her eyes open wide. "You're paying twenty-two hundred dollars a month for six hundred and ten square feet?"

"Can you believe it? And Sarah says this is cheap. I can't imagine what an expensive place costs."

"At least you have street-facing windows." MJ walks to one of the two narrow living room windows and squints at 18th Street through the dirty pane. "Oh! That looks like the movers."

Two young, nicely muscled guys wearing College Hunks t-shirts are standing by my U-Haul. "Are you Randy?" one of the impossibly gorgeous guys asks.

"Yes." I feel myself blushing. "You must be the movers."

"I'm Evan, and this is Dimitri." I look to the ground so his chocolate eyes don't turn me to salt. "If you could steer us to the apartment and open the U-Haul, we'll get started."

After showing them where everything can be found, MJ grabs my arm. "College Hunks? How could you hire people who wear their sin on their shirts?"

"It's not a sin to be a hunk, MJ. Besides, they're the cheapest movers in Washington."

"No one better come expecting special favors just because they lifted the couch. Honestly, Randy! I worry this city could put a strain on your reputation. You don't need to start off with people whispering behind your back."

On the contrary, these hunks are exactly what I need. Well, I should probably start with guys closer to my league. Having a handsome guy at my side would realize at least some of my moving goals. MJ can never understand this.

The truck is unpacked in three hours, the movers making good use of their bulging muscles. Dmitri caught me looking at Evan's butt as he lifted the last box and gave me a sly smile.

I turned away in a blaze of heat, still afraid someone would discover I was gay.

Throughout the afternoon, MJ decided on furniture placement, which pictures to hang, and the arrangement of everything in the closets, kitchen drawers, and cabinets. She's a big help, but nothing about this apartment is mine. It screams Mary Jo Klerken – with a hefty dose of Mother – from the teaspoons to the toilet paper. We finally stopped working long after sundown with almost everything unpacked and put in its (MJ's) place.

"I can't lift another thing," MJ announces as she falls onto the couch.

"We've gotten almost everything unpacked and put away, and I can finish the rest later. Nothing more to do tonight. Thanks for all your help."

"Don't mention it. Now, will I get to sleep in the bed? Or are you relegating your guest to the couch?"

Given the experiences of the last few days, I should have anticipated this question. "Shouldn't I get the bed in my own apartment?" I start to say and then think better. I don't want an argument. Or worse, another discussion of immaculate conception. "You can have the bed."

She smiles like a small child.

The Friday morning sun rises on my brand new home. I sit up on the couch/Randy's-bed-for-the-night, looking in awe at the first thing I can call my own. MJ is already dressed and reading her Bible in the kitchen.

"Good morning!" Her sing-song voice is eternally cheerful, which, of course, goes hand-in-hand with annoying. "I knew you would sleep late." It's only 6:30. "Would you like me to make some breakfast?"

"Thanks for the offer, but the cupboards are bare. Maybe we should go out this morning."

"I should be at the airport by 4:00, so earlier is better."

"That's today?" She giggles while I feel a rush of panic for my impending independence. Her departure means I am truly on my own. "Well, let's do McDonald's this morning and then some sightseeing before your flight. Sound good?"

My nervousness goes unnoticed. "Sure. We should see some memorials."

Spending four days with MJ has been eye-opening. She's nice enough, and I think her heart is in the right place, but I don't know why she's my friend. Maybe it's because we've known one another almost all our lives, two single people who don't mesh well with others. Now, as I begin to stretch my wings, I struggle to find a connection while also fearing her absence.

The afternoon finds us on a park bench near the Lincoln Memorial. "Are you nervous about starting life alone in such a big city?" MJ asks. Her demeanor hints she is about to start a serious conversation.

"I wasn't until today. There's something about knowing you'll leave this afternoon that makes this real for me."

"I know. I was thinking the same thing." MJ shifts to face my direction. "I'll go back to Minot, and everything will be just as it always has been. Except you won't be there. It's not that we spent so much time together. I just liked knowing you were close by."

"Yeah." There's a quiet pause while we both think about what it means to go our separate ways. "Hey, MJ. I can't remember how we met. Can you?"

"I sure can. It was kindergarten. We made construction paper animals, and you were afraid to get your clothes dirty. I had to glue all the pieces after you cut them out. Don't you remember?"

"No, I don't. It sounds like us, though!"

"Yep. It's always been that way. You are afraid to take something on, and I come in to do it for you. I even asked Sandy Bowman to senior prom for you. I'm like your other mother!"

It hits me she just said what I've been thinking. MJ has made decisions and taken on actions that I should have been doing myself. Mother did the same. And Dad. And Millie. In fact, I can't think of a time when I had to do anything on my own. People have treated me like a child my entire life. And I have let them. Or encouraged them.

"You just became distant for a moment," MJ breaks into my thoughts. "What are you thinking?"

I look at her, not sure I know how to have such a deep conversation. But I know I should be more open with people. This is a good time to start.

"I've been thinking about how everyone decides things for me. My whole life, I haven't made any significant decisions on my own. It's why I never left Minot for college, even though I should have. I could have gone to St. Olaf, like my parents and my siblings. But it was easier to stay home, let Mother make the decisions, and change nothing."

"Is that so bad? You've had people to care for you your whole life. I think that's pretty special."

"Sure. And I'm grateful. It's just that I'm nearly 33 years old now. Mother and Dad are gone. Who will take care of me if I don't start doing it myself?"

"Very true. You're out here on your own, so you sorta need to be independent."

"Sometimes, I imagine a fairy godmother appears to teach me all the things I need to know and guide me through life. Wouldn't it be nice to have someone to take care of us, like Cinderella?"

MJ frowns. "That's not real life, Randy. You can't count on

fairies and magic. We can only look to Jesus. Just remember, the Lord is here to watch over you." She takes my hand and smiles. "And you can always call on me."

"Thanks, MJ. I appreciate you saying that. The strange thing is, I'm not scared. I'm not worried about being alone. Or finding new friends. Or learning to live in a new place." I pause for a moment to collect my thoughts and feelings. "The truth is, I'm overwhelmed. There are so many new things I don't know which one to face first. I believe I can handle each of these by themselves. Together, they are a bit too much."

"You shouldn't worry so much, Randy. It will all work out."

I pause for another moment, trying to decide if I should ask this next question. "Do you mind if I ask you something kind of personal?"

MJ sits upright, instantly defensive. "You can ask. I won't promise an answer if it's improper."

"No, nothing like that. I was just wondering. Do you think I'm good-looking?"

"That's a strange question. I thought you were gay."

"Yes, I'm still gay. I mean, do you think anyone will find me attractive?" I look at my feet. "No one in Minot ever asked me out. At least not guys, anyway. I don't have big muscles, or great hair, or a chiseled face. I wonder if someone will take notice of a run-of-the-mill guy like me."

MJ gives me a forced smile. "I think you're a good-looking fella, Randy. I mean, as gay guys go. Just don't get antsy about dating right now. You're not sinning as long as you don't act on your unnatural inclinations."

I gave her an opportunity to cross the line, and she took it. Better to let this go, or it will ruin our final hours together. "Okay."

"I think you're taking on too many challenges at once. Nothing will come to you beyond your ability to handle it.

Jesus promised that. When I'm faced with a wall of things like you are, I try to deal with only the one closest to my face. You know? Take the present situation and deal with it rather than trying to see everything at once."

I take a moment to let that sink in. "Seems like good advice, MJ. Thank you."

"No thanks necessary. Now, we need to collect my things from your apartment, so I can fly home. Your new life will finally begin when you get me out of your hair!" That makes us laugh, and she gives me a huge hug.

Our walk home takes us through two of Washington's most beautiful neighborhoods, Foggy Bottom and Dupont Circle, on our way to Adams Morgan. MJ gets a little strange when we pass the fountain in Dupont Circle. Several gay men sunbathe in Speedos, holding hands and generally showing affection.

"It's hard for me to look at *that*," MJ admits. She's making the scrunched-up face for which she's known. "Wearing skimpy clothes and pretending they're normal people. I just don't like it."

"They could be everyday, regular guys," I say, trying to keep the conversation from going down a dark hole. "In fact, that could be me, you know. Definitely not wearing a Speedo! But maybe with a boyfriend. My Prince Charming!"

"I don't think so, Randy." She is very sure of herself as she speaks. "One of the reasons you won't go to hell is you stay away from the sins of the lifestyle. You live a celibate life, as the Lord intended."

MJ walks forward with a faint smile and her chin high, belying the moral superiority she owns so proudly. I don't have the energy to challenge her. We just had this great conversation, and once again, she reminds me why it's time to let her go.

A few hours later, I'm waving to the back of MJ's head in a

taxi window. It's the first moment I am truly on my own. The weight of her constant judgment lifts from my shoulders... only to be replaced by the weight of aloneness.

This isn't the same as being lonely; I've felt that when surrounded by friends and family. There's an adultness to being alone that's a new sensation. Even the months after Mother and Dad died, the familiar house kept me company. Here, the rooms of my tiny home are unfamiliar, even if the out-of-place objects have shared my life for years. I should rearrange things to my liking instead of MJ's preferences. Maybe that's the first step toward owning my future.

That can wait for another day. Right now, I want to lie on my own couch and watch TV.

Some things never change.

NINE

Here You Come Again

I used to love Whack-a-Mole. Marty and I often went to Planet Pizza on Monday afternoons just to beat the crap out of those cheeky critters. Somehow, Marty's mole mallet always managed to whack my nuts no matter how hard I tried to avoid it. He told everyone we were going to whack off. I didn't understand the expression until I argued with Paul Missler over the correct hand gesture to show 'whacking off.' It's just another innocent thing Marty managed to ruin in my childhood. Like the game we played in Friedlander's orchard to see who could use his thumb to pop the most cherries off their stems in 30 seconds.

I still don't understand how a person uses their thumb for any other kind of cherry-popping.

Anyway, my first month in Washington is like a nonstop Whack-a-Mole game. Just when I think I know where something is, it pops up in a different place. Take CVS. From 17th Street, I learned to turn left on P Street to get there. Until I accidentally turned right once and ended up at CVS. Or the time I tried to find groceries on Columbia Road and ended up at CVS. Or the time I accidentally exited the subway at Woodley Park and ended up at CVS.

It's not much different in my apartment – thanks to MJ. I open every kitchen drawer whenever I want a fork. She rearranged my dresser, so I can't find my socks. I miss the days when everything was in its proper place and stayed there.

The subway is less crowded this afternoon. I guess people got an early start on their Labor Day weekend festivities. Back in Minot, there weren't many choices for holiday activities. I might have gone swimming or helped Mother and Dad host a cook-out, surrounded by family and friends without any effort. Washington has a million options for the holiday weekend, but I have no friends.

Now I feel lonely *and* alone.

The internal pity party is at full tilt as I mindlessly enter the Spanish Safeway and slam my cart into the back of another shopper. "Qué carajo!? Mira por donde vas, chico blanco!" the woman yells at me.

I've had just enough high school Spanish to know she said something about a white boy. I pull a few words of apology from a dusty corner of my memory. "Lo siento. Tomaré sopa y palitos de pan."

"Dumbass," she says in clear English before walking off in a huff.

"Your Spanish isn't so good, is it?" comes a voice from behind me. The resonant baritone belongs to a guy my age, tall with Tiffany blue eyes, full lips, and long, dark hair.

"That's all I could remember from high school," I say, blushing.

"Well, after your apology, you told her you'll have soup and breadsticks. It was the waitress treatment that probably set her off." His eyes and laugh sparkle in unison.

"Oh, no! I didn't mean to do that! I was trying to apologize! Should I go find her?"

"Don't worry. After what she said to you, I'm sure she'll get over it." His charming confidence persuades me. "I'm Julio, by the way."

"Thanks, Julio." I look at the ground and then turn to continue shopping.

"Uhm, okay. Nice to meet you, random shopper," he says playfully.

"You, too."

Why can't a fairy godmother burst from behind the kumquats and tell me what to say? This is the first time a cute guy has noticed me; all I do is walk away. I could have made a friend! A cute friend! Ugh!

Fifteen minutes later, I'm in the checkout line, wondering if cinnamon or peppermint will make my breath smell better. Dolly Parton's "Here You Come Again" plays in my head when there's a light tap on my shoulder. Julio is behind me, practically glowing with charisma.

"We meet again." He should be on a magazine cover.

"Yeah." It was hard enough to have one conversation with this guy without blushing myself into a fireball. I turn my gaze to the gum display. "Thanks for your help back there."

"No worries. I trust the rest of your shopping was free from physical altercations and insults." Could his laugh be any cuter? He's definitely out of my league.

"Yes, I'm fine. I probably won't speak a word of Spanish for the rest of my life!" I rearrange my groceries on the conveyor, impatient for the cashier to finish.

Julio perseveres. "Hot dogs. Hamburgers. Chips. It looks like you're having a Labor Day party. Can I come?"

"No." That sounded mean. Try again. "I mean, there's no party. This is just my regular stuff." The cashier finishes, and I quickly swipe my card before grabbing the two bags.

"Okay. Maybe another time." He lifts his hand to say something. "Uhm...."

I half-turn my head, avoiding eye contact, and say, "Thanks, again for your help. Have a good weekend." And, with that, the door closes behind me. Any potential for a new friend is forever shelved with the canned goods.

I blew it! BLEW IT! I can't even manage life when it taps me on the shoulder. Tonight I'm going to wallow in self-pity in front of the TV. Hot dogs nuked. Chip bag opened. TV on. The arms of my recliner will, once again, stand in for a boyfriend.

And it's another Friday night at Randy's house.

My failure to engage with Julio haunts me the entire weekend. I see little point in leaving home just to have the same scene play out in a different location. Easy activities like watching TV and eating frozen dinners now seem more like regressive behavior than comfort. I spend three days alone in my apartment, slowly drowning in self-pity.

The progressive build from loneliness to homesickness reaches its peak on Monday night when I'm faced with the end of the holiday weekend. No calls. No visits. No invitations. I have Minot on my mind, and I start to think this move was a mistake. The reality that my home and family are gone makes it worse. There's nothing more for me in North Dakota than here.

A last pass through the kitchen confirms I've eaten all the groceries and then some.

"Salagadoola mechicka boola, Bibbidi-bobbidi-boo!" I turn my hands in circles repeating the magic words Cinderella's fairy godmother sang, hoping it will create food. Nothing. The cupboards are still bare, and Prince Charming isn't outside my door.

"Any woodland critters want to be my friend?" I yell to the empty kitchen.

There's a faint squeaking somewhere in the ceiling. Maybe I shouldn't call forth creatures that may already be living in my walls. My grumbling tummy and I had best return to our recliner for one more movie night.

Cinderella, Mother's favorite movie, is now in my head – and the DVD player. A couple of hours cheering on someone who actually *had* a fairy godmother sounds good. I became a child again, singing along with every song and pretending to be the enchanted titular character. My sleep is visited by dreams of a fairy godmother. She takes me shopping, introduces me to the gay community, and finds me a boyfriend. Life is perfect under her kind watch. If only dreams could last forever.

The next couple of weeks pass like all the others. Breakfast. Work. Dinner. TV. Sleep. Repeat. I have officially developed a rut. It's the same one I was in when Mother and Dad were alive.

By the end of September, I hear Mother's voice telling me to take an active role in making a change, or this new life will be for naught. "You can sit at the stop and go light watching life drive past, or you can turn the corner and take off," she used to say. Good advice.

Of the four criteria I used to pick DC – 1) big city; 2) gay community; 3) subway; and 4) interesting – the only one I've actually taken advantage of is the subway. This weekend I promise to tackle one or more of the other three.

A week planning my big Saturday night, and the best I can come up with is supper in a (cheap) restaurant. At least I'm out of the house. I'm hungry for a steak, but probably not in this neighborhood. Half the places in Adams Morgan serve foreign food I'm afraid to eat. The only pizza parlor is called Mellow Mushroom. It sounds like something having to do with drugs, so I avoid going in.

Wandering the streets aimlessly brings me to... a CVS. Of course. This one is on 17th Street in the heart of Washington's gay district. I pretend my fairy godmother led me here for some great adventure.

"Excuse me," I say to an older man walking past. "Is there a steakhouse in this neighborhood?"

He gives me a smirk. "Is there a steakhouse? You mean *the* steakhouse. I'll send you up there, but you have to tell Doris she owes me a drink for handing her a fresh twinky."

I try not to show my confusion. "Doris. Got it."

It turns out I'm two blocks from the gayest restaurant in DC. Annie's Paramount Steak House sits bathed in rainbow colors at the corner of R Street. (Thank you, Fairy God-mother!) The short, squatty building looks like a queer mother ship, with rainbow bunting and tables full of men enjoying themselves behind the extended porch's large windows. The jam-packed menu posted at the entrance says this won't be a cheap dinner, but it clicks off all my criteria.

The host (hostess?) towers over a small podium just inside the door. He sports a brown and blue Swiss Miss dress with a full petticoat and white stockings leading to Army combat boots. This contrasts with an extra-heavy coating of rouge, oversize hoop earrings, and spray glitter in his graying, crew-cut hair and beard.

"Welcome to Annie's, my little pretty! Looks like we finally have fresh meat!" he yells over his shoulder with a deep, bel-lowing laugh. "I'm Doris. Anyone joining you this fine even-ing?"

"No," I say, blushing and looking to the ground. "It's just me. A guy at CVS sent me and said you owe him a drink."

"You don't say? Well, I don't recognize your cute little ass. Is this your first time in the Emerald City?"

I nod.

"Welcome to Oz! You'll definitely be the catch-of-the-day

around here!" he laughs. "Let's get you a seat by the front windows so you can advertise your goods. Lucky for you, the Bears of Bethesda are seated at the next table. They're the east coast's most famous thruple."

"What's a thruple?" I ask like a small child.

Doris gently takes my hand. "A thruple happens when two people love each other very much and then discover they're both bottoms!" She roars as if this were the funniest joke ever told. I still don't understand, and it must show. "Don't worry, sweetie. These are lovely guys – as long as you don't try to feed them." Doris grabs a menu and puts his long arm around my shoulders. "Follow me," he smiles, "and walk this way."

Doris walks the short distance like he's in a fashion show. I do my regular walk. We come to a front corner table where three large guys with gray beards and flannel shirts have just started their meal. Two look to be 60 or so, and the third is probably in his 40s. I guess this is a thruple.

"Girls!" Doris announces. They all look at me. "I've got an addition to tonight's menu. Let me introduce..." he looks at me, bewildered. "Uh, what's your name?"

"Randy."

"Rrrrrandy," complete with a full curtsy. "Randy, this is Dave, Belle, and Casey." He sweeps his hand across the air to present the table.

"Howdy, Mr. Randy," the Goliath-sized man drawls in Southern sweetness. "I'm Merle. People just call me Belle, as in Southern Belle." His large, warm smile radiates pure kindness. "You new to DC?"

"Yes. I just moved here a few weeks ago."

Doris interjects in a stage whisper, a hand to the side of his mouth, "We've got ourselves a *virgin* here." I blush.

"Pay no attention to Doris," Casey says, rolling his big, brown eyes. "She also claims to be a virgin. But that hole has been entered more times than the Lincoln Tunnel!" They all laugh while Doris feigns offense.

"Where you from, and what do you do, darlin'?" Merle/ Belle asks.

"I'm from Minot, North Dakota, and now I work at the US Treasury."

"You're a G-man! Davy, here, is with the Air Force." He points across the table to the man resembling Winnie the Pooh.

"You're with the Air Force? I thought you were...." I stop myself before sounding foolish.

"You thought I was what? A hand model? A ballet dancer? Rosie O'Donnell's twin?" Dave gives me a devilish grin.

"Hush up, you," Merle/Belle says, swatting at Dave. "Don't pay him no nevermind. He's just teasin'."

Doris takes my arm. "Maybe you girls can convince our naive little Munchkin to sashay in this year's High Heel Race. A pair of heels would lift and separate his fine tushie – and I'd pay money to see that!" More good-hearted laughter.

"Careful, Doris, or you'll scare him off," Casey says, coming to my defense.

"Well, I'm going to seat this delectable cub at the next table if you girls want to talk after dinner."

"DORIS!" yells a booming voice at the front door. "The girls and I haven't had a drink in nearly five minutes, and we're about to become mischievous. We need to be seated NOW!"

"Oh, horsefeathers!" Doris swears. "It's the Brothel. All I need is a night of drunken drag queens taking all the attention off *me*!" He yells over his shoulder, "Coming, Jayne. Don't get your titties in a twist!" Doris points to my seat and runs back to the door.

"Nice to meet you all," I say, waving.

"It's y'all," Merle/Belle drawls. "And welcome to Washington."

I sit with my back to the Bears of Bethesda even as I chastise myself for being rude. This is where my fairy godmother could help. She would also explain how a "thruple" works. They seem happy and normal as I overhear conversations about their dog, garbage collection day, painting the living room, and other mundane things.

They have what I want. I mean, I only want *one* partner. But aside from that, I want to meet a man who does ordinary things with me in our average house. Nothing fancy. He's content to live life enjoying the little things. And he likes steak. I guess thruples can do that, too.

And soon enough, the entire month of September is gone. I've read several books that have been on my list for years. And I talked with Julio, Doris, and the three Bears, so that's a positive. The downside is I haven't made any actual friends or done anything with other people for a full two months. I begin to wonder if this isn't just my personality. Maybe I need people to tell me what to do because I'm not interested in deciding for myself. And that makes me homesick.

TEN

Fashion Queen of Minot

October is beginning to look like a repeat of September. I walk out my door each day to see 18th Street filled with folks shopping, going to restaurants, or hanging with friends, at any time of the day or night. It's a constant sea of humanity that can't even see me. I don't feel any closer to living an exciting life than eighteen months ago when Mother suggested this folly.

My Thursday commute home is clouded by feelings of loneliness and failure. What made me think I could escape Minot and suddenly have friends and adventures? I've never been outgoing or adventurous. Even my old friends back home don't call. And what do I know about being gay? I don't know any *actual* gay people, and the only gay place I've ever been is Annie's Steakhouse. And I sat alone.

I exit the subway station to find myself in Dupont Circle. "Wrong stop, stupid," I whisper to myself. "You can't even manage the subway."

I'll walk the extra blocks to Adams Morgan, using the time to plan my Minot return. Maybe I was destined to live in North Dakota my whole life. It wasn't so bad. I could get my old job back and find a little apartment downtown. It might even feel like a whole new experience. Right?

My head is deep in thought when I somehow run smack-dab into a tree. A couple of bluebirds circle my head, but I don't think there's any real damage. I'm more embarrassed than injured. A poster for the 17th Street High Heel Drag Race taped to the tree kept my forehead from a permanent bark impression.

High Heel Drag Race? Didn't Doris, the hostess; or host? – I'll go with hostess – at Annie's Paramount Steak House mention this? I distinctly remember he said running this race would make my butt look good. The miracle poster gets folded in my backpack for later consideration, and I continue home.

A Hamburger Helper dinner spurs further thought about the race. Do I have the guts to dress up as a woman and run a race? The articles online say it's lots of fun. But Randy Larson as a drag queen? On the one hand, I could meet new friends and have a great night. On the other hand, I could be a total joke. It's only one-tenth of a mile, meaning I won't even need to do any physical training. And Doris recommended it.

It's strange to think I could do something like this. It would be a giant leap – maybe the kind of leap I need. I could put off my return to Minot long enough to give this a try, right?

I wish I had someone to turn to for advice.

Twenty-four hours later and I can't stop thinking about the race. There would be some challenges. First, I don't know anything about dressing as a woman. The best-case scenario would involve working with friends to develop my look, buy clothes and whatnot, and create the final product. However, that would require having friends. If Mother were still alive, I could... No, that wouldn't happen. This is where a fairy godmother would come in handy.

Okay. Absent the fairy godmother, what do I know about women's appearance? I have a few faint memories of Mother and Granny getting dolled up for church with lipstick and eye shadow. Granny often had her hair in curlers. And there are women's fashion magazines. I could tape some pictures to my mirror and try to replicate the look.

This is ridiculous. I don't know anything about makeup, dresses, or any other stuff necessary to turn me into a woman. I should call Millie. We haven't talked much since I moved, and I miss her. Besides, she always wears nice clothes and makeup. People *have* called her the Fashion Queen of Minot.

"Oh, my gosh! Randy! Big city boy! How the heck are ya? Have you met any famous people? Did you get to Arlington Cemetery yet?" She always knows how to get a conversation rolling.

"Hi, Millie. Is this a good time to talk?"

"Of course, silly! The kids are all done with their home-work, and I finally got them settled on a Disney movie. Dave can take his turn being a parent for once, the fat lump. I can chat a spell as long as he doesn't yell for more popcorn. My life is an endless circle of making food, buying food, and making more food. I always seem to catch myself coming and going. Lordy! Hey, is something wrong, dearie?"

"No. Everything's fine. The job is good. Washington is amazing."

"I've never been, you know. It must be so glamorous! Are there movie stars everywhere? Did you visit the Air and Space Museum like I told you? Did you meet Melania Trump? I hear she bought the most perfect boobs. Of course, they're fake. Probably better than the pointy bosoms Minnie Seavers got a few years ago. The tramp of Bavaria Drive, I tell you what! She could put an eye out with those things! She still tells everybody they're real. And I'm Dolly Parton! Golly!"

"No, I haven't met anyone at the White House. I walk near

it when I go to work, which is pretty cool. But that's about it."

"Oh, you know I tell everyone you're famous now. Working at the United States Treasury, and all. Those little toads over at the public schools office say you're just a peon like you were here. I give 'em what for. I mean, do they look out their window and see the President sitting in his office? I don't think so! Do you ever wave hello? I mean, just to be friendly?"

"Millie, my cubicle is in the basement and doesn't even have any windows. I'm just a number cruncher."

"Pshaw! I'll have none of that! Why, you have a gorgeous apartment in that fancy neighborhood. What is it? Morgan Stanley?"

"Adams Morgan."

"I knew it was one of the presidents! And I told Mona Sewell that the Supreme Court sometimes asks you for financial advice. I did. But she was all like, 'He weren't nobody in Minot, so how do you s'pose he's suddenly high falutin, rubbing elbows with J. Edgar Hoover and everybody?' Sometimes I don't know why I bother with her. Lordy!"

"I haven't rubbed elbows with any dead people yet." This conversation is not doing my ego any favors. "Anyhoo, I need some advice."

"Well, you came to the right place. Seems everybody's always asking me for advice about something. It's my burden, I guess. Just the other day, Junior Friedlander drove up by me in a brand spanking new Ford Ranger, askin' if I thought he got the right color interior. I told him there on the spot that he ain't worked a day in six years, and he shouldn't spend poor Becky's money on toys like that when she's been wearin' the same worn-out dress since the 90s! Don't much matter what color the interior is when you put trash like that behind the wheel. I tell you what."

"Well, you always knew your fashion."

"Ain't that the truth. If it weren't for Laurie Shilling's daddy inheriting so much money when his uncle died, I would have been voted the best-dressed girl in our class. People always said I shoulda been an Avon lady 'cause my fashion sense is so good. Truer words, am I right?"

"Well, that's kind of why I called you. I'm thinking of running in the annual High Heel Race. It's kind of a big thing. But I have to dress up in drag to do it. Can you help me?"

"Sakes alive! Randy Larson gettin' dolled up as a lady! If that don't take the cake! I always said you have high cheekbones and would make a beautiful woman. Honest to gosh! This is where it helps to carry a few extra pounds to provide some curves."

I ignore the unintentional dig about my weight. "I knew you could help. Where do I start? I don't own a thing I can use."

"You're tellin' me! I've seen your wardrobe. Best thing I coulda done was take you shopping before you moved off to Washington, but you just wouldn't have it. Do you still have them pants from Sears? I always told you to march your butt to the other end of the mall and get real fashion from the JCPenney. You never did listen!"

"I know, I know. Right now, I need to get a dress and stuff. My other clothes are just fine."

"This could cost you a pretty penny, you know. Good thing you came to me. I know how to be glamorous on a budget. I tried to tell that Sharon Heitkamp she wasted her money on them fancy rags from Macy's because she just ended up giving them away to the Salvation Army when she wouldn't quit eating macaroons. Blew up like that little girl in Willie Wonka! Shucks! That's it! You need to go to the Salvation Army. Best to find one in a fancy neighborhood. All those rich people get rid of their clothes every few weeks, and the stuff will be like brand new."

"That's a good idea."

Millie goes on about some scandal at the Dairy Queen involving a banana split and the cheerleading squad. I tune her out to do a quick internet search for a thrift store. "St. Alban's Opportunity Shop is part of a church," comes out of my mouth before I notice she's still talking.

"Oh. Well, I guess the Dairy Queen story can wait for another time." I broke a cardinal rule: she wasn't finished talking. I can usually get away with this once. "You say this place is part of a church? Even better. Give the money right back to the good Lord, I say. Besides, there must be rich people all over Washington. You could find a perfectly good Givucci dress. Or something fancy by Velma Wang or Donna Klarmen. We're talking all the big names of fashion. No more Toughskins for you!"

Mental note: remember all the designer names. "Okay. So, I'll go there for a dress and shoes. What about hair and makeup?"

"Don't skimp on the makeup, or you'll get the pink eye and end up dead. Too bad you don't have an Avon lady. Anyhoo, you need to go where they sell all the best stuff: Walgreens. Maybelline is top-of-the-line. Got that? And don't get it from Walmart 'cause they sell factory rejects. Only Walgreens. All the Miss Americas wear Maybelline, and we know how pretty they are."

"Right. Maybelline from Walgreens." I frantically write as she talks.

"And there should be a million wig stores in Washington. Doesn't everybody wear a wig there? And probably nice ones. Not like Loretta Stevens from the third pew at church. She thinks nobody can tell, but we all know that chihuahua on her head ain't the real stuff. Lordy, there are days I swear she had to pull it from the cat's mouth just before she left the house. Honest to Pete!"

"So, how do I style it?"

She puts her hand over the phone. *"I get one darn minute a day to put my feet up and talk on the phone, Dave! Can't you just figure this out without me having to march in there and take over?"* A muffled response. Millie takes her hand away. "Honey, one of the kids just threw up all over Dave, and you know how squeamish he is about puke. If I had a nickel for every time one of those little demons barfed all over me! Lordy! Good luck with the new duds! I'm sure you'll be the spitting image of Liz Taylor herself!"

"Thanks, Millie. But...." She hung up.

My trusty, yellow legal pad now contains the designer names and stores where I can get Millie's recommendations. A second page lists everything I think I'll need: dress, heels, wig, makeup. Is there a store to buy boobs? That has to be enough to get started. It's a lot of information, but I can do this.

My mind drifts to a picture of me as Elizabeth Taylor. I'm stunning in a simple, black dress with a white mink stole draped casually over my shoulders. This is the 1960s Taylor I always loved. Soon I'll be walking down 17th Street, and people *will* think Elizabeth Taylor came back to life!

ELEVEN

Five Dollars of Fabulous

St. Alban's Opportunity Shop is in a quaint, old building next to the National Cathedral. There are neat displays of clothing, shoes, furniture, knick-knacks, and an extensive selection of books. Definitely better than the Restore Thrift Store in Minot. Maybe Millie was right about rich people giving up their clothes. I'll have to remember it the next time I shop for 'real' outfits.

The women's section is divided between casual and formal, with a smattering of coats and shoes. If I'm going to wear a dress, it should be something elegant from the formal section. There's no sense in wasting the occasion.

The evening gown section sparkles blue, silver, and red against the fluorescent lights. I wonder what Mother would choose if she were here. My imagined style – flashy yet elegant – is probably too much for her. However, a few scream 1980s luxury Mother would enjoy – think *Dynasty* or *Dallas*.

Thumbing through the fancy dresses, I realize this could be harder than I imagined. Problem number one: I know nothing about dress sizes. The numbers on the tags are a mystery and offer no comparison to men's sizes. Why can't it just say 'large?'

"Can I help you?" comes a woman's monotone voice from behind. I turn to see a pasty, pie-shaped face, expressionless and unmarred by makeup, framed by shoulder-length, greasy hair the color of cooked chicken liver.

"Oh, hello. I guess I could use some help. Do you know what size I am?"

"For which section of the store?" she says with no inflection.

I blink several times quickly and ponder the inquiry. "Is this a trick question?"

"Are you shopping for traditionally male or female clothes?"

I look at my feet, embarrassed to say why I'm here. "Women's, please." She has no reaction. "I know my size in men's clothes, but I've never bought a dress before. I kind of like these." My arm is draped with some sparkling treasures.

She grabs the dresses and gives them a quick glance. "Some of these might fit. What's your waist size?"

"Thirty-four." I look at my feet again. "I'm not really the type to exercise much."

She purses her lips and looks me over, walking around behind to get the complete picture. "It's hard to say, exactly. You could start with a 16 and go up or down from there."

"Are any of these a 16? It's so hard for me to tell."

"The one with silver sequins is a 14. You can try it on. The others are all sized four to eight. Far too small for your figure. Are you going to a formal event?"

I thought this might be embarrassing, but she's taking it seriously. Men must come in to buy dresses for various reasons, and no one thinks it's strange. I'm oddly comforted.

"I'm going to run the High Heel Race."

"I've heard of it. Never been, though." Her head remains focused on my face, but her eyes look at my dress selection. "Seems like you want something flashy, yes?"

"Maybe. Can I try these on?"

In the dressing room, I remove all my clothes and wiggle into the silver dress. The back is baggy and cuts low to expose a risqué amount of skin. The front is tight on my stomach and chest, with the zipper-puller-thingy hanging prominently near my throat like a necklace. Nothing is comfortable or elegant. I take a deep breath, determined to make the best of this.

"Well?" I exit the dressing room with my arms out like a *Price Is Right* model, though the look is more like Jesus on the cross.

"Is this your first time in drag, my dear?" She still manages to say everything without a single facial expression or vocal inflection change.

"Yes. Believe it or not, I've never tried on a dress before."

"Clearly. We ladies zip our clothes in the back."

That explains why the zipper-puller-thingy is at my throat. How was I supposed to know that? "I'll be right back."

Flipped around, the dress looks a bit better. Sort of. What little chest hair I have is sticking out above the neckline. It's still too tight in the stomach and hips, but the chest is better. I doubt the original owner of this dress had a tiny bump in her crotch. And how am I supposed to zip the back?

The clerk is patiently awaiting my return. "Pardon my nakedness, but I can't get it zipped."

"I figured. We all have that problem. I'll show you a trick later." She reaches behind me and attempts to zip the dress. "It's going to be tight. You have what we call a little junk in your trunk. This dress doesn't have room for the extra. Let's find something in size 16."

For the next 15 minutes, we rummage through the hit-or-miss collection of frocks made between 1950 and today. Not many grab my attention. In the end, there are only four possibilities: two blues, a pink with sequins, and a green taffeta.

The sequins on the pink dress give me a dozen or so tiny

cuts just trying it on. I'm not sure how women ever wear these vicious disks from hell. One of the blues is too small in the waist (note to self: lose a little weight). The other blue is a 1960s mini-dress that barely covers my butt cheeks. It's fun and sexy.

I strut out of the dressing room this time as Blue Jesus on the cross. The clerk's facial expression changes when I attempt a Hollywood smile and raise my arms above my head.

"Sir, we prefer you wear underwear when trying on clothes. It seems your twig and berries are basking in the sunlight."

I look down to see my entire wiener and full bush surveying the somewhat crowded store. I double over and swing around only to have my moon rise on three ladies in the sunglass section. The involuntary shriek I emit ensures the other shoppers are alerted to the viewing.

"I'd like to say that's the first time I've seen such a thing happen, but I can't," the clerk attempts to be helpful.

And I thought purchasing the dress would be the humiliating part. I sit for a moment pondering how Mother would have handled this situation. She might have said, "Well, the good news is they've now seen everything. You might as well go back out there 'cause you ain't got nothing more to show." That's pretty much true.

The last dress is staring at me from the dressing room hook. It's green taffeta with poofy sleeves, shoulder pads, and a wide, frilly, white lace adorning the neck. I can see this being popular with the Minot Lutheran women. It even accommodates my tummy. Though it's not the Elizabeth Taylor dress I imagined, I still look elegant. There's a *Golden Girls* sophistication that reminds me of home.

This time, I walk out to model but forgo the attempts at runway posture.

"Green is a nice color on you." As the clerk gives her first fashion assessment, I notice her baggy, beige, tunic-style dress that probably came from a sale bin toward the back. Taken with a grain of salt, as Mother would say.

"I guess." I hold a few poses in front of the mirror and imagine myself as a full-blown lady.

"Remember, the taffeta will wrinkle easily," the clerk warns. "The ample pleats should hide that somewhat, but don't sit down without smoothing out the backside."

"Got it." Ample pleats also hide my wiener bump. "This reminds me of the church ladies back home." I leave out the part about *The Golden Girls*. "It's so beautiful and fits me perfectly."

She thinks for a moment. "Well, if it reminds you of the church, I'll give it to you for half price. Call it my contribution to your success at the Drag Race."

I can only smile. It's hard to believe a person helps me buy a dress, doesn't mock me, and even shows extra kindness. Maybe the Drag Race will be a turning point.

"Let me show you our shoes," she says, leading me to a selection of formerly elegant footwear that now displays the scuffs and scratches of use.

After picking through the entire collection, I find only one pair in my size: flats with red sequins and a low heel. They're a bit worn, reminding me of Dorothy's ruby slippers in *The Wizard of Oz*. Possibly the ones she used to mow the lawn.

"You can have those for five dollars," the clerk tells me. "I haven't served a woman with feet that big since I started."

I walk out with my head high, entertaining grand visions of myself as a beautiful woman, mysterious in my green dress yet elegant in sequined shoes. Strangers will stop to stare. Women will comment on my impeccable style. Men will ask for my phone number. And *Washingtonian* magazine will call to do a spread on me, the woman who transformed DC fashion.

Now I'm officially excited about the race!

My Wednesday outing to Marie's Beauty Supply on Capitol Hill requires leaving work a few minutes early. The small shop has thousands of hairpieces in every length and color, fighting for attention along the crowded shelves.

This time, I start with professional help from the get-go. The girl behind the counter looks like a young boy and has a tight buzz cut that's probably helpful for wearing wigs.

"Could you help me find the perfect hair for my drag debut?" I ask.

Her bright eyes light up when she sees I'm a guy. "What's you lookin' for, hun?"

"Well, I'm going to run the High Heel Race next week, and I need something fabulous."

"We specialize in fabulous! Every good drag queen on the east coast gets their hair from us. You're my favorite customer!" she says with a wink and a smile while tightly grabbing my hand. "My name's Veronica, but you can call me Ronnie. That was my dad's way of getting someone with his name when all his kids was girls. Now, just tell me how close you wanna be to god, and we can get you fitted."

"Oh. Nice to meet you, Ronnie. I'm Randy." It's a little weird she's still holding my hand. I hope this isn't leading her on. "Am I supposed to pray about the wig before I decide on one?"

"No, silly! My customers always say, 'the higher the hair, the closer to god.' I think it's a southern thing. Wanna start there and see where it goes?"

"I'm from the north, so we don't really think along those lines. Though I remember several women in the church whose hair stood a good eight inches above their heads. What would you suggest?"

"Well, 'fabulous' is the usual order around here. So you

can go normal fabulous or super fabulous." Her hands reach high above her head. "And do you want real human hair?"

"Human hair sounds expensive. Is it?"

"You pay for what you get, darlin'. Synthetic hair don't feel the same as the real stuff."

"I see." Now I'm a little nervous. After getting such great deals on clothes, I'm afraid to splurge on a wig, especially if this could be a one-time thing. "Maybe we should start with my budget."

"Of course. Was you thinking eight hundred or so?"

"Dollars? No! I can manage twenty-five or thirty, at most."

She does a complete one-eighty and pulls me toward the section marked SALE in giant, red letters. "We gonna do our best in this section. You might need to lower your expectations a bit, just sayin'."

The sale wigs look like wet mud plastered against the wall. The colors range from Used Motor Oil to Fresh Rabbit Turd, and many are already cut in a 1920s bob. Even the sale prices are more than I want to spend. I definitely can't afford to be a Rose Nyland blonde.

"Do you need to tease it up, or could you work with something cut close to your face?" Ronnie points at a few relatively unoffensive wigs, but none realize my vision.

"It would be better to go up, at least a bit. Are there any with long hair?"

She scans the collection and thinks hard. "This section gets picked over fast. It's WYSIWYG. What-you-see-is-what-you-get."

In the back corner, near the top of the wall, hangs a long wig that needs some attention. "What about that one?" I point.

Ronnie grabs a step ladder and pulls the wig from its hook. Up close, it looks more tattered than from a distance. It even has some dust on it. And I'm pretty sure a spider dropped out. "We've had this one for at least eight years. Nobody will buy it. We all call it 'Annie.' You know, the orphan."

"What color is it?" I honestly can't tell.

"The staff likes to say it's Wet Dog Food. I don't know what the professionals would say. Let's put it on you."

She reaches the wig to my head, and I hold up my hand. "Can we check for more spiders first?" She gives it a vigorous shake, and I see one more spider parachute to the ground in a cloud of dust.

"I can't guarantee they're all gone, but I promise to kill any more I see." She pulls it tight on my head. The hair drapes unevenly down past my shoulders. It's a little patchy on top like a woman headed for baldness in about three years. Ronnie takes me to a mirror, hikes up the hair, and piles it on my head.

"See. We can get this a teensy bit closer to god. You've got lots to work with. Tease it."

All I see is Charlie Brown's Christmas tree. I can't envision this complimenting my dress and shoes. "How much is it?"

"Nobody wants this poor thing. It's been sitting around here for years." She scratches her head and thinks. "I'll sell it to you for five dollars. Plus tax. Does that work?"

Five dollars? The price is perfect, but can I ever get it to look good? "You really think I could do something with this?"

"Let's put it this way: what you can do is equivalent to the amount you paid. You got five dollars of fabulous, honey."

"I guess I'll take it," I sigh.

She carefully wraps it in paper and gently places Annie in a bag. "Maybe someday you drop by with a picture of the final product? We all want to know Annie went to a good home."

"Yes, I will. Thank you."

After spending almost no money on fake hair, I make my way home to research self-styling options. If Mother could take care of her own hair between trips to the beauty parlor, I certainly can.

TWELVE

Beauty Takes Time

I've got four days to become proficient in cutting and styling hair, doing makeup, and turning an average guy into a fabulous woman. The problem is I've never trimmed the hair on a dog's butt, let alone brought a wig closer to god. I don't even own hair products. At the risk of being a pest, it might be helpful to talk with Millie again.

"Two weeks in a row? How did I get so lucky!"

"Hi, Millie. Got a minute to talk?"

"You know I love ya to death. But I got three kids in Halloween costumes chomping at the bit to get to the church trick-or-treat party. Little Zach is dressed as Kermit the Frog. He's just cuter than nipples on a bumblebee! I tried to get Jolene to be Miss Piggy, but that girl has a mind of her own. She had to be Wonder Woman, and I could easier lasso the moon than change her mind. Annabel is supposed to be a cowgirl, but she looks more like a lesbian used car saleswoman! As I live and breathe! So, can we take care of your problem in two minutes or less?"

"Sure," I speak as quickly as possible. "I bought a cheap, somewhat tattered wig that I need to trim and tease to the heavens. Can you give me some guidance real quick?"

"Lordy, Randy! How is that a two-minute conversation? Beauty takes time! You think I accomplish this look in two minutes every morning? A novice like you could take all week!"

"I'm sorry. Maybe you could give me the *Cliffs Notes* version."

"That's all I got time for. I'm gonna give you a shopping list, so write it down." I quickly grab my legal pad while she continues to talk. "Hair scissors. Get them at Walgreens. Only Walgreens. The Walmart ones aren't sharp enough to dent a marshmallow. Teasing combs are at Walmart. Walgreens makes the cheap ones that break off at the handle on the first use. And buy some Dippity-do. Lots of it. It would be best to get that from Jane's Beauty Supply if you could get back to Minot. Jane would be tickled pink to see you! She'd show you pictures of her new grandbaby, who has to be the ugliest little demon ever dropped on this earth! I tell ya, there isn't a looker in that entire godforsaken family. Honest to gosh!"

"Okay. I wrote it all down. That's all?"

"And a hairdryer. The fancy ones they use in salons are the best. You know, the big ball ones with a million air holes that sit on your head for half an hour. Those can set a curl, I tell you what! Too bad you'll have to make do with something hand-held." She pulls the phone away from her mouth. "*Get off your brother's flipper, Annabel! Cowgirls do not rustle up frogs! Jolene! Is that vomit on your shoes? Who threw up? Dave! We got a puker. Figure out who it was, and I'll be right there!*" She comes back breathless. "I gotta go, Randy. I swear, if Zach has the holler tail again, he can just sit in the corner. A river of vomit cannot keep us from the party. Good luck!"

"Thanks," I try to say quickly, but she's already gone.

Don't tell Millie, but I went to Walgreens for everything on the list. I know she was specific about the stores, but I can't wander all over Washington just to find a Walmart. How much difference can there be?

I ask permission to leave work an hour and a half early on Tuesday, the big day. My boss mentioned the High Heel Race earlier in the break room, so he knows it's happening.

"Do you have special plans tonight, Randy?" Mr. Evans asks innocently, not connecting me with the most prominent gay event of all time.

"Uhm. I'm going out with friends. I have some things to do before I leave. I'll make up the time later if that's okay." I don't have the nerve to tell him – or anyone – about my evening plans. Maybe I'm still a little ashamed of being gay. Or doing drag.

"Don't worry about it. Hours come and go. Have a good evening."

The unadorned hairpiece greets me at 4:00, stretched atop a coffee can on the kitchen table. It looks sad and lonely. My fingers caress the brittle brown beast as I take a deep breath. "Git 'er done" is the best pep talk I can muster.

Cheap scissors slice through the strands of faded beauty — a little snip here, a little clip there. Actually, it's more like chewing through each strand. The recommended scissors aren't sharp enough to cut construction paper. And the coffee can is a poor approximation of my head as it fails to hold the wig in place while I trim. Halfway through each cut, I notice the wig has slid toward whatever side is being cropped.

The straight and even form I envisioned looks more like teeth on *Where the Wild Things Are* monsters. The wig is a crossed pattern of slashes, gashes, peaks, and valleys. And the thinning spots are still painfully obvious, like a mortally wounded Cousin Itt. I'll need to tease it high to cover for the imperfections.

Dippity-do, the stalwart miracle worker of hair products

that should cover a multitude of sins, is liberally applied from scalp to tip. The more I use, the better it should hold when teased up. Unfortunately, instead of lifting and holding, it's sagging and dripping. More Dippity-do makes the wig look to be covered in green vegetable oil. I try to tease it again, but all that goop causes the comb's handle to break. Millie was right about the Walgreens combs.

Now I'm looking at a stringy, mud-colored, hairy alien that could easily be mistaken for a dirty mop head. "You're ruining it!" I yell at myself. The problem is I don't have time to start over, so I move on to an improvised Plan B: finger curls.

MJ forgot two bobby pins when she left, so I can use those to set the curls. Pull a few strands straight out, wind in a circular pattern, and pin them to the longer hair. Voilá! The bobby pin slides off the lubrication and falls to the floor, the hair hanging listlessly. After three more attempts, I just gave up.

Thirty minutes later, the heavily-treated wig is on my head. None of the finger curls held, so I pinned the hair in two places to keep it out of my eyes. I'm a dead ringer for Edna Turnblad – Divine's version – as she hunched over an ironing board. Sweaty. Greasy. Stringy. Unsexy.

The thrift store dress is carefully slid over my head, mindful of wrinkling the taffeta, though catching several grease stains from the Dippity-do. The tattered, red sequined heels, just a bit too small, and a yellow sunflower purse I saved from someone's trash complete the outfit. It looked more elegant in my mind. The person in my mirror is a white trash, trailer park drag queen only North Dakota could have produced.

"Well, Randy," I say to myself, "you did your best with the talents you've been given." I take a quick selfie to commemorate the occasion and promise myself no one will ever see it.

One final deep breath and I walk out the door.

Thirteen

We Are Family

I changed my clothes three times before settling on the green Toughskins jeans with a blue and yellow pinstripe button-down shirt. MJ and Millie, seated in the front row on either side of me, gave little thought to their average, everyday school outfits. They – nor anyone else, for that matter – could grasp the magnitude of this historic event. I mean, I changed my clothes *three times* to get precisely the right look!

Minot has sent only one winner to the Miss North Dakota pageant during my lifetime: Kay Picconatto. In August 1999, barely two months since her glorious triumph on the Williston stage, our native beauty queen visited First Lutheran Church. She came to the monthly potluck to give an inspirational speech and sing "Journey to the Past," her winning pageant song (I mouthed along as she sang).

From the moment Kay Picconatto took her place next to the Wurlitzer upright piano in the Fellowship Hall, I knew she was royalty. Our front row seats caught every sparkle of her red sequin evening dress. Red heels, perfectly matched to her dress, and mile-high hair made her 12 feet tall in my adolescent mind.

Kay Picconatto was beauty incarnate.

Twenty years later, I stand before the mirror, hoping to see Kay's reflection – or at least her essence – in my getup. I'm willing to accept the Minot beauty queen torch passed to my generation. However, with fry cook hair topping a green dress, yellow purse, and red shoes, I look more like an ad for the free lunch program than a pageant winner. Any individual piece – except the hair – looks great alone. Together they define 'trashy.'

Sorry to disappoint you, Kay.

I square my shoulders and inhale like I'm about to scuba dive before walking out the door. Heads turn the moment I hit the sidewalk. Passersby appear unable to reconcile my appearance with what they believe can exist in this world. Fingers are pointed. Cats are called. Laughter is made. I'm reminded of my poor aesthetic choices and beautician skills with each amorphous strut.

Three facts dominate my mind as I slog a mile down 18th Street to the starting line:

1. Wigs are hot. The river of brow sweat is mixing with Dippity-do to form a toxic eye irritant.

2. I'm an average guy in the looks department. As a woman – as *this* woman – I defy description. Maybe something from a coroner's report? I'm not looking for pity, just stating a fact.

3. How am I supposed to find a boyfriend dressed like this?

Dad always said I could make rays of sunshine stream from a cow's butt for all the lollipops and rainbows I have in my daydreams. If there ever was a time for wide-eyed optimism, it would be now.

The Dupont Circle neighborhood vibrates with a spectacular array of sights and sounds unique to the gay community. The streetlights seem a little brighter in Dupont. Halloween decorations and orange twinkle lights hang from the windows of staid old buildings where the gay elite make their lives. Laughter is the language of their happiness. And I am enveloped by the wave of queer humanity, pulled deeper into a sea of drag queens. Tall ones. Short ones. Fat ones. Hairy ones. Gorgeous models. Nightmares in heels. It's a fabulous goulash of spandex, hair spray, and sequins!

The sheer spectrum of drag boosts my confidence. It's abundantly clear some people do shock-inducing drag that was never meant to be beautiful. Many sport makeup at least as hideous as mine – though they probably intended this outcome. Where I have them all beat is my hair. Nothing can compare to the greasy mop leaving stains on my lacy collar.

I learn this is not really a race from the get-go. Well, for some highly competitive types, they run it to win. But for most, this is a sashay down the avenue. I find myself in the middle of a nebulous Max Factor blob two blocks from the starting line. The crowded street resembles a cattle chute where oversize egos compete for attention and the space to be seen.

The starter pistol crack inspires most queens to move slowly forward, waving at fans and hurling insults at everyone else.

"Hail Mary, full of grace, come and sit upon my face," intones one incredibly ornate nun.

"You trashy motherfuckers are all my slaves!" a dominatrix Ivanka Trump reminds the crowd.

The Tin Man, bent slightly at the waist with a rocket-sized dildo protruding from his backside, pleads for an oil can.

We move slowly as a single, crawling amoeba slinking down 17th Street. Parade watchers fill the sidewalks, some in drag with others in a spectacular array of Halloween costumes, from the risqué to the sublime. Somewhere a group begins singing "We Are Family." The entire crowd is soon belting along – myself included – lost in revelry and the feeling we are among our people. I can't believe I'm here! No one is speaking directly to me, but I'm part of a new community unlike any other.

The finish line becomes a human bottleneck where a motherly lesbian notices my naiveté, grabs my hand, and pulls me toward her. "Better get off to the side before the mob crushes you!" She gets me to the sidewalk and stops to take in the whole picture.

"Jesus, Mary, and Joseph! Diane!" she yells to her partner a few feet away. "We got a Rose Nyland abortion here!" Her belly laugh is infectious.

I smile as Diane walks over. "That has to be after-birth in your hair. Nothing else has that much keratin!" She tries to touch my wig but stops short when she sees the stains on my dress. "A-plus for creativity, man!"

I'm standing in front of CVS as the crowd flow pushes me back up 17th Street. I let it take me along, simultaneously feeling like an outsider and the family's newest member.

FOURTEEN

Pussy Liqueur

"Ooo, gurl! This ain't no break down lane." A seven-foot Grace Jones queen slams into my side, knocking me off balance. "Git your ass off the highway!"

The glitter and lights must have hypnotized me. I blink twice, trying to focus on the Nubian Goddess in the sleek, black dress, her close-cropped hair reaching to the deep night sky. Her fierce scowl says I nearly ruined the entire get-up. I'm unsure how to respond since there were no angry drag queens roaming the streets of Minot.

My muttered apology meets her back as she's already ripping into a perfectly coiffed Lucille Ball. "Bitch, you owe me for three nights of hard drinking."

Lucy gives it back. "Something tells me you don't love Lucy." They both laugh and shower each other with air kisses. I clearly don't understand the culture.

A striking guy dressed as Matthew Broderick in *Ferris Bueller's Day Off* invades my space next. The drag Sarah Jessica Parker hooked solidly on his arm appears moments away from passing out in the street.

She laughs loudly in my face. "I promise not to puke on your head, dearie, since it seems that already happened a couple of times tonight, huh? Matthew!"

"Call me Ferris!" he whines.

She smacks his chest. "I'll call you Fairy. Now, give this poor, homeless drag queen a dollar. No one should ever have to look like that!"

Grace Jones is right. I need to get off the road. A steady flow of people goes into a small door at Dupont Italian Kitchen, and I let the current carry me inside.

A flight of narrow stairs leads to a crowded space known as the DIK Bar. It's packed with drag racers, their admirers, and a smattering of shirtless young guys looking for Mr. Right Now. The roar of 100 drag queens, all trying to be the most prominent, loudest royal in the room, is deafening.

And then there was me. Not fabulous. Not pretty. Not thin. Apparently looking like a pile of homeless vomit.

And not noticed.

I slip between sweaty bodies to the bar. It's a big night, and I won't let a few drunken gals take me down. I plan to have two lite beers. *Two.* Inches from my face, the bartender can't see me. I wave and say, "Hey!" He looks through me to wait on the queens behind. It could be a very long night.

"Heavens to RuPaul! Did some drunken party girl lose her cookies on your head?"

The most enormous boobs I've ever seen, encased in Kay Picconatto's red sequin evening gown, are staring me right in the eyes.

"Up here, Sugar. My eyes are up here," says the candy apple red lips as my face turns the same color. My neck cracks as I crane to meet her stare. Long, gaudy earrings brush her shoulders beneath a classy, platinum blond wig. "Can't get that little prick's attention? Let Mama give it a try."

The Amazonian princess puts hands on her hips and bellows like a drill sergeant, "Whose tiny dick does a girl have to suck to get a drink around here?!?"

The bartender immediately comes over, sporting a sly smile. "Aren't you Jayne Mansfield?"

"What was your first clue, the hair or the tits?" she says with a sexy smile, lightly touching her hair.

"Your feet."

"Bitch!"

"What'll it be, Miss Mansfield?"

"My friend and I will have vodka tonics – heavy on the vodka with the slightest whisper of tonic. Make them doubles. No. Triples. I don't have enough knee pads to keep coming back here for refills." He laughs as she reaches across the bar and grabs his crotch. "When you're good to Mama... you know the rest." He winks and runs to make our drinks.

"Thank you," I say meekly as I fumble through my purse for cash. I have no idea what a vodka drink costs. Especially a triple. Just the thought of it makes me tipsy.

"I'm paying, doll. I always get the first round." She flashes a monstrous smile. "Let's call this a shot of courage to help you get a little hottie to buy the rest."

I'm definitely blushing, and my inexperience is on full display. Can she tell I'm new to all this?

"You're Jayne Mansfield?" I stammer, awestruck.

"This year. Last year I was Loni Anderson, but she doesn't have the name recognition to get me gigs. Gotta pay the bills. And who might you be, darlin'?"

Before I answer, the bartender arrives with our drinks. Miss Mansfield passes him two 20s and says with a wink, "Keep the change. Now you owe me. And a Mansfield always collects her debts."

We lock arms as she uses her enormous frame to part the gay sea toward her group by the windows.

"Settle down, you festering twats!" The group is deferentially silent. Jayne points a long, elegantly manicured finger at each person around the table. "Let me introduce you to the

Brothel. Here's Joan, Bette, Bette, Marilyn, Cher, and Lea De-Laria. The leather Santa Claus working his magic over there is John, who was with us until his divining rod prick pointed at that muscle stud."

"Well, don't we sound like a cliché caravan?" Bette Midler comments sarcastically.

Joan Crawford raises one eyebrow and looks me over from my cheap Dorothy pumps to my dripping wig. "What's your name, little ragamuffin?"

I raise my chin in an air of haughtiness. "You can call me Snoopy Shawnee."

The realization I should have said the name aloud before committing to it slams into me. Snoopy Shawnee. I read somewhere a drag name is your first dog and the street where you were born. Snoopy and Shawnee go together, according to the formula. I swear it sounded fabulous in my head.

Bette Midler gives a tight-lipped frown like she took a bite of a dog poop pizza. Joan Crawford's head is tilted back to keep from vomiting. Even Lea DeLaria has become a living Munch painting.

My head drops a bit, and I look from face to face. I've rendered everyone speechless without even saying "twat!" This was a win until a greasy hair curl detached itself from the pack and skidded slowly down my forehead onto my nose. No wins here.

Cher wags a finger at me while smiling with only the right side of her mouth. "Penny Pingleton is permanently, positively, punished." Now both sides of her face are smiling deviously.

Jayne Mansfield cackles. "Oh my god! She IS the love child of Edna Turnblad and Blanche Devereaux! Honey, next time this posse is coming over to put you together right."

"And give you a proper name!" Bette Davis adds. "You sound like the uncredited character in every John Wayne movie. The one who gets shot first! As the senior member of this bordello and the one who has had the most to drink, I hereby christen you," she pauses to think, "Pussy Liqueur."

"Here's to Pussy Liqueur, the fiercest snatch in Dupont!" Jayne says, raising her drink. They all clink glasses and laugh hysterically.

So, Snoopy Shawnee and Pussy Liqueur are my only options? They both have some cute factors. Like Mrs. Andersen's dog, Pancake, we all thought had such a cute name until he was run over by a truck. Regardless, this crowd of alpha queens has taken a liking to me. My chest burns with the warmth of acceptance. Or alcohol.

My drink seems to be empty. Staring quizzically into the dry cup, I barely notice Santa John has sidled up next to me, arm wrapping my waist. His other hand refreshes my drink while a third hand(?) grabs my butt like he's about to get laid. My vision is blurred, but I think he's licking his lips and growling at me, sort of like an English bulldog with a bad cold.

Jayne wedges between us. "Easy there, Saint Dick. Run along and check on Prancer." John spies a shirtless twink and wanders off. "So, what's a nice girl like you doing in a place like this?"

"I moved here three months ago," I say, holding up four fingers. "I came from, uh, North of Dakota. That's the north one."

"Oh, dear god! And you stumbled into the Drag Race like Alice through the looking glass! After a fall such as this, you'll think nothing of tumbling down the stairs!"

Did she just quote Lewis Carroll? Is this room tilting a bit to the left?

"I wanted to experienth D-Thee's gay culture." How in tarnation did I get dog hair on my tongue? I put three fingers deep in my mouth but can't find the hair. Jayne stares at me like I just grew another head. By the way, this drink is much better than the first – more lime.

"Are you slurring after only one drink?" Jayne seems more amused than shocked.

"No. I mutht have licked a dog thomewhere after Santa gave me his drink."

"It gets better after the third one. Here, take mine, and I'll get another." Jayne hands me her special triple vodka tonic. Let's see, a triple and a double and a triple is... I realize complex addition such as this will require using both hands. That means putting my drink down. I stare blankly at the space between the glass and my other hand. What was I doing?

Lea DeLaria eyes me with a mix of pity and wonder. "Here you go, kid. Take my stool. I'm hitting the road anyway."

It feels so good to sit down. Between my (absolutely gorgeous!) sequined heels and an unknowable number of drinks, I've had enough standing for one night.

Joan, Bette, Bette, Marilyn, and Cher all turn their attention to me.

"Maybe you should have a little something to eat, doll," Cher says with genuine concern. She slides a bowl of mixed nuts in my direction.

"When I'm drinking, all I think of is putting nuts in my mouth!" Marilyn can barely get the lines out before erupting in an unflattering cackle.

Bette Davis falls off her stool, yelling from the floor, "I just peed, Cher! Jesus! Get the mop!"

They all howl and slap their thighs. What a great bunch of gals. Hey! How did I manage to finish my drink already? It must have been mostly ice.

So, this is what it feels like to belong. To be at the center of the gay universe in the world's capital. I sit for a quiet internal moment to bask in the light of community, a light that appears to get brighter. No one has a face anymore. I can only squint and see long rainbow spikes and halos. Maybe my contacts fell out. Do I wear contacts? There are beiges, and browns, and reds, and blues, and the occasional penis. Is that a penis? Santa John must be next to me again.

"Alright, girls, I think Miss Liqueur has had enough liquor for one night. Let's be good witches and get her home." Jayne has my left side, and Cher has my right. I rest my head in someone's sturdy bosom.

My stomach hurts from laughing so hard. My mind blurs thoughts, and I can't tell if I'm speaking aloud or to myself. I definitely need to Google Lea DeLaria when I get home. I think one of my boobs is in my armpit. Who knew Florence Henderson could be such a bitch? Cher is so lovely. This taxi smells like a wet dog. How many steps do I have to climb to my apartment? Did I really leave my underwear on the floor?

There's no place like home.

I'm sure my half-open eyes see Jayne Mansfield tucking me in and kissing my forehead. As she turns to walk away, I say, "Are you my fairy godmother?" I giggle myself to sleep before she can answer.

FIFTEEN

Brown Bottle Flu

So, we're back where we started. I'm staring at my besmirched reflection, contributing to my nausea. At the same time, a gargantuan Jayne Mansfield drag queen sits in my kitchen. She apparently spent the night nursing me through my first hangover. It was a nice gesture, but I would rather be alone.

"If I looked that bad, I certainly wouldn't stand before a mirror." The inappropriately loud voice nearly causes involuntary defecation.

"Why are you back in my room?" I squeak. "I thought you went to make breakfast!"

"Just checking to see if you can stand. Last night I had a sense you could use a mother. Looking at you today," she dramatically eyes me from head to toe, "I was right."

That reminds me, I'm standing in only my underwear. Not the nice ones worn by magazine models, but tattered tighty-whities that are no longer tight or white. They hang on me like a soiled diaper. My hands instinctively move to cover my crotch.

"Oh, puh-leeze! Don't be demure around me. I've seen more dicks than my urologist!" She rolls her eyes. "What say we retire to the kitchen? I'll teach you to make my famous breakfast martini, and you can cook up some eggs to settle your tummy."

My hands and feet make no attempt at movement. "Food would probably be good. And maybe a little privacy." My hands remain over my crotch. "Oh, and do you know what time it is?"

"Does anybody really know what time it is?" She throws her head back and laughs, but I don't get it. Jayne sighs. "It's 1:30, dear. You slept right past the morning."

"1:30! You mean I missed work?!" This shocking revelation makes me forget I'm all-but-naked as I hysterically flail my arms and pace the room. "I'm so fired! How could you let me sleep through my job?"

"It was *my* responsibility to raise you from your drunken coma?" Jayne shakes her head. "Well, that's a lot to expect of a girl on her first sleepover, isn't it? Stop fussing and relax. I can't even count the number of things I've blown off because of the brown bottle flu."

I've never missed a day of work in my life, even when I had that terrible bug with the nonstop vomiting and diarrhea. It was so bad the interns presented me with a ceremonial toilet seat. But I was on the job.

"I have never missed a day of work. EVER!"

"Are you going to explode right here on the spot?" Jayne has a concerned look she may have learned in an acting class. "Take a deep breath. Let's get you into the kitchen and have some of those eggs."

How did things go so wrong? It's the middle of a Wednesday afternoon, and I'm lounging around the apartment instead of working! I was so snookered last night that I lost my sense of responsibility. A drag queen has taken over my apartment. And I'm standing naked as a jaybird while this stranger tells me to calm down. This is the worst day of my life!

Deep breath. The bedroom mirror throws back my shame

in vivid color. The innocent Midwestern boy with a developing Buddha belly and Charlie Brown head is not enhanced by disfiguring makeup and a sweaty mangle of hair shedding Dippity-do flakes.

And I'm wearing nothing but moth-eaten underwear.

"Poor thing. You're a hideous drag queen, and you missed a day of work," Jayne lowers her head and takes a good look at my crotch. "And you've got no bragging rights. God didn't give you much to work with, did he?"

I blush and reposition my hands. "I'm not sure what I'm supposed to have, but this one does the job." Jayne turns and leaves with a little chuckle. Humiliation gives me the strength to cross the room for gym shorts and a long t-shirt. I don't need to be reminded being hungover is about the only kind of hung I will ever be.

Jayne sits at the kitchen table, filing her nails while I make a plate of scrambled eggs, toast, coffee, and two Tylenol (her suggestion). It looks better than it smells, and my stomach is still grumbling from last night.

An airplane vodka emerges from her purse and is poured into my coffee. "Hair of the dog." She smiles. I raise my hand to object, and she puts a finger to my lips. "Listen to your fairy godmother. Now drink up."

My meal is slowly ingested as Jayne continues with her nails, gently chuckling to herself. With one bite left, she's suddenly chatty.

"Oh, this reminds me of breakfast at Joan Crawford's place the morning after a particularly wild bender. She made her daughter Christina and me these gigantic garlic and peach omelets, the consistency of pureed oysters, with Limburger cheese. Boy, that sure brought my gag reflex back to life!"

This good Midwestern boy can conjure the scent of Limburger cheese just by hearing the word "limb." I knock my chair to the floor in a mad dash for the commode. Everything

I just ate – and every drink from last night – is emptied into the bowl with a smell worse than, well, Limburger cheese.

I slump back into the kitchen chair, feeling admittedly better. My stomach has quit speaking in tongues, and my head no longer feels like it's bouncing in the dryer on high heat. The spiked coffee remains unfinished.

"You can thank me later," Jayne says wryly. "That story works better than a stomach pump."

My good sense returns with the hangover's remission. "I had best call my boss and explain why I didn't come to work today."

"Let me guess. You're going to tell him you put on your finest drag last night and got so snot-slingin' drunk you couldn't haul your sorry ass to work?"

"Well, not in those exact words." I think for a moment. "I can't lie to my boss! Honesty is always the best policy."

"Such a sweet platitude," she mockingly says, clicking her perfectly manicured nails on the Formica tabletop. "Let's take a look down this path of complete honesty. You confess you're rougher than a badger's foreskin from a drunken Tuesday night drag outing. He logically assumes you will begin missing Monday and Friday mornings, as Sunday and Thursday are prime party nights. And what if there's a Wednesday night drink special? There goes Thursday. Or a Tuesday night drag competition? Bye, bye Wednesday. Pretty soon, you're down to working a day or two per week until your cocaine habit takes over."

My mouth drops open. That's an oddly specific prediction. "He'll really think that?"

"It's a story as old as time. Now I'm going to tell you what to say, and you're going to repeat it word-for-word. Got it?" I nod. "Scamper off and find your phone. Mama will get you through this call with your boss."

"Are you sure I shouldn't just tell him the truth?" I ask,

hoping to change her mind.

"On second thought, let's tell him you were in a sling, a bear was fisting you, and now you're in the hospital with a severe intestinal blockage."

"A bear? What?"

"Forget it. So much to learn. Just call your boss and repeat what I say. No ad-libbing."

He gave me his cell number, but I call the office to be polite. "Hello? Mr. Evans? This is Randy Larson."

Jayne begins whispering words, and I repeat them.

"I'm sorry I missed work today. In fact, I just woke up a few minutes ago. You see, I started feeling feverish last night, so I went to bed early. During the middle of the night, I woke with terrible chills, explosive diarrhea, and projectile vomiting all over the walls. I'll probably have to repaint." I give her an are-you-serious look. "I was awake half the night before falling asleep again at six am. I never heard my alarm. I'm so sorry."

Mr. Evans is understanding, saying he hopes I feel better. He tells me to take another sick day if I need it.

"Thank you, but I should be fine tomorrow. See you then."

I can't believe I just lied to my boss. This feels like a slippery slope toward more significant indiscretions. What's going to be my next story? Jayne Mansfield came back to life and moved in with me?

"See. It's not so bad," she says in a motherly voice that may have also been learned in an acting class. "You could have added a bit more detail about diarrhea and vomit. You know, to give the story color. But, que sera, sera. A little white lie never hurt anyone." I look at her with a weary face. She ignores me. "So, what are we going to do now? Some light shopping? Afternoon cocktails on 17th Street? Maybe a little happy ending massage?" Her face looks like a puppy waiting for a walk.

"What are you talking about? I'm not doing anything!"

"Nothing?! On this perfectly glorious afternoon? The birds are singing, the flowers are blooming, and the crack whores haven't hit the streets yet. You want to pass up all this?"

"I feel like crap from last night, and I need the afternoon to recover. I still have to work tomorrow. I'm thinking a Netflix binge or something like that."

Jayne raises one eyebrow and crosses her arms over her chest. I'm a little afraid. "You would have me, the great Jayne Mansfield, sit in this shithole apartment for an entire day doing absolutely nothing? Like common trash? Or a Federal Government employee? I think not."

I ignore the insult. "You're free to do whatever you want. Or you can just leave. I need to stay here."

"Pshaw. You don't know what you need. Today is your lucky day. Miss Jayne graciously allows you to escort her on an indulgent afternoon in the Nation's Capital. Free of charge."

"And I have no say in this plan?"

"I only need to look at you to see poor choices are your specialty. Chop, chop! We're going out!"

Somehow, I don't think I have a choice.

SIXTEEN

Dreadfully Average

Jayne's horror film screams interrupt my shower bliss. She pledged to find a shirt and jeans appropriate for an afternoon out, and I assume she found the Toughskins. While I'm still not on board with leaving the apartment, it's better than arguing with a self-righteous drag queen all day.

When I return to the bedroom, she has laid out fresh clothes – no Toughskins. A pair of my JCPenney tighty-whities is folded into an indeterminate woodland creature shape with a ChapStick erection. She chuckles over her creation.

"Put this on, with or without the ChapStick, and I'll help with your hair. To the best of my ability, mind you. There's not much to work with. We just can't have another disaster like last night."

Modesty prevents me from removing the towel around my waist. "Can you give me a little privacy?"

"No, I absolutely cannot. How am I supposed to make you fabulous if you keep secrets? Now, drop that towel and let me take a look at you."

I once fantasized about a similar situation where I was a spy captured by a Mexican drug lord. Somehow I was wearing a Creekside Inn towel, and he was Ricky Martin's twin brother.

Anyway, Jayne has managed to ruin that fantasy, of which I will never speak again.

"Drop it," she commands.

My hand loosens its grip on the towel. I don't know why I'm listening to her. Nothing good can come from this. I haven't been naked in front of anyone since I took swimming classes at the YMCA.

"Let's go, Peter Pan. Unless you're hiding an anaconda, I doubt there will be any surprises."

My teeth and eyes clench as the towel drops. "There. Happy?" It's on the floor, and I'm standing butt naked in front of Jayne Mansfield as she bends to closely examine my wiener. No more secrets.

"Well, it is a bit small." She squints. "And you have enough bush to be a Republican! We've got our work cut out for us."

Yep. Bad idea. It's one thing to be naked and flopping in the wind – if there was wind – and if I was actually big enough to flop. But it's another thing altogether to be inspected and evaluated. With squinting, no less! Is my wiener really that small?

"Let's start with basic gay hygiene," she says, still squinting. "We are going to take a machete to that underbrush."

"What? You're going to do what?"

"Let me put it this way: your Vienna sausage is covered by a foot-long bun."

"Huh?"

"Your needle is in a haystack."

"I don't get it."

"Your tiny, little penis is suffocating under all that hair!" she yells. "I can add inches to your schwanzstucker with just a few clips. Let me get my purse."

Jayne walks out as I look down at my wiener. My old friend barely peeks out from his wiry nest. I've never had a problem with his size or ability to do what he's supposed to do. Now he's being scrutinized for who he is. He must feel shame and pity because I think he just shrunk.

Jayne returns with a beautician's shears and an electric hair trimmer. Where does she find room for everything in that tiny clutch? She grabs my wiener like a tow rope and pulls me across the room. I'm pretty sure Cinderella's fairy godmother never pulled her around by any part of her body.

"Ouch! Watch the nails!"

She gives me a fierce look, and I'm reminded she is holding scissors in front of my wiener.

"Now, this won't hurt a bit. You just stand there and let ol' Jayne take care of everything." She squints again.

"Do you need glasses?" I ask nervously.

"Only for seeing. But I'll be honest. I'm not sure I can tell the difference between the weeds and the grass with or without glasses. Why don't you hold your little pecker while I do the trimming?"

Touch myself in front of someone? Is she kidding? I shift my weight and look to the side.

"Fine. We'll just take our chances. Now turn your head and cough."

I glance down to see if she's serious when she brusquely grabs a fistful of pubic hair.

"Ow! Do you have to pull so hard?"

"Don't be a baby. Beauty is pain; pain is beauty. This won't take long."

She pulls the hair until it's straight and clips off a fistful of my strength. Nearly all the hair is gone when she comes back at it with the electric trimmer. She shaves my entire nether region down to the bare skin.

I've had that hair since I was 13! Never trimmed it; never shaved it. I was so proud to have it. What makes her think getting rid of it is an improvement? I'm sad, indignant, and a little cold.

Next, she takes my wiener in her falcon-like talons and presses it flat against my belly. She's fumbling around my balls with the trimmer, barely able to see for the press-on nails covering everything. Someone can put it back on if she cuts off my penis, right?

That's when I notice another sensation. I'm not sure if this is supposed to be erotic, but I'm getting aroused. Maybe it's the buzzing of the trimmer. Or the feeling of her hand on the underside of my wiener. Or just that I haven't jerked off in three days. Whatever the reason, I'm suddenly hard.

Jayne arches one eyebrow as she stops the clippers and slowly raises her head to look at me.

"Is that really necessary?" she says sarcastically.

"I'm so sorry! It's not my fault. It just happened. I'm not really enjoying this. Honest!"

"Let's get something straight." She stares disapprovingly at my stiffy. "Or another something straight. I'm not giving you a handy. Or putting my mouth anywhere near your prick. In fact, I never want to see this little display again in my whole life. Ever!"

"I'm sorry. It won't happen again. It's just...."

"Get over yourself. At least we know the little guy works properly." She cocks her head and stares directly at my fully erect penis. It's making a valiant – though fruitless – effort to be taller. "While I've got your attention, let's measure this puppy. Good information to have, right?"

"Uhm. I'm fine with an approximation."

Jayne pulls a soft tape measure from her purse and unrolls it. Just a little.

"You must measure the top, starting from the base of your schlong," she says in a schoolmarm's voice, putting the tape against my torso and laying it along the top of my wiener. More squinting. "Five-and-a-quarter inches." She then wraps the tape around the middle to measure girth. "Four and a half inches. Honey, if we are to believe scientific studies, you are dreadfully average. Not big, not small. Just middle-of-the-road. Unremarkable. Ordinary. Commonplace. Garden variety. Dime-a-dozen."

"Okay! I get it. I'm nothing to write home about."

"Well, I honestly don't know anyone who would write home about such a thing, but to each his own." She cocks her head. "You're a strange one."

"How can this be average? I thought most guys had at least seven inches."

"Maybe they grow 'em big up near Canada, but that's not what the rest of the world has. You just never see the small ones because nobody has fantasies about average guys." She gives me a half-smile and looks to the side. "Present company excluded, of course."

She is doing absolutely nothing for my self-esteem. Now I know I have an 'average' wiener, and no one wants to see it. What am I supposed to do with that information?

"All done." She's continued shaving my balls while I obsess over every word she says. "Now we can see what we're working with."

I feel like an eight-year-old boy at his first physical exam. "Can I get dressed now? We need to do something other than obsess on my shortcomings."

"Yes. Methinks we need an adventure in clothes shopping, n'est pas?"

"What's wrong with my clothes?"

"Tell me, did your mother buy your clothes for you? And was she a nun who spent all her days watching *Stand By Me* on a loop?"

"All my colors match perfectly."

"Oh, sweetie. Your current wardrobe says, 'I still eat paste.' You need pants that say, 'You couldn't pay for a finer ass than this!' Let's be honest. There isn't much we can do about your front, so let's concentrate on enhancing your rear assets." She throws her head back and laughs, again amusing herself.

"Do you really think I have a nice ass? Uh, butt."

She gives me a condescending look. "You can say 'ass.' It's not like your mother, the nun, is here. And, yes, you have a decent hiney. It's like an end-of-season strawberry that's got just a few more days before it turns."

I really need to learn where her compliments are.

"Grab your Amex Black card! We're going to Pentagon City!"

SEVENTEEN

Stand Clear of the Closing Doors

"You have a whole fucking list of rules just to get on the Metro? Who does that?" Jayne has little patience for proper social order.

The Metro is one of the primary reasons I came to Washington. And, three months on, it still feels like a special treat. Swiping my card, riding the escalator, and hearing "Stand clear of the closing doors" still give me goosebumps. Minot offers nothing comparable.

My subway experience has led me to create commonsense guidelines ensuring an enjoyable excursion. Mother always said it's good to have personal rules about things to avoid unpleasantness. And vomit. Any rational adult would do the same.

First, one must always sit. I don't have 'subway balance.' You know how some guys pee at urinals without holding their wieners? Some people can stand upright on moving trains without holding onto bars – subway balance. I can't do either of those things.

Why not just hold one of the rails? That's the second rule:

never touch any surface. The dregs of humanity have wiped their snotty mitts on practically everything, and it's disgusting. I've seen it, and it's too gross for further commentary.

Rule number three: the seat must face the direction of train movement. This is an unbreakable regulation discovered firsthand back in April. And it has to be the second seat back because the first one is too close to the side-facing bench. I could end up pressed against a strange person, or someone could spill coffee on my shoe. It's all common sense.

Finally, and this one is optional, sit in the window seat. It's fun to look out. I know we're underground most of the time, and the tunnels are dark. I imagine fantastical creatures roaming beyond the window in this mysterious world beneath the streets. There's nothing wrong with an active imagination.

"Rules create pleasant experiences," I say smugly. This is the first time I've felt in control since meeting Jayne.

"Darling, a crowded subway is the only place I can count on getting felt up! Why would I sit and remove any possibility of adventure? A person with your stunted endowment should take it where he can get it." She lowers her head and squints toward my zipper. The feeling of control evaporates.

"Can we *please* stop talking about the size of my wiener?"

"Small penis, short fuse, I guess." Jayne flaps her hands dismissively and walks onto the train. "Okay, Miss Stickler McSticky, show me where we're required to sit."

The Woodley Park red line isn't crowded at 3:30 on a Wednesday, so finding the appropriate seats is easy.

"Take those two seats over there." I point to the second set on the right. "Let me have the window."

"But of course, your royal highness," she says mockingly.

Jayne's sashay to the seat involves a repeated loop of "Pardon me, excuse me" to ensure she receives adequate attention despite having a clear aisle. The other five passengers take no notice. Once seated, she looks around the train, commenting on the other passengers. Loudly.

"Now there's a nice family from Rabbit Hole, Iowa, seeing the Nation's Capital for the first time. Notice how they think October 28 is still shorts season. White ones, even! Not that you can tell where the shorts end and their pasty, disgusting skin begins. And everyone got new vacation Crocs just for the trip!"

"Can you please keep your voice down? Everyone can hear you." I try to keep my head low.

"And that visitor over there must be from Milwaukee. She had her hair did with the Packers Football Helmet Special just for this trip. Jesus Christ! Not even a gun-toting, Republican lesbian would think of sporting that coiffure!"

"Jayne!"

"Oh, *puh-leeze*! No one is even aware we're here. I could stand up and sing the entire second act of *Gypsy*, and not one person would throw me a rose. Not one, I tell you!" She begins to stand, and I pull her back to the seat. "What a dreary existence."

The train enters Metro Center before she can create another spectacle. I give her shoulder a little tap, but she ignores me.

"Hurry! We transfer here," I say, pushing her out of the train. My arm sports a bright red Jayne handprint for the effort.

"No more pushing! These expensive heels are meant for a runway, not a track and field event." She gives me the evil eye before her expression changes to condescension. "You don't know where you're going, do you?"

"This whole trip is your idea. I've never taken the Metro to Virginia. So, yes, I'm winging it. Where's the connecting train?"

"Do I look like a fucking prairie dog to you? I only travel above ground. If we had taken a Lyft as I suggested...."

"I have exactly $126 of extra money each month, and I don't want to spend it on Lyft. There's nothing wrong with the subway. Now help me find the blue line." I look frantically for signage to take me out of this argument. "There! We have to go downstairs."

Metro Center is much busier than Woodley Park, and the arriving train has few empty spots. The only empty adjacent seats are the first set, a clear violation of my rules. This is better than standing since no one is on the side-facing bench. So I make the rule exception and slide to the window with Jayne next to me.

A statuesque sailor with military-cut dark hair and bottomless brown eyes glides into the side-facing seat in front of me. He's wearing the tight, white uniform that may or may not appear in some of my personal fantasies. My face burns with bashfulness.

Jayne elbows me hard and nods her wig toward the way-out-of-my-league sailor. Wink, wink. She couldn't be more obvious if she hung a neon sign over his head. I coyly ignore her. No luck. She puts a hand on my left leg and pulls it toward her, my knee leaning against the sailor's leg. Nothing could be more awkward.

The weak smile crossing his lips says he's aware of our physical connection. And he leaves his leg right there. My muscles freeze.

"Why don't you say hello?" comes Jayne's stage whisper. "Ask for his name. Say something pithy. Make out a little." Another elbow to my ribs.

I grit my teeth and open my eyes wide, staring her down. She looks undeterred. My focus turns to hunting for fantastical creatures in the subway tunnel.

"Pssst!" is followed by another elbow to the ribs. She won't stop.

Then the athletic leg hugging my knee gives me two gentle

pushes. I turn to see that the sailor has fixed his dazzling, Cocoa Puffs eyes on me.

"You look lost. Are you visiting DC?" intones the James Earl Jones voice emanating from the god-like being. He smiles.

"No," croaks the average boy from Minot. "I live here. I mean, not on the train, but in the city. It's my first trip to vagina. I mean, Virginia." The longest 10 seconds of my life.

"Where are you headed?"

"Petunia. Or, rather, Pentagon City."

"I'm going to the Pentagon. It's the stop right before yours. Just go one more after I leave, and you're there." He flashes a perfect smile and practically pats himself on the back for being a Good Samaritan. "Are you shopping for something special?"

"Tell him you're buying condoms. Trojan Magnum XL," comes the stage whisperer again. I turn beet red as the sailor flashes Jayne a Hollywood smile.

"Just buying some new clothes. Winter is coming."

"Oh! *Game of Thrones* fan! Very cool." Apparently, I said something to impress him. "My name's Derek, by the way."

"Randy." The most enormous, warm hand engulfs my stubby paw. I gaze into his eyes and shiver a little.

"Ooh! Big hands!" Nothing escapes Jayne's commentary. I shoot her a murderous look.

"You must be new to DC if you've never come out to Virginia. How long have you lived here?"

"Three days. I mean, months. I'm all up in Madams Organ." Jayne stomps on my foot.

"You mean Adams Morgan," he says with a devious grin. What beautiful teeth he has.

"Oh. Yeah. I'm not really into women's organs." Why won't my mouth work?!?

Derek chuckles. "You're funny. Well, if it means anything, I'm not really into women's organs either." I swear on my mother's grave, his eye twinkled!

"Get his number!" Jayne hisses with all the subtlety of a prompter to a deaf and forgetful stage actor. I nervously look out the window, trying not to take the bait.

Derek puts his hand on my leg. "Well, this is my stop. You think I could give you a call? Maybe get your number?" This time he blushes and quickly removes his hand.

Jayne elbows me again. I know I'm going to have a bruise. "Yeah. Sure. It's, uhm, 701-555-0121."

Derek types my number on his phone with the ease of someone who has done this many times. "Great. I'll call you." He floats from his seat, pauses, and looks back at me. "Randy." And then he's gone.

"Well, well, well. Look who's wearing her big-girl panties now! You can thank me later." Jayne shines her nails on her dress.

"What just happened?" I ask in a way that sounds more like a statement.

"I just got you laid," Jayne replies arrogantly. "Or possibly a date. Well, that's if he calls you, of course. Let's just call it subway titillation, and then you don't owe me as much."

"Owe *you*? For humiliating *me*?" Jayne clutches her necklace at my sudden irritability.

"I thought you liked him. I was doing you a favor." And she counters my irritation with righteous indignation. "Besides, I'm not the one who said 'vagina.'"

"No! That's not the point!" I'm feeling a level of frustration I rarely experience. "I want to meet a guy on my own terms, not because you forced me to talk to him. I'm not comfortable moving so fast!"

Jayne adjusts her bosom before wagging a finger in my face. "Private thoughts are much more sinful than public actions. I'm only repeating what Jesus said. And you don't want to piss off Jesus, do you?"

I can't speak. It's as if MJ came back to DC and gave me the mirror image of her lecture in the truck. I've never really been able to stand up to MJ, and I'm suddenly in the same situation with Jayne. My shoulders droop as I realize I'm beaten.

"Personally, I like sailors. Those uniforms have no secrets," she says with a wink.

"What if he's a serial killer or something?"

"Ask him to wait until after sex to kill you. Then, you're both satisfied."

And it's Jayne for the win.

EIGHTEEN

Emerald City, Virginia

"Let me guess. That dopey stare and glisten of drool say you're picking out curtains for your new home with Derek. Hmmm?" Jayne is walking so fast that I have trouble keeping up.

Yes, I'm still mad. Jayne embarrassed me. But, I did get hit on by a hot sailor who took my phone number. Of course, I'm decorating our new home!

"No! Why would I spend time thinking about our new curtains?" I try to act cool. "It's no big thing. I mean, he hasn't even called yet."

"You gave him your number five minutes ago! I'm betting on two days. Three maybe. There are rules about these kinds of things, so give it a rest."

"Three days! Could it really take three days? I can't wait that long! Why didn't I ask for his number, too?"

"One military hunk notices you, and suddenly you're a drama queen. Sheesh! File it away for tonight when you're alone. For now, there are some new frocks in your immediate future."

We emerge from a long hallway into the glimmering atrium of Fashion Centre at Pentagon City. It's like walking into the Emerald City.

"It's just a mall, not the Emerald City," Jayne says, reading my mind.

"Should we start at Sears or go right to JCPenney?" I ask, like a child on his first trip to Walt Disney World.

"Jesus, Mary, and Anderson Cooper!" Jayne completely stops, turning her head sharply to reveal a demonic glare worthy of a Biblical tale. "Don't you *ever* use those filthy words in my presence again! Now get on your knees and give me 24 Hail Neiman Marcus's to repent for your sins."

I roll my eyes. "Fine. You choose the store. But remember, I only have $126 of discretionary money for this venture."

"You didn't bring a credit card? On a fashion excursion? I will not stand beside some dirty checkout desk breathing the same air as a minimum wage employee while you pay with dimes and pennies."

"Yes, I have a credit card. And I can charge exactly $126. That's my budget. If I spend more, I can't pay it off."

Jayne laughs so hard she snorts. "You pay off your credit card every month? Who does that?"

"Actually, I just did some quick math," I tell her indignantly, "and we can only spend $48 today. I used some of my slush fund to buy a dress and Pussy hair."

So this is what 'rolling on the floor laughing' looks like. I think she even pushed out a fart.

"Get up! Let's just get this over with."

I grab Jayne's arm and pull her up as she wipes her eyes with a lacy hanky. "You said Pussy hair!" She begins to chortle again.

"Fine." I look around for a store I can possibly afford. "I'm going to Macy's."

This is when I learn her blood-curdling scream means: A) her arm has been severed; B) she just saw a person decapitated with a machete; C) someone is wearing clothes from a discount chain, or D) all of the above.

The answer is likely D.

Jayne poses with one hand stretched toward me, the other on her hip as if she was about to lip-sync, "Stop! In the Name of Love." I stand frozen. Nearly everyone in the atrium has also turned their attention our way.

"NOT THERE!" The horror in her voice would be more appropriate if I were about to step into a bear trap. "We will start at Hugo Boss and Armani and work our way down. But not *that* far down. We are not SAVAGES!" She composes herself and gracefully steps on the escalator. Scene over.

The Hugo Boss store is a sea of price tags with large numbers. Who spends $78 on a plain t-shirt? The only thing I can afford is the free cologne sample.

"Let's start with the basics. You need new skivvies. They have stuff here that will accentuate the good stuff and guarantee you get laid." She picks up a package of red, low-rise trunks with random black markings. "This says sexy."

"This says forty-two dollars. That's a lot to spend for something that spends its day hugging my smelly butt. If I buy now, our shopping trip is over."

She tosses the underwear in my face. "With that attitude, no one will ever see you naked again." Her eye catches the jeans section. She knows exactly what she wants. "These turquoise Candiani jeans compensate for all the places you come up short." She stares at my crotch. "And they lift your tushie nearly to eye level. Perfection."

"Have you looked at me? There is no way I can squeeze into slim-fit jeans."

"They come in regular fit if it's absolutely necessary. Maybe someone could work on losing a few pounds, hmmm?" And the insults keep coming.

"These are $178! For one pair of jeans! If you added up all the jeans I've ever owned, it wouldn't come to that much! No. Definitely not."

"Try them on. You'll go from roly-poly to slim and sexy in an instant. The dressing room is over there."

"I can't afford any of this. We need to leave."

She grabs my shoulders and spins me to face a gorgeous young clerk with flawless mocha skin, shaggy dark hair styled to perfection, and an ultra-bright smile that guarantees he gets what he wants.

"Can I help you find something?" he says, batting his doe eyes.

"See! Ask the waiter if he likes your ass in those jeans." Jayne flicks her hand in my direction and walks to the shirts.

"My friend says these jeans would look good on me, but...."

"Absolutely," he says while evaluating my lower body. "They will enhance your best assets. Why don't you try this pair instead?" He grabs a larger pair off the rack. "More your size. Go over there and put them on."

He's too cute for me to resist, so I take the jeans and walk into the dressing room. A moment later, I'm being inspected by this adorable dreamboat who has me considering infidelity in my new relationship with Derek.

"Let's spruce up your window display." He hikes the front of the pants, so a package magically appears – though I'm pretty sure it's empty. "Perfect."

I look in the mirror. They do make me look great. "You really think so?"

"That is an ass I would take home to mother." He winks at me.

"I'll take one in turquoise and one in regular blue. And the underwear." I say breathlessly.

"You got it, stud."

He swaggers to the register, carefully folds my new duds in tissue paper, and places them in an embossed bag that probably cost more than my shoes. I'm staring at him like a cartoon character hit by an anvil.

"That's $423.87," he says with that Ultra Brite smile. "Would you like to use a card?"

My brain is yelling to walk away and save myself from financial ruin. My nether region is already planning the second time we'll have sex. This is not a fair contest.

"I'll use Amex."

It's funny how fast regret can set in.

I try to hand him my card, but the sexy god is texting with someone, completely ignoring me. He smiles at his phone as he reaches for my card, never looking up. He runs the card, puts the receipt in the bag, and hands me my clothes and Amex, all while staring at his phone.

"Thanks, and come again." No eye contact.

Is this what a one-night stand feels like? I see Jayne at the other end of the store holding a $225 shirt aloft. She has the face of a child who wants money for the ice cream truck.

"We're leaving. I just spent far too much because I thought I might get a date with the sales guy. No more impulse spending."

"Well, I hope you're better in the sack than you are at buying clothes. Did you really think that guy was interested in you?"

"Actually, yes. He touched my waist! And winked at me."

"And took $400 from you. That's called prostitution, honey." She suddenly seems maternal. "Let's get some ice cream. You're buying."

I never argue with ice cream. We walk up to the Baskin-Robbins counter, and I don't bother checking the choices.

"I'd like a large cup of vanilla."

I can feel the hot breath of condescension on my neck as the scooper turns to fill my order.

"Vanilla? All the sexy underwear in the world can't do much for a guy who is vanilla." She makes a clucking sound with her tongue. "And I guess we'll start losing some weight tomorrow, huh?"

"This was your idea! Besides, vanilla is my favorite flavor, and ice cream always makes me feel better. Give me a break. I've had a hard two days."

Jayne rolls her eyes.

"What are you getting?" I ask, trying to be polite.

"Oh, darlin', I'm on a diet. I'll wait over on that bench for you to get your great big, steaming bowl of ordinary." She walks off.

"That's $6.25," the scooper says without irony as she hands me a somewhat skimpy bowl of blandness. That's the price of *two* lite beers in Minot!

I carry my disappointment and ice cream to the seat next to Jayne. She's scoping out the other shoppers like a voyeuristic psychic.

"See that woman over there? The one wearing the Walmart exercise pants with the thighs nearly worn away. That didn't happen from exercise. You are on the fast track to being her in about six months." Jayne is doing her best to ruin my ice cream, but she fails to understand the hardships a North Dakotan will endure for this frozen dessert. I continue eating. "Congratulations! I've decided to make you my pet project."

"Your project? I don't need that much help."

"It would take an entire army of drag queens to fix all that's wrong with you. Eat up, if you must. We've got work to do."

There's something almost atheistic about eating ice cream too fast, but Jayne propels me forward. The moment my spoon hits the cup's bottom, she grabs my arm and drags me back to the Metro stop.

The ride is a blur. I can hear the American Express card gently weeping in my wallet, and the new clothes seem to be throwing a party in the Hugo Boss bag. Jayne is talking fast and incessantly. The only way I will survive this excursion is to enter a comatose state until I can lock myself in the bedroom at home.

A downside to being comatose is that the drag queen is now in charge. Maybe she told me what she was planning, but the smear of sound from her mouth never made a lasting impression. No matter. I snap out of my stupor just as I see the words "Friendship Heights" at the top of the escalator.

"What are we doing here?"

"You agreed to hit one more store, and I agreed to go slumming at Bloomingdale's. I call that a lopsided win on your part." She lets out an enormous sigh. "As long as you scamper right on past the sale racks, we just might find one acceptable shirt in the designer section."

I grab her arm as we enter the mall. "Jayne, I can't afford this."

She turns and puts her hands on her hips in what is clearly a lecture stance. "Darling, you can't afford *not* to. Just look at yourself! People have been tossing quarters at you all day like you're some sort of Skid Row reject. Just being in such close proximity has tarnished my reputation that no amount of elbow grease will erase. This is a national emergency!"

Two days ago, I was happy to have clean Wrangler jeans hanging in the closet. Today I'm the cause of a national emergency.

"Okay, but I may ask for a part-time job application while we're in the store. There is truly no way to pay off today's little outing."

Jayne begins her power walk through the store. "No worries. I can do a few verses from 'It's a Hard Knock Life' for the store manager, and you're practically guaranteed a janitorial position. I honestly don't know why you feel the need to be so dramatic!"

She accentuates this little speech by cackling and throwing her arms up like Endora. That's enough distraction to make me pass the sale rack and sail right into the designer section.

Let's suffice it to say there was much begging, pleading, demeaning, cajoling, fighting, name-calling, and crying over the next 15 minutes. It ended with me carrying a Bloomingdale's bag packed with two Armani shirts.

My American Express was inconsolable on the ride home.

Nineteen

Truth Serum

One of my church friends bought a puppy cam a couple of years ago. She adopted a four-month-old golden retriever and couldn't stand being away from him. So, she wasted countless work hours staring at streaming videos featuring the mundane activities of a baby dog. Not that he could do much from the confines of his metal crate, but the yawning, stretching, and sleeping must have been fascinating TV. As far as I know, she still watches while she 'works.'

I'm considering a puppy cam for homebound drag queens.

It's been three days since I first woke to find Jayne in my apartment – and she's still with me. In fact, I now have three identical red sequin gowns hanging on the living room curtain rod. Five Styrofoam heads adorned with blond wigs, a toolbox that serves as a makeup kit, and a pile of women's undergarments cover most of the remaining floor space. She has completely overtaken my living room and bathroom.

Jayne is seated at the kitchen table when I wake every morning and on the couch when I get home. The ubiquitous red sequin gown with matching heels and full makeup always look fresh. In fact, it's the only thing she wears. I don't know what she does after I close my bedroom door at night or when

I'm gone at work. I'm afraid to ask – but I think I should.

On the other hand, maybe CVS sells drag queen cams.

Work was particularly trying today. In fact, it's been a tough week; no thanks to Jayne, and I could use an evening alone. As the key slides into the lock, I maintain a glimmer of hope the apartment will be empty.

"TGIF!" screams the voice loud enough to signal approaching ships.

"Hi, Jayne. You're still here, huh?"

"Where else would I be?" That sounded like a serious question. "You look exhausted, like you haven't slept in days. I know how you feel! Come sit with me for a quick moment before you make us drinks."

She excitedly pats the cushion next to her. I sit in the chair across the room, attempting to assert my independence. It's a futile gesture, but I feel better.

"I've had such a day," she sighs with dramatic flair. "It was just nonstop! My feet are killing me! At least you get to sit on your ass at a cushy desk for eight hours. Try wearing these fabulous pumps, day-in and day-out!"

"You could take them off."

"And ruin the outfit? Now I ask you, which of those is worse?"

I stare blankly at the floor. Jayne's need to talk is matched only by her need to be heard. I keep forgetting neither of these requires my vocal participation.

"I have a great idea! Why don't you come up with a special concoction to wet our whistles?"

"My choice? Before Tuesday night, all I ever had was lite beer, but I'll give it a try." A little voice inside me recommends caution. "I'll only have one of whatever we drink. There can't be a repeat of Tuesday's inebriation." Jayne offers a crooked smile.

Along with the clothes we bought on Wednesday, Jayne

insisted I stock a proper "fag bar." That (expensive) little trip included: vodka, gin, whiskey, bourbon, vermouth, tonic water, Aperol, tequila, angostura bitters, olives, lemons, limes, maraschino cherries, and something called rye. Each had to be the largest size bottle available. My kitchen is an alcoholic's dream.

"What do you think if we line the bottles up alphabetically and mix the first three or four? Tonight would be," I point to bottles as I quickly alphabetize, "angostura bitters, Aperol, bourbon, and gin. We could try a different letter set each night."

Yes, I had a rough week. But something is exciting about becoming a bartender.

"Well, aren't you the creative one! You'll make a fantastic bartender." She pauses. "Tonight, let's start at the end of the alphabet with vermouth, vodka, and olives. Dirty." She begins filing her nails. "Do whatever you want with those ingredients."

Jayne stays in the living room as I move to the kitchen to make our drinks. This might be a good time to ask her how long she plans to stay with me. We're in separate rooms and won't make eye contact. I can do this.

"Jayne, can I ask you something?" A drop of sweat rolls from my armpit.

"I was thinking the same thing," she yells. "Once you make those drinks, we can yak for hours!"

Just then, my phone rings. Probably someone from Minot who, like me, has nothing to do at 6:30 on a Friday night. Strange. It's from the DC area code.

"Hello?"

"Hi. Randy?"

"Yes. Who's calling, please?"

"Uh, this is Derek. We met on the Metro the other day."

My mouth silently shrieks, "IT'S DEREK!!!"

Jayne sits up straight and adjusts her bosom. "On speaker!" she mouths, pointing at the phone. I unwisely comply.

"You still there? I'm the sailor. We sat next to one another. Do you remember?"

"You better answer him," Jayne chimes in, loud enough to be heard, "or he will move on to the next guy on his list."

"Uhm, hi, Derek. I, uh, sure. I mean, I couldn't forget meeting you. How you doin'?"

Jayne rolls her eyes. "This is going to end badly."

"Did I call at a bad time? It sounds like you have company. I can call later." Derek keeps trying.

"Of course, it's a bad time," Jayne starts her running commentary. "Tell him it's Friday night, and you're just counting your toes like you always do. You're only on number three, so you could be busy for a while."

I give her the universal signal for 'shut up,' but she shrugs and mouths, "I don't understand."

"No, it's not a bad time at all. My friend Jayne and I were about to drink dinner. No! I mean, make a drink or something, and maybe eat dinner."

"Okay. I wondered if you would like to go to dinner tomorrow night. I know it's last minute, but I couldn't get up the nerve to call you sooner."

Jayne clutches her pearls, looking horrified. "Well, that little hussy! There's barely enough time to shop for new clothes and get your hair done! Talk about inconsiderate." She thinks for a moment. "Tell him to take you to Marcel's. You'll feel better about being a cheap whore if he springs for an expensive dinner."

I put my hand over the phone. "Shut up! You're going to ruin this for me!"

"Well, somebody's sitting on swollen hemorrhoids." She sharply turns her head toward the window.

"Yes, I'd love to eat you. I mean, have you for dinner. With dinner. What time?"

"How about 7:30? You like Mexican? I can meet you at Lauriol Plaza on 18th and T Streets. Sound good?"

Jayne begins flailing her arms and shaking her head. I turn away.

"That's perfect. I can walk there from my place."

"Great. See you then."

"Bye, Berek. Uh, Derek."

"Well, he's a cheap one, isn't he? Mexican food on the first date! I tried to warn you. All the beans and cheese will have you bloated and gassy. He'll be sorry for his poor culinary selection once he's balls deep in your exploding manhole!"

I've heard nothing she said. "I have a date!"

She ignores my love-struck dumb face. "And he's betting the off-brand tequila will limber you up like Simone Biles sitting spread-eagle on the vertical bar." She pretends to fan herself frantically. "A girl can dream, can't she?"

"Jayne, I just got a date with the most beautiful man on the whole planet! I'm going on a date tomorrow!!" Even an acerbic drag queen can't bring me down.

"It's a good thing we got you some appropriate clothes to wear 'cause there's no time to shop. It'll take the entire day to get you properly crimped, curled, and douched for an evening of savage bodice-ripping."

Jayne probably continued talking, but I heard nothing. I was lost in a vision of myself as the Disney Cinderella entering the ball. Maybe I should buy glass slippers.

"Snap out of it, Cinder-fella. Tonight, we must celebrate!" Jayne pumps her palms toward the ceiling. "Darling, let me walk you through making martinis, so you don't fuck it up. We'll make both drinks in the same shaker and then split it." She pauses to think. "For two of us, you'll need 10 shots of vodka. No, make it 12."

I begin pouring as she watches over my shoulder. "Remember,

I'm not getting drunk."

"Of course not!" Jayne feigns surprise. "You just use the barest whisper of vermouth – that's the stuff that makes you drunk – two tablespoons of olive juice, and a twist of lemon. Shake gently. Pour into glasses and add two olives each. It's practically all fruits and vegetables!"

The martinis are so enormous I serve them in water glasses. Jayne says it's an unpardonable sin to treat a martini this way, but she'll overlook it in light of the happy news – and the fact I'm an unwashed rube. I'm pretty sure I should be insulted.

"Let's play a game," I offer as a way to pass the time without thinking incessantly of Derek.

"Truth or Dare." Jayne gives me an eyebrows-raised look that encapsulates innocence and evil in equal measure.

"I was thinking euchre. Or Monopoly. I even have Chutes and Ladders. Any of these sound good?"

"And will we also be listening to Lawrence Welk?"

My mind wanders to where we can find some of his recordings when I see she isn't serious.

"We will play Truth or Dare. Unless you have something to hide," Jayne says definitively.

"No. I have nothing to hide. Just stuff I don't want to share with you. Those are two different things."

I take a beer-like chug of martini. Bad idea. My face becomes Lucille Ball on her first taste of Vitameatavegamin, full-body shudder and all.

"You can take the girl out of Minot, but you can't take the two-for-one-draft-night-at-the-Redneck-Saloon out of the girl," she says, shaking her head. "You have to sip it for at least the first half of the glass. After that, it's fine to chug like you're at a frat party until you pass out."

I take a little sip, followed by a head and shoulder shimmy. "I made these a little strong."

"You're gay."

I guess that explanation suffices. Another sip and another shudder. "It would probably go down better if I drank it faster. This seems like an acquired taste."

"Suit yourself. I think of it more as a truth serum. And speaking of which, you said you wanted to play Truth or Dare."

"I did? Well, if I'm drinking truth serum, I don't think I have a choice." My glass is nearly empty, and the world is losing focus. Just because clear drinks look like water doesn't mean they should be imbibed similarly.

"What'll it be, little puppy? Truth or dare?" Jayne looks down at her nails, hiding a devious grin that says she doesn't care which one I pick. Either way, I'm going to be screwed.

"Truth. Better to start with truth." I throw back the last of my martini and notice that Jayne hasn't even touched hers. "Aren't you going to drink your martini?"

"This is *your* martini. You just finished drinking mine, you greedy little shit."

"Oh. I'm sorry. They both looked the same. I'll make you another as soon as I finish my drink." I reach across the table and take the other martini.

"No worries. Happens all the time." She rubs her hands together and looks me straight in the eye. "You said Truth." Then her mouth makes a closed-lip, curly smile only Dr. Seuss could draw. "What is the extent of your sexual experience?"

"That's a comprehensive and personal question."

"You're the one who chose truth. Besides, we might need to have The Talk before your date tomorrow night. It would be good to know where you're starting from."

Jayne sits back on the couch, crosses her legs, and places her hands on her lap. She's clearly expecting copious details.

"Fine."

Martinis are absolutely truth serum. And inhibition inhibitors.

Should I try to say that aloud to see if I'm drunk? Jayne is still staring at me. I better answer the question.

"I kissed Millie once when we were in the fifth grade. It was a dare at a party. She used that great big, slimy, sloppy tongue of hers, and I thought it was gross."

"That's it?"

I furrow my brow like I'm thinking hard. I wonder if I look like I'm thinking hard. I should think about thinking more often.

"You were saying," she drawls.

"Oh, right. Well, on this band trip in high school, I, uh, I kind of lost my virginity. That's it."

Jayne's eyes become flying saucers without the flashing lights. "That's it? You drop the words 'kind of lost my virginity' and expect me to just let it drop? Fess up on the details, bitch."

"I don't know. What else can I say?"

"Oh, maybe add a few details. Paint with some color. Give a full and accurate description of his dick."

"Details. Right. Well, I was sitting on the bus next to Ken Lambert, and we were coming home from an away football game. Those are the games that aren't at home. That's why they're called 'away.'"

"Stick to the story, Betty White. I'll figure out the context on my own."

"Yes, sir. Ma'am." Her glare causes me to shudder harder than the martini. I decide to speak faster. "So, he fell asleep and sort of slid over, so his head rested on my shoulder. We were just friends. And he's straight. Anyway, most of the trip was on country roads, so the bus was bouncing quite a bit. And he was sleeping with his head on my shoulder. Uhm, anyway, with all of that, I kinda, sorta made a mess in my pants. Fortunately, it was dark, and I just ran to my car and drove home when we got back to the school. No one saw. It wasn't a good experience."

Jayne had slowly moved forward in her seat until she was sitting on the edge of the couch, resting her head on her hands as I told the story. As soon as I finished, she threw back her head and let out a cackle that nearly broke the windows, falling on the floor and laughing until her sides hurt. Several times I was afraid she had quit breathing. Then she would belt out another cackle, and it all started anew.

After nearly five minutes of watching this display (and nervously drinking the remainder of my martini), Jayne finally pulled herself back onto the couch.

"I have no words!" She starts laughing again.

"To be fair, there weren't many operas." Pause. "Oprahs." Words are eluding me. I double my efforts to finish the sentence. "Operafortunititties for a gay guy in a itty-bitty, teeny-tiny town in the North of Dakota." I'm frustrated, a bit embarrassed, and struggling with language skills. "And that's in North Dakota, even!"

"You're fucking trashed!" More laughter.

"I am not trashy! There is no way I could be drunk twice in one week. I'm fucking fine." I stand and immediately fall on my ass just in front of the chair. Ooo, this isn't good.

"Fucking fine?" She has clearly found great humor at my expense. "I've never heard you swear. Not once. You're trashed, Missy. So, before you pass out, tell me you've never even kissed a guy?"

"No. Just Millie. And MJ's dog. He was thuch a goo boy." Melancholy creeps in.

"What happens if ol' Derek wants to do the nasty tomorrow night? Do you even know what to expect?"

I sit up straight. "I didn't not even think about that! It's only on our firtht date! Jesus on the cross! Help me!"

Jayne gives me a stern look. "Get up off that floor and put your ass in the chair. I'm getting you some water." She walks toward the kitchen. "Christ! You give the girl 12 shots of vodka, and she's flat out on the floor! You better build some tolerance, little lady," she yells over her shoulder and continues to mutter as she walks.

I know the chair is behind me, but I can't seem to find it. I simultaneously twist my shoulders to the left and head to the right, but it's not any closer. Maybe if I roll over on my side, I'll have a better visual. I put all my weight on the left side of my body and slam into the carpet. Nope. No chair here.

"What are you doing? You look like a worm trying to turn into a butterfly. I said, get up!"

Jayne grabs my arms, pulls me to the couch, and throws me down with my head on a pillow. My feet are still on the floor next to me. I really doubt I could manage this position if I weren't so drunk.

"Drink this."

I take the glass of water and lift it to my lips, pouring the entire thing onto my chin and chest. Goddamned gravity!

Jayne grabs the glass, lets out a dramatic sigh, and returns for a refill. This time she sits me upright and holds it as I take a few sips.

"You're tho good to me," I say in my best child-like voice.

I suddenly remember I wanted to talk with Jayne about why she is always at my apartment. And why she's always in drag. Is there a "he" under all that makeup? I do a dramatic head swing to the left and raise my finger.

"Hey! I have a inquiring inquisition for you. Why are you never gone from here? Don't you got like a plathe with your own furniture and clothes and stuff?"

Jayne reaches down, puts an arm around my waist, and lifts me up. "Time for you to go to bed." She helps me to my room and lays me in bed. My half-open eyes see Jayne Mansfield tucking me in and kissing my forehead.

As she turns to walk away, I say, "Good night, my fairy godmother."

I giggle myself to sleep.

TWENTY

Braunschweiger, Maybe?

Maybe I should roll into a different position. My left arm is numb, and the right may no longer be attached. Hello, legs! Can you hear me? Is my arm down there? No response. What if Jayne cut off my arms and legs, and I'm tied up in a basement somewhere? Have I been kidnapped?

It figures I would get caught up with a homicidal drag queen. Did Mother warn me about this once?

Wait! Am I still in bed? Possibly. Is the bed underwater? My face feels like it's in a puddle. I hope it's not drool. Or vomit. I'd rather be underwater. Oh, god! I've had my limbs hacked off by a killer drag queen, and my torso is tied to a vomit-soaked mattress! It's just what Mother predicted!

An unidentified body part moves, followed by a squeak.

"I thought I heard the bed creak... and not in that don't-mind-me-I'm-plowing-this-field kind of way," Jayne bellows as she walks into the bedroom. Her voice brings to mind Elvia Allman as Lucy and Ethel's boss in the chocolate factory. If my tongue ever re-hydrates, I'll tell her this comparison.

"Jesus! How did you get into that position? I'm not sure which of these is an arm and which is a leg!" I hear her approach the bed. "Oh, but honey, I know what that appendage is!"

"Nnnnthp." That's all I got.

I feel grabbing, hitting, pinching, bending, and straightening. As my vision slowly returns, I see I'm lying on my back below the judgmental eyes attached to the loud voice.

"Twice this week, I've had to nurse your sorry ass back from a hangover. I thought those days were behind me after Marilyn Monroe quit throwing slumber parties. I didn't sign up to be your damned nursemaid."

She sits me up and puts two pillows behind my back, forcing me to stay upright. A cold, wet washcloth wipes my face and hair. Two fingers force my mouth open, toss in a couple of Tylenol, and fill the dehydrated cavern with water. I somehow manage to swallow.

"I've drawn you a bath. Maybe we can soak you back to health." I feel her wrench me to my feet and drag me to the bathroom. There's further tugging, contorting, and rustling. Suddenly, I'm feeling air that tells me I'm naked.

The bath was probably warm once but is now on the chilly side of tepid. I sink into the water until I'm just short of drowning. This is the first good sensation since I became conscious.

"Oh, Jayne. I feel terrible."

"That's nothing. You should see how you look."

"What time is it? I didn't sleep through the entire day again, did I?"

"It's 2:15. You broke your own record from just three days ago. I admire your competitive spirit!" She does a half-hearted fist pump.

"I've got a date tonight! I can't go out with Derek when I'm so hungover!" My whining voice is annoying even to me. "This is a disaster!"

"Perez Hilton is a disaster. You're just a hot mess." I think this is intended to make me feel better, but it's not helping. "Jayne will get you fixed up. You just soak here for a bit, and I'll find some food and a little hair of the dog."

She leaves the bathroom, and I slip down under the water. I could stay here all day. A few minutes later, Jayne returns with a plate of scrambled eggs and a glass of water. My stomach may be gurgling, but I'm always hungry. I grab the water and drink it in one gulp.

"What the hell?!?" I nearly choke on my drink.

"Hair of the dog, my child. It does a body good."

"You gave me a glass of straight vodka? I had enough alcohol last night to cover the entire year. No more booze!"

"Suit yourself. Joan Crawford always told me to start my morning with the same drink that ended the last evening. The hair of the dog that bit you. Millions of old wives can't be wrong!" Her face shows she truly believes in the healing power of excessive drinking.

The Tylenol does its work on my headache while the vodka softens perceptions. The combination serves to even the world to a very tolerable plane. Maybe there is some truth in that old platitude. I stay in the bath for nearly an hour before standing becomes an option.

Back in the bedroom, Jayne has once again laid out clothes for me. This look is decidedly casual: sweatpants, Minot State University sweatshirt, sports socks, and JCPenney tighty-whities folded into a different nondescript woodland animal. This time she put the ChapStick entering the rear of the animal. Subtle.

"I thought I would be wearing my new underwear."

"That's for tonight. You can't spend the day in a fine pair of skivvies like those only to have them smell of ass for your date. You can wear them after your pre-dinner shower."

I can't argue with that logic. Besides, the couch and TV are calling my name.

"You know we have to do your hair, right? That gargantuan task could take a couple of hours, so don't get too comfortable."

"I just need to rest." Her words start to sink in. "What exactly do you have planned for my hair?"

"I will perform miracles on that Midwestern mop such that you cause whispers wherever you walk."

"Oh."

We flip through Netflix and decide on an old movie: *All About Eve*. Actually, *we* didn't decide on it, but I've never seen it, and there's no energy to argue with the diva. Jayne says every gay should know this film and be able to quote lines on cue.

Maybe someone should write a book listing everything we gays are supposed to know.

By now, it's 5:30. Ninety minutes to prepare. Jayne has apparently mapped out the next hour-and-a-half, so my freshness doesn't fade before 7:30.

"Sweatshirt off and have a seat in the kitchen chair." She brings a white towel (did I already own this?), rubber gloves, and a strange hairbrush. The smell of peroxide soon overwhelms me, and I think I know what she's doing.

"You're going to color my hair?"

"Add color *to* your hair, my dear. That washed-out mane of yours is a cross between wet cement, corn silk near the end of the season, and dog shit. What word describes this hair color on your driver's license?"

I shrug. "Braunschweiger, maybe?"

Jayne stands frozen with a blank expression.

"You know my date is in two hours, don't you? That's not enough time to color my hair, shower, and get dressed. Besides, I think it's fine just as is."

"Says the man with Wrangler jeans in his closet. Just look at me. I'm an expert in hair color!" She gently pats her hair and strikes a sex kitten pose. I don't know what's under that wig, but the outer layer is admittedly fabulous.

"You can't screw this up!"

"Shut up and close your eyes."

After much snipping, swearing (Jayne), painting, pulling, more swearing (also Jayne), waiting, and near-fainting from fumes, I'm finally allowed to open my eyes.

"Go shower that out. And no looking before it's washed!" I run to the bathroom as Jayne yells behind me, "And make sure you wash your cooter three times!"

I fight every instinct and don't look in the mirror. Wash, wash, wash. Condition, condition, condition. Scrub, scrub, scrub. Cooter, cooter, cooter (whatever that is). Done.

Jayne is waiting on the other side of the shower curtain when I finish. "A little towel-drying, and I'll finish the rest with the hairdryer. Then you can look."

The whole process takes minutes because, well, there isn't much hair to work with. I'm not going bald, by any stretch of the imagination, but I keep my hair short – civilian short.

"Mirror, mirror on the wall. Who's the foxiest stud of all?" She makes a grand gesture toward the mirror.

Staring back at me is a lightly highlighted, beautifully feathered North Dakotan who suddenly has big-city style. I LOVE IT!

"This is amazing! I can't believe you did all that in just over an hour. Thank you!"

"Well, I always say, 'If your hair doesn't look good, he's never going to grab a fistful and shove your face into the pillow.'"

Fifteen minutes later, I'm dressed in Hugo Boss underwear and jeans, perfectly matched with an Armani shirt. I still have little to show upfront, but my butt has never looked better. The socks and shoes are the best I can do on short notice.

"Stop admiring yourself and get going. Remember, no beans, and go easy on the cheese. If you decide to bring him home, he'll never know I'm here. Just have fun. Oh, and take these." She tosses me two condoms; one is a Magnum XL.

"This will fall off as soon as I put it on." I smile.

"If you let him 'accidentally' see it before you do the nasty, he will think he's getting more than he bargained for. It's the illusion that counts. Now, don't do anything I would do."

She gives me air kisses, and I'm out the door.

TWENTY-ONE

One of These Things
Is Not Like the Other

It's incredible what new clothes and hair color can do for one's confidence. I'm strutting down 18th Street like Frank Sinatra in *Guys and Dolls*, feeling every bit as classy. I swear traffic stops, and people lean out apartment windows just to watch me go by.

I feel so good I've forgotten to be nervous; until just now. My inner voice reminds me I'm going on the first date I've ever had with a man – a gorgeous man who has probably dated more guys this week than I will my entire life. This deluded person asked *me* out after mere moments on a train. What if he never got a good look at me? What if he mixed up my number with another one he got that day and thinks I'm someone else?

My gait loses some of its assuredness. The butt that is undoubtedly the inspiration for sculptors worldwide begins to sag. The shoulders that boldly displayed Armani's best become rounded and droop from the additional weight. I suddenly remember I'm just an average North Dakotan.

While my brain proceeds with its usual work to undermine

confidence, my feet have continued forward. At 7:31, I'm standing at the entrance to Lauriol Plaza. Derek, waiting at the host desk, breaks into a warm smile. At least he recognizes me, so that's a plus. I manage a smile that may give the appearance I'm holding in a belch.

"You look fantastic!" he says with a twinkle in his sparkling, brown eyes. His simple beige sweater, tight enough to reveal a swimmer's pecs, broadcasts a hot/casual vibe perfectly accented by his glistening hazel hair.

"You, too," I squeak, catching a glimpse of the bulge in his jeans. I assume one of us can use the Magnum XL condom.

"Did you walk here?"

"Uhm, yeah. I just live up the street a few blocks in Adams Morgan." I get flustered and point in the wrong direction. "I've always wanted to eat here."

"Cool. It's my favorite restaurant. I like everything on the menu, especially with you here."

His gorgeous brown eyes stare so deep inside me that I visibly shudder. Is that the look people give when they want to have sex? Jayne's voice is in my head, warning against beans and cheese and reminding me of my inexperience. Does the sweat show through my shirt?

The host arrives looking like he's going to sing "One of These Things Is Not Like the Other." Derek motions me ahead, placing his hand on the small of my back. Can he feel the goosebumps? We nearly reach our table at the far end of the dining room when I hear an inimitable cackle that freezes the sweat running from my armpits. I know that laugh.

Jayne Mansfield!

No one can miss the gargantuan drag queen laughing loudly at the next table. I shake my head, squeezing my eyes shut. She couldn't possibly be here! I open my eyes, and she's still there in all her screaming red glory. Her dining partner is the drag Cher from the other night. How the hell did they manage to get the table right beside us?

Derek seats me directly behind the buxom busybody. I can feel her wig hairs tickling my neck, and I shudder again. Nothing good can come from this.

"Did I ask if you like Mexican food when we talked the other night?" Derek asks, effortlessly starting a conversation. I nod. "Good. I was afraid I made a mistake."

"Who doesn't like Mexican food?" I say, trying to be nonchalant while fearing Jayne will move to our table.

"No beans!" comes a loud voice from behind me. She doesn't need to physically sit at our table to be part of our conversation.

"So, do you live nearby?" I try to deflect his attention.

"I'm on Capitol Hill. It's a great neighborhood and an easy Metro ride to work. I lived in Silver Spring when I first got here, but all the construction got on my nerves, and I wanted to be around some of the city's history. Have you been to the Hill?"

"Not really. I stay in Adams Morgan and Dupont, mostly. Sometimes Georgetown."

The server appears, standing with his thigh touching Derek's arm and his back to me. "Can I get you guys some drinks?"

I've had so much alcohol this week that I'm not sure I can handle more. Besides, I don't know anything beyond lite beer. Well, and whatever concoctions Jayne has been feeding me. My eyes dart from the menu to nearby tables, trying unsuccessfully to recognize drinks other than water.

"Stay away from the tequila," comes a stage whisper from behind. "It'll knock you on your ass."

I wish she would shut up. Better yet, go home! How will I ever explain her to Derek?

"What's your favorite?" Derek asks.

"Uhm, I don't really, uh, have one." I fidget with the menu.

"I'll just have what you have."

"Okay, then. We'll take two Roca Patrón silver margaritas on the rocks. No salt."

The server slides his hand from Derek's shoulder to the top of his chest and nods. "You got it, stud." I think he winks.

"Somebody knows his booze!" Jayne says over her shoulder. "But I told you to avoid the tequila. You never listen to a thing I say."

"I've never had a margarita before," I admit to Derek. "What's in it?"

"It's basically tequila, lime juice, and Cointreau. I thought everyone drank them. We can change our order."

And have the waiter back to fondle my date again? I don't think so.

"No. It's fine. Tequila is a new one for me. It's just, uh, we don't have many Mexican restaurants in North Dakota."

"You're from North Dakota? I know you've only been here for a few months, but I didn't know where you came from. That's pretty far out! Did you live near Mount Rushmore?"

"No. That's South Dakota."

"Oh, right. You were near Yellowstone."

"Uh, that's in Wyoming."

"Mount Saint Helens?"

"Washington State."

Derek shakes his head. "I guess I don't know my geography. So, tell me, what's North Dakota like?"

I want to tell him about Minot, my friends, and life with my parents. But, somehow, I feel more like an alien from an exotically boring place than an actual human. His stare suggests I'm being studied.

"Oh, it's cold and dark much of the year. There are lots of Lutherans. It's not terribly interesting." Let's hope that sums it up to his satisfaction. "Where are you from?"

"I grew up in Orlando. Talk about places that aren't

interesting! It's literally a Mickey Mouse town!"

"That's funny," I giggle. "I've never been to Florida. It must be nice to have sun all year. Why did you leave?"

"I studied engineering at the University of Florida after joining the Navy and got put on a ship for two years. After that, I re-enlisted, and they stationed me here for office work. So, really, I didn't make any decisions. They were all made for me."

The server arrives and hands both our drinks to Derek, managing to touch his hand and giggle coyly. "Did you decide on dinner?"

Derek looks at me, and I just shrug. "I'll have whatever you're having. It's all new to me."

"Okay, then. We'll have the bean burrito. That comes with refried beans and pickled bean salad, correct?"

"Yes. And it goes great with our bean dip as an appetizer."

"Perfect. We'll have that."

"You'll be sorry!" comes the sing-song voice from behind. I turn bright red.

We spend two hours eating and talking, sharing our experiences of moving from home, and learning about life in DC. Jayne's interjections, though always biting and sarcastic, become fewer throughout the evening. I clean my plate like a good Midwestern boy, eating every bean. It's washed down with two margaritas, a tasty drink that has already made me tipsy.

"Would you like another drink? We can stay here or drop in one of the Dupont bars."

"I'm fine for now," I say, trying not to move my head and confirm inebriation.

"Invite him to your place, dummy!" comes the loudest stage whisper a person could muster without screaming. "Do I have to do *everything*?"

While Jayne encourages promiscuity, Derek pays for

dinner and gives me a wink. Everything seems to point toward a bedroom escapade. I'm interested, but I don't know how to let him know.

"We could take a walk," I suggest.

"Sure. We could go to Adams Morgan and maybe end up at your place?"

I wasn't expecting him to be so forward. He stands and reaches for my hand, which I hold up for him to kiss. Derek looks confused by the gesture and pulls my entire arm to help me up. Actually, that's better than a kiss because I can't manage an upright position on my own. I turn to notice Jayne is gone.

We walk up 18th Street, admiring the architecture and peering in apartment windows. He has a deep, charming laugh that warms me. He takes my arm in his, a romantic gesture I appreciate more for balance assistance. As we approach my apartment, I point to my tiny home.

"Shall we go up?" he says as if he already lives here.

I have a flashback to the disaster I left earlier in the evening. The place hasn't been cleaned in over a week. Parts of Pussy Liqueur's outfit are lounging about, and I'm sure there is pubic hair on the bathroom floor following the deforestation session. But how can I decline?

"My place is a mess. The maid comes next week." He laughs at that one.

"No worries. I'm sure it's fine."

As I open the door, I feel his massive hand on the small of my back. This time it quickly slides down to my butt, lightly squeezing the left cheek. My wiener jumps to attention, probably to guard against any further attacks.

I leave the lights off to hide the disastrous state of my home. Derek likely interprets this as mood lighting and an invitation to start the party.

With his hand still on my butt, he asks, "So, where's the bedroom?"

"Just over here," I say as he leads me through the apartment with the night vision of a cat – in heat. He finds the bedroom door without running into a thing.

"So, this is where the magic happens, huh?" he says with a wink.

"Oh, I'm not a magician," I reply seriously.

His right hand flips on the overhead light while his left hand guides my butt toward the bed. He's a man who knows – and gets – what he wants.

We reach the bed, and he turns me around. His large hands softly touch both sides of my face as he pulls me in for a kiss. Not wanting him to do all the work, I move my head forward to assist. We smash our front teeth with a cracking sound that may signal dental work is necessary.

Derek pulls his head back in surprise. "I'm sorry. That was a little clumsy." He smiles, and I'm relieved all his teeth are intact.

"No, it was my fault. I'm nervous." I push my tongue against my front teeth to ensure they are still solidly attached.

"Because it's your first time?" he says with a kind smile.

Do I smell of virginity? "Uh, well, I guess so. I mean, I've kissed someone once, but none of the other stuff. Is that okay?"

"I find it a turn-on. Actually, I knew the moment I saw you on the Metro, so don't be embarrassed. It's kind of a thing I like to do. You know, help cute virgins. Now, let's try again. I'll go easy."

This time I let him find my mouth. His full lips press against mine as his tongue gently parts my teeth. It isn't all slimy and gross like Millie's was. I'm staring directly into his eyes, which he would know if he had his open. He pulls me so close I can distinctly feel the protuberance in his Levis.

Derek takes a step back, just as I was about to try kissing with my eyes closed. "Do you want to undress me? Most guys enjoy doing that." He spreads his arms in an invitation to take whatever I want.

"Sure." I lift his beautiful sweater from the bottom, and the neck gets caught on his head. His arms are still in the sleeves, so he can't help me. I pull harder and hear a ripping sound. We both stand completely still. I can see there are large holes in both armpits. Maybe more damage to the neck.

"I'll take it from here," he says, much nicer than I expected. He removes the remainder of his sweater, revealing enormous pecs and either a four- or six-pack. I make a note to count them later.

He reaches over to lift my shirt, returning the favor. I move my arm to assist, and my elbow slams into his nose. He falls back, wincing and holding his sneezer.

"Is it bleeding?" he asks.

I look closely. "No. It's good. Maybe you'll have a black eye or swollen nose in the morning, but it's fine for now." I wonder how much more damage I can do before we even get to the naked part.

At this point, Derek seems to dispense with formalities. He roughly unfastens my pants and stoops to pull them down. I lift my right leg to step out, crashing into his forehead. He slams backward into the floor. That one will definitely leave a mark. I decide to finish removing my clothes without assistance.

Derek must have decided the same as he removes his pants and socks. I'm completely naked, with five-and-a-quarter inches of rock-hard manhood pointing directly at Derek. He is standing a safe distance away with about seven inches of disinterested dick pointing directly at the floor. Maybe it doesn't like what I have to offer.

"After our somewhat debilitating wrestling match, I could use a little help here." He stands with hands on his hips, looking expectantly at me. The furrow in my brow tells him I don't understand. "Help me get hard?"

"Uh, okay." I grab his wiener and pull like I'm trying to save him from falling over a cliff.

"Easy, tiger! It's not a tow rope. Maybe you should use your mouth."

Now is the wrong time to realize I should have watched more porn. Yes, I have seen a few videos in my day, but there weren't many, and I didn't usually last through the end of the first scene. Further, I haven't ever put into practice what I saw. Now he's asking me to use my mouth; all I can imagine is a Popsicle.

From a kneeling vantage point, I get a good look at his wiener. It is magnificent – easily twice the size of mine. I put it in my mouth and go to town on the imagined frozen dessert.

"Teeth!" he says, in obvious pain.

"Sorry!" Okay, so I can't use my teeth. Maybe I should take the word "suck" more literally. I go in with a power that would make Mother's Electrolux jealous.

Derek takes a step back, uncoupling from my misguided vacuum technique. "I think I can get it up on my own. You pull the bedsheets back and get a condom."

I turn the bed down and go to my jeans for the condoms. He has a full erection when I turn back – no thanks to me. My jaw may have actually hit the floor. The seven inches of softness are now more like nine or 10 with the girth of a pop can. He is indisputably the size of a horse (and I've seen horses with erections).

I reach out with the condoms, and he takes the Magnum XL. Obviously. Watching him wrap that monster in latex is a show in itself. His hands work like a surgeon's as they unroll the rubber and cover the beast in one smooth move. It's almost balletic.

He gently walks me to the bed and lays me on my back as I stare at his amazing body. Then he grabs my ankles and lifts them over my head, knees at eye level.

From this semi-upside-down perspective, I come to two realizations: 1. I am far too chubby to be in this position. 2. He intends to put that gargantuan wiener in my butt. I let out a whimper that sounds too much like "Mommy."

Sorry. There's a third realization: 3. I had *way too many* beans for dinner.

"Derek. I don't want to ruin the mood, but I've never done this. I don't even know how to start. Maybe we could do some warm-up exercises or light stretching?"

"You're just nervous. I promise to be gentle and go slow. I like teaching you how to get fucked."

His face is so earnest that I want to believe him. Then I catch a glimpse of his wiener again. It looks like the genitalia version of the Kraken. And my stomach makes a noise similar to a pack of rats retreating from a fire.

"Well, I appreciate that. It's just that I imagined my first time would be with someone a little more, uh, average. You know?"

He smiles proudly. "I've never seen another one like mine. And I've slept with a lot of guys. *A lot.*" He leans back to ensure we both get a good view of his wiener. "Usually, they can't wait to hop on."

"I guess we can try. If you promise to be careful." At that moment, my stomach rumbles loudly, and the rats change direction. "We can stop anytime if it hurts too much, right?"

"Deal." He winks.

The beautiful man who has smiled at me all evening, put his amazingly agile tongue in my mouth, and whose lips have been pressed against my own, now dives in and uses those very same body parts on the restless intestinal rat pack's only escape hatch. And I don't remember how carefully I cleaned said hatch after it last expelled its contents.

"Whoa! What are you doing?" I find myself saying involuntarily.

He looks at me so I can just see his eyes over my belly. "Rimming. Do you like it?"

"Uh, I wasn't sure what you were doing down there." I can't say I *like* what he's doing because I'm worried about other things. The intestinal movement has increased, and I'm breaking into a sweat.

He dives back in, tongue thrusting aggressively. Maybe pointing my hole to the ceiling is encouraging the gas to rise. Of all the inopportune times for a fart! I clench my butt hole as hard as possible to keep anything from escaping.

"Hey! Relax! You can't clench like that, or you'll cut off my tongue." He gives me a faint smile and goes back in for more drilling. This time he puts his right hand on my balls very lightly, and it tickles.

Yes, I said tickles. So much so that I let out a little giggle. This causes me to lose concentration – and some muscular control. I feel the rats on the move again. A second later, I let loose a fart with enough force to rattle the windows. I think the wind moved his hair.

Derek abruptly sits up and shakes his head. He looks like a person who awakened in mid-colonoscopy, seeing the size of the probing device for the first time.

"Beans," I say, blushing.

"Well, that's a first." He shakes his head like a cartoon character. "Let's move on to the main course before any more of that manages to escape." I'll give him credit for being tenacious.

For the next 15 minutes, we try six different positions and use an entire bottle of lube. At no point does he ever manage to get any part of his wiener into any part of my body. It's just a matter of physics. Nothing we do can negate his camel being too big to thread my needle, so to speak.

Was it wrong to use a Biblical reference in this situation?

After one particularly gymnastic attempt – and possibly

the liberation of a little more gas – he finally gives up. "You know, I'm just going to go home and take care of myself. Maybe put some ice on these bruises." He rubs his forehead. "At least you can tell people you got to spend a few hours with this." He sweeps his hands from head to toe and ends with a bicep flex.

He certainly is a magnificent specimen of a human being.

Derek gets dressed, including the sweater that now has exit holes for two additional arms, and walks to the door. I lay on the bed, covered in lube, staring at the space he used to occupy.

"I had fun tonight, Derek," I say with a weak smile.

"Yeah. This is definitely one for my memoir. I'll let myself out."

As the door slams, I can finally release the breath I'd been holding all evening. As well as the remainder of the pent-up gas. It's the first moment I've felt relaxed. That is until my closet door bursts open, and Jayne makes a grand entrance.

"I saw the whole thing!" she says with an enthusiastic mixture of fascination and disgust. "Olympic pole vaulters should have so much to work with!"

"How long have you been in my closet?" I scream.

"From the get-go. I saw the trapeze act, the lion tamer, the flame thrower, and the contortionist. You know, I nearly appointed myself Ring Master and came out to direct the show if he hadn't given up so soon. I thought he had a stronger competitive spirit. What a shame!"

"I'm so humiliated!" I start to cry.

"Now, there, there," she says as she sits beside me on the bed. "There was no way to know his cock has its own zip code. One would have to be a professional to handle such a thing. But I did warn you about the beans. You nearly blew his entire face off!" She falls beside me, laughing hysterically.

"I feel like such a rube. My first date imploded on itself,

and I didn't even lose my virginity!"

"Exploded!" she says, gasping for air.

"You're not helping!"

"Oh, honey," Jayne says in her fake motherly voice. She reaches to pat my arm and notices every inch of me is covered in lube. "There, there," she coos without touching me.

"I knew this would happen!" I continue crying. "This whole move has been a failure. Why did I think I could become a different person just by moving to Washington?" I blow my nose into my greasy sheets. "I was going to move back to Minot before the Drag Race, but I decided to give it one more try. Well, I failed again!"

"Stop with this nonsense! You can't move back to Lutheranville just because of one hilariously disastrous date." Jayne unsuccessfully attempts to contain her laughter. "Tomorrow, we'll run right out and buy you some toys. You know, to limber you up a bit. We can fix this. Why, after just a couple of weeks on Jayne's Dildo Diet, you'll be turning tricks in the back room of the Eagle like a professional."

"I don't want to be a professional. I just want to enjoy it. And I want someone to *like* me!"

"You can have both, little man. Trust me with this one."

I roll over, still naked and sticky, and cry into my pillow. There is no consoling me tonight.

TWENTY-TWO

Life, Independence, and Relationships

The sun's first rays turn the tent walls a pale pink. I know it's too early to get up, but I like watching the transformation of night into day. It's even sweeter with my boyfriend spooning me from behind as we share a sleeping bag and pillow. I don't want this week of camping to end.

I feel some movement, and I think Erik must be awake, too.

"You awake?" I ask him quietly.

"Yeah. I've been waiting for you to open your eyes for nearly an hour."

"That's so sweet," I whisper. "I can't believe we have to leave today. It's been such a great week with you."

Erik moves his hands down my chest and gently holds my hips as I feel him press his wiener against my butt. "Since it's our last morning, do you want to have sex?"

"Really?" I ask, surprised. Erik hasn't indicated an interest in sex all week, so this is a new turn of events.

"I was hoping we could do it at least once before we leave." He starts grinding his hips into my backside, and I realize there's more to him than I imagined. It feels like he has something the length of a ruler trying to make its way into my butt. I start to sweat.

"Take your pants down," he says in a sexy voice. And I oblige. "Now, take mine down," he commands.

I roll over to see the person behind me isn't Erik.

"Derek! How the hell did you get here?" I yell.

"What's all the commotion?" Jayne bellows as she bursts into my room.

"Jayne?" Her giant red presence startles me. I rub my eyes and stretch. "That was the strangest dream."

"Judging from the tiny, little bump in the sheets, it must have been a good one," she says, pointing a freshly painted nail toward my crotch. "I assume you took care of the...," she pauses and makes a tossing motion with her hand, "... last night before sleeping."

"What? No! I mean, that's none of your business. I'm not talking to you about that." I pull the blanket tight to my neck. "I was just having a dream when you invaded my room. Nothing was going on."

"Uh-huh. You mean you didn't spank the monkey last night after your horrifying, gut-wrenching, unmitigated failure with the Prince of Hungness?" She shakes her head in a dramatic show of disappointment.

"I just wasn't feeling it after everything that happened. Besides, the dream was about my fifth-grade camping trip. Somehow Derek ended up in it."

"That was your little cock reminding you to give him some attention. You can't introduce him to Derek and his mighty domino and then walk away without so much as a stroke. All that pent-up energy could make you go blind! Now, I'll just close the door and give you a few minutes to make the little guy happy. Take all the time you need. Nothing like a little spritz in the morning to make you feel fresh." She starts to leave and then turns back, speaking in a low and foreboding voice, "And make sure you clean up after yourself."

The door closes. There are no boundaries with Jayne. Yes, I probably should have given the little guy some attention before going to sleep. Not that it's her business. The combination of tequila and humiliation didn't make me feel very sexy, so I just went to sleep. I reach down and rub a bit; last night's dream begins playing in my head. I guess I could do this.

"Use the lube!" comes the drill sergeant from the other side of the door.

"Oh, for the love of Pete!" I yell back.

Jayne opens the door and pokes her massive head inside. "Once, just once, I would like to hear you tell me to fuck off. I honestly don't know how you made it this far in life with such a bland vocabulary." She closes the door as loudly as possible.

I'll be lucky to get started, let alone finish.

Three-and-a-half minutes later, I walk into the kitchen, where Jayne sits at the table.

"Wash your hands."

I give her the side-eye while taking eggs, cheese, sausage, and bread from the fridge.

"What's with all the fat and carbs?" she says while looking over *The Washington Post*. "Aren't we on a diet?"

"No, *we* are not on a diet. I always have a sausage and cheese omelet with toast on Sundays. Then I watch *CBS Sunday Morning*, take a shower, and go for a walk. That's what I always do. That's what I'm going to do," I say defiantly.

"Don't mind me. I'm just your life coach. Or fairy godmother." She pauses with a look that says a brilliant thought is about to form. "Or fairy coach," she says with a wry smile. "Your fairy coach will sit over here and watch you eat until you're so large you can only get around in one of those scooters. It can't be long now." She goes back to reading *The Washington Post*.

It's easier to ignore her than I expected.

"I'm going for a walk," I tell Jayne around 11:00 am. "I'll probably be gone for a couple of hours." No response. "Want to come with?"

Jayne drops the newspaper in her lap and strikes an indignant pose. "You expect me to walk all over creation in these incredibly gorgeous yet highly impractical shoes?" Her expression says it's a serious question, but I decide silence is the best answer. "Besides, I didn't get much sleep last night with all the gaseous explosions coming from your bedroom. Just when I would be nodding off, BOOM! Another hydrogen – or was it methane? – bomb would drop. I'll just rest my bones right here on the couch, thank you."

"Suit yourself."

I finally have some alone time.

November in Washington is the kind of gorgeous that lifts my spirits. The leaves are wearing the bright reds, yellows, and oranges that signal the coming winter. The low-humidity air carries a chill. It's so beautiful I could walk the entire day. I meander up Connecticut Avenue to Chevy Chase, across to Bethesda, and back down Wisconsin Avenue, stopping at the National Cathedral's gardens.

My brain is in overdrive, trying to process the events of the last week. In just seven days, I've created my first drag persona, ran the High Heel Race, met Jayne (did she move in with me?), had my first real date, and made a valiant effort at sex. These would go on the pro side if I were making a decision list.

The con side says my drag was a nightmare, the High Heel Race turned into a drunken disaster, I met Jayne (did she move in with me?), and I made spectacular failures of my first date and attempt at sex. Oh, and I went into debt for clothes that should have made my life better but didn't.

All of the good stuff comes with an equal measure of bad. The thought of returning to Minot creeps back like an omen. I'm no closer to becoming an independent gay man than I was when I moved here. I went to a huge event but didn't make any friends — unless you count Jayne. Is she a friend, a fairy godmother, a roommate, or simply a bad influence?

And then there's Derek. My accidental boyfriend – if one date means he's my boyfriend – is handsome, intelligent, nice, and, well, other things. Dinner wasn't a complete failure, I guess. He seemed to have fun, and the food was good. The sex was an experience. Maybe I can work on it, like Jayne said. I mean, I'd like to try it again.

I have so many questions about life, independence, and relationships. I could talk with Jayne, but her style is a little rough for me. MJ has no experience with these, so she is definitely the wrong person to ask. Maybe I could get Millie's advice. She certainly has the experience. Besides, I haven't talked with her since she guided me through my Pussy makeover. Or something like that.

"Hi, Millie. It's me."

"Randy! As I live and breathe! Isn't this a nice surprise? We just got home from church, and I haven't even gotten my pantyhose off. Hold a sec." She throws the phone down, and I hear her rustling clothes, yelling at the kids, the dog, and her husband. I don't know how she does it.

"Okay, I'm back," she says breathlessly. "Oh, shoot. Hold on." She covers the phone and screams loud enough to be heard in space. *Just put the VapoRub on her chest and then give her a good finger-full to eat. She won't want it but do it anyhow. That cough ain't goin' nowhere if she don't eat some."* More rustling, and she's back on the phone. "Lordy, I don't get a minute's rest. Annabel has the croup, and Dave acts like he's never seen Vicks before. I swear I should just get in the car and drive 'til I fall off the end of the earth."

"Is this a bad time? I can call later."

"I just run from one emergency to the next. Don't much matter what time you call, it's all the same. Why, today in church Rose Eicherson was supposed to have a volunteer bring cookies for the reception after the service. Wouldn't you know, she decided to leave town for the weekend and didn't tell no one until the last minute. Of all the nerve! So, I'm baking a batch of my famous chocolate chips at 8:30 this morning while shepherding my little flock through the morning routine, and we nearly missed Sunday school. Shoot! It's a good thing I can whip those up in my sleep, or we would have had a disaster on our hands. I tell you what!"

"It sounds stressful."

"Don't I know it! I guess it's just my lot. People keep putting the problems of the world on my shoulders, and I keep carrying 'em. What about you? What are you up to, hun?"

"I've been taking a walk, and now I'm sitting in the garden at the National Cathedral. It's a beautiful day."

"The National Cathedral!" She breathes deep. "Isn't that the cat's pajamas! It must be like sittin' in the Lord's living room! Can you see the Pope? I hear he goes there all the time."

"I think it's an Episcopalian church."

"Same difference. All the fancy hats and stuff, without all the Hail Marys. You just live the high life, don't you?"

"Not exactly. Things always sound more glamorous than they are." I pause. But not long enough to let Millie start talking again. "So, last night, I had my first date."

"A date? A real date? Why, Randy Larson! Now, that's a first! Tell me everything! I must have a full-body description, every word he said and what he does for a living. The whole kit and caboodle. Don't skip any details!"

"His name is Derek, and he's in the Navy."

"The Navy! Ooh, there's something about a man in a military uniform that gets me all hot and bothered. Well, except for Ralph Greiser's son. That boy is a P-I-G slob. He is. A girl would have to be right desperate, maybe even on her death bed, to marry the likes of him. Ralph and Irma shoulda stopped at six kids, I always say. Or quit being Catholic. Golly!"

"Derek is very handsome. Tall with dark hair. Hollywood smile. And a huge, uh, divining rod, if you know what I mean."

"Why, Randy Larson! You went out and got you some nookie, didn't you? As I live and breathe! Now I gotta pay Dave a quarter. He bet me you'd have sex in the first six months of living in Washington, and I told him to jump in a lake. Boys will be boys, ain't that so?"

"Don't pay him yet. We tried to do lots of things, but I made a mess of it. Nothing was ever finished if you get my drift. I think I have lots to learn."

"Nothin' to be ashamed of there, mister. Why, when Dave and I first married, he thought he knew everything. Truth be told, he didn't know nothin'! I had to give him a map of my down-there, and he still kept puttin' it in the wrong place. I don't know how many times I had to say, 'that's the exit,' before he finally got it right." She gasps and then lets out a laugh. "I forget! You were probably lookin' for the exit, weren't you?" She gets a kick out of that.

I laugh nervously. "Yeah, well. It was the other way around. He found the exit, but his massive battering ram was no match for my defenses. The door just wouldn't open." That makes her laugh harder. "He finally gave up and left. We haven't spoken today. I don't know what to do."

"That's a new one for me, Mr. Larson. Oh, you poor thing. I've never tried the back door, mind you, but I hear it takes a bit of work. Rumor has it Melinda Baumgartner and her husband do that all the time. Ain't my business, and I've never asked. A body can do whatever she wants. Who am I to judge? It's just not my cup of tea."

"I really like this guy, but I don't know what to do. Should I call him? Should I wait for him to call me? Did I screw this up?" I feel out of breath.

"Slow down, there. This is not the end of the world. Sounds like you maybe weren't compatible, you know, in the birds-and-the-bees department. Or what do they say when both the birds are boys? Anyhoo, people say that's why Veronica Higgenbothen keeps having affairs with every new guy in town. She and Bubba just don't fit together right. If you ask me, she probably wants kielbasa, and he's offering Vienna sausage. Or maybe she just can't find it for that great big beer belly he's so proud of. Shoot!"

"That could be it. The incompatibility thing, I mean. As I said, he has a very big you-know-what, and I don't know if I can ever handle such a thing."

"That big, huh? My imagination is running wild if you must know the truth. Are we talking regular flashlight or one of those heavy-duty camping things?"

"We're talking lighthouse!"

She gasps. "Shut your mouth! It sounds like Mount Rushmore: fun to climb on once, but you never have the energy to go back and try again. I say you chalk it up to experience. No tellin' what that would do to you over time. Oh, hold on a sec, will you?" She half covers the phone again. *"Jolene just threw up? I thought Annabel was the sick one. What do you mean you can't handle it? And Zach needs a wipe? Diarrhea? Hold your horses, Dave."* She comes back to me. "Looks like we got stuff flying out of every end in this house. If I don't get out there, Dave will start puking himself. Don't be a stranger!" She hangs up.

So much for getting advice on returning to Minot. I should have led with that rather than titillating her with descriptions of Derek. But she might be right about him. Maybe Derek is a nice guy, but do I want to spend all my time figuring out what to do with his awesome wiener every time we have sex? Just saying it that way makes me want to move on. It also makes me a little horny.

I sit back on the park bench and take a long look at the Cathedral. The afternoon sun makes the stone facade glow with a reassuring light. When I sat down, the stone looked gray. Now the sun turns it the color of a sandy beach. Funny how things can look better after a little time.

Maybe this is the real sign. I need to give myself some credit for having the courage to try new things. Stumbling is just a part of walking the path. I can give this DC life some more time to help me grow.

TWENTY-THREE

Failures, Farts, and Friends

I return to find Jayne sitting on the couch right where I left her. She's reading *People* magazine with her legs curled under her, like a cat that has made itself at home. She doesn't bother looking up to greet me. Also cat-like.

"Did you see if the swamped got drained?" she says sarcastically.

"I had a lovely walk through Chevy Chase, Friendship Heights, and around the Cathedral. Even sat in the Cathedral gardens for a bit and enjoyed the nice weather. I need to take more time like that."

"Well, to each his own." She sounds bored. "And how was your afternoon, dear Jayne? Why, thank you for asking! I read a bit and rested my bones from a busy week." The sarcastic way she made the conversation about her takes some luster off my mood. "And I'm flummoxed by the condition of this cramped tenement! Oh, by the way, you may have a rat in the kitchen."

"A rat?"

"Could be. Or maybe it's your dog."

I'll deal with the rat thing later. "You know, you could clean a bit since you've been living here for nearly a week."

Jayne slowly lowers her magazine and gives me a deathly stare. It's terribly frightening and completely unreadable at the same time.

I do one of those cartoon gulps and forge ahead. "I've been wondering what your home looks like. And where it is. I mean, you do have a home of your own, don't you?"

Just as she raises her finger to speak, my phone rings.

"It's Derek!" I shriek.

"Well, answer it!" She goes from Norman Bates to Annette Funicello before my phone rings again. "Let's see what the big-boned buffoon has to say for himself. Oh, and ask him for some dick pics." She fans herself at high speed. "For your archives."

"Hello?"

"Hi, Randy. It's Derek."

"Hi, Derek. I hoped you would call today. It's, uhm, so nice to hear your voice!"

"That's sweet, Randy. How's your day been?"

"I just got back from a long walk. Kind of a slow day, I guess."

"Great. Well, I didn't want to wait too long before calling you. I like to get right to things so they don't sit unresolved, you know?"

"Oh, sure." I'm barely listening as I plan our next date. He takes me to Olive Garden, where I order the Tour of Italy plate. Derek gets the chicken alfredo because he's on a diet.

"I'm sorry about the way things ended last night. I don't normally run out like that. It just got kinda awkward."

"Yeah, I'm sorry, too. I guess I have a lot to learn, huh?" I laugh a little, but I swear I can hear Derek nodding in agreement.

"You're a nice guy, Randy. I didn't realize you were *so* inexperienced, and I'm sorry if I pushed you a little too hard. Guys like you are usually my thing, but this was definitely something different."

"Don't worry about that. I had a nice time and wanted to do, uhm, that stuff with you. I'll work on it. Maybe we could try again?"

"Yeah, about that. Uhm, it's probably better if this is just a one-time thing, you know? You're a great guy, but I don't think we're cut out to be a couple. We're different people, that's all. You'll be a great catch for the right person."

"Oh." I'll need the Tour of Italy in a to-go box.

We only had one date, so this could hardly be called a relationship. Oh, and the conversation on the Metro. So, two dates. Yet, I still feel like I'm being dumped.

"Maybe I'll see you on the Metro again someday." He pauses. "I gotta get going. Take care, Randy."

"Okay. Bye, Derek." He had already hung up by the time I managed the words. My arm drops to my side, and I stare at the floor. One strike, and I'm out.

"So, he gave you the boot, huh? The old heave-ho. Showed ya the door," Jayne says with the delicacy of a nurse announcing venereal disease testing results over a loudspeaker to an auditorium of horny teenagers.

"I guess that's what it was. Our relationship was just getting started." I sigh. "At least he had the decency to call me, so I know my first date was a failure."

"Let's look on the bright side – you got to play with his anaconda! And you scared it away. Vanquished your foe, or something like that." Neither one of us knows where this is going. "Chalk it up to experience, and let's move on. We need to get you prepared for the next one to come along." Jayne jumps up, grabs her purse, and walks to my bedroom.

"What are you doing?" I follow her like a sad puppy.

Jayne sits on the bed and pulls a large silver pen from her purse. She holds it in front of her devious smile.

"A pen?"

"Darling, this is an implement of self-gratification. Instructional model." She gives me a crooked smile.

"A what?"

"A vibrator, silly! You put this in your arse, turn it on, and it's like your own fireworks show! This is the petite size. I think of it as training wheels to prepare you for the real ride." She looks at the shiny object. "Come to think of it, this is almost exactly the same size as your little guy. Well, if yours was a little longer. And thicker. Whatever."

She places the shiny tubular device in my hand. It feels like metallic danger.

"What do I do with this?"

"As I said, it's the small size. We need to work you up to something realistic – maybe even Derek-sized." She smiles devilishly. "Get on the bed, and let's give this a spin." She pats the bed next to her.

"You want me to put this in my butt while you watch?" I can tell from her expression that she sees nothing wrong with this scenario. "Besides, I don't know if that's what I want to do. Maybe I'm not the one who, you know, receives the vibrator."

"You're a top?" Jayne breaks into hysterical laughter. "Even if that were true – and pigs have been known to fly – most people end up playing both positions at some point. This is a good way to prepare you to play catcher. Trust me."

"Fine." I put it on my bedside table. "I'll think about it. Maybe I'll try it when I have a little privacy. *IF* I ever have privacy again."

Jayne lets out a grunt. "Always the difficult one, she is." She walks back to the living room and yells to me, "Let's watch an old movie!"

I've had enough disappointment today, so I don't return to the question of Jayne's living situation. It will save for another day.

No one ever calls a government job exciting. I arrive at nine every day, do what I'm told, and leave at five. It's predictable. And for me, predictable is exciting. Besides, I get to walk into the massive stone building on 15th Street, right next to the White House, like it's normal. And normal is my other idea of excitement.

On Wednesday, Jeremy Monroe, who started two weeks before me in the department down the hall, stopped by my cubicle to say hi. He never seemed the let's-be-friends type of guy. I think we met once in the elevator, exchanged a few pleasantries, as Midwesterners do, and that was it. His visit is a pleasant surprise.

"How ya doin', Randy?" he says with a friendly smile.

"Just fine. I learned a new set of regulations today, so I can now run a different batch of reports. I'd call that a win."

"It was much easier back home, wasn't it?"

"Yeah. Some days I miss Minot Public Schools and the endless parade of purchase orders. Then I remember that I live in Washington, DC, and all this seems like a dream job."

"You're from North Dakota?"

"Yep. You're the first person here who's known where Minot is!"

"That's 'cause I'm a Mason City boy. Just finished my master's degree at Iowa State before landing this job. It took me 28 years to get out of Iowa, but I finally made it."

"Thirty-two years for me. This is a big change from my little town."

"I hear ya. So, have you had many chances to explore the city? Maybe do some tourist things before you become a jaded Washingtonian."

"Actually, I haven't done much of anything. I mostly stay in my neighborhood or come to work. What about you?"

"I live in Arlington, so I only come into the city on workdays. I think I should get out to explore some more before winter. Would you want to hit a Smithsonian museum this weekend, maybe?" He runs his hands through his dishwater-blond hair, and I take the opportunity to notice his chest. He's farm-boy strong.

Wait! Did he just ask me on a date? I still don't know when someone is interested – or gay, even. Maybe it's just a let's-hang-out thing. Nothing in his eyes or smile gives me a clue.

"That would be great, Jeremy. I'm free on Saturday."

"Perfect. Do you have a museum you always wanted to see?"

"Actually, it would be so cool to see Dorothy's ruby slippers at the American History Museum. I know there's lots of other stuff, but I've always been a *Wizard of Oz* fan. Would that be okay?"

"Sure. I've heard it's a fun place. Let's meet there at 10:30 Saturday morning. We can make a day of it."

"Sounds like fun. Thanks!"

As Jeremy walks back to his office, I give him the once-over. Nicely pressed khakis. Clean white shirt. His hair looks soft. I never expected to move all the way to Washington just to date another Midwesterner. And this one came to me without the help of a fairy godmother!

I don't see Jeremy again for the rest of the week. That's not unusual since we don't work in the same division, but I keep hoping he will come by. And I decide not to tell Jayne about my potential new beau. No need for a repeat of the restaurant fiasco.

With the it-could-be-a-date with Jeremy coming up, my ears are filled with the call of the vibrator. It whispers to me like the ring to Gollum, and I do my best to resist its temptation. Will it really make me better at sex? Something about it seems immoral. Vulgar, even. Do people really shove vibrating silver obelisks up their butts?

It's Friday night at 10:00. I've just gone to bed, as usual. Jayne is doing whatever Jayne does when I close my bedroom door. My date – or not date – with Jeremy is tomorrow, and the vibrator's call becomes insistent.

Come to me, young Larson. I can show you the secret to eternal happiness. Or at least give you the key to the back door.

Okay, fine. It's now or never, I guess.

I pull the device from the nightstand. It's smooth, shiny, and a bit cold, only about six inches long and somewhat thin. It doesn't look like any wiener I've ever seen. And I don't understand the vibration part. There aren't any buttons to turn on.

As I feel around the polished surface, I notice something on the bottom. A slight turn and the whole thing starts vibrating. It's an even, gentle oscillation that speeds up if I turn the button further. I press it against my hand when my wiener suddenly pops up, asking for attention. I begin to understand its appeal when I rub it lightly against my jeans.

Pants come down. Lube slathers the end of the vibrator. And now what? How am I supposed to get this thing into the place it's meant to go? Is this really a one-person job?

Maybe seated is the wrong position. If I put my feet up by my head, like Derek did with me last weekend, it would open up easy access. The problem is, I'm not a gymnast. If Derek hadn't put his entire body weight into the task, I still wouldn't know what my ankles look like.

I could use some assistance. The Winnie the Pooh bear Mother bought me when I was three is sitting in the corner. He's quite large. If I could prop him under my lower back, he would hold me as I raise my feet. That will leave the back door wide open and, well, whatever happens next.

Pooh is seated on the bed between my legs, facing me. His

permanent grin is a hungry snarl like I'm a pot of honey. I lie down, bring my knees to my chest, and get a good grip on my ankles. As I pull them to my head, I can see Pooh looking at me over my erect wiener, and I swear he licked his lips.

That's when the fart escapes. For the love of Sunday morning! I just farted in Pooh's face!

"Sorry, guy. If it's any consolation, that happened the last time I was in this position." He seems to shrug.

My ankles are finally at my ears. Pooh's nose is directly in front of my butthole; one eyebrow raised like he's giving me a careful rectal exam. I let go of my right ankle to reach the vibrator, and my balance is thrown. I roll off the bed and slam onto the floor. Pooh is now turned in my direction. Did he just shake his head?

"It's harder than it looks," I tell him.

Back on the bed and repeat the same steps. This time I keep the vibrator in my right hand while performing the gymnastics. Some of the lube gets wiped on Pooh's face when I accidentally hit him during the leg lift. I can see him smiling from my gynecological position, the lube forming an unsavory line of drool next to his mouth.

"You just hold me there," I say to the inanimate object.

I reach down, and the vibrator slips in like it was meant to be there. My hand is covered in lube, making it difficult to turn the vibration on. I grab it with my fist and give a hard twist as far as it will go.

"OH MY GOD!!" I scream.

Jayne bursts into the room. There I am. Legs over my head. Pooh's arms resting on either side of my butt like he's pushing me forward. His nose pressed against a high-speed implement of self-gratification. Both of us covered in lube. And Pooh is now sporting a toothy smile.

"Well, you're a nasty little fucker," she says in a smoky voice. "It seems we have quite the party going on here."

I let out a little yelp and pull the vibrator from my butt. "You didn't tell me it has multiple speeds! I nearly drilled through my intestines!"

"Oh, honey. That's nothing. The professional model is called The Jackhammer. This is just a tickler."

I sit up and instinctively grab Pooh to cover my nakedness.

"And what's up with the stuffed animal? I didn't know you were into bears. K-I-N-K-Y."

"It's not what it looks like. He's just here to put me in position."

"That's exactly what it looks like." She gives me a devilish grin.

"Get out!" I'm totally humiliated. "This was such a bad idea!"

"Well, at least you didn't fart in Pooh's face."

I flip over and bury my head in the pillow.

TWENTY-FOUR

Nobody Promised More Than a Pair of Shoes

"You can't spend the entire day walking. You'll get hemorrhoids!"

"Walking is not what causes hemorrhoids, Jayne." I finally get to roll my eyes at her.

"Well, I'm no ass doctor. Just an experienced user." Jayne cracks herself up, as usual. "I know I've gotten hemorrhoids every time I walk too much. It's scientifically proven."

"Let's test your theory. You spend this gorgeous Saturday walking with me, and I'll personally check you for hemorrhoids."

Jayne makes an exaggerated gagging motion until the choking pressure causes her to fart. Her stare dares me to notice the gaseous release. I say nothing.

"If a walk precipitates you giving my fine ass the once-over, I'll spend the afternoon watching the fleas and bedbugs duke it out for ownership of this couch. You go on without me."

And, without telling a single lie, I secure Jayne's unwitting blessing for a day with Jeremy. Actually, she blessed the walk.

The rest is the logical extension of her approval.

"Just to be clear, you're going to spend the day on my couch in my apartment that I pay for. You might also eat my food and drink my booze. Does this sound right to you?"

Jayne gives me a blank stare. "Yes. That sounds like a good plan."

We desperately need to talk about this living situation.

The Constitution Avenue door of the American History Museum is swarming with tourists when I arrive. Does every sightseer in a University of Whatever ball cap have to be *here* today?

"Randy!" comes a voice from behind. I see Jeremy speed walking in skinny jeans with holes in the knees. The oversize Iowa State sweatshirt is a level of casual I haven't seen. He looks even younger than usual.

"Hi, Jeremy!" He doesn't seem to notice *my* killer jeans and Armani shirt.

"Ready to take a trip to Oz?" he teases.

"I hope we can see everything. The museum looks awfully crowded."

We walk into the main hall, barely able to move for the crush of tourists. All I want is to see the ruby slippers. Everything else is just a sideshow.

"Maybe we could find the slippers first and then move to a less crowded section," I propose.

"Good plan. Grab a map."

The third floor slippers exhibit is a sea of people. The world is full of Dorothy Gale fans, I guess. When we finally get close, I'm disappointed. The worn, dusty shoes are small, not exactly the shining icons I expected.

"I thought it would be a bigger deal, you know?"

"What do you mean? These are great! I had no idea her feet were so small." Jeremy makes the most of the situation.

"I guess. Maybe I had expected a bigger exhibit. Something to make them larger than life, like they are in my head."

"Could your expectations be too high? Nobody promised more than a pair of shoes."

He's right. I always get my hopes up for things to be more extraordinary than they are.

"You're right. I think these are national treasures. But they don't deserve their own building." I give him a sly smile.

"There you go. Why don't we make this a tour of all the iconic gay memorabilia? Then you can aggregate it into one fabulous experience!"

He twirls around and slams into a family wearing matching Ohio State jerseys. I give him high marks for trying.

We see as much as the crowds will allow. Jeremy is chatty. Fun. Comfortable. He's just enough of a nerd to understand me. Yet, his wholesome good looks have me daydreaming of evenings cuddled on the couch, watching sappy Netflix love stories. I sneak peeks at his jawline, the soft torso that's neither fat nor intimidating, and the bulbous curve of his butt in comfy jeans.

By 2:00, we've had enough.

"Wanna grab some lunch?" he asks.

At Elephant and Castle, we both order The Standard burger. And two lite beers. It's like we're on the same wavelength. Jeremy tells me about growing up in Iowa, a story that parallels my own. His father also served in the military, and his mother was a teacher. And he's Lutheran. Everything is perfect.

"So, are you dating anyone?" he finally asks.

"Not exactly. I had a date last weekend, but it didn't go well. We won't be seeing each other again."

"That's too bad. Was it just mismatched personalities?"

I haven't thought of an answer to this. Today is only the second date I've ever had, and I want there to be many more. Do I open up and tell him my statistically average wiener didn't get along with Derek's monstrous serpent? That my butt was decidedly hostile to visitors? That I farted in his face?

"Yeah, you could position it that way." Jayne would appreciate the double entendre.

"No worries. There are lots of girls out there. You know, we should set you up with a Tinder profile."

There are probably a handful of scenarios in which my face would look as it does right now. Maybe if I walked into the living room to find my mother French-kissing the neighbor's Rottweiler. Or if I reached into a bag of chips and found an alien's hairy hand. Or if I sat on the toilet and suddenly felt someone breathing heavily on my butt from inside the bowl.

"Now, that's a look! Did you have a bad experience with Tinder?" Jeremy may be teasing but suddenly decides to back away. "Don't feel like I'm pushing you or anything."

"Oh, sorry. No. Uhm, I'm not exactly sure what Tinder is."

Most people don't know how much a Rottweiler drools.

"Seriously? I thought everyone used a dating app. You must be a real traditionalist." He smiles. "Some of my friends got actual girlfriends from it, not just hookups. But there are other ways to meet people."

"I guess dating apps aren't really my thing. But if I used one, it probably wouldn't be Tinder."

"What, like Christian Mingle?" He laughs cautiously.

"No, I don't think that one sounds helpful. It's just that I don't, uh, date like that. I mean, I, uhm, don't date women."

"Oh, you're gay," Jeremy says without batting an eye or even looking surprised. "Sorry. I didn't know. I always make the mistake of assuming people are straight."

"I just thought everyone knew. Sorry. I should have told you."

"Why? Were you supposed to introduce yourself as Gay Randy? That's ridiculous. There are all sorts of people. Some are gay. Some are straight. Some do a little of both. I'm fine with all of it." He disarms me with that smile.

"Sure. I guess. So, you're not gay?" I venture sheepishly.

"No. I've only dated women and see myself marrying a woman someday. Right now, I'm single. You thought I was gay?"

"It's hard to tell, I guess. Or maybe I just made an assumption. I'm so new to all of this."

"You're not the first one to mistake me for gay. I'm never offended. To be honest, I've had a few experiences with guys. You know, sexually. But it was just letting off steam or something like that. Haven't you had experiences with women?"

He is throwing so much at me that it's hard to keep up. He's straight. He thought I was straight. He's had sex with guys. He doesn't care that I'm gay. As much as I hate to admit it, Jayne would be helpful right now.

"Well, no, I haven't had experience with women. I've never been interested." His sincerity encourages me to keep talking. "And, if we're honest, I haven't had much experience with men, either."

"That's too bad. Why not? You're a cute guy, in my humble opinion."

I really want to run around like Rudolph the Red-Nosed Reindeer yelling, "He said I'm cute! He said I'm cute!" But I realize he's just being nice. We're having a conversation like real friends, and I should enjoy that.

"Thanks. I spent my whole life in a small town and never came out to most people. I always knew, but it wasn't something to discuss. And I didn't want to lead some girl on just to provide me with cover. It was better not to date. That is until I moved here. Now I'm happy to find a guy."

"Have you ever had sex with a guy?" he asks gently.

"That depends. We did some stuff last weekend but never finished up, if you know what I mean."

Jeremy gives me a sly smile. "Yes, I know what you mean. I've had a few of those very frustrating dates myself."

"I guess I could use a little practice. It seems my skills are underdeveloped."

"You're in luck! Sex is one skill that's fun to practice!" We both laugh, and I still find myself looking into his eyes. "What exactly is your issue?"

That's a personal question. And an embarrassing one. I don't want to share specific details about last weekend's botched escapades.

"Well, he wasn't too happy with my oral skills," I say, pointing to my clenched smile. "Teeth."

"Teeth is a big one," he agrees. "You can do some real damage that way. Where are you going to get your practice?"

"I guess I should get a gay dating app. If I could have a few more liaisons, I could get some practice without trying to find a boyfriend."

"That's the best situation. No strings. Everybody gets what they want, and there's no worry about long-term commitment."

"Yeah. That's it. I just don't know how to find people like that."

Jeremy sits back in the booth and puts his hands on the table in front of him. "Well, I have a penis. You could use it for some practice. And I can guarantee you there isn't a relationship thought in my head."

This time my face resembles jumping from an airplane and realizing there's no parachute.

"What? You're kidding, right?"

He breaks into a big smile. "Yeah. Just kidding." Jeremy shifts in his seat. "Let's get the check and get out of here. We could walk down to the Lincoln Memorial and take in the

World War II Memorial on the way."

We spend the next three hours touring most of the memorials on the Mall before walking past The Kennedy Center into Georgetown. We're both exhausted.

"This has been a great day, Randy. Thanks for being my exploration buddy!" Jeremy comes in close for a big hug. I meekly hug back but still expect him to drop another bomb.

"I had a great time. Thanks for the suggestion. Let's do it again."

"Sure thing. I think I'm just going to take a Lyft from here. It's not far to my place, but I don't want to walk anymore. How are you getting home?"

I may be tired, but I could use time to clear my head. "I'll walk back through Dupont Circle. It shouldn't take more than half an hour or so to get home."

And, with that, we go our separate ways. Just two guys spending some time together. Like normal people.

TWENTY-FIVE

Well, When You Say It Like That

I drag myself into the apartment at 7:30, tired and happy. Some people have a dog that greets them, wagging its tail and panting for attention. I've never had a dog.

Well, until now.

Jayne is standing so close to the door I nearly hit her.

"What the hell?" I yell.

"What the hell to you!" she screams back. "Here I sit, alone, all day long. You're out doing god-knows-what with god-knows-who and not so much as a text to let me know you're okay. Has it come to this?" She throws her right hand to her forehead, palm facing out.

As I push past her, she's following so close I can feel her breath on my neck.

"Since when do I need your approval for how and with whom I spend my time?"

"Well, I never! After all I've done for you!" She is walking in a circle, frantically waving her hands. "And for my sacrifices, I'm treated like a maid!"

Surveying the room, I see a week's worth of dirty clothes

– hers and mine – strewn on the floor and chairs. The remainders of at least four meals sit decomposing next to wigs and feminine undergarments. And there is clearly a coat of dust forming a kind of topsoil over everything.

"Maybe your exceptional housekeeping habits suggest you're the maid." I'm proud of myself for that little zinger.

Jayne comes in close and points a finger at my nose. "Little Miss Take-a-Poo-on-Pooh certainly ate some feisty pills today, didn't she?"

"What are you talking about?"

"The chubby little cubby and I have been talking. It's not like I had anyone else clamoring for my attention. The poor thing needed a Valium after your little derrière debacle last night. Think of the children!"

My cheeks burn, leaving me speechless.

"That's what I thought," she says sharply. "Now sit yourself down and tell me about your day. Maybe you need a drink?"

"No, I don't need a drink." I sit on the couch, and Jayne throws her full weight into sitting so close she's nearly on my lap. "I had a very nice day being a tourist in my new city. Most of the time was spent at the American History Museum. I even saw Dorothy's slippers."

"Go on," she says suspiciously.

"Lunch was at Elephant and Castle."

"What did you have?"

This is important? "A burger and a lite beer."

"Go on."

"And then we walked the Mall...."

"WE?!? You said we! Aha! I knew it! Who was this little tramp?"

I just can't seem to keep my mouth shut, can I? I'm flustered and blushing.

"If you must know, I spent the day with Jeremy from work.

We had a very nice time."

"Was this a date? Is that why you were drilling for fudge and gassing Pooh last night?"

"No! It wasn't a date. He's straight."

She puts her fingers up for air quotes. "Straight, huh?"

"Yes. 100% straight." I know this is sort of a lie, and somehow Jayne also seems to know.

She purses her lips and pushes them to the side of her face. "Let me see if I follow. You asked a guy from work for a tourist date?"

"He asked me."

"Oh! *He* asked *you*. But he's straight. I see."

"That wasn't completely clear when we set up our date. I mean, he never said it was a date. He just came by my desk on Wednesday...."

"Wednesday! You hid this from me for half the week?!" How did my day with a friend suddenly become all about her? "I feel so betrayed by all the secrets. And the lies. And the flatulence."

I'm never going to live down the Pooh incident.

"Look, Jayne. I didn't tell you because I didn't want you to show up like the last time. I just want my own dating life, you know?"

She pulls out an emery board and aggressively files the undersides of her nails, careful not to disturb the impeccably painted tops. The whole thing couldn't be more dramatic if set to music and danced with a chorus of tuxedo-clad gentlemen.

"I'm sorry. I should have told you." I suddenly feel remorseful, and I have no idea why.

She stops her sanding project and looks me in the eye. Her face softens in a way I haven't seen. "Randy, I'm here to help you. Remember, fairy godmothers are finite gifts, so we need to make the most of our time together." She puts her hand on my arm and gently pats it.

"What do you mean?"

She pulls her arm away and returns to her usual devious grin. "So, let me guess. He asked you to do the bus-and-truck tour of DC, and you immediately started picking out your wedding dress. Please tell me I'm singing at the ceremony! I do an amazing and very touching version of 'Mony, Mony' that's been the hit at dozens of nuptials."

"There's probably more truth in that than I want to admit. I mean, the first part. Not the 'Mony, Mony' part."

"I could do a verse for you right now," she says, grinning like a small child and rising to diva position.

"No. Sit down. This is about me."

"Suit yourself." She smooths out her dress and crosses her legs. "When did he finally tell you he's straight?"

"We were talking about dating, and he suggested Tinder because he thought I was straight."

"*He* thought *you* were straight? How many of his senses are impaired?"

"I'm trying to tell a story here." Jayne makes a zipping motion over her lips, and I continue. "Then I asked if he's straight, and he told me. But he said there had been a few times when he fooled around with guys. It's very confusing."

"Oh! Let me finish that conversation. He then told you he wouldn't mind letting you give him the occasional knob slobber if you are so inclined. Just to do you a favor."

"How did you know that?"

"Puh-leeze! Since it started being fashionable for straight guys to have a little gay action on their resumes, we've been the target of horny bromosexuals everywhere."

"It wasn't like that. I said I needed practice giving, you know, the mouth stuff, and he offered his wiener as a place for me to get some experience. Like coaching."

"Well, when you say it like that." She slowly shakes her head.

"It sounds worse when I say it aloud."

"Look. There's nothing wrong with having a little romp with a straight guy. It can be fun, actually. But don't let yourself start thinking it's a dating relationship, 'cause it ain't. This is just a guy using one of your holes to get his rocks off. No strings attached. Capisce?"

"I know."

"No, you don't know. Girls like you always get so emotional whenever a little jizz flies, and pretty soon, you're calling yourself 'Mrs.' It's a story as old as time."

Maybe she's right. I did spend the day imagining a long-term dating relationship with Jeremy. Even after he told me he was straight, I couldn't help but think that way.

"So, what do I do?"

"Well, you could take him up on the offer and see where it goes. Judging from your performance last weekend, you may need months of rehearsal before you're ready for the stage again. Can you manage it without getting all worked into a lovesick tizzy?"

"I think so."

"Just know I can't spend every night drying your tears. A girl doesn't look like this without getting the proper amount of beauty sleep." She brushes her hands together. "Now, let's pick out a movie."

Maybe this is an old story for Jayne, but it's all new to me. I can't concentrate on the movie as I wonder what it means to have a no-strings dating situation. Is that what I really want? Does it make me more independent? I'm more confused now than I was earlier.

TWENTY-SIX

Jezebel!

I can honestly say Jayne has helped develop my confidence and self-esteem these last few weeks, though I hate to admit it. She believes in the tough love approach. Whenever I say or do something she disapproves of, I get a sarcastic insult or a chastising lecture, always laden with profanity. On the flip side, I'm learning about relationships, how to mix drinks, and discovering a treasure trove of old movies I've never seen.

We still haven't had a conversation about our living situation. I think Jayne sleeps on the couch every night, though she never lets me see her asleep. And she never removes her drag. She must do something during the day, but I haven't dared to ask. In fact, I haven't asked much. She thinks of herself as my fairy godmother, and I let her run my life. At least I'm learning about the gay community, even if I'm not asserting my independence much.

For her part, Jayne is learning to embrace my frugal lifestyle. Somewhat. She must have lots of money the way she encourages me to spend.

Work, too, is becoming more comfortable. I can see a path to promotion as I get better at my current position. People are helpful if I'm friendly. My boss even occasionally compliments me. That never happened in Minot. Who knew the Federal Government could be kind?

I feel more like a Washingtonian every day. And a grown-up. This could be some of Jayne's doing, but it's enough to keep me from thinking of returning to Minot so often.

And then there's Jeremy. I haven't seen him since our play date over two weeks ago. We text occasionally. Nothing important. It's usually something we said or did at the Smithsonian. I want to continue our friendship. However, my little crush on him keeps me from going too far. I don't want to scare him off.

A text from Jeremy interrupts my self-reflection. It should have interrupted my work.

Hey, Randy. What up?

Just regulatory stuff. You?

I'm bored. And stiff. Can't wait to get out of this chair and end the day.

I hear you.

What are you doing tonight?

It's Thursday. Do I tell him that's the night Jayne and I make hamburgers and watch a Bette Davis movie? She made enough to go a full year before choosing another actress. It's become a little tradition.

No plans.

Wanna order a pizza at my place? I have a big coupon.

I start to sweat. My feelings aren't his, so this could be another innocent hangout. I shouldn't read anything into it. It's just a pizza with a friend, right?

Sure. When?

I'm thinking around seven.

I'll be there.

It's already four. This little exchange means I won't get any more work done today. I spend the next hour worrying about what I'll say and do this evening. And what to tell Jayne.

Should I be honest with her? Will I get to his place and find she has somehow climbed a tree in sequins and heels and is now staring in the window? I still don't trust her after the Mexican restaurant fiasco.

"Hello, darlin'," Jayne yells as I open the door. There's only a half-hour to shower and change before leaving again. I hate to disappoint her when she's so excited to see me.

"Hi. Can't talk right now," I say as I continue toward the bathroom. "I've got to take a shower."

"This is odd behavior. Sneaky, even." Jayne follows me to the bathroom, completely filling the door frame. She looks like a cat who has trapped a mouse but is not yet ready to eat it.

"Shower? Odd?" Could I sound any more guilty? "I take showers all the time. And there's no way to sneak a shower in this little apartment." I avoid looking at her as I remove my clothes.

"Since when do you take a shower at this time of day? Did you get particularly sweaty at work? Maybe get an oil stain fixing the fleet of Treasury cars? Accidentally get sprayed by a skunk at the copy machine? Hmmm?"

"Can I please have some privacy to shower?" I turn to face her, and she breaks into a tight, crooked grin. Somehow, I've become comfortable undressing in front of her. I always regret it.

"Looks like we're a little chubby this afternoon, huh?"

I don't know where this is going, but she is clearly searching for the jugular.

"I haven't gained any weight. I don't think. You know I've always had a little belly."

"That's not the chub I'm talking about." She points her perfectly manicured, fire engine red fingernail toward my mid-section and moves it in a circle. "Getting a little excited?"

"What?" I look down. My little wiener is looking plump. And sticking out more than usual. It must be anticipating the evening with Jeremy. I look at her indignantly and put my hands over my crotch. "That's ridiculous! It's no different than usual."

"Of course not, dear. You've always been a show-er." Another sly smile.

"Please let me clean up like any other average, normal person would do after a long day at work!" I step into the tub and make a deliberate show of closing the curtain. A slam would have been better, but what do you do with a curtain?

"I'll be waiting in the living room. Alone. Passing the time with thoughts of the movie you promised we would watch together." She seems to be walking away, talking over her shoulder. "Just saying a prayer to Proud Mary, thanking her for the friend who always stays in with me on Thursday nights. Don't mind me."

I put Jayne out of my mind long enough to shower and dress with five minutes to spare. I'm wearing my ass-enhancing jeans, sure to set off a string of questions from my captor. The inevitable confrontation must be brief.

"This is quite the ensemble for an evening on the Davenport. Or are we going out tonight?" Jayne picks up *People* magazine and begins to flip the pages as if disinterested. "I thought we were watching *Jezebel*," she says without looking at me.

I take a deep breath before speaking as fast as possible. "I'm going out. Jeremy asked me to come over for pizza. We'll probably just watch a movie. Nothing with Bette Davis, though. Those are saved just for you. I won't be late. See you later." I turn toward the door.

"JEZEBEL!" she yells in her best Madea voice.

I can't look at her. "I heard you. We can watch it next week."

"*YOU* are the Jezebel," she says, dripping with indignation. "You shameless, wicked, two-timing, whoring hussy! Making promises to me and then following your mediocre, ordinary, middle-of-the-road, completely average penis whenever it sees an interesting guy."

She never misses an opportunity to point out my lack of phallic exceptionalism.

"Do you always have to insult me?" I ask, still looking away.

"Insult you? I'm the one home alone while you're getting plowed by this straight monster!"

"Plowed?" I turn to her, flustered. "No! Why did you say that? Plowed? It's just pizza and a movie. Nothing sexual." I give her an exaggerated head shake. "Where do you get these ideas? Plowed! Jeez! He didn't even hint at a plowing when he texted me." I should stop saying "plowed," but I can't help myself.

"You have texts?" She suddenly perks up. "How incriminating."

"They are completely innocent."

Jayne sits upright. "If they're so innocent, let me see your phone. I'm an excellent judge of subtext and innuendo. Mama Jayne will even translate his words for you if necessary."

Fortunately, Jeremy's texts are entirely harmless. Showing her my phone is the quickest way to get out the door. I stand next to her and thrust the phone in her face.

Jayne pretends to use a magnifying glass as she studies the messages. "Aha! I told you. This is one devious little fucker."

"Devious? He just asked me to come by for pizza."

"How can you be so naïve?" She shakes her head before turning it sharply to the side in a dramatic move to feign offense. "The first thing he tells you is he's stiff. *Stiff*!"

"His back is stiff. From sitting in a chair all day. It's totally normal."

"Uhm, hmmm. To the untrained eye, that could be the case. And I might be inclined to believe it if he didn't also tell you he has a 'big coupon.'" She makes air quotes with her fingers. "You know. Stiff big coupon. It's obvious." She's delighted with herself for these sleuthing skills.

"How do you get something salacious from 'big coupon?'" I make the same finger motions in a lame attempt to mock her. It doesn't work.

"And what's the significance of seven?"

"What? Seven o'clock? It's a time most people eat dinner, I guess."

"And not an indication of the size of his 'coupon?'" More air quotes.

"This is ridiculous. I'm leaving now and will be home later with stories of pepperoni and a bad 90s movie." I open the door.

"Don't let his seven-inch pepperoni get its grease on your nice Armani shirt!" she yells as I slam the door.

I'll prove her wrong. Tonight will be pizza and a movie. Nothing in his texts suggests anything else. She is so smug and controlling!

Unless... Could I have missed the signals? Was "big coupon" a sexual reference? That seems like a stretch. And since I've never seen his "coupon," I don't know if seven is a relevant number. Could be. And what if he did have a stiffy at work today? It happens to me all the time.

No! I'm not letting her get in my head. This is an innocent evening between two friends. Nothing more. We'll have a great time like we did at the Smithsonian.

Jeremy's place is a boxy, first-floor studio in a new complex adjacent to the Clarendon Metro stop. I think it's called a studio with an alcove because there's an open room for his bed away from the living area. All the spaces are small, and it looks like a can of beige paint exploded over everything. There isn't a single picture or personal item displayed anywhere. In fact, there's barely any furniture.

"Wow, this certainly is an apartment, Jeremy. How did you find it?"

"Apartments.com. No Realtor fees. The rents are too high in the District. But I can afford a corner unit like this out here and still live next to the Metro."

"I used an expensive real estate agent and barely got an hour of her time. She forced me into an old building that takes half my income, and the place isn't as nice as yours."

Jeremy pays the pizza delivery guy while I sit on the world's smallest couch. So far, everything seems normal. Just two guys hanging out.

"I hope you like pepperoni."

"I'm from North Dakota, remember? We don't do fancy pizza. It's just pepperoni and cheese."

"The way the gods intended it!"

"Amen!"

We laugh and gorge ourselves on pizza and lite beer. Jeremy is a nice guy. Conversations center around work, people at the Treasury, things we wish we had learned in college, and that kind of thing. There's never a moment of silence or awkwardness.

I can't help but think it's a shame he's not gay. What a great husband he would make.

After about 90 minutes, Jeremy innocently drops a bomb right in the middle of the room.

"So, have you gotten any more practice on your oral skills since I last saw you?" He's looking out the window, not directly catching my eye.

"Uh, no. I guess not. I haven't had any dates, if that's what you mean."

"Dates... or friends. Whatever. Didn't you say you wanted to get better after your last date?"

It's almost as if this scene is playing exactly as Jayne predicted. I'm not sure how to proceed.

"Yeah, I guess I could use improvement. There will be other opportunities." I search my brain for something witty to say. Nothing.

Jeremy is sitting in the chair next to the couch. The living area is so tiny that the chair is practically *on* the couch. I notice he has spread his legs as wide as possible. This is a little more than one would usually find comfortable. He catches my eye and moves his hand into his lap. It just sits there over his crotch.

"Same with me. I haven't had a date in several months. It really sucks being a single guy." I'm not good with subtlety.

"Being single isn't so bad. I've been single my whole life. Never had a boyfriend." I thought this would be encouraging, but it's just sad. "Have you ever been in a relationship?"

"I dated this girl my last two years of college, and we did long-distance while I was in grad school. We broke up when I moved here. It's hard to maintain a relationship from several hundred miles apart."

"I'll bet."

"And expensive. For what they pay us, I can't afford to get on a plane every weekend." He slides down a bit in the chair, his hand still over his crotch.

My brain is in overdrive. I'm searching unsuccessfully for something to say. Anything. I kinda wish Jayne were here. Actually, it would be a nightmare if Jayne were here, but I could use some advice. Should I change the subject? Or do I see if this can go to the next level? And what is this next level? Subconsciously, I'm interested in something sexual. But consciously, I don't know what that is.

The whole time I'm having this little conversation in my head, I've been staring directly at Jeremy's hand-covered crotch. I quickly turn away as I realize he knows what I'm looking at.

"You mind if I take off my shirt?" Jeremy asks. "It's so warm in here. Besides, I can show you my tattoo." He sits forward and slips his shirt over his head. Even *I* saw this porn scene. "Here it is," he says, pointing at a small Tigger etched on the upper left side of his chest. "I have always been a fan of bouncy, trouncy, flouncy, pouncy." He laughs.

"That's cool. I've got a big, stuffed Pooh in my bedroom." I imagine Pooh sitting at home wondering why I haven't called.

"Feel it. The ink is raised a bit." He leans forward.

I move an inch, close enough for our legs to touch. My sweaty right hand trembles as it reaches for his chest and rubs the tattoo.

"I always thought they were smooth," I say quietly.

He puts his hand over mine and presses it against the tattoo as he slowly sits back in his chair. "Randy, you can explore more than the tattoo, you know," he says in a friendly, guys-hanging-out way. His hand guides mine across his chest, and then he lets go. I don't move from where he left me. "I was serious when I said you can use me for practice. It's okay."

"Don't you think that's a little weird?" My hand is still pressed against his chest. "And shouldn't we close the curtains?"

"For starters, I haven't bought curtains yet." I notice the picture window looking into a well-lit parking lot. "Don't worry. No one looks in. And, second, there's nothing weird. It's fun for both of us. Just two friends hanging out. Go on. Give it a try." He leans back in the chair and closes his eyes.

I'm frozen, staring at the half-naked guy in front of me. What am I supposed to do with him? I know I *want* to do something with him. Sort of. I just don't know how to go about doing it. I have full-on permission – encouragement, even – and I still feel strange about going forward. So, I just stare.

Jeremy opens his eyes. "What's the matter?"

"I don't know. I've never been in this situation before."

"Haven't you ever watched porn?"

"Yes. I mean, some. It's never been a big thing for me." I can't believe I'm embarrassed to admit I don't spend much time with porn.

"Oh." He thinks for a moment. "What if I direct you? You know, tell you what to do. Would that help?"

"I suppose."

Jeremy stands up, removes his shoes, socks, pants, and underwear, and sits back down completely naked. He has a nice body – nothing like Derek's – that's relatable and almost familiar.

"There. How's that?"

"Fine, I guess."

What kind of answer is that to a handsome guy sitting naked in front of me? I try to think of something that will help. Have I ever seen a porn situation like this? Nothing apropos comes to mind.

Okay, I know this is weird, but the only thing coming to mind is the cast of *Sesame Street* singing a catchy group number on the front stoop. It's something about sunny days. It bears no relationship to the current situation but plays on a loop. If Jayne were here, she would tell me I'm deranged. And it would be true. This moment is stressful enough without associating Muppets with naked men. But, if *Sesame Street* is the best I can do, I'll run with it.

Jeremy's touch shocks me back to reality. "Why don't you get on the floor here," he points to the spot between his knees, "and we can get things started."

I sit on the floor with my face directly in front of his crotch. Just as with Derek before him, Jeremy shows no physical excitement whatsoever. His lovely wiener is drooping serenely over his balls. Is it afraid?

I might think clearer if the singing Muppets would shut

up. I don't know what lesson *Sesame Street* characters can teach me in this situation.

Or? Cookie Monster seems orally fixated. I picture him shoving Jeremy's wiener in his mouth while he munches and yells, "Yum!"

I don't know why, but I suddenly become Cookie Monster. "Cookie!" I yell in a gravelly voice as I shove my face in Jeremy's crotch.

He jumps back in surprise. "What the hell? Cookie?"

I look up at him, resting my chin in his pubic hair, and say, "Me love cookie." I dive in and chomp on his wiener like it was one of Millie's chocolate chip specials. I even make all the "nom, nom" noises.

Jeremy laughs and settles back. "Not to burst your bubble, but I've never had a sexual fantasy of Cookie Monster giving me head. Maybe you could just do it without going into character. I'm not much into role play."

"Oh."

So, I'm sitting cross-legged on the floor with Jeremy's wiener in my mouth. Now what? Derek said not to use teeth. What if I wrapped my lips around my teeth like when I was a kid and wanted to pretend I was toothless? Then I add the suction of my mother's Electrolux. Without sound effects.

I feel Jeremy's hands grab my head and stop me. "Well, at least we got rid of the Muppets. Maybe you're taking the idea of sucking a bit literally. It's the motion that makes the whole thing work. No need to turn into a toothless cleaning machine. Just be gentle."

Jeremy gently moves my head as I go back to work, more carefully this time. His physical response clearly shows I'm doing something right. I let him guide me as my mind drifts back to Cookie Monster and the gang. I'm playing the *Sesame Street* theme song in my head and having a great time. If this is how it's supposed to work, I'm all for it.

Just as the cast gets to the song's second verse, I suddenly feel my mouth filling with semen. What the hell!?! This tastes terrible! I should have concentrated so I could see this coming. Jeremy still has my head in his hands, so I can't go anywhere. And I'm not swallowing this disgusting stuff. My eyes dart back and forth, looking for some way out.

A few seconds later, Jeremy lets go. I sit up and look to him for guidance.

"You can spit in the bathroom if you want," he offers.

I run to the bathroom, slamming the door behind me. As I'm washing the nastiness out of my mouth, I hear, "Psssst!" I look around the small, empty room. "Over here," comes a stage whisper from the window. The unmistakable blonde wig presses close to the screen.

"Jayne! What are you doing here?" I say, trying to keep to a soft whisper.

"You think I would let you go off to this unescorted? I followed you, dummy!" She shakes her head. "And who leaves their curtains open like that? Did the brute cum in your mouth?"

I nod.

"Straight guys! They always think their spunk is welcome wherever they want to put it. Well! He needs to learn the code of conduct. There should have been a warning! Personally, I prefer they yell 'fore!' or 'incoming!'" Her big smile lights up the window. "Let's make sure you get a thorough rinse."

"What should I do?"

"Let's get you home. You can either attempt to squeeze your ample behind through this window and run for it, or you can go out there and tell him he can't ever do that to you again, and you're leaving."

Her tone of voice says there's only one choice. I open the bathroom door to find Jeremy dressed and flipping through television channels.

"You good?" he asks.

"I'm fine. I've never had anyone do that in my mouth, you know."

"Yeah. I was planning to warn you, but it just sneaked up on me. You know how that happens, right? No harm, no foul."

I guess there's no harm, but I wanted more say in the matter.

"I think I'll head home. Early morning tomorrow, you know."

"Okay. Thanks for coming over. Let's do it again, yes?" He waves to me without getting up.

"Sure," I say, not knowing what else I should add.

When I get outside, Jayne is waiting for me. "Did you give him a piece of your mind?"

"Not really."

"You could have at least taken pizza to go after what you went through."

"I mean, it wasn't terrible. I got some practice, didn't I?"

She puts her arm around my shoulders. "Yes, you got some practice. You also got a taste of what men are like. I mean that literally and figuratively." She laughs at her little pun. "They've got one thing on their mind, and they'll do or say anything to ensure that one thing happens. Especially the straight ones. We need to get you some Listerine, and we'll have a safe sex discussion later."

"Thank you." I give her a hug.

"Don't mention it. Now, why don't you pay for our cab home? My delicate constitution can't handle another Metro ride."

TWENTY-SEVEN

A Midwestern Outlook on Life

"But I don't even play the guitar!" I yell, squinting at the man's Grand Ole Opry name tag: Bubba!

"Tell it to the audience," he says in a thick, Southern drawl. "Your name is next on the program, and you've got the requisite number of rhinestones on your jumpsuit to put you in the Hall of Fame. Now get out there!"

"Let me see that."

I grab his program. Dolly Parton just finished her set, and the next act is Virgin Vern and the Fellatio Five. I'll be damned! That's me!

"Aw, you folks have been great," Dolly gushes to the packed auditorium. "But I'm just the warm-up act. The guy you really came to hear is coming out now. Give it up for Virgin Vern!"

The spotlight floods me with hot brightness, and the crowd goes crazy. Behind me, the Fellatio Five kick off our greatest hit, "Your Wiener Dog Done Dogged My Wiener." Somehow, I know they're coming to the part where I'm supposed to sing, but I can't remember the words. Sweat drips into my eyes as I adjust my gleaming white guitar.

And then... nothing. The music stops. The audience is

hushed, waiting for my first notes. I'm looking out at 2,400 adoring faces and....

I fart. Loudly. The force is so great it blows rhinestones from the back of my jumper and right into the mouth of the Fellatio Five bass player. He yells something about not swallowing and runs off the stage.

"Well, fuck me! You do have a nice singing voice," Jayne roars, her butt covering half my pillow as she sits on the side of the bed.

In a blink, I'm upright and sweating in the middle of the room.

"What are you doing?" I scream.

"Easy, Patsy Cline. I heard you singing and came in to see about recording an album of duets."

"I was having a nightmare." She pulls me onto the bed next to her and hugs my shoulder.

"I'll say. The song was something about a wiener dog. The lyrics need work, but I know a guy."

I'm barely conscious and already know this should be a day off. I guess one sick day wouldn't hurt.

"So, it's a day off?" Jayne looks like a puppy expecting a walk.

"Yup."

"Fabulous!" She's up and pacing. "We can spend the entire day shopping – at the good stores. Then, we can come home and burn all your old clothes in a ritual fire dance. Order will be restored to the universe."

My sigh drips with exhaustion. "Yes, I'm taking the day off. But we're not shopping. I'm still paying off our trip back in October. Maybe we could take in some free stuff."

"Free? Like the flip-flops and cutoff people?" She grabs her necklace in horror.

"I really want to see all the monuments. It's my fifth month here, and I've only seen a handful of them. How about I set the agenda for once?"

"A cup of coffee will set you right. Besides, you know it's December, don't you? There must be five feet of snow on the ground. I'm too delicate to be out in the cold."

"It's going to be 50 degrees and sunny today." She rolls her eyes. "It's a perfect day to take in the sights. What do you say? You never do stuff like this with me."

"You get showered and dressed, and I'll see if I can move my calendar around. It's never a good idea to spring something like this on a lady." She stomps out, and I scurry to the shower, finally feeling hopeful.

After arguing, pleading, swearing, begging, and some minor negotiating, we finally leave at eleven.

"Let me change to my walking shoes," Jayne says as the final indication she's going. I stop myself before wondering aloud if she will change the sequined evening dress she's been wearing every moment since we met.

She sits on the couch, removes her red sequined heels, and puts on another identical pair.

"I thought you were wearing walking shoes."

"That's what these are. The other pair is formal."

"I see no difference."

"And that, my dear, is why you are destined to walk in my considerable shadow. There is clearly no similarity between formal attire and common walking shoes." She stands indignantly and motions toward the door. "Let's be on with it."

There are few tourists in the city between Thanksgiving and Christmas, making it the perfect time to visit iconic Washington landmarks. Walking also gives us time to talk like we never do at home. Perhaps the warm sun has me in a good mood. Regardless, I'm genuinely enjoying Jayne's company.

"You don't talk about South Dakota much," Jayne notes.

"That's because I'm from *North* Dakota."

She gives me a blank stare. "I thought they were one again after President Reagan tore down the wall." Shrug. "Don't you ever feel homesick?"

"Not really."

The notion of moving back to Minot has largely left my mind. I occasionally think about friends who still live there, but I don't miss the town or wish I could go back.

"Don't you miss your friends?"

"A little, I guess. Most everyone I called 'friends' were just people from school. It's not that we had things in common other than being the same age. And I didn't have many friends from college since I lived at home and missed all the social activities. In fact, I didn't do much with anyone other than Mother and Dad, I guess."

"Do you miss them, your parents?"

"Sure. They were good people, and I enjoyed being with them. But everyone has their time to go. It's just the way things are."

"Is this a Midwestern outlook on life?"

"Probably. There's no sense in sitting around being sad all the time. Things change. People have their time. We are thankful for that, and then we move on."

Jayne stops and looks at me, hand on her chest. "I've never heard anyone speak like that." She seems genuinely touched by the sentiment. "Is everyone in the fly-over states so cold and unsentimental? I'll bet children go missing for days before anyone notices. What about all the lost puppies and kittens?" And now she's back in character.

"I'm not unsentimental," I snap indignantly.

"Really? There's barely a personal item or memento in your entire apartment. You have only one picture of your family, and it's from Christmas 2005. Where are the family heirlooms? Grandma's costume jewelry? A ticket stub from your first burlesque show?"

"What?"

"Shouldn't you have something that reminds you of the past? Warm and fuzzy remembrances of a special day gone by?"

"I use Mother's oven mitts. And Grandma Larson's mop bucket. The furniture you lounge on all day is from back home. I have lots of stuff!" We start walking again, but it feels like Jayne is ruining the day.

"I'm not trying to snap your girdle, Randy. I don't understand what makes you tick. What excites you? What upsets you? What turns you on?" She pauses. "*Other* than Pooh."

"Very funny." I look at her and roll my eyes. "I'm an uncomplicated individual who doesn't need much."

"Uncomplicated is that guy over there wearing a Green Bay Packers hat, sweatshirt, and well-worn sweatpants. That's uncomplicated." She stares like he's a car accident. "No, that's horrifying!"

"I see nothing wrong with it."

Jayne grabs my arm, and we come to a halt.

"You want to know what's wrong with that? Where's the pageantry? Where's the flare? Where are the subtleties masked by pancake makeup and heavy sarcasm? Where's the glitter? Where's the fucking life?" She's suddenly a full-on dramatic diva.

"Maybe that's not who I am."

"But you're gay! G-A-Y! Rainbow flags and boozy brunches! Your entire genetic code is a rainbow. Embrace it! Live for it!" She begins spinning in circles with her hands in the air. "Rejoice! For the goddess of disco and tight jeans has created you in her image!"

I look around to see who's watching this spectacle. We're alone next to the Tidal Basin.

"Do you think I need to have all these things in order to be truly gay? Or happy?"

"Honey. Since the dawn of time, we queers have been decorating caves, cutting hair, doing nails, and making cocktails for the entire world. We declare what is 'in' and what is 'out,' what is beautiful and what is hideous. We *are* pop culture. And *you* are one of *us*. Therefore, by association, you must be fabulous!"

Jayne sees herself as an evangelist. But, as with all evangelists, you must sift through mounds of crap to find the one kernel of truth. And I think I just heard it.

"So, by your verbose...."

"Let's use the word *loquacious*, please."

"Fine. By your *long-winded* explanation," I say emphatically as she rolls her eyes, "the person I am is already the definition of gay. It's in my pink and green —"

"Pink and purple."

"Pink and purple DNA. I may not do hair or nails, but I can do gay math." I cross my arms and look at her smugly.

Jayne is flummoxed. She has uttered something true that doesn't align with what she set out to say. She stares at me. Then at the sidewalk. Then at the Tidal Basin. I can see her mind's wheels spinning furiously.

"Did I misinterpret what you were saying?" I ask, not so innocently.

"When you look at me, don't you see the perfect picture of fabulousness?" She does a slow sashay around me with her chin in the air.

"Yes, you are clearly fabulous." She grins at the compliment, even if it is forced. "Does that mean I have to be a drag queen to be fabulous?"

Jayne makes a face like Fay Wray before King Kong first lifts her.

"I've seen you in drag. Heavens to Paul Lynde, that can never happen again! There isn't enough vodka to get that image out of my brain!"

"My point. I thought it would be fun, but it's not something I want to do again."

"And I just heard RuPaul breathe a sigh of relief."

"Knock it off. I'm trying to be serious here. Am I expected to follow all of the stereotypical depictions of gay people if I'm accepted as one of the clan? I really want to know the answer to this. Because, if I have to do drag or become a hairdresser, I don't want to keep trying."

That hit Jayne hard. "We're having *that* kind of conversation, are we? You want to know how you fit into the world."

"I guess. I mean, I didn't fit in Minot. And I don't seem to fit in Washington. Where's my home?"

Jayne takes a moment to think this one over before responding. I'm relieved. It's better to have a thoughtful conversation than to be insulted for the rest of the day.

"Let me ask you a question, Miss Randy. You came to Washington to find a gay community."

"And my independence."

"Okay. Let's say these things are coming along." I nod with her. "So, what does a happy life look like for you?"

I bite my lip and shift my eyes from side to side. No one has ever asked me this.

"I used to think I would stay in my parents' home, work at the school system, and go to church functions until retirement. That seemed like a good life. But when Mother and Dad died, I realized I was living *their* life. The stable job and home are great – and I still want that – but I need to find something for the part of me that's gay. And the part that wants to experience all a big city has to offer." I pause for a moment. "I guess I just want a good job, a supportive husband, and a comfortable place to live. It's not far removed from before, just in a different community."

Jayne's shoulders drop a bit. "That's all?"

"Yes. That's all." Saying it aloud gives me calm.

I lead us to a park bench where we sit. The conversation has been tiring. Or emotionally taxing. Jayne's expression tells me it's not over.

"Why don't you feel you fit into the Washington gay community?" she asks innocently.

"I don't know."

I think for a moment about my experiences thus far. Until I met Jayne, I was utterly invisible to every guy I saw. I'm a lightweight drunk. I can't afford expensive clothes or fancy vacations. And my two dates made clear I'm not good in bed. Oh, and I'm an ugly drag queen.

"I don't expect to be voted Queen of the Fairies." She smiles at my attempt to be campy.

"I take back what I said before. You don't have to do drag or be the most fabulous person in the room to have the full gay experience." She crosses her legs and leans in my direction with her arm behind my back. "You *do* have to be comfortable in your own skin. There are a hundred other gays out there just like you. A thousand, even. They're looking for friends and boyfriends in the same ways you are. And they have the same doubts about their ability to fit into the community."

"You really think so?"

"I know so. I've seen your kind. Well, I crossed the street so I could observe them from a safe distance. They don't seem terrible, your people. I just don't appreciate the questionable wardrobe choices and thoughtless hairstyles." She chuckles a little.

"So, I'm good as I am?"

"Darling! There *are* minimum standards. You may not afford the finest clothing, but you cannot continue to wear the Orphan Annie collection currently in your closet. It just won't do. And you must get better at sex. No matter how itsy bitsy, teeny-weeny...."

"Enough already!"

"Still touchy about our dangling chad, are we?" She wags her finger at me. "Don't let anyone make fun of you because of your miniature schnauzer."

"No one makes fun of it except you! I was never self-conscious until you told me I'm average."

"Well, 'average' might be a stretch." She rolls her eyes. "Statistically speaking, I guess you could be right. Regardless, we just have to find you the right guy who can appreciate all the other things you have to offer."

Her teasing gives me license to broach the topic of Jayne's life. My voice sticks as I try to form the words.

"So, Jayne. What about you?"

"What about me?" she says innocently.

"Well, what's your name? I mean, your *real* name?"

"Jayne." Blank stare.

"No, not your drag name. What's your name when you're not in drag?"

"Not in drag?" She furrows her brow. "Jayne."

"Fine. Do you have your own apartment or a job? What do you do all day?" My frustration is showing.

"Of course, I have an apartment."

"But you're living with me!"

"It's only temporary, puppy. Just until you get on your feet." She pats my arm and stands. "Now, let's get home before cocktail hour ends." I have no option but to follow her determined march and leave the rest of my questions unanswered.

"My feet are killing me!" the diva complains upon entering *my* apartment. "I've got to get out of these shoes." She sits on the couch, removes the walking shoes, and replaces them with her formal pair. "Aaahhh. Much better."

My shoes come off; no replacement pair necessary.

"Mama's feeling parched. How long does a girl have to wait for a drink in this joint?"

"The last time you asked for drinks, I ended up passed out in a puddle of drool. Let's not repeat that, shall we?"

"Fine. No martinis. I'll guide you to a milder, more genteel drink called an Old Fashioned. People drank these all the time in olden days and never got drunk. Thus, the name!"

"Fine," I say on the way to the kitchen. "How do I make them?"

"You can make for both of us in the same glass, then split it. Start with 12 ounces of whiskey. Add one teaspoon of water, two dashes of angostura bitters, and two sugar cubes. Stir."

"I don't have sugar cubes."

"Sometimes, I swear I'm living on a deserted island! Just use a teaspoon of regular sugar, then. I guess we'll slum it tonight."

"Are you sure 12 ounces is right? This is a very full glass."

"You're right. We should go with an even 16. Use a bigger glass."

There is no need to further describe tonight's festivities. Suffice it to say, Jayne insisted the Old Fashioned I drank was hers and refused to sip from the one she deemed as mine. So, I drank both. My bed did not get used.

TWENTY-EIGHT

With an S or a Z?

"C'mon, Randy! We can swim off the rocks just past the boat launch."

"I don't know, Erik. Mother said the rocks are slippery and sharp in that area. We should go back to the beach."

"Dude! You gotta trust me! Besides, I don't wanna swim with all the old people anymore."

"What if we get hurt?"

"We won't. C'mon! We don't need bathing suits by the rocks!"

His broad smile cemented my crush, so I followed. Boys always make bad decisions for love.

Erik climbed the few steps to the top of the rocks, dropped his swimsuit to his ankles, and dived into the bright water. Not far behind, I hesitated a moment before removing my trunks. That's when my feet slipped, and I tumbled backward onto the jagged rocks, slamming my head into a sharp edge.

"Are you okay?" Erik yelled.

My face was in a puddle of water, feet above me, with my torso twisted into a human spiral. I felt spiders crawling on my paralyzed arms.

"Help me, Erik!" may be my dying words.

"No, dear, not Erik. It's Jayne. J-A-Y-N-E. And in this situation, I fear you may be beyond help."

A single light ray enters my eye. Nothing looks, feels, or smells familiar. Where am I? My wet face is smashed into a rock-hard pillow. An object, shaped somewhat like my chair, hangs on the wall like a piece of art. Everything smells of dust.

And I think a cockroach just ran into my hair.

"Hello! Are you in there? Did you sleep well?" The voice and all-encompassing shadow confirm Jayne is standing over me. My body won't move.

"Where am I?" slips out of my cotton-dry mouth.

"On your living room floor, if you can call it that. Not much living going on here. Anyhoo, you're right where you insisted I leave you last night. I thought it a bad idea, but there's no arguing when the Lightweight Champion has been hitting the bottle as hard as you did. And, for the record, you can be a fucking nasty drunk."

My vision starts to clear. My feet are twisted and resting on the couch above me as my head soaks in a drool puddle. A contortionist would marvel at my work.

And I hate that this feels familiar.

"Help me. Please."

"Oh, for the love of Cirque du Soleil!" Jayne grabs my arm, roughly dragging me toward the couch.

"Ow! Gently! Please!"

"Joan Crawford was never so hungover. I hate to say it, but you have a drinking problem. Trust me, I've seen it a million times before." She helps me upright, the entire room finally visible. "I'll get you some coffee. And a breath mint."

The clock says 3:15. Judging from the sun, it's the afternoon. I look down, yesterday's clothes barely recognizable. My jeans are soaked – apparently, I didn't get up to pee.

History tells me Jayne never brings a mug of undoctored coffee. "It's just coffee." She always reads my mind. "I could barely sleep last night for your liver weeping and wailing, so I left out the enhancements. Anyhoo, how ya feelin'?"

"Seriously?"

"I would say you look like the guy on the Starbucks sidewalk, but I can't embellish enough to bring you up to that level." She sits in the chair and looks around innocently. "What day does the maid come?"

"Let me finish this coffee, and I'll take a shower. And maybe you could speak a little softer."

As I nurse the black sludge, Jayne forces two Tylenol and an antacid on me. She also suggests an enema, but I decline. After 30 or so minutes of unprecedented silence, I drag myself to the bathroom.

Jayne, perfectly coiffed and smelling like Chanel No. 5, is still in the chair when I return. The shower, clean sweatpants, and coffee have improved my general sense of being. I feel slightly less ragged and beaten reclining on the couch.

"It's only 4:30," she offers. "We could still get to the mall for a little light shopping before dining in Georgetown. What say you?"

"Let's just stay home for the night. Maybe order Chinese?"

"I can live with that last part. But it is Saturday night. Shouldn't we be out on the town, making a few new friends? Having some laughs? Getting laid?"

"None of that even sounds possible."

"Tell you what. You order Chinese, and we'll discuss our evening options after we've eaten." She looks at me with bright, anxious eyes. I have a feeling we'll end up at a bar whether I want to or not.

I must admit, a little Chinese food and six Tylenol make me feel much better. And it's only 7:30.

"Were you serious about going out for the evening? I'm feeling better now."

Jayne is at the door before I can blink. "Well, I'm ready."

"Not so fast! I still need to change. Give me a few minutes."

I return in my other pair of nice jeans and my other Armani shirt. Jayne no longer seems impressed.

"Where to?" I ask.

"You need to visit the mother ship."

JR's is one of the oldest gay bars in Washington. It's in the heart of Dupont Circle on 17th Street, just up from P Street. Everyone gets there at one time or another, so my visit was inevitable. I've never dared to walk in alone, so I'm happy to have Jayne by my side.

The bar is almost over-capacity. It's populated by twinks, cubs, bears, daddies, sons, leather daddies, drag queens, and the occasional real woman. (Thank you, Jayne, for defining each label, including 'real woman.') I see guys from 18 to 120, all drinking and talking with friends while keeping a cruising eye open for fresh meat. Jayne uses me as a battering ram to break through the wall of queer humanity surrounding the bar.

"I'm only drinking lite beer tonight," I warn.

"Fine. Suit yourself. I'm sure Armani *designed* that shirt to go with lite beer." She rolls her eyes. "I'm stopping by the little girl's room to freshen up. Meet me over by the window where more people can take in my fabulousness."

She squeezes through the crowd and disappears somewhere toward the back of the bar.

The bartender actually notices and serves me the lite beer.

Maybe it's the Armani talking. I look around and can't see Jayne anywhere. It's hard to lose nearly seven feet of red sequins, but I've done it before. I walk to the window and lean against the drink rail.

"You here alone?" comes a raspy voice from behind.

An older man wearing leather pants that probably once fit him squints at me through thick glasses. His matching leather vest strains to hold a forest of unruly gray chest hair. I find myself wedged between his considerable beer belly and the drink rail, unable to retreat like the silver hair ring withdrawing from the crown of his head.

"I'm here with my friend, Jayne. She went to the bathroom a few minutes ago." I try to turn away, but I'm trapped.

"Of course she did," he smirks. "I haven't seen you here before. New?"

"It's my first time at JR's. I've been in Washington for a few months." Answering his first question was polite. Answering his second must have signaled interest. He puts his hand around my waist and leans in; the alcohol on his breath reminds me of my own smell from a few hours ago.

"Every newbie should have a mentor," he says with a wink. I manage a faint smile. "My name's Dean. You?"

"Randy." I can't seem to stop giving him attention.

"Well, Randy, can I buy you another round? Lite beer, is it?"

"No. I'm sticking to just this one. I had a tad too much last night and don't want a repeat hangover."

"Someone was a naughty boy, was he?"

"No. Well, maybe."

What would Jayne do in this situation? This guy is clearly older than I want. And he's too aggressive. How would Jayne get out of this?

"What kind of naughty things did you do last night, hmmm? Maybe we could have a replay of the best stuff?"

"That's not exactly what I meant. I just got drunk." Think, Randy. Think.

"Nothing wrong with a little nip of the bottle, now, is there?" He rubs the entire length of my arm with his hand and grins.

I take a deep breath and do my best to channel my fairy godmother. "So, how old are you?" I say, looking directly at him. That should end the conversation.

Dean smiles to show the teeth of a lifelong smoker. "How old do you think I am?"

I pretend to inspect him while I compose a response. "75 or so."

"Ouch! You think I'm *that* old!" He looks to the ceiling. "It must be the lighting. I'm 39."

Channel Jayne. Channel Jayne. "How long have you been 39?" I'm proud of myself for that one.

"Oh, my," he says sheepishly. "I have been holding at 39 for a few short years. Not too many, mind you. And what's your age?"

"I'm 12. I've been 12 for 21 years now. That makes me a minor."

He takes his hand off my arm and leans back. "There's no need to be rude! Bitch!" His retreat gives me breathing space.

I feel a little bad – and a little proud – about this. It was harsh. Not as sharp as Jayne would have been, but it was severe. I'm learning to handle things on my own for the first time.

The bar is full, but not so much that Jayne shouldn't stand out in the crowd. I push my way to the back, looking past the shirtless bodies for the gargantuan red beacon. She's not in the bathroom – either of them. And she's not upstairs. Maybe she found a boyfriend.

It's probably time for me to leave, anyway. I'm pushing to the door when I see *him*. Six feet of mocha-colored skin, longish dark brown hair parted in the middle, and full lips that look like he's pouting. The most beautiful man in the world is standing at the end of the bar.

He glances up with Tiffany blue eyes – shocking against the dark tones of his skin and hair – to catch me staring. Those amazing lips part slightly to reveal a curious smile that says he knows I see him. And he's happy about that.

What do I do now? If I don't talk with him, I'll regret not taking the chance. But I don't know what to say. Where is Jayne? I can't do this on my own. This is too much! I'm going to leave.

My eyes continue staring as I approach the exit. Just as I'm about to pass, he shouts over the noise, "Are you leaving?"

I freeze, eyes fixed on his. "Yeah."

"Oh. I thought you would introduce yourself this time. Maybe stop for a moment before you go?"

My wobbly legs move toward him, hand extended. "Randy. Randy Larson."

"Hi, Randy Larson." His unbelievably white smile is large and genuine as he shakes my hand. "Julio Rodriguez."

Someone suddenly and gruffly pulls me toward the door. I disconnect from the wavelength I shared with Julio. Jayne drags me down the sidewalk, talking so fast that breathing seems impossible.

"This place has just gone to hell! There was a time when a girl could expect to have all her drinks paid for by competing suitors. Not anymore. Barely a single one of those hormone-injected, protein-powder-puff erectile dysfunctions even looked at me. Me!" I try to look back at Julio, but the door has closed. "I'm never letting you pick the bar again, missy. Next time we hit the Eagle."

"Stop, Jayne!" We're standing in front of JR's, creating a logjam in the river of gay humanity flowing down 17th Street.

"We can't stop here! This beaver is not meant to build a dam!" She pulls me into CVS, safely away from the crowds.

"Whatever possessed you to stop me right in the middle of a brilliant rant? I was working into an Academy Award-winning performance!"

"You pulled me away from my dream man! How could you do that?"

"I cock-blocked you? Seriously? In my defense, I'm not wearing my glasses. You know how hard it is to see your little soldier, even when he's standing at attention. There was no way to know he had something going on!" She fans herself quickly with her hand.

"I'm serious!" I sound like a pleading child. "I just met a guy. All we got to do was exchange names. He seemed so perfect."

"And what is Casanova's name?"

"Julio Rodriguez."

"With an S or a Z?"

"What? How should I know? It's not like he spelled it out or anything."

"You wanna go back inside? It would be terrible if Prince Charming thought his little Cinderella ran from the ball to get away from him." She feigns a horror film scream.

"I can't just leave. Let me see if he's still there so I can apologize for running out."

We return to the magic spot where Julio sat just moments ago. The barstool is empty. The crowd is too dense to find him.

"This is terrible! What if I never see him again!? Julio was so perfect for me." I may sound like a middle school brat.

"Do you really think whining will win you any awards?" Jayne lectures. "I mean, *maybe* a Tony, but none of the big ones."

"I want to go home."

Back at the apartment, Jayne shows a little remorse. "Maybe I could help you find your little playmate."

"How are you going to find him?"

Jayne thinks for a moment, eyes to the ground, before curling into her Grinch smile. "We'll have brunch!"

"Brunch?"

"Yes! Brunch! I'll invite the whole Brothel, and we can employ their collective snooping resources to find your little Julio." She believes this is a brilliant idea.

"Who is this gang of sleuths?"

"You know them. Joan, Bette, Bette, Marilyn, and Cher. The Brothel!"

"You want us to host five people for brunch? In this apartment?"

"It's perfect! We'll get them liquored up and hatch a plot to find your dreamboat. It can't miss!"

"When would we do this?"

"Tomorrow, of course. No time like the present to find a guy who gave *you* a second look."

"Tomorrow? When will we clean? And buy food? And make food? There isn't enough time. It's nearly midnight now."

"Don't be silly. No serious brunch starts before 1:00. That's plenty of time to take care of everything. You just go to bed and get your much-needed beauty sleep. I'll call the girls."

"I don't know, Jayne. You really think we can do this?"

"When have I ever led you astray?" She stares intently, daring me to challenge her. "Just do as I say, and all will be fabulous!"

I slink off to bed, alternating between dreams of my new beau and nightmares of the brunch to come.

TWENTY-NINE

What a Dump

Cleaning for brunch would be a breeze if we both participated. While I frantically run the sweeper, scrub the bathroom, and scour the kitchen, Jayne follows behind, pointing out every spot I miss.

She opens a kitchen cabinet and grimaces. "Don't forget to re-wash all the glasses. I can practically see the lip balm of your ancestors permanently embedded in the dime-store glass."

"Fine. I'll do that if you finish cleaning the bathroom."

"Really?" Her voice dropped an octave. "These hands have never swabbed a toilet. And they never shall. Besides, every smudge, dandruff flake, and disembodied pubic hair decorating that place is yours. I'll be on the sofa inspecting from afar."

Somehow, everything is cleaned by eleven. Jayne finished the *National Enquirer*.

"What about food?" I ask.

"At this late hour, we can't possibly put together a proper menu. You should have thought of this sooner!" She ignores my grimace. "I say we cut our losses. Go grab some nice pastries at Safeway and see that the drinks are good and strong. They all met you as Pussy Liqueur, so they'll understand brunch is not in your DNA."

The food is laid out by 12:53, with seven minutes to spare. Jayne has continued to read *People* on the couch showing little concern for the time.

"It looks like we pulled it off," I brag.

"Maybe you should put the pastries in the fridge. Don't want them to go stale."

"Stale? Everyone will be here in five minutes."

"Wherever did you get that idea?"

"Our brunch starts at one. That's what you told them, isn't it?"

"Of course, I told them one. Which means everyone will arrive by three."

"Three? Why would they come late?"

"Three o'clock isn't late. Five would be late."

"I don't understand."

"Brunch is on Gay People Time. That means arrival is 60 to 90 minutes after the published start. When the guests are drag queens, add 30 minutes. Did no one in North Fuck-a-Moose teach you how to entertain?" She goes back to reading her magazine.

The next thing I know, Jayne is shaking my shoulders with the force of a six-foot, nine-inch drag queen late for cocktails. It's just before three.

"Brunch started at one, and you're in here snoozing like we were at a Meg Ryan film fest!"

I'm immediately awake. "Is everyone here?"

"Of course not. It's only 2:55."

"Why did you wake me like that if no one is here?"

"The hostess needs to be prompt. The guests are on their own time."

And, on cue, there's a knock at the door. Jayne takes a reclining sex kitten pose on the couch and motions for me to get the door. Five drag queens greet me, each clamoring to be the center of attention. It sounds like lunch recess at an elementary school.

"Hello, ladies. Come on in!" I only know this group from one drunken encounter at the Drag Race. It's suddenly intimidating, and I lose all confidence.

Joan Crawford enters first, extending a hand to show an immaculate manicure. Opalescent pink. "Enchanté." I reach up to shake her hand.

"Kiss her weathered craw, or the bitch will never stay!" Jayne yells from across the room.

My kiss on her hand is met with a tight smile that reflects the gesture's inadequacy. "So, this is where Pussy Liqueur lives. Fitting." She glides into the room, each patronizing step decrying the floor's cheap finish.

Bette Midler is next. She's wearing a pink and blue mermaid outfit, revealing an amazingly shapely figure. "Don't mind her. She's 20 years past menopause and still pretends she's on the rag once a month. She'll loosen up when she starts drinking. Again." I'm amazed that Bette can walk with a flipper covering her feet.

"I'm happy to be invited to brunch, but I'm on a diet," Marilyn Monroe says in her breathy voice. "No carbs. Except for alcohol. And those don't count." She's wearing the stunning white dress from *The Seven Year Itch*. I attempt to apologize for the pastries, but she makes a beeline for the drink table before I can speak.

"Hi, Pussy. It's great to see you again." Cher is so kind, though I wish she would call me Randy. Her long, dark hair and bell-bottom pants suggest the 1960s Cher. She kisses me on the cheek and boops my nose.

Bette Davis, reprising her *Baby Jane* frock, must be in a mood. "I had nothing better to do. Get me a drink, will you?" She stands at the door, surveys the apartment, and grunts disapprovingly. "What a dump."

My little place is cramped. Jayne, Bette, Bette, and Marilyn are shoulder-to-shoulder on the couch, with Joan enjoying the chair alone. Cher and I are forced to sit in the uncomfortable kitchen chairs with our knees pressed together.

"It's nice to have the whole brothel together again!" Cher exclaims, barely able to contain her delight.

"Yeah. A real cunt fest." Bette Davis' mood continues.

"At least Cher was able to wear something from a different era today," snaps Joan. "Davis has been in that same Baby Jane crap since I met her. Really? *One* film?" Davis flips her middle finger and looks around the room, showing it to each one in turn.

"It helps that I'm the one who's had the longest career." Cher sends a zinger while maintaining her innocent smile.

Bette Midler doesn't want to miss out on the catty fun. "And what's up with Miss Tits Ahoy over here," pointing at Marilyn. "Since when did she give up carbs?"

"Since I tried to wear my blue sequin dress and saw I look like a sack of potatoes." Marilyn gulps down the last of her bloody Mary and begins making a second.

"Otherwise known as Jayne Mansfield," shoots Joan.

"Why such a twat today, Joan?" Jayne asks. "Vibrator battery die last night?"

"That explains why my smoke detector didn't go off this morning when Marilyn burned her toast," Midler quips.

"I thought you weren't eating carbs," Jayne notes, looking at Marilyn.

"I can eat *toasted* bread. The carbs are burned up in the toaster," she replies, never looking up from her drink creation.

"Keep at it," Joan warns, "and you, too, can have an ass like Davis here. It's a life-sized map of Texas!"

"With a big, puckering crater for San Antonio!" Jayne adds. Everyone cackles except Davis.

Cher looks at me. "So, how is the new life in Washington?"

"I see you had the good sense to give up drag," Joan mumbles into her drink. "Your country thanks you."

"Well..." I start.

"He's having such a time," Jayne answers for me, anxious to control the narrative. "There was the attempted jackhammering by a horse-hung sailor, rimming by a lascivious Pooh bear, and he had his pie hole creamed by a sneaky straight fucker. And he's turned into a Crawford-like alcoholic who blacks out on the first sip of vodka." She shakes her head. "It hasn't been pretty."

"You poor thing," Marilyn says as she swallows the last of her third bloody. "The first sip?"

"Sounds like my type," Davis says as she exhales her cigarette smoke. "I've changed my mind. We can be friends."

Jayne cracks a devious smile. "And we've discovered he's got a...." She holds her thumb and pointer finger about an inch apart.

"He's got a tiny tallywhacker?" Marilyn gasps.

"Baby boner?"

"Teeny weenie?"

"Wee willy?"

"Meager member?"

"Paltry pecker?"

"Trifling tool?"

This continues until Davis sees I'm beyond embarrassed and shuts it down. "So, his family jewels are cubic zirconia. The world can always use a good bottom."

"About that," Jayne continues. "Despite Pooh's best efforts, he's closed up tighter than a born-again at a chastity convention. No offense, Cher."

"It's Chaz now," Cher sighs.

"Jesus Christ!" Crawford growls. "I've got a Jon Hamm dildo in my purse. Let's lube this boy up and show him how it works."

I grab my chair, nervous that this band of divas will actually teach their misguided sex-ed class. "I would rather you didn't try to shove a plastic wiener in my butt!"

"Plastic? You think I can't afford silicone?" Joan sternly wags her finger. "No dildo for you."

"Believe me," Jayne says. "I tried vibrator therapy with him. That's what led to his sexual obsession with stuffed animals."

"I don't have an obsession with stuffed animals!" I protest.

Jayne's look tells me I shouldn't correct her. "And he's become uncontrollably flatulent!"

"Oh, honey! Haven't we all!" Davis says with a smoker's laugh.

"Not me! I've never flatulated. Ever!" A tipsy Marilyn interjects.

Midler pats her on the shoulder. "Dear, you really should slow down. Instead of a fourth bloody, why don't I make you a nice martini?" Marilyn giggles and nods.

Jayne stands and walks to the center of the room. "And that gets us to the real reason you've been invited here today. It seems Miss Randy met a man last night at JR's."

"Tell me it isn't so!" Midler gasps, clutching her bosom. "Why would he ever be in such a pedestrian place like JR's? I once got crabs just walking past the joint."

"Jayne said we had to go." I'm not letting her control the narrative on this one.

"It's not so bad," Crawford chimes in. "Last time I was there, I got gang-banged in the bathroom. How many players are on a gay soccer team?"

"Joan," comes Davis's smoky voice, "the closest you ever got to a gang is a guest appearance on *The Little Rascals*."

"Ladies!" Jayne claps her hands sharply. "Let's stay on topic so we can help poor Randy before Marilyn passes out."

Midler covers Marilyn's ears and whispers loudly to the

room, "We probably have 15 minutes. Tops."

"So, as I said, Randy met a man at JR's last night. They talked for a few seconds, and then Randy abruptly ran out for no reason at all."

"Jayne!" I can't believe she's messing this up so badly. "Let me. I saw this gorgeous guy at the bar and decided to say hello. All we managed to do was exchange names before Miss Mansfield, here, grabbed my arm and dragged me out. When I went back a few minutes later, he was gone. Now I don't know how to find him."

"Boy, if you could turn back time," Cher quips.

Davis takes a drag on her cigarette. "We need a full-body description if we're to determine the worthiness of this goose chase. Every inch."

"He's got brown hair, parted in the middle, that hangs down to his eyes. Perfect eyes. Tiffany blue." It makes me shudder just to think of his eyes.

Joan looks at Davis. "Is he ever going to get to the inches part?" Davis shrugs and takes another drag on her cigarette.

"What's his name?" Marilyn asks.

"Julio Rodriguez."

"With an S or a Z?" Midler wants to know.

"That's what I asked last night," Jayne says, affirming her worth. "Can you believe he doesn't know?!"

Midler agrees. "It seems a logical follow-up question to 'What's your name?' and 'What will I get when I unwrap your package?'"

"How would I get that information? I mean, the S or Z part. It was a 60-second conversation. I don't know anything about him, really."

"We're supposed to help you find someone named Julio Rodriguez when you don't know where he lives, what he does, or even if he spells his name with an S or a Z?" Joan grunts. "It's an impossible task. Who do you think we are? CIA?"

"Come on, girls! You've all slept with someone who knows someone who could get us into a database with names and pictures." Jayne may have a point here. "The guy has a common name; I get that. Maybe we could find him if we narrow it down by having pictures attached to guys in a certain age range."

"Did anyone bother to do a Google search yet?" Cher asks naively.

"Of course! Randy did that as soon as he finished spanking the monkey last night, didn't you?"

"Well, no." Randy blushes. "And no monkeys were spanked. You started talking about doing a brunch today, and it completely slipped my mind. We could do a search now."

"Let's all go to the computer building together so we can see how it's done," Davis suggests. "Do we have to go far? I didn't bring the right shoes for walking."

"They always say you can't have tits and brains," Crawford drones. "No one ever said you can't *not* have tits and *not* have brains."

Everyone looks around, puzzled, except for Marilyn, who laughs in a high-pitched whinny. "I've got tits to spare. You can borrow some of mine, dear Bette."

"No argument from me," Midler adds.

While they continue to discuss the cause and effect of tits and brains, I get my laptop from the bedroom. Marilyn is gracious enough to move her drink so I can put it on the coffee table.

"Ask it if his name ends in S or Z," Davis offers.

"I'll just try typing it both ways." I get millions of hits, regardless of the spelling. Even adding 'Washington, DC' doesn't help.

"What if you ask The Facebook?" Joan throws out while continuing to down her drink(s) from the comfort of the chair.

"Good idea. Does anyone have an account we can use?" I

ask. "I don't have any social media."

"I'll sign in," Marilyn offers. "My username is ReginaldAl-thertonAKAMarilyn."

Davis gives her a disgusted look. "Your name is Reginald Altherton? Fuck me! I would have emerged from the womb with signed name-change papers if someone did that to me."

Marilyn ignores her. "The password is m-y-p-a-s-s-w-o-r-d." She giggles. None of the others seem to see any problem with this.

"You have 19,800 friends!" Cher exclaims, leaning over the screen.

"I've been known to offer a friendly hand to a few fellas, here and there." Another giggle.

She types in Julio Rodriguez and limits the search to Washington, DC. Immediately I see the faces of the three dozen or so guys with that name. One, however, stands out as familiar.

"Click on that guy," I tell her.

His profile shows the face of the handsome man I met last night with a rainbow flag in the background. It must be him. He lives in the District, and it says he works at the Omni Shoreham. That's just across the bridge from Adams Morgan. He's practically in the neighborhood!

"Tell me if he has any nudes," Joan throws in from her perch.

"He is quite handsome," Cher says, patting my back. "We've got to help you reel this one in."

"Truer words have never been said," Jayne adds, finally returning to her role as leader of this little pack. "We've got to devise a scheme by which Woody LittlePecker here can land in the arms of our Prince Valiant. Any ideas?"

Midler is very enthusiastic. "Let's all go to the Omni right now and spy on him. We could get some dirt and blackmail the guy into taking a date with our micro-dicked friend."

I'm covering my face with my hands as Davis continues

this madness. "What if I entice him to fuck me in the broom closet? Cher could bust in with a camera after an appropriate amount of time for me to get to know him, of course, and take compromising pictures. She promises not to release them if he goes on a date with Johnny DickBeSmall, here."

"Why would he take a dried-out cunt like you into a cleaning closet?" Joan digs. "We should use Marilyn. She's got the tits."

"I'll admit I may have seen better days, but I'm still not to be had for the price of a cocktail, like a salted peanut," Davis hisses. "Or Marilyn Monroe."

"Do you have any original material? Or is it all from your dreadful films?" Joan shoots back.

"I've got great tits!" Jayne interjects. "Why not use me?"

"You do have great tits," Cher adds. "But don't you think this guy is more into dick? Does anyone have a dick that would entice him?"

They all sit silently, uncomfortable with the ramifications of answering that question. Finally, Jayne says, "I guess we'll have to use Randy as the bait. Despite his shortcomings." They all nod in agreement.

"You're going to use *me* as bait to get dirt on the guy so he will go on a date with *me*?" I say, trying to summarize their conversation while showing its inherent flaws.

They all nod in agreement. Again.

"What say we wander over to the Omni right now?" Joan suggests. "It would be nice if we could do *something* interesting today."

"There's no need for all of you to get involved on my behalf," I plead, trying to avert an almost certain disaster.

Jayne stands and sharply claps her hands. "So, it's settled. We're all going to the Omni. Chop, chop, girls. We've got a man to catch!"

And, with that, everyone stands to leave. Marilyn, of

course, needs some assistance. Once everyone has visited the bathroom, freshened up their makeup, finished the last of their drink (or started a new one), and generally insulted one another with abandon, we are ready to leave – nearly two hours later!

THIRTY

Finally, a Little Grandeur

My apartment is, at most, five blocks from the Omni. It's an easy six-minute walk on a typical day. However, shepherding a gaggle of drunken drag queens this distance is much like herding cats. We stop for rests, insults, complaints, more insults, encouraging lectures, demeaning lectures, still more insults, and drink refills from the flasks each carries in her purse. And the occasional question, directed at me, about what it's like to have such a tiny wiener.

The walk takes 75 minutes.

The drag menagerie comes to a full stop upon entering the hotel lobby. "Finally, a little grandeur," Joan remarks. "Why did we waste our afternoon in that shithole when we could have been here?"

She isn't wrong, so I take no offense.

"It wouldn't hurt to dust the chandeliers every decade or so," Davis notes disapprovingly.

The Omni Shoreham is one of the oldest and grandest hotels in Washington. I've walked past but never imagined I would go inside. Its palatial lobby is filled with ornate, plush seating areas lit by antique chandeliers. The highly polished stone floors reflect the ceiling arches and give the impression a person could ice skate from one end to the other. I feel like I've entered Windsor Castle.

Jayne points to an array of chairs and couches at the far end of the lobby. "Let's have a seat over there and plan our strategy."

She chose the remotest spot so my attention-seeking friends could get the most exposure. The staff and guests stare in silent awe – or horror – as our glitzy group snakes its way across the expansive lobby. Each of the queens puts on airs, suggesting she owns the place. Nothing seems to miss their discerning eyes, from highly critical deconstructions of the decor to some staff's lax grooming habits.

"In my day, a place like this would have been classy," Bette Davis notes, looking down her nose.

Joan nods. "Remember when the Beverly Hilton used to be nice? What is this world coming to?"

"I was the headliner at a White Party in Miami once," Marilyn offers. "Or maybe it was just an acid trip on Venice Beach. It's all a little fuzzy."

"Well, I was mentioned in a headline *after* a White Party in Miami," Jayne barks, not to be outdone. "I wouldn't mind going back to the Dade County Jail just to say hello to the boys."

We're settling in the secluded seating area when Marilyn asks the question on everyone's mind except mine: "Will someone be coming by for our drink orders?" Heads nod in agreement.

"I'm just here to find Julio," I say, relieved they're no longer drinking my personal liquor stash. I've never been around people who drink as much *water* as this group imbibes alcohol.

Cher takes charge of the mission. "Randy, you go to the front desk and ask about Julio. Maybe they can direct you since we don't even know what he does."

"I'll put money on toilet-cleaner," Crawford growls. Several heads bob in agreement.

Davis rolls her eyes. "And you all made fun of me about trapping him in the mop closet. It's probably his office."

I ignore the stream of demeaning comments, choosing to acknowledge only Cher. "Good idea." The desk clerk, a middle-aged lady with press-on nails that would make any task impossible, watches me approach.

"I'm trying to find someone who works here," comes with the urgency of reporting a fire. "At least, I think he works here. He's very handsome. I only met him once. And I don't know if it's an S or a Z. It all happened very quickly. And then Jayne pulled me out the door."

The clerk puts her hand on mine and smiles. "Sir, let's slow down and go back to the beginning. You're looking for someone?"

"Yes." I take a deep breath. "Does a guy named Julio Rodriguez work here?"

"You're looking for Julio?"

"Yes. But I don't know if he spells Rodriguez with an S or a Z. Does that matter?"

"Our Guest Services Manager is named Julio Rodriguez. Could it be him?"

"Maybe. I need to see his face. Does he work on Sundays?"

"You're in luck. He happens to be in today. Who should I say is calling?"

My collar feels tight as I realize this is actually happening. "Randy Larson. We met last night at JR's."

The clerk winks at me while punching four numbers into the phone. "Mr. Rodriguez? This is Lorraine at the front desk. There's a Mr. Larson, Randy Larson, here to see you. He says you met last night." There's a short pause. "Yes, I'll tell him. Thank you."

I must look like a child waiting for a cookie. She can't help but laugh. "He's on his way. Please, have a seat. It will only be a moment."

"Thank you."

My palms are sweating profusely. The last 24 hours have gone by so fast that I haven't had time to think about what I'm doing. Jayne pushed things forward like she always does. Now I'm about to be face-to-face with the incredible guy I met last night. What if he no longer thinks I'm attractive? What if he never did? Maybe he was so drunk he thought I was someone else. Perhaps he was just talking with me to be nice. He felt sorry for me because I was alone. This is going to be a disaster! I shouldn't have come here.

As my head fills with every insecurity I can imagine, I feel a hand on my shoulder. "Randy?"

I turn to see a tall, dark-haired man with piercing blue eyes standing next to me. He smiles in recognition while I blush. "You're Julio. From last night, right?"

"Yes. I can't believe you found me here! Did I tell you this is where I work?"

"No. No. I just trolled Facebook for you. I hope you don't mind."

"Normally, I would be a little weirded out by a stalker. But this time, I'm glad you were persistent." His smile increases its wattage. "What happened last night? You introduced yourself and then ran out. I was afraid I said something wrong."

I shake my head vigorously. "No! It wasn't you. My friend, Jayne, dragged me out the door. I came back a few minutes later, but you were gone." I want to tell him how disappointed I was, but that sounds desperate.

"Yeah, we decided to leave. Nothing good was going to happen after you left."

A smoky voice from across the lobby yells, "How many inches?" My face burns as Julio looks in their direction.

"Do you know the drag queens over there?" he asks

innocently. "They seem to be staring at us."

"Yes and no," I stammer.

"No worries. We get that kind of thing all the time." I'm not relieved. "Anyway, I don't really have time to talk right now. Could I get your phone number and call you later?" He pulls out his phone and hands it to me. "Just punch in your digits." Another smile.

A different voice from across the room yells, "S or Z?" I'll never live this down.

I put my number in his phone and hand it back. He immediately calls me. "There. You have my number, too."

"Thanks," I say, afraid to look directly into his eyes. I start to save his name in my contacts and stop short. "Oh, I gotta ask...."

"It's with a Z." Big smile. "I'll call you later. Thanks for coming by, stalker." I look at my feet. "And for bringing your entourage with you." He laughs and lightly touches my arm.

All I can manage is, "Bye."

I'm frozen watching him return to his office, imagining his walk in slow motion.

Twelve clicking heels remind me I'm not alone. I turn to see the entire Brothel staring at me like inquisitive cats. I give them a thumbs-up.

"He is quite the looker," Midler says. "One of the finest asses I've ever seen! I'd wrap my tail fin around him any day."

"Big hands," Joan coos.

"You got some good taste for a guy who can't even decorate his own apartment." Coming from Bette Davis, I'll call that a compliment.

"Does anyone else need a drink?" Marilyn asks.

Cher jumps up and down quickly. "Let's stay here and hit the bar. It's a classy place, and we're classy broads. What say you, bitches?"

They all turn for the bar, but I'm not in the mood. "You go

ahead without me. I'm going home. Thanks for helping me to-day. I couldn't have done it without you."

"Sure thing, Toots," Midler says as she gently slugs my arm. "We'll come out for you anytime. Just call!"

As I walk to the door, warm from a day filled with new friends and a potential new boyfriend, I hear someone ask, too loudly, "Did we ever hear how many inches?"

THIRTY-ONE

A Person I Don't Like

The walk home is peaceful after a noisy (and boozy) day with six oversize personalities. I try filling my mind with thoughts of Julio, but the Brothel is still in my head. Jayne and her friends commandeered my day and nearly ruined my brief encounter with a potential boyfriend. Maybe they had the best of intentions, but how can I tell? There was never time for me to think before plans went into action.

In fact, I can't remember when I last had time to myself. Jayne has been living in my apartment – uninvited – since October 29. That's 40 days! Noah was on the ark for 40 days while God flooded the earth. It seems an apt comparison.

The past 40 days have seen me drunk more times than I can remember, continuously overspending my budget, missing work (both planned and unplanned!), and descending into domestic uncleanliness that Mother would deem heretical. More people have seen me naked during this time than in the previous 32 years! Nothing in my life reminds me of the person I was just a year ago. I don't even wear the same clothes. And Jayne is at the center of it all.

Jayne Mansfield is my Biblical flood.

Frustration turns to anger. Jayne can be nurturing, but

240

mostly she's pushy and selfish, dragging me into whatever debauchery she wants for herself. Maybe I want life to go back to what it was before she arrived. I had a new job and home with frugal dinners in front of the television. The occasional lite beer was my only alcohol, and no one made fun of my body or forced me to have sex. Things used to be better.

Jayne and I need to talk. I must get a grip on my life before it spins out of control. If Jayne continues living with me, she needs to learn my rules. She needs to respect my wishes. And she needs to pay rent!

Wait. Do I want Jayne living with me? She has slept on my couch for 40 nights. My only living space has become a drag queen's dressing room that is never clean. My bathroom overflows with sequins, hairspray, and hand-washed lady things I must move to use the toilet or shower. Jayne never buys food or alcohol, yet she's happy to devour mine. And she's always following me.

Am I so weak I let this person walk on me, taking over my life? How did I allow this to happen?

I'm suddenly home, barely aware of how I got here. The anger has fueled an urge to clean, to regain control of some part of my life. Piles of dishes are washed, the floors are swept and mopped, and five loads of laundry are cleaned. Every space is decluttered. The bathroom, a truly disgusting room even after cleaning this morning, is scoured to spotless.

It's nearly 10:00 when I finally collapse onto the couch. I admire the tiny home I've made for myself. A clean home. The couch and chair are placed just as Mother would have, with homemade afghans draped over the back of each. And my bed has the same sheets and comforter I used in Minot. The two pieces of Walmart art my parents bought 25 years ago – an unnamed mountain scene and a trout swimming upstream – adorn the walls of the living room.

This apartment is a miniature version of our North Dakota

home in many respects. The furniture, decorations, bedding, dishes, and kitchen utensils are direct transplants. MJ and I arranged everything similar to the Minot house such that Mother and Dad would feel comfortable here. It's like the old saying, "The more things change, the more they stay the same."

My mind stops in mid-thought. Did I really move to Washington just to recreate the life I had in Minot? My plan was to live in a way I couldn't back home; to be independent. This apartment shows no signs of independence. Have I failed?

"Shouldn't you be in bed?" Jayne's booming voice startles me.

"Jayne! I never heard you come in. Have you been drinking with the girls this entire time?"

"Well, we started at three. Only seven hours of boozing, I'm embarrassed to say. There was a time I would have said that was just getting started. I must be aging."

"Did you stay at the Omni?"

"No. Midler decided to perform an entire show set that was not appreciated by the other patrons. Troglodytes! So little class." She throws her hands in the air. "We wandered into a couple of other holes-in-the-wall before the fun fizzled out. So, I'm home."

"Ah. It's been quiet here." I'm still thinking about the comparisons with my old life, which makes me upset again.

Jayne surveys the apartment. "Quiet? How could you hear yourself think with the maid in a cleaning frenzy?" She wipes a finger across the coffee table. "You could get two-and-a-half stars on AirBnB in this condition. Do I now have to use coasters?"

"Can we talk?" I say with a little sigh.

"That's never a good start." She sits next to me on the couch and looks expectantly.

"Do you know we've been living together for 40 days?"

"No wonder I feel like a caged animal!"

"Very funny. But I'm serious. You showed up after the High Heel Race and never left. I don't remember you ever asking to live in my home. And we never discussed what the future would be. It just happened. Now we're inseparable roommates whose lives are twisted together like we're married."

"I'm waiting for the bad part of this conversation." Jayne starts filing her nails.

"Don't you get it? This is all messed up."

She stops filing and puts her hand on her waist. "Jesus Fucking Christ, Randy! I'm waiting for you to lay into me about taking over your life, and you just keep whining on with passive-aggressive statements that never get at how you feel. You're upset. Angry, even. Am I supposed to take the lead on bitching at myself?"

"I thought I was clear."

"Clear as a Dead Sea mud facial. Are you telling me to take a hike? Vamoose? Don't-let-the-door-hit-you-in-the-ass kind of sayonara?"

"That's a little harsh."

She's full-on yelling at me now. "You think that's harsh? I could give you a tongue-lashing that would make your dead grandmother sit up and rub her bony ass. It only becomes severe when there's truth behind it. Now, don't just sit there patting me on the leg. Slap my fucking face! Kick my ass, bitch!"

I feel my entire body getting hot. Tears stream from my eyes, dripping onto my shirt. My teeth are clenched. This is the first time I've ever been irate!

"You have ruined my life! Ever since you got here, you make me do uncomfortable and embarrassing things! You force me to drink too much. You're trying to make me into a sexual deviant. Now I'm self-conscious about the size of my wiener. And you're turning me into a person I don't like." I pound my fist into my leg. "I want you to leave!"

It all came out so fast, and with such malice I nearly fainted. It's hard to catch my breath. Did I really say all that to Jayne?

She is sitting perfectly still, staring into my face. Her expression shows nothing. No shock. No offense. No anger. It's like I injected her whole body with Botox.

I look at my feet and wipe tears from my face. The anger subsides as fast as it came, leaving me exhausted. "Say something," I plead. "Please."

Jayne sits back on the couch and smooths her dress. She slowly and deliberately crosses her legs and stretches her right arm along the back of the couch. She looks comfortable.

"Your delivery was out-of-control. The crying is a nice touch but should be left for the end. Start with 'Go fuck yourself.' That's always an icebreaker. Maybe throw in, 'Your mother was a whore.' Nothing stings like a good insult to the parental units."

"What?" I feel like I'm making MJ's constipation face.

"Another good line to use on a drag queen, 'You're becoming un-tucked, like a tiny, baby turtle trying to push its head through a curtain of sequins.' I've used that several times and nearly cleared the room." She throws her head back and laughs at the memory. "In fact, you never made a single comment on the size of my ass or feet, the color of my hair, or my inadequate abilities in the sack. So many wasted opportunities!"

"I don't understand. I just yelled at you to get out of my life, and you're criticizing my delivery? Did you hear anything I said?"

"Of course I did, dear. You thanked me for helping you grow up."

"I did what?"

"Randy, you moved to Washington for a reason. You

wanted to be part of a community – the gay community. You wanted to make new friends. You wanted to see what you might be missing in the big world beyond Minot. You didn't move to this great city just to live the same life you had in North Dakota."

I can't speak. It's like she knows me better than I do.

"Once you got here, you were unsure how to achieve all you wanted to do. So, you set up your life in the only way you knew. That's why your apartment looks like your dead mother decorated. And why you sit home every night watching TV. It's also why you decided, on your own, to run in the High Heel Race. It was the first step that allowed us to meet."

"But... my independence. You make all the decisions!"

"Independence is overrated, my dear. We all need friends and people we can count on. I'm your fairy godmother, right?" I frown. "As such, I'm here to guide you to a better life. It seems to be working, from my vantage point."

"But don't you have your own life? Your own place to live?"

"What I have will still be there when I'm done here. In the meantime, we have more work to do."

"Like what?"

"Like this dreadful apartment. It's nice to see it somewhat clean, for once. You know, I nearly broke a hip sliding on the grease in your kitchen the other day." The bossy drag queen returns. "But the decor has gotta go."

"What's wrong with the decor?"

"It's fine if you're 75 and living in Fargo."

"Minot."

"Minot. Even worse! You move to this hipster part of DC and drag in parts of Idaho on your shoe!"

"North Dakota."

"North Dakota! I keep trying to help, and you insist on taking things down a notch. For the sake of us both, we need to make some changes. How about starting with the old lady afghans? Do they have to be on the back of the furniture?"

"Mother always kept them there, so it's easy to wrap up on cold nights."

"You can't get your fat ass off the couch and walk to the closet? You're not in a nursing home."

"I guess we could put them away. They're rarely used anyway."

"Good. Now let's talk about the layout of the living room. The TV is directly in front of the only window that looks at your neighbor's apartment. We should push it to the other wall, giving you a clear shot into his space. Maybe he walks around in his birthday suit all day, and you've never seen it!"

"I'm not going to spy on my neighbors! Besides, they could look back."

"I don't see a telescope pointing this way, so he's not going to see anything." She holds up her index finger and thumb for the second time today, about an inch apart. "Don't you want to know what he's got going on?"

"No." Well, it would be fun to see him naked, but I'm not admitting that to Jayne.

She begins moving furniture. For 30 minutes, we push the few pieces I have to new spots, evaluate, move again, criticize, and move again. There are only so many configurations possible in this space. We try every one of them.

"Jayne, it's nearly midnight, and I have to be at work in the morning. Can we just stop for the night?"

"If you can sleep with unfinished business, I can."

I walk to my room and collapse onto the bed. Today has been one of the longest of my life!

THIRTY-TWO

Cockroaches and Ass Crack

"It's the law," Jayne says over Monday morning coffee. "No argument."

"The law? Whose law?"

"I have run from the law, run afoul of the law, and had run-ins with the law. I know the law. You wait three days."

"That's ridiculous! I want to call Julio today," I whine. "What if I wait too long, and he loses interest?"

"He hasn't seen you naked, so I doubt he's lost interest yet. You must follow the three-day law if you want a serious relationship. End of discussion." Jayne unfolds the *Washington Post* in front of her face.

"Fine. I'll wait. But this better not ruin my chances."

My anger has subsided from last night, and I'm a little embarrassed to bring up the subject. I wish I hadn't gotten so emotional with Jayne. We have unresolved questions about our living situation that should be discussed calmly. Unlike the urgency to contact Julio, Jayne's conversation can wait a few days.

I'm sitting at my desk a few hours later when I get the first text from Julio. He apparently knows nothing of the three-day law. The vibration jolts my entire body like a heart defibrillator, and I drop the phone when I see his name.

Hey, stalker.

Hi. Should I apologize for that again?

No! Just teasing. What up?

I'm at work for three more hours. Groggy from being up late.

Hot date?

No! Just cleaning my apartment.

I should do that, too.

It sounds more fun than it is.

Cute! Can I see you this week?

He wants to see *me*? It's hard to believe that after I invaded his workspace with a gaggle of drunken drag queens and admitted to stalking him online. My sweaty hands are now shaking.

Sure. When?

Thursday night?

The last time I had a Thursday night date, I missed work on Friday. Oh, and there was the whole humiliating put-that-in-my-butt-and-I'll-fart-in-your-face thing. Maybe Thursday is a bad omen.

Thursday is a school night. What about Friday?

That works. But wait five days? Can we have lunch before then? I really want to see you.

He really wants to see me? Is this real? Now my face and pits are sweating along with my hands. No one has ever been this interested in me.

Sure. Can you come to the Metro Center area? My lunch is too short to come up your way.

I can. How about Wednesday?

That's good. Noon at District Taco on F St?

It's a date. See you then, cutie. ;)

Everyone in the department probably heard me exhale. He wanted to see me, and he called me cute! The lunch idea was a good one. There won't be any drinking, and I only have an hour, so not much can go wrong. And I don't need to tell Jayne since it's happening during the workday. Lots of wins here.

Jayne has rearranged the apartment again by the time I get home. All the furniture is moved. Pictures are re-hung. The surround sound for the TV is even suspended on the wall. Does she have power tools in her purse? Though I won't admit it to her, the place looks nice.

"Well? I did my best, considering what I had to work with. Do you like it?" Jayne looks like a child who just used the toilet for the first time. And I know this is not an honest question. It's a statement – a demand.

"I guess."

"That's hardly a ringing endorsement! I nearly broke my perfect little ass dragging this Gothic furniture all over the room. Bette Davis had to come help me. Oh, on an unrelated note, we're out of vodka, vermouth, gin, bourbon, and bitters. And olives."

I give her a stare, and she looks to the ceiling, attempting to appear innocent.

"I guess it's fine. It doesn't look like my apartment, though."

"Exactly! That's the beauty of it! It looks like the home of someone with style and taste. Scratch that. Stylish placement of tasteless crap. If I can make do with it, so can you."

I walk into the kitchen and see she has moved all the contents of the cabinets and drawers. "Was it necessary to completely reorganize my system?" I ask.

"What system? Your way made no sense. I couldn't find a thing."

"Yes, but I could. How will I get what I need when nothing is in its proper spot? Besides, when was the last time you cooked anything?" I'm frustrated now. It's one thing to move the furniture. Putting the utensils in the drawer clearly meant for potholders is entirely different!

"Did someone get his man-boobs caught in the subway door?"

"What? I don't have man-boobs!"

"Of course, you don't, dear. Those are just sad little pecs." She grabs me by the shoulders and turns me toward the kitchen cabinets. "Now, let me show you how I put the right piece in the right place."

Jayne gives me a tour of each drawer and cabinet. I must admit, she has impeccable organizational skills. Her arrangement makes far more sense than the way Mother did it. Hence, my mixed-up kitchen methodology.

"A professional chef would be happy here! Not that *you* know any more about cooking than I do. The only thing you really need to find is the microwave."

"Okay! You win. The place is better."

"You could have started with those words. Should we repeat them so I can set my ringtone?"

"Don't push it." I wonder if I will ever find a spoon for my morning cereal. "Is there anything else I need to know?"

"The bedroom and bath should be self-explanatory. Oh, and I put Pooh in a special place next to the bed." She winks. "But we still need to add a little color." Jayne starts walking to the living room as she talks. "Some paint here and there. Maybe custom blinds. A coat of stain on the floors. Nothing big."

"You know I rent this place, don't you? I'm not putting money into an apartment I don't own."

She puts her arm on my shoulder and guides me to the couch. "Now that you're regularly entertaining...."

"I am?"

"It's important your home be a showplace. Or at least

somewhere north of crack den. I'm sure you'll agree an upgrade is in order for some of these flea market rejects. A few new pieces of designer furniture. A set of Riedel hand-blown wine glasses. A martini glass that doesn't double as a mop bucket. The basics, I tell you."

"How much is all this going to cost?" I know it sounds like I'm interested in hearing more, but this is just a ploy to take control of the conversation. She knows my financial situation.

"Did I mention there's a sale at Scandinavian Designs?"

"That's not an answer. Besides, I'm about to pay off the debt you forced on me last October, and I can start with a clean slate."

"You mean we have some room on our credit card? And you didn't tell me? These secrets are ruining our relationship!" Jayne dramatically throws the back of her hand to her forehead. "How will we ever come back from this?"

"*Our* credit card? Is your name on it? Have you made any payments?"

She peeks her eye from behind her hand. "This line of questioning suggests you'd like to compromise. Fine. I can be reasonable. Only one piece of furniture." She slowly brings her hand down and looks at me expectantly. "The chair groans when you sit, and I fear the couch is suicidal. She could throw herself from the window at any moment!"

"I know these two pieces are old, but they belonged to my parents. How can I get rid of heirlooms?"

She smiles. "So, it's settled. You agree to recycle the worn-out family Davenport, and I'll lower my expectation to something from West Elm. Wasn't that easy?" She lightly punches my shoulder.

Jayne runs to the bedroom for my laptop before I can lodge any further complaints. I know she's right. This furniture was purchased before I was born and has been recovered two or three times. I just don't know how I can afford new things right now.

She puts the computer on the coffee table and claps her hands twice. "Take us to the place with the West Elm furniture," she commands.

"How do you live without using a computer? I'll do it." I open the West Elm site. Everything looks so fancy. And expensive.

"There! There! That's it. Tell it to show me the Zander sofa."

I click on the picture and see the most beautiful piece of furniture imaginable. It's exactly what I like. Sleek. Plenty of cushions. Long enough for a nap. And $1,500.

"When can they deliver it?" she asks excitedly.

"This costs $1,500! I can't afford fancy furniture on my salary. We should look at the sale page. Or maybe check out Sears."

She gasps and stares directly into my eyes like a snake charmer. "The important thing isn't the price. It's the style. Your entire home would come together with this piece. And a complementing Dennes chair. No man could resist you!"

"The chair is an additional $1,200. You want me to put $2,700 on my credit card?"

"Quite frankly, I don't care if you pay for it from your penny jar. You're the accountant. Account!"

The pictures are nice. These pieces would bring style to my home, and it's a huge step toward being my own man. And they would last the rest of my life.

"It says there is zero percent interest financing on purchases this big. And they deliver for free." I make the MJ face. "Maybe I could do it."

"Yes! We're on the road to respectable now! Have it delivered tomorrow."

I can't explain what happened next. Yes, Jayne put the idea in my head and pushed me hard to spend the money. But, somehow, this feels like my own decision. It's something I want to do. The furniture is exactly what I want, even if I didn't know I wanted it. And the free financing will help me pay it off over time. I fill out the credit forms, add the items to the delivery basket, and submit the order.

And, in a flash, I spent more money on two places to sit than on my first car. The car *was* barely running and cost me a fortune in repairs. But it's the principle of the thing.

Jayne looks closely at the confirmation email. "It says the furniture will be delivered at noon on Wednesday. I can't be here to accept it. I have an appointment at the beauty parlor for a massage, facial, and wig refresher. It's practically an emergency medical appointment. You'll have to come home on your lunch hour."

What just happened? I scheduled a furniture delivery at precisely the same time as my lunch with Julio! What am I going to do? I can't back out of the date, or it might signal I'm not interested in him. And it would mean my first date is Friday night. I don't want another disaster like the one with Derek.

"Is there a problem?" Jayne is staring at me in her probing way.

"No. No problem. Why do you ask if there's a problem?"

"Because you look constipated. That means your brain is working. What is it?"

"Nothing. It's just that it's hard for me to get back here on Wednesday afternoon."

"Because?"

"Because I've got a thing. A thing that can't be changed. You know how that is. Maybe we can do this another day."

"Another day? Haven't I endured enough? I can't spend another day sitting on this sofa crawling with cockroaches and smelling of ass crack! It's so demeaning to a girl of my stature!" She takes a deep breath, ready to continue her tirade, when she suddenly stops. The Cheshire Cat grin I've seen many times spreads across her face. "There's something big you're not telling me, isn't there?"

"What? Big? No! Of course not."

"Hmmm. Don't you take your lunch every day at noon?" she coos.

"You know I do. Most people do. It's a normal time. I have to eat then, or my blood sugar drops, and I get shaky."

"So, your Wednesday plans must include lunch, n'est pas?"

I feel like I'm playing a dangerous game of cat-and-mouse. "Yes, I imagine I'll eat lunch at noon on Wednesday. It's just a normal day. So, I'll have a normal lunch. I also have a meeting."

"A meeting? In or out of the office?"

"It's just a meeting. Regular meeting. Only at lunch. Out someplace. But why is this important to you?" I'm sweating now, and Jayne can smell my fear.

She leans in close. "Your entry-level, proletarian, mundane, servile, lowly, and poorly-paid position doesn't warrant a business lunch. This must be personal." She sits back and makes herself comfortable, contrasting my extreme discomfort. "Does this little lunch meeting include any gymnastics? Say, the sort you might do with, oh, I don't know, Pooh?"

I jump off the couch. "I'm not having sex with him at lunch!"

"Aha! So, you have a date!" She is quite pleased with herself.

"It's not a date. I mean, it's a lunch date. And it's nothing. We're just eating lunch. On a lunch date. I mean, not a date." I'm flustered and making things worse.

"You have a date with Mr. How-Many-Inches and didn't plan to tell me? First, you hide that we have bazillions of dollars available on our credit card, and now this! What has our relationship come to?" She gingerly falls prostrate on the couch, careful not to mess her wig or smear her makeup.

I sit on the floor next to her and breathe deeply. I could put my foot down and assert my independence, but I can't risk upsetting her so she shows up like she did the last time. Tactfulness will be my win.

"This is an important lunch for me. It's the first time Julio and I will talk. Get to know one another. Our whole relationship could hinge on this one hour."

Jayne sits up and composes herself. "That is precisely why you need to consult with Fairy Jayne before you careen headlong into a disaster. Again. I hate to sound like one of those people who knows everything, but I do. If you had followed my advice the last time, you wouldn't have blown an ass hurricane into the face of your donkey-dicked suitor and might now be married and living in a castle somewhere in the Virginia hills."

"That seems a bit dramatic."

"Dramatic? Moi?" She does her best Norma Desmond impersonation. "Maybe if you had a flare for the dramatic, you wouldn't have to worry about a little lunch date. Now, let's make our plans."

"What plans? It's just lunch!"

"Just lunch says the boy. And Pooh is just a 'friend.' We need to plan our strategy."

"There is no *we* in my lunch with Julio. You can't come! I need to do this on my own."

"Where will this lunch-to-which-I-am-not-invited be held?"

"I don't want you to know."

"Dear god! Tell me you're not taking him to a dive where you order at the counter!"

I hesitate. It's definitely one of those places. "Well, yes, orders are placed at the counter. But District Taco is a very hip place to go."

"District Taco? Again, with the Mexican food! Have you told him of your gas problem?"

"What? I don't have a gas problem! Besides, it's just lunch. I can go back to my desk and fart all afternoon if I want. This place is inexpensive and trendy. I thought it would be impressive to take him there."

Jayne thinks for a moment. "You might be right. This could be a good place. If you let him order first, he might pay. Otherwise, he will give you a clear signal that you're splitting the bill. Perfect for a cheap bastard like you."

I hadn't thought of this upside. After spending $2,700 on furniture, I can't afford to pay for his tacos. Or mine.

"You realize this requires new clothes," Jayne says dryly. "Everything you own is so two-months-ago."

"No new clothes. I'll be at work, so he won't expect anything fancy. It'll be casual."

"Fine. I'll continue to think about what you need. We can discuss strategy tomorrow. Right now, it's time for *Wheel of Fortune*." Jayne stretches to a comfortable position, ready to end our conversation.

If I watch TV with her, she wins. There will be plotting and planning until I do precisely what she wants. I must take charge.

"We don't need to discuss strategy tomorrow. I've got this." My confidence may be misplaced.

Jayne swats at the air. "It only takes one look at you to see...."

"I said I've got this," I reply steadily. "This is my lunch date, and I'll wear what I want. More importantly, I'll wear what I can afford. Which is something already hanging in my closet." Jayne looks stunned. "Now the conversation is finished," I continue. "Go ahead and put on *Wheel of Fortune*."

"Well, I never."

Me neither. Until now.

THIRTY-THREE

Say It with Feeling

Jayne insists I cancel my Wednesday lunch because she will need a 24-hour, on-call chiropractor if she spends another minute on the old couch. It's controlling behavior, but I won't let her stop me. Julio and I can find another solution. I text him when I reach work.

Good morning, Mr. Rodriguez!

Hi there, handsome. What up?

I have a little problem with our lunch date tomorrow.

You're not ditching me, are you?

No! I ordered furniture for noon delivery. I have to let them in.

New furniture? Fancy!

Not fancy. Just nice. Could we move our lunch?

What if we meet at your place and I help with the delivery? We could grab a quick bite at Chipotle after.

Is this guy real? He's willing to move furniture on our first date? And get cheap fast food?

Really? You want to help?

Absolutely. Anything for you.

That's so nice. I'll text you my address. See you at noon!

Have a great day, cutie.

My eyes sparkle like an enamored Disney princess waiting for Julio, the perfectly coiffed, handsome knight, to take me to my fairytale life.

The afternoon is a mixture of work and Julio daydreams until Jeremy appears as I'm putting on my coat to leave.

"Hey, Randy. Heading out?"

Oh, lord. He's the last person I want to see. "Yep. I can't wait to get home. It was a long day."

"It was. Mind if I walk with you?"

I have a strange feeling about this. We both catch the subway at Metro Center, so it's not odd that we would walk together. It just hasn't happened before. My sense is there's something else.

"Sure," I say. Yes, I'm avoiding confrontation.

We spend the five-minute walk going over the work day. There's some new gossip about his boss and an intern going around. Another Starbucks may open next door. And I tell Jeremy about the furniture I just bought.

"You know, I've never seen your apartment," he remarks. I guess I gave him the lead-in when I mentioned the furniture.

"It's not much. Certainly not a modern place like yours. And the new furniture won't be there until tomorrow."

"I could swing by now and take a look. Even without the new stuff. I've got nothing going on this evening."

Is he speaking in code? It feels like code. What if he wants a 'practice session?' This is one of those times when Jayne's insight would be helpful.

"I guess you could come by for a few minutes," I reply, not wanting to be rude. I wish I were more assertive. The last time we got together, he had way more fun than I did. And then there's Julio. It will feel weird doing something with Jeremy tonight before seeing Julio a few hours later.

As we approach my door, I realize Jayne will likely be home. How do I explain her to Jeremy? Do I just say, "This is my friend, the gargantuan drag queen?" Or maybe she will hide again and watch us going at it. I hope we don't go at it. Really.

I'm a nervous wreck. I can't think fast enough to change the course of this encounter. I'll tell Jeremy that Jayne is a friend visiting from Minot. Wait. An Amazonian drag queen from North Dakota is staying in my apartment? That sounds ridiculous, even for me.

We stop at my door, and I take a deep breath. "I'm not sure what we'll find when I open the door," I say, trying to prepare him for sequins and Chanel No. 5.

"No worries. I'm not good at keeping my place clean, either. Especially when I'm not expecting a guest."

I make a point of dropping my keys before noisily turning the lock. It's worse than I thought. Jayne isn't home, but her dresses, wigs, and feminine unmentionables are strewn about the living room.

"What's with all the women's clothes?" Jeremy asks. "You have a roommate?" He steps up to a dress that hangs taller than he is.

"Uh, no. Just a friend visiting."

"She must be huge! I've never seen a dress like this." Jeremy is awestruck.

"Yeah. You could say she's tall in the saddle. Anyway, this is where the new furniture will be. You'll just have to imagine it looking better," I say nervously.

Jeremy does a self-guided tour until he reaches the bedroom door.

"Nice Pooh bear."

"He's just a childhood relic. A constant reminder of more innocent days." Pooh gives me a wink.

Jeremy walks in and sits on the bed. Clearly, he planned this moment.

"So," he says with a swagger, "you want to get in a little practice?" His hand moves to his belt and starts playing with the buckle.

"Oh. I didn't know we would be doing that." I try to act surprised and disinterested.

"I thought it was obvious why I came all the way up here."

"Sure. I guess. You said you wanted to see my apartment. Like I said, it's not much."

"Yeah, it's nice," he says quickly. "So, you wanna do this?"

I shift my weight nervously. "You see, I have a lunch date tomorrow. Like, a *date* date. New guy. It would feel weird to do this with you before I see him."

Jeremy gives me a condescending look. "Really? That's not until tomorrow. And it has nothing to do with this. We're just buds." He tries unsuccessfully to hide his frustration.

"It might be fun and all, but I'm not any better than I was the last time." No response. The veiled threat of teeth isn't enough to make him leave. "Anyway, I don't want to do this today. I know it's not cheating. It's not like he's my boyfriend or anything. I just don't feel comfortable. That's all."

"Okay. Uhm. I was just doing this as a favor to *you*. No skin off my back either way." He's clearly miffed. "I guess I'll go then." Jeremy stands and walks to the door. He turns before leaving. "You could have told me before I came all the way up here. It was a huge waste of my time for nothing."

"I'm sorry, Jeremy. I didn't know."

Jeremy walks out the door, angry with me. While I feel bad about it, there's a part of me that's proud I didn't just cave and follow his lead. If only I could have done it sooner.

Jayne bursts from the bedroom at that moment, looking like she was shot from the top of a champagne bottle. "I saw the whole thing!" She's out of breath from running 12 feet.

"Where were you?"

"The closet. Where else?"

"I knew I should have checked there."

"What a dirtbag! He's an arrogant, fucking piece of trash! How can you think he's your friend? And why were you planning to have a little nookie the night before you meet up with Julio? You're just a little slut!"

Does this mean she's mad at Jeremy or at me?

"I didn't plan this! He wanted to walk to the subway. It just went from there. I never planned to do anything with him again after that night in his apartment."

"Well, I'm pleased to hear that. This guy is a grade-A fuck-wad with shit for brains. If I didn't just have my hair done, I would go out there and beat his ass all the way back to Virginia!"

"Thanks for having my back. No need to chase after him."

"You held your ground, didn't you? I'm so proud!" Jayne walks over and gives me a bear hug. "But you should have called him a fucking shithead."

"You know I don't talk that way."

Jayne steps back and wags her finger at me. "This isn't Sunday school, Miss Prim-and-Proper. You need to expand your vocabulary. I'm tired of all these little kid words you use."

"Kid words?"

"Yes! Like wiener. Say penis. Cock. Dick. Schlong. Mr. Happy. Anything but wiener, for fuck's sake!"

"And you also want me to say the F word, I suppose?"

"Fuck the F word! The word is FUCK! Say it!"

"No! I can't say that. I'll say the other words you said, but I can't say the F word."

Jayne is on fire now. She begins screaming at the top of her lungs. "You fucking say fuck, or I'll fucking scream until all of fucking northwest fucking DC tells me to shut the fuck up!"

"I'm not saying that word!" We're yelling so loudly I'm sure the neighbors can hear – and are amused.

"What word?"

"Fu... Oh, shit! I almost said it!"

"Haha! You said shit! You fucking said shit! Randy is a fucking potty mouth!" Jayne dances around in a circle. It's sort of an offensive Native American dance parody combined with disco and hand jive. If I weren't so mortified, I'd film it.

"Quiet down! The neighbors will think I'm a dirty person!"

"The neighbors? Which ones? The ones across the hall who told their dog to take its own fucking walk this morning? Or the ones next door who literally yell 'fuck' when they fuck. Every fucking night." She's glaring at me, determined to win this one.

Deep breath. "If I say it, can we end this conversation?"

"Yes. I want you to say, 'Fucking Mary had a fucking little fucking lamb whose fucking fleece was white as fucking snow.' And say it with *feeling*."

Mother would be so ashamed of me. I take another deep breath and half-whisper, "Fuck."

Jayne falls to the floor, laughing. "That's it? No emotion? No feistiness? Where are the fireworks, glitter, and glamour?"

"FUCK!!!" I scream. We are both stunned to silence.

After about 30 seconds, Jayne picks herself off the floor and smooths her dress. "So, you wanna order Chinese?"

THIRTY-FOUR

Lips and Assholes

"Looks like everyone is punctual," Julio says with a florescent smile. He's waiting with the furniture movers just outside my building.

"Except me," I smile and wave.

The Minot heirloom couch and chair are unceremoniously removed, and the new stuff is delivered. They even place it where *I* want, for a change. The new pieces make the apartment look grown-up.

"West Elm. Very fancy."

"Thanks, Julio." He pats me on the back. "A friend suggested Scandinavian Designs, but it was too expensive. I can barely afford this stuff. Now that it's here, I'm glad I bought it."

"Yeah. It looks great. This makes my place look like a college dorm."

"I'm sure your apartment is beautiful!" I say, trying not to sound hopeful. "This was old family furniture that wore out. Sunday School teachers taught us to put away childish ways once we became men. Maybe the couch was one of my childish things."

"I remember when I bought my first new chair. It was hard

to see the hand-me-down loveseat go, but it was time. I'm happy to be here for your furniture rite of passage." He puts his arm around my shoulder. "Shall we walk to the Woodley Park Chipotle? Lunch is my treat since you spent all your pennies on furniture."

I want to be flattered, but Jayne's voice is in my head: "If the guy pays out, you put out." I don't want our first time to be a quickie in the bathroom after lunch.

"I don't expect you to buy. You were nice to be flexible when I nearly screwed everything up."

"This little outing is my pleasure." He removes his arm from my shoulder as we start up the street.

Julio makes easy conversation on the short walk. I learn he's originally from Brooklyn, New York, has lived on Capitol Hill for two years, and has a degree in business management from the University of Maryland. And he loves his job. He seems like a genuinely happy person.

I get a table while Julio orders our food. The place is small and casual. The only available seats are in the back corner, somewhat private.

"Taco salads and diet sodas for each of us," he says, putting the food on the table. "Seems we like the same things."

"I guess so. Except your soda is my pop."

That makes him laugh. "And your couch is my sofa! We're really from different worlds, aren't we?"

"Yeah, pretty much."

"Just curious. When is your birthday?"

"December 29, 1986."

"You're a Capricorn!" His face takes on a charming glow. "That's perfect. I'm a Virgo. September 8, 1988. Capricorns and Virgos are considered the most compatible. Sounds like a good omen!"

"And you're 31?"

"Yep. I'm an old man. I mean, not quite as old as almost

33, but close." He winks. "To be honest, I don't mind aging. A John Denver lyric said, 'It turns me on to think of growing old.' That's exactly how I feel."

"You like John Denver? He's always been one of my favorites. That lyric's from 'Poems, Prayers, and Promises,' isn't it?"

"Well, you *are* an old man if you know that." I like that he feels comfortable teasing me.

"It's nice to meet someone my age."

Julio cocks his head to the side. "You don't remember, do you? We already met."

"Yeah, I know. But that night at JR's was so fast, it doesn't count."

"No. I'm talking about before that. Around Labor Day." He pauses. "You don't remember me?"

I'm confused. I'd certainly remember meeting Julio. There wasn't anything special about Labor Day weekend.

"No, I don't remember meeting you. Where were we?"

"You physically assaulted – and then insulted – a woman in the Spanish Safeway. I was behind you and heard your terrible Spanish. Something about ordering soup and bread. You made me laugh."

Oh, my god! Yes, there was something with a woman and my poor Spanish that weekend. And some guy told me what I said. He was tall with Tiffany blue eyes. I drop my fork.

"That was you?"

Julio winks. "One and the same. I followed you to the checkout line and tried to get your number, but you ran off. I spent months going back there, hoping we would run into one another again. When you appeared at JR's, I couldn't believe my luck. It felt like fate."

"You've been looking for me ever since September?"

"Yes. Something about you made my heart beat faster. I felt warm all over. It was like love at first sight. I mean, if you believe in that sort of thing." Now he's blushing. "Sorry. I'm sort of a romantic."

"Love at first sight? With me? I don't get it." I should be excited. This gorgeous man just told me he obsessed over me for months. He kept returning to the place where our paths first crossed, searching for me. It's like a fairy tale. But I just don't understand how someone like him would be interested in someone like me.

"El corazón quiere lo que el corazón quiere," he says, staring into my eyes.

"What does that mean? You know my Spanish isn't so good."

"The heart wants what the heart wants."

We sit looking into one another's eyes for several seconds. And my heart beats faster and faster. It's trying to tell me what it wants.

Julio clears his throat. "We should get back to work. I've already taken too long for lunch." He stands and clears the table while I sit, unable to comprehend what just happened.

"Let me walk you to the Metro," Julio offers as he pulls my chair back from the table.

We walk in blissful silence, each contemplating what our little lunch could mean. Once, his hand brushes against mine, accidentally. It might as well have been a live electrical wire for the jolt it sent.

"Here is where we say adiós," he says, taking my hand. "I'm looking forward to our date on Friday night." He kisses the back of my hand, turns, and walks away.

Marcia Brady once was kissed on the cheek by Desi Arnaz, Jr., and she said she would never wash her cheek again. That always seemed ridiculous to me – until now. I can feel his soft, full lips against my skin for the entire afternoon. It's like time stopped the moment he touched my fingers.

My mood is so good that even seeing Jeremy in the hall doesn't bring me down. He is clearly uncomfortable and probably wants to avoid me for as long as possible.

"Hi, Jeremy," I say with a slight smile.

"Hi, Randy. Uh, about last night. I..."

It could be Julio's interest inspired a boost of confidence. Or maybe spending the last couple of months living with a sassy drag queen has rubbed off. Or possibly Jayne finally convinced me to expand my vocabulary. Whatever it is, I find myself controlling the conversation.

"Yes, Jeremy. About last night. Fuck off, you fucking fuck."

And with that, I continue down the hall. Jeremy stands, stunned, and says nothing more. Mother may not be proud of me, but I am. And Jayne will be.

Jayne is lounging Cleopatra-like on the new couch when I get home. She purportedly spent the day at a spa, but I don't see any difference in her wig, clothes, or makeup. Not that I ever notice a difference.

"Welcome home, dear credit-card-holder-in-good-standing!" she sings. "Look how comfortable I am!" She sweeps her arms wide like a *Price Is Right* model introducing the new furniture.

"You must like it."

"It's fabulous. Not a lump, stain, or bedbug anywhere. These tits were meant to be coddled like this." She pops a bonbon in her mouth and licks her fingers like she's in a porn video.

"I prefer you don't eat there, please. It would be nice to keep the furniture in good condition for as long as possible."

"Of course, dear. Let me just finish this last one." She repeats the seductive snacking and tosses the empty box in the general direction of the kitchen. "So, you must have canceled your lunch with Prince Pretty Pants since you were here for the furniture delivery. That, and I coincidentally had lunch at District Taco and didn't see you." She looks so smug.

"As a matter of fact, Julio met me here and helped with the delivery. We had lunch at Chipotle on Connecticut Ave. Too bad. We wanted to invite you along." I shoot back a toothy, fake smile as I watch hers drop slowly off her chin. "Thank you for hiding your wigs and dresses in the closet, by the way."

"You mean you went forward with this foolishness and didn't tell me? I thought I expressly forbid it."

"Forbid? Foolishness? I met an amazing man who gave up our first lunch date to help me with furniture delivery. And then we enjoyed a cheap meal because he wanted to spend time with me. And he touched my hand. And he treated me with kindness. I call that my lucky day."

Jayne snorts. "Well, let's hear the details of how you broke in the couch with your sexual escapades before scarfing down a salmonella-stuffed taco." She pretends to file her nails.

"Nothing happened. He was a perfect gentleman. I swear it was like a Disney movie. In fact, he even bought lunch because I spent so much on the furniture. No sex was required. And he kissed my hand when we had to part." I give her a bright smile. "He's the most wonderful man I've ever met."

"Hmmph. You've run into the guy twice, and now he's your knight in shining armor."

"The funny thing is I met him over Labor Day, and I didn't remember. We talked at the Spanish Safeway, he tried to give me his number, but I ran out."

Jayne waves her hand. "Means nothing. It was a BJ experience."

"What? I didn't do that! It was just a chance meeting at the grocery!"

"Jesus! B.J. *Before Jayne*. Any dating you did Before Jayne doesn't count."

"There was no date! I was buying groceries. And how did

a conversation about me get turned into something about you?"

"Darling, *every* conversation is about me. You should know that by now. Maybe if you had started by asking about *my* day, this whole thing would have played out differently."

"Let me tell you how that would have gone. I'd greet you and politely ask about your day. You would tell me how difficult it was to sit on this new couch – one that had not been properly broken in – and read an outdated issue of *People* magazine for nine hours. And then you would tell me to make us enormous drinks that could tranquilize elephants. And I would follow your commands, pass out in a puddle of my own drool, and miss work again on a Thursday. Sound right?"

"Somebody's sassy," Jayne sneers with a hint of pride.

"Oh, and I told Jeremy to fuck off."

I turn and walk to the kitchen.

"Well, slap my ass and call me Sally. Will there be details with this announcement?"

Ignoring her is the only way to maintain the upper hand. "I'm making hot dogs for dinner. With potato chips. You want any?"

"Hot dogs? Again? You know those are just phallic encasements of the lips and assholes from random animals found dead on the roadside."

"You had me at phallic," I say from the kitchen.

"What?"

"I said, you had me at fucking phallic. Now, do you want a hot dog?"

Jayne breaks into a proud smile. "Touché, bitch! My little pupil is learning!"

I don't let her see my satisfied smile.

THIRTY-FIVE

Existential Questions

Midwesterners rarely need alarm clocks. We awaken five minutes before any alarm could ring to greet the day with a stretch and a smile. This is especially true on the Friday of my first 'real' date with Julio. As consciousness replaces slumber, I snuggle the last warmth from the blankets before opening my eyes. The air is fresh with the scent of something that seems out of place in December. Gardenia? Lilac? Chanel No. 5?

"Are you awake?" Jayne yells in her outdoor voice.

"AHH!" My scream sounds like a small child who just saw a ghost. And Chanel No. 5 is out of place here any time of the year.

Jayne sits on the bed with her face an inch from mine. "I thought you'd never wake."

"What are you doing in my bedroom? It's only 6:00!"

"I came to check on you and thought I saw the tiniest little mouse move under the sheets. Turns out it was – what is that Beatles song? Oh, yes. Morning Wood. I'd call it more of a sapling. A sprout, even. See? It's still there." She pokes my wiener, uh, dick, with her finger.

"Stop it!"

"I'd say he's feeling neglected. He's heard all about this Julio guy, and they haven't met. Poor itsy bitsy little fella."

"We could enjoy a quiet morning if you turn your volume down seven or so notches. How about it?"

"Oh, darlin', these melodious pipes have but one volume. I could sing a rousing wake-up song if you'd like. 'Welcome to the Jungle,' perhaps?"

"What drag queen sings Guns N' Roses?"

"We all have our side gigs."

"I'll pass." I try to sit up, but Jayne has me pinned inside the blanket. "Do you actually have a reason for being in here?"

"Not really. I missed you."

"Very sweet, but we just talked a few hours ago. And now I need to pee." Jayne kisses my forehead and quietly leaves the room. My phone buzzes before I get to the bathroom.

Hey, cutie! We still on for tonight?

Hi, Julio. Yes. We're on.

Great! I made a 7:30 reservation at Ophelia's Fish House. Meet me at the Eastern Market Metro stop at 7:15, and we'll walk from there.

Sounds good. I'm looking forward to seeing you.

Me too! BTW, it's my treat tonight.

Accountants never discuss money in a text.

You're adorable. See you tonight.

Julio Rodriguez thinks I'm adorable. *Adorable!*

My return home is met by Jayne lounging on the couch, flipping through the latest *National Inquirer*. She looks up, contorts her face into something that could be interpreted as a friendly greeting, and raises her martini glass.

"Welcome home, little bean-counter," she says with more musical lilt than usual. "How was the day in the salt mines?"

"I had a great day. But now I need to...."

"Why, yes. My day was fine as well. Thank you ever so much for asking." She looks back down at her magazine. "Could you get mama a refill on this puppy? Dry." She holds out her glass without looking up.

"You finished your first martini already? It's only 5:30."

"Was that my first? I lost count. Well, it *is* cocktail hour. Chop! Chop! I can't be expected to make all the drinks."

Time is tight, but I can quickly mix my friend a drink. I move like someone has pushed my fast-forward button.

"Do I hear you skimping on the vodka?" Jayne yells from her perch. "Real gays keep the drinks stiff and the stiffies stiffer." She cracks herself up with that one.

"You're not joining me?" she asks as I hand her the over-charged martini glass.

"I have to shower and change for my date! There's no time to get drunk first."

"Cheers!" she yells with a slur as I close the bathroom door. "Salut! Feliz Navidad! Bon voyage! Down the hatch!"

This is odd. I poke my head out the door to give her a wary glance. "How much have you had to drink today?"

"That's an existential question with no real answer, isn't it? Sort of like, who made the universe? Or what day is it? Or who let the dogs out? Unanswerable questions."

I'd take care of her if I wasn't in a rush. There's barely enough time to prepare for the most important night of my life, and I don't need to babysit a soused drag queen.

"You noticed it, too?" Jayne appears in the bathroom door-way as I put the finishing touches on my hair. Her cloven hooves never seem to make a sound, ensuring she startles me whenever she approaches.

"Notice what?"

"It's only natural for your looks to fade once you're over 30. I'm just one of the fortunate few who have escaped such tragedy." And another martini bites the dust.

"Can I get out of here without ego-deflating insults to-night? This date is really important to me."

"Suit yourself," she mumbles. "I'd rather have a cat with a stomach virus take a runny dump on my face than ruin your night."

"Thank you, I think. Want to give me a pep talk before I go? I could use your advice for this first date."

Jayne has already returned to the couch, reclined with her eyes closed. "Don't take any wooden nickels." The snores begin almost immediately.

It would have been nice to hear encouraging words before I go, but this will have to do. It almost feels like she's acting this way to sabotage my date. I quietly close the door so as not to wake the great drag one and hear more negativity.

THIRTY-SIX

Tastes Like Chicken

The Eastern Market Metro escalator rises to reveal the magical world of Capitol Hill. Inch by inch, I see a black leather newsboy cap, luminescent smile, Navy pea coat, and black jeans that comprise my handsome date. Somehow, the black clothing and shiny dark hair whimsically floating below the stylish cap draw attention to his impossibly blue eyes.

"Julio!"

"Randy! Welcome to Capitol Hill." Julio hugs me like we've known one another forever.

"It's a different world over here. Am I underdressed?" It feels as though my repeat clothes look shabby compared to Julio's movie star getup.

"Not at all," he says, putting his arm around my shoulder. "You could wear clown shoes and a red wig for all I care. I finally found the man from Safeway, and that's all that's important. Now, shall we make our way to dinner? It's just down the street."

Julio tells me about the neighborhood stores and restaurants as we walk. Little of what he says stays with me because my brain keeps repeating, "I finally found the man from Safeway," in my head. This guy is incredible.

Our server seats us by the window at an intimate corner table with a deep red cloth and a single candle. Julio must have requested the spot by the way the waiter winks at him. It's very romantic. The twinkling Christmas lights hanging outside sparkle on the window and give everything a fairytale glow.

"If you don't mind," Julio says sheepishly, "I'd like to order for us tonight. I've been plotting a romantic meal all week."

"That would be nice. This small-town boy is open to whatever surprises you have in store." Speaking those words makes me feel like an adult, even if I'm not sure I mean them.

Julio orders oysters to start, followed by matching meals: shrimp & crab bisque, Caesar salad, pan-roasted branzino, and the chef's choice dessert. A bottle of New Zealand sauvignon blanc complements his deliberate culinary selections.

"Everything in this meal is new to me," I say with a smile. "Well, I've had shrimp, but the rest is an adventure."

"I'm not sure you can call it adventurous. I'll confess I've had everything before, and the chef prepares them to perfection. I hope you'll like each course."

When the oysters arrive, I look at the slimy blobs of sinus infection and try not to gag.

"These are oysters? Mother kept two cans of them in the pantry for over 20 years planning for a recipe she didn't get around to making. I guess I never saw what was inside the cans. They went in the trash when I moved." Closer inspection does not make the oysters more appetizing. And how did they get the shells into the cans? "These don't look like the pictures."

Julio laughs. "They can be an acquired taste. Are you okay with trying one?"

"I guess."

He picks up an oyster and spoons some sauce on top. "This is called mignonette. It's just vinegar and shallots. I think oysters taste best with it."

"Is a shallot another type of fish?"

He laughs. "No. It's like an onion." He returns to the food lesson while I try to imagine how good onions and raw fish can be. "Now slide the spoon under the oyster to make sure it's disconnected from the shell, and then slurp it up!"

He slides the slimy creature in his mouth, chews a couple of times, and then swallows. The whole thing looks disgusting, but Julio appears happy.

"Am I supposed to chew it?"

"A little, if you want. Some people just swallow. Chewing a couple of times brings out the briny flavor."

I put the oyster in my mouth, chew twice, and swallow. It's definitely a Vitameatavegamin moment. My eyes are squished closed, nose crinkled, lips pursed, and a full-body shudder shakes me from head to toe. To my credit, I don't vomit.

Julio gives me a wary look. "That bad?"

I force a weak smile. "I've had worse."

This is true. As a child, I once ate a 'Tootsie Roll' the neighbor's dog dropped on the sidewalk. Mother never understood why I quit eating candy for nearly eight years.

"It seems people either love or hate them – no middle ground."

"You actually like them?"

"Yeah, I like them. But don't eat any more on my account. I promise the rest of the food will be mainstream. And all of it will be dead."

"Dead? What do you mean? Was the oyster alive?"

"Of course, silly. Didn't you know that?"

I hold the arms of the chair in a death grip, hoping to keep the bile down. "No," I manage to say. "Let's talk about something else."

The wine arrives at that moment. Julio tastes it, tells the

server it's delicious, and we each get a glass. Another first. I've never had wine.

Julio holds his glass up. "A toast. To new food and new friends." We clink glasses.

The wine is slightly sweet with a biting aftertaste. Again, I shudder.

"You don't like the wine?" He looks concerned all his choices will lead to convulsions.

"It's not that. I feel so foolish. You see, I've never had wine. Or oysters. Or bran-muffin fish." Julio laughs. "The tastes are different, that's all." To show my commitment to adventurous eating, I take another sip of the wine. "I think I like this. What's it called? Onion plank?"

He laughs again. "Sauvignon blanc. It's French, but I like the varietal from New Zealand best. We can get something different to drink if you want. What do you usually have?"

"Well, until recently, I only drank lite beer. A couple of months ago, I was introduced to many new drinks, mostly martinis. And I haven't had many of them. I'm not a big drinker, I guess. But I like the wine. Or, I will once I've had more of it."

"That's refreshing. Most of the guys I meet still drink like they were in college. I like to drink to enjoy the flavors. And I like to pair drinks with food. I'm not good at it, but it's fun to try different flavors together and see how they speak to one another." He blushes a little.

"That sounds interesting. You can teach me." There's a little awkward pause as we realize how different we are. "Where are you from?"

"My family is Puerto Rican. They moved to Miami just before I was born, so, technically, I'm from Florida. But we moved to Brooklyn, New York, when I was four, so I think of myself as a New Yorker. I liked DC when I went to the University of Maryland, so I've stayed ever since. What about you?"

I told him about Minot, my parents, and my siblings. It's a short story. He finds it fascinating because North Dakota is as foreign to him as Puerto Rico, New York, and Miami are to me. People who have never been to that part of the country can't imagine the beautiful wildlife and rocky terrain of the upper Midwest. He has a million questions about the people, traditions, food, weather, and anything that comes to mind.

The conversation continues through the bisque (my favorite), Caesar salad (too salty), and branzino (tastes like chicken). It's so easy to talk with Julio. He smiles and laughs more than anyone I know. And he's interested in all the little things about me. My job. My family. My thoughts. It's hard to believe I've known him for less than a week.

As the food and wine disappear, the conversation slows to simple smiles. A short, round man in a white coat interrupts our teenage ogling.

"How was your meal, Julio?" he asks with a friendly pat on the back.

"Chef Gregorio! It was incredible, as always. Chef, this is my friend, Randy. Randy, this is Chef Gregorio Martinez. He made our dinner tonight."

I shake his hand. "I really enjoyed the meal," I tell him.

"Anything for my friend Julio. He told me he was bringing a special guest tonight. I'm happy he shared my food with you."

"Thanks, Chef," Julio says, blushing. "This is the best restaurant in Washington."

"The pastry chef is putting the final touches on dessert, as requested. If I don't eat it myself, your Baked Alaska should be here in just a moment. Now you boys enjoy your evening and come back soon." He pats Julio on the shoulder and walks back to the kitchen.

"You know the chef? I'm so impressed!"

"Full disclosure: I was a waiter here all through college. He was so nice and treated everyone like family. Still does. So, I come here every chance I get."

That's when our dessert arrives. When the server lights the giant white mound afire, I'm so impressed I want to applaud! Julio explains the outer layer is meringue, covering a sponge cake layer, covering a mound of strawberry and vanilla ice cream.

"How did you know I'm genetically required to have ice cream every night?"

He laughs. "That's the potential boyfriend test. Anyone who says no to ice cream is immediately cast aside."

"So, I passed?" It slipped out of my mouth before I could contemplate the ramifications of asking.

"Yes. You passed. More than passed. You're at the top of every list."

We leave the restaurant after two luxurious and filling hours. Julio puts his arm around my shoulder and pulls me close. "Did you enjoy the meal?"

"It was the best! I've never had such good food! Well, except the oysters. Thank you, Julio."

He hugs me tighter. This reminds me that Jayne says I'm expected to have sex if he pays. Even though I'm nervous, I wouldn't think of it as an obligation.

"Well, here's the Metro," he says, walking us toward the escalator. "I had a great time with you, Randy."

"Oh, are we done?" I wonder if he has decided he doesn't really like me. Or maybe he doesn't find me physically attractive.

"I thought about inviting you back to my place. But I don't want to put any pressure on our first date. You know. Take it slow. I really like you, and I don't want to screw it up by making this a physical thing right at the beginning. Is that okay with you?"

His eyes are so blue. And deep. And caring.

"I like that," is all I manage to say.

He hugs me tight and softly kisses my forehead. Somehow – I don't know how – I rode the subway home and found myself in the apartment.

"You didn't spend the night?" Jayne bellows from the living room. She's standing in the middle of the room, holding a fresh martini. "You must have split the tab."

"Jayne!" I wrap my arms around her colossal frame, nearly knocking the drink from her hand. "It was such a magical night!"

"Hope it was better than mine. Right after you left, Davis and I went on a bender – you know how that bitch can knock 'em back. I got bored with her saggy ass when she ran out of gin. Anyhoo, tell me about your date."

"It was an incredible meal. And he knows the chef. And he ordered for me. And I tried oysters, which I didn't like, and white wine, and Baked Alaska. And he kissed my forehead. And he told me we shouldn't ruin the start of our relationship by sleeping together on the first date." I'm out of breath.

"Slow down, turnip. I've never seen you so excited."

"He's my Prince Charming!"

We sit like slumber party girlfriends and talk for two more hours. I tell her everything about Julio, and she just listens and nods. No catty digs at his name or asking the size of his wiener. We just talk until I'm too tired to say another word.

Jayne walks me to my bed and tucks me in, kissing my forehead just like she did the first night I met her. As she walks away, I say, "Good night, my fairy godmother."

All is right with the world.

THIRTY-SEVEN

Adult Relationship

The Washington Metro system is engulfed in sparks and flames just as I leave work. Miraculously, Julio appears at my station on his white stallion, reaches for my hand, and swoops me into his lap.

"I'll get you home, my love," he says in a James Earl Jones voice.

My flowing blond hair whimsically flutters in the wind as we ride the steed up Connecticut Avenue. Hillary Clinton waves from the veranda of her mansion.

"Bill and I are so happy for you, Randy!" she yells. I wave back.

A text ding sounds as we approach Dupont Circle, and the horse abruptly stops.

"I think that's my phone," the stallion says. "Randy, be a doll and read the text to me. This old gray mare just ain't what she used to be, and now I can't see anything without my glasses."

I sit bolt upright in bed, looking for the source of the dinging sound. Only spammers would wake me from beautiful dreams at 7:30 on a Saturday morning. My fists rub the sleep from my eyes as I see the phone is lit with Julio's name.

Good morning, cutie!

What? Jayne and I decided I would be the first to text him today so he could see how much I liked him. True to form, he takes the lead before I have a chance.

Good morning, Julio.

Did I wake you?

Yes. I was dreaming.

Sorry. I tried to hold off, but I couldn't stop thinking about you. Was it a nice dream?

Perfect. I planned to text you this morning. As usual, you beat me to it.

Like I said, I couldn't stop thinking about you. What are your plans today?

No plans.

Great! Want to come on an Exploration Day with me?

What's that?

I like to take days to explore places I've never been to. Today I was thinking of Old Town Alexandria. Have you been there?

No. I would love to see it. When?

Meet me on the Metro Center Blue Line platform at 10. We'll make a day of it.

I'll be there.

Jayne is sitting at the kitchen table as I float from my bedroom. "Good morning, sleepyhead," she says without looking up from her magazine. "Did I hear you texting already?"

"You can hear me texting?"

She looks directly into my eyes. "I hear – and see – all. Don't you forget it." There's a dramatic pause allowing her words to sink in. "What's in your bed that's got you all smiles? Pooh put his paw in your Jockey shorts?"

"Julio texted me. He wants to spend the day exploring

Alexandria." My bowl of Cocoa Puffs looks extra tasty this morning.

"That little whore! He didn't even let you text him first. Is there no decency any longer?"

"Can you believe he likes me so much?"

"Maybe he's a keeper. There's still much to be learned. Remind me, how many inches?"

"I wondered when that would come up." Milk dribbles down my front. I should slow the sugary feeding frenzy. "I told you, I haven't seen him naked or had sex with him. I don't have any idea what's under his clothes."

"No idea?" Jayne puts her magazine on the table, suddenly interested in the morning tutorial. "Haven't you looked for the signs of what's to come, so to speak?"

"What signs?" This is likely to be a long conversation.

"Large hands. Big feet. A significant but not unattractive nose. All these point to a man with a notable appendage. Does he have any of these desirable characteristics?"

I picture Julio but only see his smile. "I don't know. He's tall. I guess his hands and feet are normal for a guy his height. And there's nothing memorable about the size of his nose. Maybe he's just average."

"Tall guy, huh? There's one more certain test. How close is the length of his ring finger to the length of his middle finger? You know, the one I always use to wave hello." She aggressively flips her middle finger in my face.

"I didn't notice the length of his fingers. Why is that important?"

"It's the ultimate test. The closer those two fingers are to the same length, the larger the present in the package. You should look when you see him today." She picks up the magazine and reads as if this were just another normal breakfast conversation.

"Well, I don't care if it's big, small, or average. I just care about him as a person."

She looks over the top of *People*. "You say that until you're face-down in a low-thread-count pillowcase, wondering if he's ever going to put his little pecker in your hungry asshole. Then he suddenly says he's finished, and you're left unsatisfied and messy. Trust me. I know. I dated a guy like that once." Dramatic pause. "Just once."

"I don't understand the obsession with wiener size."

"For fuck's sake! Just say dick size. Or cock size. You're 32 years old and should not be saying wiener anymore. Especially now that every other word out of your mouth is fuck."

"Why do you want me to swear so much?" So much milk has dribbled down my front that I no longer look like an adult.

"Adult relationships require adult vocabulary. Now, repeat after me: Peter Pecker fucked a shitty slut with his goddamned fucking huge cock."

"That doesn't even begin to resemble a limerick. You just strung together as many swear words in one sentence as you could."

"Fuck you. It's early, and I haven't started drinking yet." She abruptly stops, raises her chin, and looks to the ceiling. "Nope. I'm pretty sure I haven't started drinking yet. Or have I? Whatever. Just promise me you won't say wiener in front of Julio."

"Fine. I promise. Can we move on to other things now? I've got to shower and dress for a day with my man."

Jayne gives me a knowing smile and wink that may contain a little encouragement.

Saturday passes with a fairy tale haze and vivid, colorful memories. Lunch at Chadwick's. Shopping at the Torpedo Factory. Snacks at Lavender Moon Cupcakery. A romantic walk through Founders Park. The sun is down before we realize we've spent the entire day laughing and talking.

"Want to go back to the District for dinner?" Julio asks.

"Sure. Any place in mind?"

"Let's go to your neighborhood. We can grab cheap burgers at Town Tavern and maybe stop by Pitchers for a drink."

"I've seen them both from the outside but never been. I guess we can call it a continuation of our Exploration Day."

He takes my hand, and we walk back to the Metro, holding hands the entire way. As we slowly stroll down King Street, I see stars twinkling in the December sky. The full moon was two days ago, but tonight it shines as if it returned to fullness just for us.

"I don't think I've ever seen anyone look happier than you do right now," Julio remarks.

I blush. My lovesick grin must look foolish. "It's been a really nice day."

"For me, too. I feel so comfortable talking with you. And you're interested in me, my work, my family. Most guys just want sex."

"That's not me. I mean, it would be great to do that. But I like having someone to talk to. You know, a person who just wants to be with me, no matter what we do. I think my parents were that way. It's a nice way to live."

We stop at the Metro entrance, and Julio turns to face me, taking both of my hands. "I like being with you, Randy Larson. And I like hearing your thoughts and dreams. It just feels right."

Our eyes are locked, emotions warming my entire body. It's like I'm aware of every beat of my heart. And then Julio leans in and kisses me. A gentle, soft kiss that reveals everything about him. It lasts only a couple of seconds before he pulls back and smiles to tell me we feel the same things.

Our hands remain clasped until we reach Town Tavern.

There aren't many people at the bar, probably because it's early. Better for us. We get seats at a table and order our burgers: classic with bacon for me and Southwest for Julio. Whenever I walk past this place, it's full of loud people, sometimes spilling into the street. The quieter atmosphere allows us to talk without shouting.

We chat and slowly sip lite beers until we both realize the bar is full, and we are shouting to hear one another. My watch says it's already 10:00. We've been at this table for three hours!

"Let's get out of here," Julio suggests.

I now have a dilemma. My apartment is only a block away, and Pitchers is just next door. I'm tired from the long day but don't want to leave Julio just yet. Do I invite him back? Do we go to another noisy bar?

"This has been a perfect day, Randy, but I'm beat. Do you mind if I just hop the subway home and we call it a night?"

My Prince Charming made the decision – the right decision – for us. "I'm good with that. I'll probably fall asleep before I even get undressed!"

"Want to do brunch tomorrow?"

"Yes!"

"I'll text you in the morning, and we can decide on a place then. So, I guess it's adiós." He pulls me close for a repeat of our earlier kiss before turning to walk away. His long-legged strides hold my attention until he is absorbed into the sidewalk crowd. Somehow, I find my way home.

Jayne is lounging on the couch with a martini when I walk in. "You were certainly gone a long time."

"Hi, Jayne. Any drunken debauchery tonight?"

"You don't know the half of it!" She sits upright, feet on the floor, leaning in to ensure proper dramatic flair. "It all started early this afternoon. Marilyn was on her tenth vodka tonic when Davis finally arrived at Mr. Henry's. That's when the drinking *really* started! Monroe got so wasted she couldn't maintain an upright position, and I don't mean that in the positive way. Her nice, shimmering pantyhose were full of holes and runs by the time she stood on the bar to replay the subway vent scene from *Seven Year Itch*. Poor thing! She didn't realize the rips had opened a window into her nether regions. The bitch pulled the dress over her face, and the whole bar saw her ding-a-ling!" Jayne doubles over, laughing hysterically.

"Oh, no! She must have been so embarrassed!" I laugh with her.

"She would have been if she wasn't three sheets to the wind. Davis and I had to pull the bitch down and carry her home. I swear on a stack of *Vogue* magazines, it was the teensiest little fuckin' pee-pee I've ever seen. And I've seen yours!"

I laugh with her while self-consciously adjusting my crotch. "Did you stay and nurse her the rest of the night?"

"Hell, no! Davis and I got her to bed and then went back out to another bar. The rest is a little fuzzy. A Secret Service agent may have been involved, so I got home early." She relaxes into the cushions and swigs her martini. "Did you have a good day with Prince Pretty Pants?"

I just give her a stupid grin and nod my head.

Jayne sits up straight and slowly puts her martini on the coffee table. "Well, fuck me. Randy's in love."

THIRTY-EIGHT

Adult Decisions Come with Adult Consequences

"Should I have the chef make us some cheesy scrambled eggs?"

"*I'm* the chef, Jayne." We both roll our eyes.

"Have it your way. But also make us some cheesy scrambled eggs." Jayne makes herself comfortable on the couch.

"I'll pass. I'm meeting Julio for brunch. He's going to text the details. I'll have coffee with you, though."

"Hmmph." Jayne stands, dramatically smooths her gown, and does an exaggerated runway walk to the kitchen. I know my lounging time is over. Either I get up and join her, or I'll be the target of verbal assaults all day.

Jayne silently stares at me until I finish my coffee. She probably feels the quiet is doing me a favor. Still, an FBI interrogation is more uncomfortable when no one asks questions. I sense an interrogation coming.

"Do you have plans today?" I ask, trying to re-establish our version of normalcy.

"Oh, I don't know. I could hang out with Joan. That is if I want to hear the bitch talk about herself all day." She sighs.

"None of my friends are as unselfish as I am. It's tiring, I tell you."

"You *are* a giver."

She lowers her head and gives me the stink eye. "Was that an unprovoked attack on my character? You've become feisty these days, and I can't tell when your comments are innocent anymore."

"If I've become feisty, it's because I learned from the best," I say, winking at her. She manages a self-satisfied smile. "From now on, I'm not taking shit from anyone."

"Well, that's quite the potty mouth for a Sunday morning. You even pronounced shit correctly."

Julio interrupts our conversation with a text.

Good morning, handsome man!

Hello! I've been waiting to hear from you. I'm starved!

Starved, huh? It's only 8:30. Who eats this early on Sunday?

This guy! Where do you want to meet?

I'm getting together with some friends from college this afternoon, so I can come your way. How about Open City at 10:30?

Where is it?

Calvert and 24th. Near the hotel. You can walk there.

Got it. I'll see you at 10:30.

I'll be the guy with his heart on his sleeve and his eyes on you.

"That's so corny! Send him an eye roll emoji." Jayne is behind me, reading the texts as if they were for her.

"I think it's sweet. And maybe you could ask before reading my personal messages?"

She throws her hands up. "Well, I hope he's not after your money, or there's going to be a rude awakening!" She pauses a moment and gets a serious look. "You really like this one, don't you?"

"Yeah," I say quietly, feeling myself blush. "I've had crushes on guys before, but this feels different. More like an adult."

"Adults have sex, missy. Until you check that box, you can't call it an adult relationship."

"Your mind has only one track. Adults have deep conversations, too."

"Fine." Jayne takes out an imaginary paper and pen. "I'll check the box for 'oral,' but only because you stretched the definition." She sits in her chair. "What do you talk about?"

"Everything. Our jobs. Family. What we want to do with our lives. Our favorite foods and music. He's an easy person to be with."

"Do you talk about me?" She looks away, pretending to be demure.

Oh, boy. This has never come up. I don't talk about her with other people, probably because she's challenging to encapsulate in words.

"Uhm, no. I've mentioned a friend named Jayne, but that's it. He doesn't know you're staying here right now."

She pauses and looks to the ceiling. "That's probably for the better. This tall drink of fabulous can be a big shock to the average person."

I turn my back long enough to refill my coffee when I hear the distinctive texting sound. "What are you doing?!" I scream.

Jayne is holding my phone, texting faster than I imagined possible. "You're going to lose this one if you keep up the junior high school romance. I just helped you become an adult couple." She hands me the phone.

Want to get in a quickie before the food comes?

"You sent this to Julio?" I'm shocked, embarrassed, and immediately angry. "Everything has been perfect! Why did you fuck it up?"

"Nice vocabulary!" I ignore her attempt at a high five.

"With my help, you'll have him slobbering on your little knob before the eggs can get scrambled."

"No! That's not what I want!"

My phone dings. *You want to have sex this morning? At the diner?*

There are cartoons where a character turns red from the toes up until he explodes with steam from his ears. That is me right now.

Jayne snatches my phone and texts before I can stop her. *Just a quick blowjob in the bathroom. Can't wait!*

Julio immediately responds. *This is what you want? I thought we would save that for a special night.*

I grab my phone and read the exchange. "JAYNE! How could you do this?" I'm sobbing. "My whole relationship is ruined!"

Jayne remains calm. "It's only ruined if he doesn't swallow. Now get in there and wash your willy thoroughly." She takes a sip of her coffee as if this calamity has never happened.

"This was a spiteful act, Jayne Mansfield. All you ever do is sabotage me! Whenever I meet a guy, you're hiding in the closet or eating at the next table. You give me bad advice. Spend all my money. Sleep on my couch. I don't understand how we got to this point!" My face is covered with tears, and I'm out of breath. All the pent-up questions and anger have exploded at once.

Jayne sits up, smooths her dress, and crosses her legs. "Let me start, Mr. Larson." She pauses for effect. "When I met you, a friendless, skanky imitation of a drag queen, you couldn't even order your own drink. Lord knows if you *had* been able to order a drink, it would have been house vodka. *House!*" She pauses to shudder at the thought of drinking such swill. "I introduced you to my posse and proceeded to spend months nurturing you. Suckled you at my very own bosom, I did. I gave up everything to take care of you. And for what? An ungrateful tongue-lashing following a sincere attempt to help your love life! The indignity of it all!" She rapidly fans herself.

"I never asked you to do anything for me. In fact, I never invited you to stay in my apartment. Or drink my alcohol. Or eat my food. You just barged in here, called yourself my fairy godmother, and proceeded to ruin every aspect of my life! Everything was fine before *you* got here. I've been too wishy-washy to confront you. Somehow, I became a doormat that you walk on. What am *I* getting out of this?" I collapse into the chair.

"Miss Randy, you've been a child for 32 years. Your mother and father took care of everything – from your subsidized housing, to your public education, to your dull and predictable social life – right up until they died. And you let them. When you moved here, you even let MJ arrange your apartment, which was dreadful, by the way. *Dreadful!* You waited for someone to step forward to be your friend. That never happened, did it? Until I came along. When have you ever taken responsibility for your own life?"

I sit there, allowing the words to sink in. Everything she says is correct. Harsh but accurate. What have I ever decided on my own? When I sold everything in Minot and moved here, I thought I was stepping into a new phase of life. But maybe I just took the old me into a new place. Instead of Mother making decisions for me, I have Jayne. And I've returned to being the same child who lives with his parents, letting them decide his life.

My whole body trembles as I know what I have to do. "You need to leave," I say quietly and calmly.

Surprise paints Jayne's face. "Leave, huh?" She stands and smooths her dress. "That's probably a good idea. I'll go hang out with the girls for a few hours until you cool down." She pauses. "Remember, adult decisions come with adult consequences."

I can't find a voice to speak, so I just nod. Jayne grabs her purse and walks silently out the door.

My good mood comes to an end, and the quiet of the room envelops me.

Jayne succeeded in killing my good mood almost before the day started. I don't know what to say to Julio after those texts, but I think it's best done in person. And I kicked my best friend out of the apartment – for good reason! – but I regret it anyway. I credit Jayne for kicking my ass and moving me toward adulthood. She also gets credit for all my hangovers and failed dates. And what if I lose Julio?

My mind is in overdrive when I arrive at the diner. Julio is waiting at a small table just inside. He looks unsure and scared.

"Good morning, Randy."

"Julio, I'm so sorry for those texts. That wasn't me."

Add confusion to his look. "Wasn't you? Who was texting from your phone?"

I sit across the table and sigh. "It was my friend, Jayne. She thought the relationship was moving too slowly and wanted to move it along. I'm sorry. I don't want to have sex with you."

Add disappointment to his look. "You don't want to have sex with me?"

"No! That's not what I meant. I mean, I don't want to have sex in a diner bathroom. Our first time needs to be special. We both agreed on that. It will happen when it's meant to be."

His face brightens. "So, we're not going to do a quickie in that disgusting bathroom over there?"

"No, we're not. You okay with that?"

"More than okay. I thought those texts seemed out of character." He walks to my chair and gives me a hug. "Is it weird that I've missed you these last 12 hours?"

"Yes, it's weird," I tease him. "But it's also the sweetest thing anyone could say."

We order brunch and return to conversations from yesterday as if we've known one another for years. He tells me about renovations at the hotel, a concert he wants to see at The Kennedy Center, and articles he read in the *Washington Post*. I tell him about John Blackstone's story this morning on shipping costs and a new regulation I learned this week that will likely double my workload. Then the conversation turns to Christmas.

"What are you doing for the holidays?" Julio asks me.

"No plans. I thought one of my siblings might invite me to spend it with them, but I haven't heard anything. That's not really a surprise, I guess. Last year I spent Christmas Day at my friend Millie's house, playing with her three kids and watching old Christmas movies. I'll probably still do the movie part this year but in my own apartment. What about you?"

"My parents want me to stay with them in Brooklyn for a few days. I'll go up there on the 24th and probably come back on the 29th. I may see some friends, but it will mostly be a quiet time with my parents."

"That sounds nice. Will they have a live tree? We always drove into the woods and cut our own tree right up to the year my parents died. I miss that tradition."

"Yeah. We get a real tree from the lot around the corner and decorate it together on Christmas Eve. It's a long-standing family ritual that goes back several generations."

"Nice."

"About that." Julio shifts uncomfortably in his chair. "I was wondering if you would like to come with me. You know. Spend Christmas with my family?"

"Meet your parents? Aren't we supposed to be dating for a while before that happens?" I'm so shocked I can't close my mouth after speaking.

"We're not announcing an engagement or anything!" Julio laughs. "I really like you. Having a few days together will give us a chance to get to know one another better. My parents are chill. They'll welcome you like you're a part of the family. Besides, they'll pass all their judgments in Spanish, so you won't know what they're saying." He winks. "And I can show you around my neighborhood. Maybe take you into Manhattan to see the Christmas lights."

"I've never been to New York."

"It's a better experience when you have a personal tour guide. What do you say?"

I thought the decision to move to Washington was a big one. And I've been cocky about my recent arrival to adulthood. But this seems more significant than everything else I've experienced my whole life. Meeting the boyfriend's parents. Vacationing in New York. Shouldn't I think about this for a few days before deciding?

"Uhm, sure. It sounds like fun." Apparently, my mouth had already made the decision. So why is it still hanging open?

Julio looks so happy he could burst. "Excellent! Oh, and one more thing. I thought we could maybe have a sleepover on Tuesday at my place. You know, get better acquainted before our road trip. You good with that?"

The rest of our brunch is a blur. I'm confident I answered his question about the sleepover. And I probably participated in some conversation for the remaining 30 minutes of our time together. Somehow, I walked home, though I don't remember a single step. This is the day my life truly changes.

THIRTY-NINE

Unconditional Acceptance
Is Dangerous Stuff

It's a rare occasion when I have an entire afternoon alone in my apartment. After the lows and highs of the morning, it's best that I keep busy with cleaning, laundry, and some reading. My emotions alternate from guilt for yelling at Jayne to excitement for the trip to New York.

The phone rings around 8:30. It's MJ. We haven't spoken since our August road trip, and I can't say I've missed her. The conversations around dating, sleeping arrangements, and other persnickety things left a bad taste in my mouth. But, she's been a life-long friend. I decide to answer just to see if there's an emergency.

"Hello, MJ," I say with the enthusiasm of a man greeting his colonoscopy doctor.

"Hi there, Randy!" The excitement in her voice feels oppressive. "It sure has been an age since we talked. Is life treating you well?"

"Some days are better'n others. I can't complain." This would have been a good time to tell her about Julio. Or Jayne. However, I'm not interested in another lecture about sins and sinners and how I should maintain celibacy. Besides, saying "I can't complain" is the Midwesterner's equivalent of an entire afternoon of conversation.

"Good to hear! I just got home from our annual Christian Singles Mingle, Ringle, and Jingle Christmas party and thought of you. That, and I'm all hopped up on Sprite. Lately, I've had a little drinking problem."

If this is a drinking problem, I wonder what she would think of my new friends.

"I'm not sure you can call excessive Sprite intake a drinking problem." I'm not in the mood for a tedious conversation. "So, what made you think of me?"

"Well, I sat next to Mark Horndecker as we played Old Testament Jeopardy, and we got to talking. You remember him? The kid from first grade who ate so much paste he had to have surgery for the bowel blockage. He's still single if you can believe it. And he makes good money as a stock boy at Walmart! I might consider dating him if it weren't for that mole near his left eye that looks like a woman's body part."

"Yeah, I remember that. Creepy."

"Isn't it? Anyhoo, he asked about you. Wondered if you still go to church now that you're in the big city. I said I don't know. So, I decided to call and ask."

"I thought you might have an emergency or something important."

"No, I'm fine. Just wondering about your church attendance and eternal salvation."

Here we go. "Uhm, no, I haven't been to church since I got here. Picking the right place is kind of a big decision, and I don't want to rush into it. I, uhm, thought about trying the Unitarian Church. But I haven't made any decisions."

"Unitarian!? Are you crazy? Those people don't believe in anything! All that unconditional acceptance and do-whatever-you-want attitude is dangerous stuff. It's a cult, just like Judaism."

"What? Judaism?" I feel my anger rising for the second time today. "I work with several Jewish people, and they hold many solid beliefs."

"Except for the divinity of our savior, Jesus Christ. Kinda hard to overlook that one."

"Yes, except for that. But you can't call them a cult just because they don't follow the New Testament. Besides, you remember Jesus was a Jew, don't you?"

"Of course, he *was*. Then he realized it was a cult and decided to create his own religion where he was the divine being and sole path to salvation."

"You realize that's the *literal* definition of a cult."

I've heard people have several defining moments in their lives. Like learning you're adopted. Or discovering you have cancer. This is emerging as one of mine – probably the second one today. In the past, I would have let MJ's comments roll off me like water off a duck's back. I just took it as harmless talk. She was never challenged, and she never learned. Today, I can't let her words stand. Maybe it's Jayne's influence, or just being around educated city people, that is pushing me to call her on the awful things she's saying.

"Randy Larson! How dare you compare Jesus to a cult leader? That's blasphemy!"

"Don't you think other religions would consider your words blasphemy? I've heard you say every denomination and sacred practice belongs to a cult if it isn't part of your conservative Lutheran tradition. I don't know much about Buddhism, but I don't think they blindly follow a single leader like Christians do." I'm on a roll and can't stop. "The same goes for the Jews. And I don't think all Catholics are going to hell just for repeating a Hail Mary or two. What you're saying is simply hurtful and untrue."

"Well, I never! I don't know what's happened to you in that place, but the Randy Larson I know wouldn't denigrate the name of Jesus like you just did! Mark Horndecker won't be happy to hear this!"

"I didn't denigrate Jesus. I'm just saying there are many perspectives out there, and you shouldn't be passing judgment on them without looking at your own truths."

There is a long silence where I think I hear MJ wiping away tears. I almost feel bad for upsetting her. Almost.

"Randy, I will say this only once. And you know I say it with a heart full of Christian grace and love. The big city has turned you into a dirty, blaspheming heathen, and you need to come home to Minot, where we can set you straight again. And I mean that in every sense of the word."

Enter the moment of definition. Not only is she a bigot, but she still looks down on me for being gay. There is no way to rectify this situation. And, quite frankly, I don't want to find one. I ponder the consequences of what I'm about to say for a brief second before taking a deep breath.

"Well, MJ, thank you for your call and your concern. You have been my friend since childhood. Now, as they say, it's time to put away childish things. I'm sorry I can't share my growth with you and have you celebrate it with me. It's probably best this be our last conversation. Take care, MJ."

I hang up the phone, releasing decades of tension in one massive exhalation. I don't feel sad, guilty, or regretful. I simply feel free. And tired.

Monday is a series of texts with Julio interrupted by some occasional work. Did I sleep well? (Sorta.) What am I having for lunch? (Tuna salad.) Don't bother to bring pajamas on Tuesday night. (Won't I get cold?) What do I want to see in New York? (Times Square.) His mother is so excited to finally meet one of Julio's boyfriends. *One* of? I don't ask for clarification on that one.

I'm greeted by an empty apartment at the end of the long day. My anger has subsided, replaced by regret. Yes, Jayne is bossy, rude, arrogant, vulgar, and an incurable drunk. But, she has taken care of me for two months, and I think I'm better because of that. I wish I hadn't told her to leave. There have to be better ways to discuss our strange relationship.

As I'm taking the last bite of another bland hot dog, the door bursts open to reveal my drag queen in shining sequins.

"Jayne's home!" she yells. "Was I gone long enough?"

I run to give her a hug. "Too long. I'm sorry I told you to leave," is muffled by her enormous breasts in my face.

"We all make mistakes. Water under the bygones, that's what I say." We settle on the couch. "Tell me about your brunch with Prince Pretty Pants! I want all the details. *All.*"

"Let me make drinks, and I'll tell you everything."

"No, honey, *I'll* make drinks – Mansfield surprise. I planned to abstain for the night to rest my liver – the poor thing has threatened to strike if I keep up my current pace – but it feels like a special occasion."

I recount the brunch details when Jayne returns with large, colorful, and tasty drinks. "And we ended with two pieces of big news."

"He has a twin brother, and they want to do a three-way?"

"Very funny. First, he invited me to spend the night tomorrow. He's going to make dinner...."

"... and then you're both going to cook!"

"Looks like it. He told me not to bring pajamas."

"You dirty whore! He cooks *and* polishes your candlestick!" She fans herself rapidly. "Does he have a brother? Doesn't even have to be a twin."

"No, he doesn't have any siblings. But I'm going to meet his parents. He's taking me to Brooklyn for five days over Christmas!"

She stares with her mouth agape. My smile feels out of place as the silent pause drags on. Did I say something wrong? My facial muscles begin to sag along with some of my enthusiasm.

After an eternity of clown-faced silence, Jayne clears her throat and smooths her perpetually perfect red dress. "That's quite the development." She won't look me in the eye. "Sometimes people date for years before getting an invitation to the holidays. This relationship is moving quite fast. Julio must be smitten, kitten."

My smile is now gone. "Uhm, I guess he is. I mean, we are. I feel the same. Isn't this a good thing?"

"Of course, it is. My little Randy is growing up right before my eyes. I didn't see it coming, so I'm slightly off-balance."

"If I'm growing up, the credit goes to you. All the lessons, the teasing, the encouragement to break out of my shell. That was you. I just took your advice, and the rest fell into place."

Jayne clears her throat. "No, the credit goes to you. You've put up with all the shit I've thrown at you. The growing up part was despite me, not because of me." Jayne's face looks a strange combination of sad and proud. There's a little moisture collecting in her eyes that she wipes away brusquely. "I'm sorry I was so rough on you."

We sit quietly, her last words hanging in the air. I want to dismiss the apology, as we Midwesterners tend to do, but I can't. I needed to hear it. Those eight words changed our relationship, putting us on nearly equal footing. And now I don't know what to do with this new development.

We turn on some movie, but I'm not watching. Jayne. Julio. MJ. Furniture. Sleepover. Christmas. Parents. Boyfriend. Is this what independence looks like? Apartment. Work. Did I finally find my place in the DC world? Debt. Subway. Sex. Have I succeeded in becoming the self-sufficient adult Mother hoped I would so many months ago?

I call Jayne my fairy godmother, but she's more like Glinda the Good Witch. She helped me to see what I already had in front of me.

FORTY

A Quick Overview

Jayne assists with packing for my overnight trip like Mother used to. She picks out my clothes, fixes my hair, and ensures the duffel bag has everything necessary for a night at Julio's. Two pairs of clean underwear: one for tomorrow and one for an unfortunate bowel discharge she believes is in my near future. Toiletries, clothes for work tomorrow, and enough condoms and lube to open my own sex store.

"Don't forget to do some limbering stretches before jumping on the hobby horse," Jayne instructs. "Nothing like pulling a groin muscle while having your groin muscle pulled!"

I have to laugh at that one. "Hey, I'm not going to find you in the window or closet again, am I?"

"No, kitten. I won't be following you. I think you're in good hands."

She kisses my forehead and pats my butt as I leave the apartment. I mean, ass. She pats my ass. I like having the attention and support. And, yes, I can see how weird it is.

Finding Julio's place is an event in itself. He lives about six blocks from the Eastern Market Metro stop on Walter Street,

303

SE, one of the shortest streets in DC. After 30 minutes of wandering about the neighborhood, taking one wrong turn after the next, I finally ask for assistance from a friendly gentleman in a stylish driving cap. I'm not sure, but he looks like the leather Santa who fed me drinks at the DIK Bar. He tells me I'm already on Walter Street, and I didn't know it.

Julio rents the narrow, two-story home from a retiree who moved to Florida. The small front porch and miniature lawn comprise the fairytale place I can picture us sharing. I stare dreamily at the rocking chairs I imagine will grace our future home before finally making my way to the door.

"I don't see why I need to know any of these boring details," Jayne insists as she sips her martini. I'm excited to tell her everything from the previous night's adventure, but she has little patience for the mundane. "He has a house so small you couldn't find it, and you met Santa Claus rocking on the porch. Blah, blah, blah. Let's fast-forward to the action. By the way, Davis wants an answer to her inches question."

"You could at least pretend to be interested. Yesterday was the biggest day of my life, and I want to share every detail with you." I immediately realize the folly of that statement. "Well, maybe not *every* detail."

"Of course, poodle. I'm all ears for your fascinating story. Now, tell me again, was the second floor above or below the first floor? And it had how many years left on the siding warranty?"

"Fine. I'll skip some of the minutiae. You have to know, though, he's an incredible cook. He made squid ink linguine with clam sauce that looked so gross I didn't think I could eat it. Then, surprise! It was amazing!"

"Inked clams? I see where this is going. He fed you pasta made from octopus jizz and covered it with sea critters that look like puckered assholes. It's obvious his mind was on something other than food."

I shake my head and determine there is no appropriate response. "By the way, I don't think your wine recommendation was good. I bought what you said, and I even paid less than five dollars. Good bargain. We each had one sip of it before Julio suggested we set it aside and try one of his. I think I saw him dump the rest of the bottle down the drain."

"What did you buy? I don't remember saying anything specific."

"I went to Trader Joe's and got the Charles Shaw merlot as you said."

"Jesus Fucking Christ! It's a wonder you both didn't die! I said *anything except Charles Shaw*. Except! Russian spies use that to poison their enemies. It is often employed to remove tacky wallpaper from the 60s! I hear the military dropped it on Vietnam in place of Napalm." She shudders and nearly spills her drink.

"Julio probably agrees with you. I'll take the note for next time."

"Let's move this news report along. You ate sexually explicit food and drank shitty wine. Got it. Honestly, you must learn how to tell a more engaging story. I want to hear about the pony ride."

"You're skipping over the best part," I insist. "We talked for over four hours before any of the other stuff. He was so interested in me. *Me*! He asked about my friends, childhood memories, life in Minot, family traditions, and what I dream about. Everything! He really wants to get to know me."

"That's a big change from wham-bam-thank-you-ma'am. In my experience, the ones who talk so much are covering for other inadequacies. Maybe – someday – you'll get to that part of the story." She rolls her eyes and tries to appear interested. "Does it feel like you have things in common?"

"Yes! He doesn't use social media much because he likes to connect with people on a personal level. And he was raised

Catholic but feels it's time to move away from the church. And, even though he grew up in New York, he still thinks it's an adventure to ride the subway. All of this is so me!"

"And he's not bothered that you masturbate to mathematical equations?"

I tilt my head and give her the side-eye. "He's fascinated by my job, thank you very much. And it's not like I do anything interesting. His work is full of stories about crazy people. I thought he would be bored with the government regulations and strings of numbers I look at all day. Not so!"

"How many boyfriends has this Romeo had? Hmmm? Guys who look like Julio leave a trail of broken hearts behind them."

"That's the thing. None. I mean, he's dated and all that. But his longest relationship was three months. He thinks people use him for his body—"

"Not that there's anything wrong with such a thing." She wags her finger in my face.

"Fine. I suppose. But he wants more. He wants to sit on the couch and watch movies. And talk about politics. And take long walks to watch the sunset. He's a romantic."

"Romantic, huh? No offense, but you aren't much the romantic sort. Not unless you consider changing the TV remote batteries a romantic gesture. Oh, and that reminds me, we're out of vodka."

I think for a moment. "You're probably right. I'm more of a pragmatist. That doesn't mean I wouldn't like a romantic to balance me out. Midwesterners don't expose our soft spots so easily."

"Speaking of soft spots...."

"You're not going to give me any privacy in the bedroom, are you?"

"Nope."

"Okay, then, just a quick overview. I told him the details of my limited experience, and he said he's nothing like those other guys. And it's true. He asked me what I wanted to do. What *I* wanted! And then he showed me how to do all that – and more – in a way that felt like he really cared."

As soon as I said "overview," Jayne started filing her nails. She wants to look disinterested, but I know she's listening to every word.

"Inches?" she insists, not looking up. "I'm asking for a friend."

"Well, he's smaller than Derek but larger than I am."

Jayne looks up and rolls her eyes. "Oh, for the love of Charles Nelson Reilly! You're saying he's somewhere between a mini Tootsie Roll and the Empire State Building?"

"That's fair."

"Davis is going to be pissed. You know she likes to get a mental picture of things. Don't think this is the last time you get asked this question."

"He's my boyfriend, and there are some things only I should know."

"Boyfriend? I guess we have moved out of the kiddie pool, haven't we?"

"Oh, Jayne!" I say like Annette Funicello in a beach movie. "I know I shouldn't go too fast, but he's perfect! We have enough in common without having everything in common. And he makes me smile. He cares about me in a way no one ever has."

"Present company excepted, I assume."

"Of course. But you know what I mean. I think I could be very happy with him."

"That's all we can ask, now, isn't it, kitten?"

We sit for a moment staring at one another before she grabs the remote and turns on the TV. "What say we watch Judy Garland tonight?"

"I'm good with that."

FORTY-ONE

May Your Tits Always Point to the Sky

Julio and I planned for Thursday night dinner, our first date since the sleepover. Unfortunately, the Omni's banquet manager came down with the flu, requiring Julio to cover a big event. He apologized repeatedly and promised to make it up to me. I'm disappointed, though I know we'll soon have five travel days to enjoy one another's company. I can spend a night at home with Jayne.

It's nice to know my new boyfriend is important.

"Would there be a world in which we have something other than hot dogs for dinner?" Jayne complains. "I saw a package of ground beef in the refrigerator that has started reassembling itself into a cow. Maybe we should cook it up? And by 'we,' you understand I will supervise from a respectable distance."

"Good idea! I could add it to a box of Hamburger Helper. You have a preference on which one? I've got bacon cheeseburger, cheesy ranch, cheddar cheese melt, and double cheeseburger."

My childhood consisted of weekly Hamburger Helper feasts.

Mother served only the original flavor, and it's been my comfort food ever since. I don't really care what the ingredients are; it tastes like love to me.

"Cheap, spoiled ground beef covered in powdered, imitation cheese? And there's a choice of seasoning? Heavens! Each flavor is a dry heave better than the last." She makes a condescending sound that crosses between a sigh and a cluck. "Make whatever you want. I suddenly remembered this was day one of my all-vodka diet. You have the cheese-ish cow extravaganza, and I'll make do with a geyser of Grey Goose."

As we each consume an extra-large portion of our chosen meal, Jayne anxiously wiggles in her chair. I can tell something is bothering her.

"Are you okay?" I ask while chewing my last delicious bite.

"Oh, puppy, we need to talk." She sits up and smooths her dress.

"What is it?" I have a terrible feeling. Jayne never says anything with such a serious tone.

She stands, lightly touches her perfect hair, and expertly adjusts her bosoms. "Why don't we retire to the living room and have a little chat."

I follow her to our usual seats, she on the couch and me in the chair. Something seems wrong, and I restlessly fidget with my shirt cuffs. "You're making me nervous," I tell her.

"No need to get your cheap knickers in a twist. Lord knows your BVDs are one fart away from disintegration. I just think we need to make a change."

"Change? You mean like you'll cook, clean, and pay for things while I sit on the couch?"

"I said change, not annihilation." Jayne clears her throat. "This little love fest has been peachy, but I must take my leave."

"Leave? You're leaving?"

She takes a deep breath. "It's not like I'm dying or anything.

Your little tirade on Sunday got me thinking about your open-ended invitation to live here."

"Open-ended?"

Jayne cocks her head. "Call it poetic license. Anyhoo, it's probably best I spend some more time in my own place and let you have some space. A little distance could be good for us. Besides, Julio will move in any day now, and I'll never have hot water for a shower."

The revelation stuns me to silence. How many times have I thought she should leave? I can't afford to keep buying her food and alcohol, and she doesn't contribute to any of my expenses. There's never any privacy. I wouldn't mind having a living room free of sequins and wigs. All this is true. And what if Julio and I start living together? How does Jayne fit in? Would we be a thruple?

At the same time, Jayne is the first gay person to take me under her wing. I might have never met Julio if it weren't for her encouragement – forced compliance? – to get out of my shell. I've grown fond of her, and I'll miss her company.

"Well? Are you going to say anything?" Jayne impatiently asks, tapping her nails.

"When will this happen?"

"Oh, I don't know. Could be next week. Could be five minutes from now. A girl needs to be spontaneous."

"Where will you go?"

"Back to my place, of course."

"You have a place?" I assumed she was homeless.

"Where do you think I go every day? I can't sit in this shithole 24-7, hoping my hepatitis vaccination still works. I have a place."

Now I'm less concerned about her leaving than getting more information about this vodka-soaked enigma. "I don't know what you do all day. Or where you came from. I really don't know anything about you. Maybe you could give me a little back story before you go?"

Jayne sighs. "Fine. There's not much to tell. I'm just a simple gal from Chicago's Gold Coast. Lake Shore Drive. My parents were doctors for the rich and famous. I grew up in a tired, marble-clad penthouse eating caviar and staring at Lake Michigan."

"Wait! You're rich?" I'm shocked. There are only so many surprises a sober person can take in a single evening.

"I just said Gold Coast, Lake Shore Drive, doctors, and penthouse, didn't I? And without even the slightest hint of sarcasm. Who knew I could pull that off?" She's proud of herself.

"I don't understand. You never seem to work and haven't offered to pay for anything since I met you."

"Stop right there! I bought your drinks the first night I met you. Don't make me out to be some cheapskate mooch!"

"Fine. But how can this be?"

"My parents were rolling in it. They were a bit too aristocratic and Catholic to have such a sissy son. So, they bought me a simple three-story townhouse in Georgetown and sent me away to this low-class, political swamp. Then they died in a plane crash when I was 20, and I started a lifetime of annual meager trust fund payments. Happily ever after. The end." Jayne brushes her hands of imaginary dust and gives me a smug smile.

I think Don Knotts gave less dramatic surprised looks than I am after hearing her story. "But..."

"I said 'the end,' didn't I?" Jayne is in no mood to continue her personal story.

"No! I have so many questions!"

Jayne stands and shakes her head. "Oh, for the love of Carol Channing!"

"Who?"

"Who? I said Carol, not Stockard!"

"Oh." Her stare threatens me to ask another question, but

I feel brave. "Just one more, please! What's your *real* name? Please tell me this time!"

"Jayne." Blank stare.

"No, not your drag name. What's your name when you're not in drag?"

"Not in drag?" She furrows her brow. "Jayne."

A folded piece of white paper greets me from the kitchen table on Friday morning. It mocks me with its simplicity causing my stomach to churn. My wet vision squints at blurry words: *May your tits always point to the sky, and may the photographer always capture your best side. Love you. Mean it. XOXOXO Jayne*

She's gone. No forwarding address. No invitation to have lunch. No see-you-later kiss goodbye. Just meaningless words and a bright red lip print. Her presence is everywhere, from the new furniture to the kitchen arrangement, but nothing left belonging to Jayne. And nothing that *is* Jayne.

She has left nothing behind – except me.

FORTY-TWO

Patron Saint of Lost Things

Time alone is both a blessing and a curse. On the one hand, no one makes fun of my pedestrian culinary habits. I like hot dogs. I really do. It's just a bonus they take so little effort to prepare. I have had the opportunity to sit on my new couch for only the second time since I bought it. No one is waiting outside the shower curtain to make a comment about some part of my body. And I've had two nights of swear-free, alcohol-free solitude.

On the other hand, I miss Jayne.

Julio can see I'm in a bit of a funk when we finally get together on Sunday evening. He seems to know me better than he should for our short time together.

"I'm taking you to dinner at Dupont Italian Kitchen," he says with his trademark toothy smile. "Nobody can feel low with a belly full of pasta!"

He's right. Well, pasta *and* my Prince Charming. Or Prince Pretty Pants, as Jayne would say. No. No! I won't think about her tonight. This is my time with Julio.

"Let's go up to the DIK Bar," I say after dinner, like an alumnus looking to relive his college days. "It was the first bar I went to after moving here, so it's got special memories."

"Sure. I love that place. I used to spend hours there looking for love... until you came along." He winks.

I hear Washington empties out around Christmas, and the deserted bar confirms it. The last time I was here, I needed Jayne to break through the crowds. Now there can't be more than a handful of guys and one lone bartender. We approach the bar for our lite beers, and I notice something familiar about the bartender.

"Hello, kids. What'll it be?" the tall man with cropped hair says from behind the bar. He looks at us with big, round eyes that may have the remnants of eyeliner smeared on the edges.

"You're new here," Julio says.

"Yep. It's my first week. Nice to have the slow nights, so I can get the hang of this place." He winks at us.

"I'm Julio, and this is Randy," he says, pointing at me. "I used to know everyone who worked here, but I haven't come by in a while."

"Nice to meet you kids. I'm Anthony. Named after Saint Anthony of Padua, the patron saint of lost things. Ain't that a kicker?!" His booming laugh is like a warm hug.

"Do I know you?" I ask. "There's something familiar about your voice."

"People always say that," Anthony replies. "I'm just one of those people everyone thinks they know, but I doubt we've met."

He deftly uncaps two beers in one motion using his freshly painted nails to flip the tops to the floor. If there's one thing Jayne taught me, opening beer bottles will ruin a virginal manicure. I can already see the scratches in Anthony's flaming red polish.

"It's odd to take a new job right before Christmas," Julio says to Anthony. "You could have waited a couple weeks and started in the new year. Why ruin your holiday?"

Anthony rubs his thumb and two fingers together. "Coming

up short. My parents saw to it I get a cash infusion every spring, but I don't have the self-control to make it last all year. So, I pick up a bartending gig to tide me over when the money gets short. It's not so bad." He shrugs and chuckles. "What are you lovebirds doing for the holidays?"

"I'm taking this guy to meet the parents." Julio beams with pride.

"Heavens to Joan Crawford! You're a bona fide couple, aren't you?" Anthony turns to me with a wink. "It's good to have someone watching out for you, isn't it, puppy?"

Julio tosses a twenty on the bar and takes our beers. "Great to meet you, Anthony. I'm sure we'll see you around." He takes my arm and leads me toward a table in the back.

"Thanks," Anthony booms. "And have fun in New York."

"You alright?" Julio asks as we sit.

"You never said we're going to New York."

Julio shrugs. "No. He probably just assumed all Puerto Ricans live in New York." He laughs. "It's not a stretch, you know."

He called me Puppy! And who says heavens to anything, let alone Joan Crawford? My brain feels like it just learned all the world's ice cream was eaten by aliens. And then they started eating the hot dogs. "I can't shake the feeling I already know the bartender."

"Is this another one of your hook-ups?" he says with a wry smile. "I see so many people that I'm always mistaking one for another. It's no big deal."

The rest of the night, I keep an eye on Anthony to see if he winks at me or gives me some clue about his identity. Nothing. He serves drinks and chats with the few poor souls who come in, but there's no sign he knows me. Why do I recognize every move he makes?

Julio and I return to my place an hour or so later and have a little romp under the covers. Actually, it started on top of the covers and moved to under the covers. But he got too hot, and we threw the covers to the floor. And then, the bottom sheet got messy, and we had to put the top sheet on the bottom to sleep. Jayne always said I should offer to sleep in the wet spot, but she didn't account for just how wet Julio can make things. But that's probably too much information. Suffice it to say, Julio is exhausted from the romp and sound asleep.

I, on the other hand, lie awake. My mind is replaying the conversation with Anthony.

Sleep finally comes when I imagine Jayne standing next to me, kissing my forehead. I whisper softly, "Good night, my fairy godmother," and drift into peaceful repose.

FORTY-THREE

Ever After

The red Toyota Camry rental glides up I-95 like Santa's sleigh making its Christmas Eve deliveries. Julio is singing unabashedly to old Lady Gaga albums – very un-Santa-like – as he expertly guides us to Brooklyn. He has a great singing voice, and I add tenor harmony when the spirit moves me. I feel as if I've known him my whole life.

Julio continues singing as I gaze at the Baltimore lights twinkling over the water. I've never been to Baltimore. Or Wilmington, or Philadelphia, two more places we will pass through on my first trip to New York. It's a true exploration week.

It's been an exploration year.

The last 12 months have brought more change than any other time in my life. For the second year in a row, I won't see my siblings during the holidays. We've gone our separate ways since Mother and Dad passed. Maybe I won't ever see them again. It's a little sad, but I don't find myself thinking of them much. And I haven't picked up the phone to call them since I sold the Minot house.

For a while, I thought Jayne would be with me for Christmas. We became strangely comfortable together in the short

317

time she lived with me. She was a cross between parent and friend, though nothing like my real parents and friends. Jayne was probably closest to a fairy godmother. A giant, foul-mouthed, sex-obsessed fairy godmother who will never get her own Disney film.

God, I miss her.

Maybe it's time to redefine and create my own family. I'd like Julio to be part of the new family, but not as a parent or fairy godmother. Partner, maybe. Husband, someday. Sounds like the next phase of my adulthood.

Five months ago, I arrived in Washington with tired furniture and a worn-out friend. I took my first apartment, started a new job, and learned about a new city. There was a drag race, a fairy godmother, some less-than-successful dates, and a new wardrobe. And then came Julio.

I am becoming the adult version of Randy, just as Mother said I should. Decisions and choices are mine – for better or worse. My childish things have been mostly put away, and I am becoming my own man. I wonder what Mother would say about all this? Would she like Julio? Would she rearrange the kitchen back to the way MJ put it?

A strong hand squeezes my knee. I turn to see the oncoming headlights sparkling on Julio's smiling teeth and eyes. His happiness fills my heart.

I also wonder what Jayne would say if she were here right now. I imagine her sitting on my couch, red sequin dress smoothed carefully over legs stretched the length of the sofa. She yells to me in her booming voice, "Stop with the fucking googly eyes and happily-ever-after daydreams. Your tits may be bigger, but you're no Cinderella. Now, be a good boy and fetch me a top-shelf double vodka martini. Up with a twist. And don't skimp on the vodka. *Never* skimp on the vodka."

Some lessons I'll never forget.

THE END

APPRECIATION

I began writing this book about six weeks before my 55th birthday. Having never undertaken such a gargantuan project, I didn't know how much time, energy, and creativity would be required. It has been a great and rewarding learning process — and one for which I will be forever grateful.

I'm fortunate to have significant support and inspiration from friends and family who served as my cheerleaders throughout the entire writing process. You inspired me to follow this outrageous dream to its completion. Thank you.

My first short stories were published by James Finn, editor of *Prism & Pen* on Medium. James encouraged me to continue writing, eventually publishing the short story that became this novel: "That Night I Ran the High Heel Race."

Hats off to my beta readers: Kelle Louaillier, Diane Stark, and Peter Stark. Your advice helped me through some difficult edits and guided me toward a stronger story. Thank you for giving so much of your time and talents.

Heartfelt gratitude goes to everyone at Atmosphere Press. You took a chance on a novice writer and gave me incredible support every step of the way. Special shout-out to Kyle McCord, Alex Kale, Chris Beale, and Ronaldo Alves, who helped me put my best foot forward.

Sometimes, life throws us lemons, and it's great friends and family who hold our hands and help us make lemonade.

I'm forever indebted to my lemonade makers: Martin Borbone, Dean Cerrato, Eric Gering, Lori Knowles, Kelle Louaillier, Maria Melone, Drew Nelson, John Perkins, Jennifer Pinck, Dan Ruffer, Dorothy Ruffer, Kevin Ruffer, Shawn Ruffer, Steve Ruffer, Diane Stark, Wendy Stark, David Styers, Terry Thomas, Randy Walther, and Annie Yang-Perez. And, as always, thank you, Mom.

I never studied creative writing in college, so I'm forever indebted to my extraordinary English teachers in high school: Anita Canterbury, Harry Boguszewski, and Candice Koehn. Who knew you were teaching me to write about drag queens?

And, capping this appreciation list is my husband of more than a quarter century, Peter Stark. We have seen our world change more times than we can count, giving us opportunities, challenges, and adventures up and down the eastern United States. Nothing I have ever achieved, or obstacle I've surmounted, could have happened without you. You are my rock and my forever love. Thank you for sharing this journey with me.

• • • •

About Atmosphere Press

Atmosphere Press is an independent, full-service publisher for excellent books in all genres and for all audiences. Learn more about what we do at atmospherepress.com.

We encourage you to check out some of Atmosphere's latest releases, which are available at Amazon.com and via order from your local bookstore:

Icarus Never Flew 'Round Here, by Matt Edwards
COMFREY, WYOMING: Maiden Voyage, by Daphne Birkmeyer
The Chimera Wolf, by P.A. Power
Umbilical, by Jane Kay
The Two-Blood Lion, by Nick Westfield
Shogun of the Heavens: The Fall of Immortals, by I.D.G. Curry
Hot Air Rising, by Matthew Taylor
30 Summers, by A.S. Randall
Delilah Recovered, by Amelia Estelle Dellos
A Prophecy in Ash, by Julie Zantopoulos
The Killer Half, by JB Blake
Ocean Lessons, by Karen Lethlean
Unrealized Fantasies, by Marilyn Whitehorse
The Mayari Chronicles: Initium, by Karen McClain
Squeeze Plays, by Jeffrey Marshall
JADA: Just Another Dead Animal, by James Morris
Hart Street and Main: Metamorphosis, by Tabitha Sprunger
Karma One, by Colleen Hollis
Ndalla's World, by Beth Franz
Adonai, by Arman Isayan
The Journey, by Khozem Poonawala
Stolen Lives, by Dee Arianne Rockwood
Waiting 'Round to Die, by Chris Grant
Unraveled: The DNA Kill Switch, by Mark Henry Thienes

About the Author

Chandler Myer published his first novel, *Jayne and the Average North Dakotan*, at the age of 57, following a 35-year career as a professional musician. The book is based on his short story, "That Night I Ran the High Heel Race," published in the Medium publication *Prism & Pen*. He has also been published in *Bear Creek Gazette*, as well as Medium publications *Rainbow*, *An Idea*, and *Atheism101*.

Myer lives in Philadelphia with his husband of more than a quarter century. He loves to walk, travel, and make friends with every dog he sees.